Street Life
To
Housewife

Street Life
To
Housewife

Kim Robinson

This edition arranged & typeset by M Brown Literary Services.

Publisher's Note:
This novel is a work of fiction. Any references to historical events, to real people, living or dead; or real locales are intended only to give the fiction a setting in historic reality. Other names, characters, places, and incidents either are the product of the author's imagination or are used fictitiously, and their resemblance, if any, to real-life counterparts is entirely coincidental.

ISBN: 978-0-9820679-3-2
June 2010
10   9   8   7   6   5   4   3   2   1

Acknowledgements

First, I give all thanks to God for gifting me with writing. To my husband, my three beautiful children, my parents, Clyde and Anna Lee Harold, aunts and Uncles and extended family. Thank you for loving me through the hard times.

My cousins who have always had my back, Tracy Glover, Kenya Glover, La Shun Broussard, Michelle Broussard, Aisha Muhammad, Asia Muhammad, La Kisha Broussard and Johnathan Broussard Jr., Poncho, Chris and Uncle Willie, Butch and Johnathan.

I dedicate this book to all the people who died before their time, but in God's time. They have gone home while we are left to deal with the horrors of the world. Melvin Broussard, Sadie Broussard, Melvin (Crickett) Paul Broussard Jr., Curley Broussard, Helen Simpson, Aunt Genevieve, Phyllis Broussard. Tina Whaley, Paul Moreland. My cousins, Jean Anne, Terry, and Clarence. Terrie Primmer, and Tracy's godson, Dallas, Sheila Perkins.

James Charles thank you for sending the photograph's that brought back so many memories, I am missing you.

To all my Internet families, thanks for the support.

Sylvia and David Pope, I would love to hear from you. Jackie Mathieu thank you for all the late nights of listening to me read my manuscript. Thank you Misherald for the typesetting and Tuesday Dube for the cover.

"As long as I live, so does this series"
Kim Robinson

Introduction

People raised without the benefit of trauma like growing up in ghettos, abuse and addictions, are considered "normal" people. They drive down the street and look down their noses at prostitutes, drug dealers, and addicts.

If these "normal" folks had to take to the streets to survive, they would most likely starve to death. No one grew up playing with Barbie and G.I. Joe dolls saying, "When I grow up I want to be a prostitute so I can sell my body, or a drug dealer so I can sell poison to people who desperately feel that they need to medicate away memories and pain."

They had dreams of being nurses and doctors who saved lives. Lawyers, airline stewardesses, the first female President of the United States just like "normal" children but somewhere along the way something happened that led their goals astray, for whatever reason they lost confidence in themselves and abandoned their dreams. They took the only roads they felt available to them.

I can't tell you every hustler's story, but I can give you some insight into a world that most people never see. I can show you why some women are not at home, married with two-point-five children and going to church every Sunday and why some men risk jail and jacker's to sell drugs, to survive.

I'm hoping that this book will inspire and enable people to change their lives. If you can say these words then you can turn your world around, "I'M STILL HERE AND I'M STILL STANDING."

If you are still alive, God has a plan for you. If you listen and be obedient, He will show you that plan. Everyone has a special gift that can be used to help others. When you utilize your gifts, you will have a wonderful and rewarding life. "All things are possible through God. I am a living breathing testament to his grace."

Kim Robinson

In writing this book my mind's eye remembers certain events in my life I dream as if in black and white movies, maybe because back in the day that was what the televisions played. Open your mind and let your eyes share my vision.

Laissez les Bon Temps Rouler

Let the Good Times Roll

1982

Bad Girls
Donna Summer

Francois let out a loud moan, his body shuddered, and it was over. The first time I had seen him it took ten minutes of conversation to put this trick "to sleep," which meant putting him at ease so that he could relax enough in my company to attain a happy ending.

Every black girl had to be adept at this in order to assuage the fears that lurked in client's minds planted by experiences, rumors and assumptions that all black girls wanted to rob them. Funny thing, it didn't stop them from taking the chance.

As a hooker, prostitute, call girl, I did not mind the talking part, it's when the client wants to touch me that I disassociated my mind from my body and hover around on the ceiling. I go into automatic pilot, robot mode, so it isn't me that they are huffing and puffing over.

I learned a lot of tricks of the trade listening to my Uncle's women while growing up. A good working girl never got off with a trick. If you did then you were the trick. Having been beaten and tortured by a few psychopaths I had a level of disdain for men who paid for my time and body. Within the first few months of my career, I mastered techniques that helped me avoid sex, while at the same time satisfying the needs of the client so they got their moneys worth.

With this particular client, work could not be avoided. Now I had to remember the other advice I had received, "Do what you got to do to get paid, stay down for your crown, and don't turn down nuthin' but yo' collar."

The $400.00 Francois paid me for two hours of my time made it worthwhile. The first hour we talked about his work and problems. Reading the paper every morning certainly paid off. I wasted a lot of time talking about current events. This also helped me appear intelligent.

If a trick just wanted to get off, he could do that on the street in the back of his car for twenty dollars. Once a client was a regular like Francois, they wanted socializing, company and compassion that they were not getting elsewhere.

Francois had been seeing me once a month for a year. Lately he called the agency every two weeks asking for me. He was trying to kiss me, again. I turned my head so his mouth fell on my cheek. He looked hurt. The slight had not gotten past him.

Too damn bad, I never kissed.

"Why won't you let me kiss you?"

I ignored the question and changed the subject. "Daddy you were good. You need to get out of the hills more often. It's rare that I get someone who isn't fat or ugly, or cares about satisfying me the way you do. If it wasn't for my tuition being due I would give you your money back."

If he believed that, he was really not the sharpest pencil in the box.

I smiled at the silver haired, Spanish, sixty year old man. He looked aw'ight for his age, but he was a client. I could not have feelings for clients.

"You are going to make a great teacher one day. You know my offer still stands." He pulled me close to him. "I could pay all your bills, put you in a nice house and you wouldn't have to do anything but focus on your studies."

Yeah right, anything but sleep with you day and night.

The thought of waking up to Francois everyday made me want to throw up. He was in the middle of his fourth divorce and was looking for wife number five.

I touched him on the side of his face, "You are so sweet, but you know I have goals that I want to achieve before I think about a serious relationship."

He really was sweet. If I let him, he would take care of me. I could live in a big house and never worry about anything. Even after the inevitable divorce, I would get a great settlement and a big alimony check. The only problem was I could never be with a client that way.

I had spent weeks with clients. The money was good. The thing that made it all right was that we negotiated my time and I knew that when that time was up I was out of there. An indefinite relationship or marriage - Naw! That would drive me nuts.

I knew all about the grief he got from his ex-wives and kids. He spent hours talking about them. I listened, not saying anything as any good psychiatrist would, should have thought about it as a profession.

I didn't blame his wives for leaving him. He was adulterous. If I was a square, I would leave him too. The funny thing was all his wives were pseudo-squares. He had a penchant for rescuing girls.

He pulled his first wife a dancer, out of Las Vegas. The second was her best friend, a hotel showgirl that he took up with shortly after his first son was born which resulted in a considerable weight gain for his first wife who divorced him.

Wife number two gave him a daughter and promptly filed for divorce when she caught him with soon to be wife number three, a bartender at the Playboy club who promptly presented him with a son before pulling her vanishing act.

The current wife had been a massage therapist who made "house calls." They had been together the longest and had two grown daughters. All of his wives had found a payday when they married Francois.

"How did you get into this business?" Francois asked

I knew it would happen one day, it always did with regulars. Eventually they wanted to know all about you and then they started getting delusions of being your rescuer. It had taken Francois a year, but like many others, he wanted to know about my life and what had landed me into prostitution.

"I really don't like talking about my life but since you're so good to me I guess I can tell you, I know you will keep it confidential. My parents were killed in a robbery when I was seven. A drug addict broke into our house in the middle of the night and shot them in the head. When I heard the gunshots, I hid under some clothes in my closet. I saw the killers face through the clothes. When he left I called the police because my parents would not wake up, the police showed me some pictures from which I identified him."

"You saw the man who killed your parents?" Francois asked.

I had a distant look on my face that told Francois I was reliving the event. "I had no other family and landed in a series of foster homes where I wasn't treated too nicely. I ran away from the last one when I was fifteen. I figured the streets couldn't be any worse than that house."

"What happened there?" Francois got a tissue from the bedside and wiped the tears from my face.

"The Father and teenage son were raping me. Almost every night they came into my room. The mother beat me because she knew."

"She beat you because her husband was raping you? She knew about it and did nothing to stop it?"

"Oh, she knew alright, sometimes she joined in."

"I don't believe such despicable people walk this world. Why didn't you tell someone?"

"Girls who told ended up in worse places. No one believed them and they were labeled troublemakers."

"Someone should have helped you."

"I looked at Francois and through my tears said, "I helped me."

"One night when my foster parents were out, the son brought home his football teammates. I heard them talking through the vent in the basement where my room was. They were pulling straws to see who would rape me first.

"My God, he planned to pass you around?"

"I threw some clothes and my piggy bank into a pillow case. I had saved my lunch money and allowance for over two years. My jar held $200.00. I climbed out the window and never looked back."

"How did you survive?"

"I hitchhiked to Venice beach. The beach held so many good memories from my childhood. My parents took me camping there every summer. My Father and I fished during school vacations. It was a place where I felt like they were still with me. I even saw them sometime."

"You mean you saw their ghost?"

"I think it was there spirit. They kept me safe. One day I was bedding down in the beach bathroom, when a man followed me in. Suddenly I saw my parents, and felt the man being lifted off of me. He went running down the beach naked, screaming at the top of his lungs. I slept in that bathroom every night for two months and nothing bad ever happened. I stashed my sleeping bag and pillowcase in a locker at the bus station during the day, and went to my under the table job at the skate store. The woman who owned the place paid me to clean up the skates and eventually I started working the rental counter. I never told her that I was homeless but she figured it out and presented me with a key and bought a bed and a radio so I could sleep in the back room."

"You poor child, my heart bleeds for you," he hugged me.

"I met some girls who were a couple of years older than me. It seemed like we had all been through hard times and opted to be on our own for one reason or another. They invited me to be their roommate. I jumped at the chance to have a roof over my head."

"How did they live? Where did they get food, shelter, and clothes?"

"There was an old guy, Mr. Charlie who rented an apartment and paid the utilities in exchange for one night with each of us every month. We did whatever it took to feed ourselves. Mr. Charlie forged birth certificates and enrolled us in school as his foster children."

"Wasn't he a nice pedophile?" Francois' voice dripped with sarcasm.

"We are all in college now and I'm proud to say getting very close to accomplishing our goals."

When I looked at Francois, there were tears in his eyes. I knew he was thinking about his spoiled daughters. He spent a fortune putting them through college and they did nothing with their sheepskins but get pregnant and marry bums that he was forced to hire at his construction company so they could keep a roof over his girls and grandchildren's heads.

"You know my daughters are grown women in their thirties and forties and if they had to take care of themselves they would starve to death. Here you are twenty-two years old and you've been taking care of yourself for seven years now. Look at you, furthering your education so you can do something with your life, something that will make a difference in spite of everything you had to survive."

"Hey, what else do I have to do? Without an education I won't ever be anything that I can feel good about."

"You deserve a break and I am going to give you one. How much money do you need to finish school?"

"Well, I have about three more years to go. I just finished community college and got into a state college this year. I don't know twenty-five grand for this semester alone. I'm taking a heavy load trying to finish quickly, books are expensive as hell."

"I don't want you to worry about any of that, hand me my jacket."

Francois wrote me a check for $30,000.00 and placed it in my hand kissing my wrist, "If you have any problems here's my card. This should allow you to concentrate on what's important. I'll give you more for next semester and if you need anything, anything at all you promise to call me."

Hook, line and sinker. I looked at the check and squeezed out a few tears, "I can't take this Francois," knowing full well there was no way I would give it back.

"Yes you can. Sparkle I throw away more than this every month on alimony and it doesn't make me feel good. Doing this for you makes me feel like my money is doing some good and I can write it off on taxes."

"The Francois College fund huh?" I laughed and hugged him.

"Maybe I'll start a foundation."

"Thank you Francois, you don't know how much this means to me, no one has ever given me this kind of help without wanting me to do something crazy." I sniffed.

"There are no strings attached. If I never see you again, which I know I will, you don't owe me a thing."

"I think you are my guardian angel." I kissed him on the forehead before raising my 5' 9" 130 pound, long-legged frame from the bed. I stepped into my five inch stilettos. "I need to freshen up and get out of here, got to pick my baby up from the sitter."

"You have a child?"

"Yeah, I didn't tell you?" I reached in my wallet and pulled out a picture of a little girl. She was about three years old, her caramel skin was close to my own complexion, and she had a head full of wavy hair. "This is my baby girl Keisa."

I picked up my leather dress, jacket, and panties and walked into the bathroom to wash up. I touched up my eyeliner, mascara, and lipstick. I didn't need foundation or powder. I took the $400.00 cash that Frank had given me upon arrival and wrapped it around the check and placed it in the hidden pocket in my jacket lining.

I smiled at the dark eyed, full mouthed, pretty girl reflected in the mirror, *Damn girl; you are good at what you do. $30,400.00 for two hours of my time was a personal best.*

I took the silver-plated two-shooter from my purse, checked that the safety was on before placing it in the pocket sewn into the nape of my neck where a 22 inch, curly wavy, human hair weave covered it. *Time to go.*

Francois was dressed. He handed me back the child's photograph along with a roll of money. He held my hand with both of his, "Do something nice for your daughter. She's very beautiful. I can tell you take good care of her. Maybe one day I can take you and Keisa on a trip to Disneyland or Knott's Berry farm?"

"Maybe, you never know what can happen in the future. I've never taken any men around her. I've never told any clients about her, so please keep this confidential. The agency doesn't know about her. I don't know why I told you."

"Don't worry Sparkle; your secret is safe with me. It is understandable that you would be protective of her in light of all you have been through."

I leaned in to kiss him on the cheek and he turned his head and tried to kiss me on the mouth. "You know better than that."

"You still won't let me kiss you?"

"Don't take it personal Francois. I usually don't even kiss on the cheek. I feel that I have to save something for later in life. One day I'm going to meet a man and he isn't going to know anything about this life, or care when I tell him. He will love me unconditionally and take me away from all of this. We'll date like normal people, and he will ask me to marry him. That is the person I want to kiss. You see I give every thing else, I have away for money. You understand don't you?"

"I understand. You know the more I get to know you, the more I like you. Who knows maybe I can be that guy for you. You keep working on your dreams; I'll do anything I can to help. No strings attached. I promise I'll be there for you," He hugged me tightly, too tightly.

When he let go I turned and headed for the door. I took one last look in the mirror on my way out the door to make sure everything was in place. Three pair of lions-head earrings, three gold chains, one with a Lions-head sporting a two carat diamond in its mouth. I loved lions, didn't hurt that I was a Leo.

I was heading for the elevator when Francois peeked out, "Hey Sparkle, I'm going to call for you next week?"

I walked back and gave him a card with my pager number, "Call me direct, you do know to keep this between you and me, right?"

He took this as a sign that I was getting closer to having a relationship with him. What I was really doing was cutting out the agency out of its forty percent. They had made enough money from me off of this client. If he was going to start calling every week that was 40 dollars an hour that I would be putting in my own pocket.

I got off the elevator and made my way through the parking lot to my little blue Nissan. I loved my little stick shift car. I realized I was still holding the money and the picture in my hand. I counted it. Oh how sweet, Francois had given me

$200 to spend on precious Keisa. I kissed the picture and returned it to my wallet where it was when I purchased it.

I didn't have any children, unlike most of my friends who had kids before we graduated high school in 1977. Why had I used Keisa's name? Maybe it was because my little cousin was on my mind. I had told my aunt that I would babysit this Saturday night. I planned to take Keisa and her brother Jay to the movies Saturday.

I turned off my radio and pushed the last button then used the key to open the hidden compartment that was welded into the center panel. If I got stopped, the police would not find any thing. I retrieved an envelope folded from a hundred dollar bill and used a gold plated, one inch fingernail to powder my nose with cocaine that would clear my head of the date I had just turned.

It was five p.m. on Friday and traffic was going to be a bear. I anticipated being on 101 for at least an hour to get from Hollywood to Compton, so that I could take my parents to dinner.

My parents were still very much alive, married, and living in the house that they bought when I was five years old. Every year the week after New Years, I used my Christmas money to treat us to dinner at our favorite restaurant, Tracton's on La Cienega Boulevard and Rodeo Road. It was a very colorful place that was owned by a boxer.

I laid my head back against the headrest and let the cocaine and the Gap Band's "Burn rubber on me," relax me. Soon I was snapping my fingers and back to the real world. On the way to the freeway, I went to the bank drive through window on Wilshire Blvd to deposit the check into my account.

I went back into my stash and removed one of three identifications. I had four bank accounts one in my real name. I never let the balance get over ten thousand for tax purposes so I would have to move some money around as soon as the check cleared. I knew better than to play with the IRS.

I was feeling the beat of The Dazz Bands "Let it Whip," as I waited in the long bank line. A man in a white Mercedes was flirting with me through his rear view mirror.

When I drove out of the bank, he was parked on the street standing next to his car waving at me. I parked and he came to my window.

"Hey pretty lady."

"Hey yourself," I smiled at the guy and assessed his expensive clothes and Rolex; I did not miss the fact that he was wearing a wedding band.

"So how long have you been married?"

"You saw that huh?"

"Yeah, what's your name?"

"Martell Sham," he said handing me his business card. And yours?"

"Sparkle." When I took the card he captured my hand and kissed the back of it."

"Aren't you a charmer? So what's really going on Martell?"

"I'm attracted to a pretty lady."

"Really now?"

"What's wrong with that?"

"What's wrong with that is you have a wife sitting at home, with all the luxuries that come with station. That means that the number one position has already been filled, where does that leave me?"

"I would not leave you anywhere, besides you don't look like a lady who would go for it anyway."

"Right, right."

"I like that. Why don't we work out the details over dinner?"

"I have a prior engagement."

"Oh, you got a man huh?"

"Nope, my engagement is with my parents. I'm taking them to dinner."

"That's so sweet. So when can we get together?"

"Sunday night good for you?"

"How about Monday?"

"That'll work. I'll call you in the afternoon."

"Don't I get your number?"

"Yeah, after we work out the details."

When I looked in my rear view mirror, Martell was watching me drive off. I wrote down his license number. So I could find out who he was.

The sky was a beautiful mixture of orange and pink as the sun went down on the smoggy, palm tree lined freeway. I loved this time of day. A few years ago I worked downtown Los Angeles in a bank and had to take this ride everyday. I always worked until the sun started to set so that I could enjoy it. When I Sometimes I just sat outside and watched the sun go down.

Rick James and Tina Marie kept me company. I was pleased to find traffic moving at a brisk clip, for after work traffic hour. I pulled into my parent's driveway in 40 minutes instead of the anticipated hour. I opened the gate and parked in the back yard and used my door key. Once inside, I got myself a glass of water, "Hello I'm here," I announced.

"You know your mother can never be ready on time," My Father said from the living room. I hugged him and kissed him on the cheek. He was wearing Russian Leather, I love that fragrance.

"You better go help her Daddy. If we ain't on time for our reservation we will be waiting all night to get in, and I'm hungry."

"Your hungry, I could eat a bear. I didn't eat lunch so that I would have extra room." He went into the bedroom, "Come on woman we got to go."

I phoned the agency to let them know that I would not be on call until Sunday night. I had made enough money to take a couple of nights off.

I called a friend who worked at the Beverly Hills police precinct and gave him the license number for Martell Sham so that he could run it. My pager had gone off several times while I was on the freeway. I checked the numbers and returned my friend Laisyv's call. We made arrangements to meet at The Speakeasy later that night for a bachelorette party.

"I'll have my parents after dinner and roll with you if you can bring me to get my car tomorrow?"

That settled I went into the living room and sat on the brown leather couch. I picked up a photo album that my

Father had been working on. That man had a camera glued to his face every since I could remember. He had a photographic diary of our lives. As I looked at the pictures, I drifted back down memory lane.

1959

You know some people say they don't remember when they were born, not me, I remember everything. It was around 10 p.m. when my Mother, Anna Lee Broussard's water broke. She had been in labor for eight hours. I heard a lot of screaming and hollering in the room, but it wasn't coming from mommy, it was coming from someone else in the hospital room. My mother yelled, "Shut up all that noise!"

There was another voice saying, "Breathe, and push." It was a tight squeeze but I made it. When I saw my mother for the first time, she looked tired, but beautiful. At first look, I thought they had made a mistake and given me to a White woman until I saw the tight curl around the edges of her auburn hair, "Oh, she's a pretty baby."

I protested when they took me out of her warm, soft arms. I was pissed as they cleaned me up, sucked stuff out my nose, and put drops in my eyes. I found myself in a room where I felt like a goldfish. Lots of people were looking at me through a glass window. When the other babies weren't crying, I could hear everything they said.

The first time I heard my Father's voice Clyde Harold Jr. was talking to my Grandmother, Helen Broussard. "Oooh she's so ugly, whaz' wrong with her head?"

My Grandmother hit him, "That's cause the head gets squeezed coming through the birth canal, the bones are not set. She's a pretty baby and she'll be just fine. You just have to keep rubbing her head to mold it."

Three days later, I left the hospital in my Father's 1951, forest green, Mercury Monterey. Home was my Grandmother's house on Hillford Avenue, off of Rosecran's and Central in Compton.

There were a lot of people holding me all the time. I could barely get any sleep. The moment I fell off, here they come, making funny faces and goo gooing at me. If they knew how ridiculous they looked, they would stop.

I was a happy baby, I always had someone to make me laugh, and most important, I was loved. I was the first grandchild born to Helen and Melvin Broussard, though they were divorced. My grandmother had a new man, Mr. Willie Bruce, so I had two Grandfathers. I had three aunts, JoAnna, Francis, Aunt Genevieve and her daughters Pat, Jeanann, and Virginia. My mom had friends all over the neighborhood. Cookie, Edna, Gwen, and Mrs. Criss were around the most.

Then there were my Uncles, Melvin Jr., who was called Cricket, cause he was short and dark, Curley, Charles who was called Butch, and Jonathan who they called Bumpy because when he was little, he would get mad and bump his head against the wall. Aunt Genevieve had son's too, Poopie, Stewart, Donny, Larry, and Terry.

My mom went off to work during the week and Mrs. Chris, who lived three doors down, babysat me until my aunt's picked me up on their way home from school.

My dad came by everyday when he got off of work. My mother and I slept in the master bedroom and on weekends the three of us stayed in the room together, sometimes we went to the house my Father shared with his mom in the projects.

In his little room, we watched his 19" portable television. The little Rascals, The Bowery Boys, westerns with John Wayne, the Lone Ranger, and Tonto, all watched my Father sleep. We were a cozy little family.

I had incentive to start walking earlier than most kids. Mr. Willie would put a can of beer down on the floor and if I walked to it, he gave me a few sips. By seven months I was toddling around sucking on every left over beer can I could get my hands on.

My parents married when I was one year old. They went downtown to the Justice of the Peace. My parent's best friends Edna and Billy stood with them as bridesmaid and best man. Afterward they had a wonderful party at Billy's house complete with cake.

My Father's Sister, who I was named after, lived with her husband and two daughters who were a few years older than me. My Fathers Mother, Theresa Prade had been abandoned by her Husband and the Father of her children when they were very young. She worked as a janitor at a school.

I was almost two years old when we moved into a two-story town house in Nickerson Garden projects off of Imperial and Central in Watt's. The living room, dining room and kitchen were downstairs, two bedrooms and the bathroom were up.

My Father had fixed up his car and was the president of a car club called The Matadors. When he got everything it just the way he wanted with custom hubcaps sporting little stars in the center and long tailpipes, wouldn't you know someone striped it right in front of our house? That was the last time he put money into that car.

My Father had been injured in Guam while in the Air Force. He somehow fell over a waterfall, the coral and rocks took the skin off of his leg. While they carried him back through the jungle, he was bitten by mosquitoes. His fever went so high it cooked the veins closed in his legs and resulted in Thrombophlebitis. (Throm-bo-fle-bite-is) It meant that his blood got too thick and clotted, so it had to be thinned with medicine. During this process, he had to be watched closely and spent weeks in the Veterans Administration hospital every few months. I thought the hospital was his other house.

One thing about my Father though, when he came home he got out and pounded the pavement until he found another job. He used his G.I. Bill to attend Trade Technical College and learned how to sew and make patterns. We had an Industrial sewing machine in our small dining area off the kitchen where he made shirts for all the hustlers who could afford tailor-made clothes.

When my Father worked or was hospitalized I stayed at my grandmothers. While my aunts and Uncles attempted to do their homework, I bugged them to let me help. To keep me occupied they gave me alphabet blocks to spell out words from books until I could identify them. By the time, I was three I was reading and learning to write.

My Father read to me at bedtime. My favorite books were Dr. Seuss. We were supposed to take turns reading the pages until I fell asleep, but he usually conked out before I did.

My grandmother often took me with her to work. She cleaned rich people's homes in Wilshire, Beverly Hills, and the San Fernando Valley, and sometimes worked at the movie studios in Burbank.

In the evenings after The Tom and Jerry show went off I sat on my Grandmother's porch waiting for my Father. He always brought me a dime store toy or some penny candy. Before he gave it to me he asked, "You been a good girl?"

No matter what had occurred that day I said, "Yes," hoping that my grandmother would forget what ever I had done to make her say, "I'm gone tell yo' Daddy."

My mother worked for an electronics company in Compton soldering circuit boards and a few evenings a week, she cleaned house for a lady who worked at Mattel Toys and always sent me Barbie dolls. I had an impressive collection. On paydays, my mother would bring me clothes for my family of dolls. For my birthday, I got four fold out cases where I could hang the doll clothes on tiny little hangers. Being the only child, I learned to entertain myself.

I decided my doll family should have a home, so I set about constructing one out of shoeboxes held together with Elmer's glue. Matchstick and single-serve cereal boxes painted with watercolors made beautiful couches and chairs. Swatches of fabric made curtains for cut out windows. An old bathroom mat was cut into carpets for the bedrooms. Cardboard folded accordion style made stairs. Spools of thread glued to circles of glass that my Father cut and sanded made nice tables.

Boy, I spent hours playing with that house, and every time I got my hands on shoe boxes I added more rooms to what soon looked like a mansion and took up a forth of the floor in my small bedroom.

I also had an entourage of imaginary friends who I later found out were not imaginary at all. They were from the other side, I was sensitive to them. Michelle, a young slave girl had been sold away from her mother at the age of seven. She was abused by a perverse master. I didn't know exactly what she meant by abused at that, time, "He hurt me," was how she put it. Whatever he did made her really mad because she stabbed him in the heart and was hung for it. Michelle told me, "People who die bad, don't stay dead." I had heard my grandmother use this phrase.

Sally, a teenaged white girl who did not like me, kept calling me "Slave," Nat Turner and 55 runaway slaves killed her whole family and all their friends. They were just about to blow out the candles on her birthday cake when the up-risers smashed their way into the plantation house.

"She can be mad all she wants, but she knows better than to mess with me. I don't take truck with her foolishness," Michelle said.

Kende, a young boy whose mother had him tied to her back while she ran from her African village, which was under attack. A spear pierced both their hearts.

Kende was telling me about the customs in his village when my parents overheard us talking one day, "They really let your Father have all the wives he wanted?"

My parents came into the room. Daddy said, "Who has a lot of wives?"

My mom was looking in the closets and under the bed, "Who are you talking to?"

"My friend from Africa says that his Father had a lot of wives."

"Where is this friend?"

I looked at them like they were crazy. Didn't they see them sitting on the bed? I opened my mouth to ask and Michelle said, "You might not want to tell them about us because you are the only one who can see us."

Kende said, "They will think you mad and send you to the crazy hospital."

"Kim, I asked you a question, did you hear me? And what are you looking at on the bed?" my mother asked.

"Huh?"

"Where did you hear that? And what are you looking at on the bed?" My Father asked.

"Oh, I guess I dreamed it. Can I have some ice cream?"

They looked to one another. They didn't believe me. My Father said, "You don't have to lie, we heard you talking to them, and I feel them."

Daddy was born with a caul or a veil over his face. A caul is a thin layer of skin. People born with this can see ghost. He had been seeing spirits all his life.

Over the years I had many friends, Ming, a Chinese girl who killed herself when she was made to work in a bad place to pay for her family's passage to America, Helga, a Jewish girl who had been locked in a room and gassed by Hitler's troops during the Holocaust.

I had live friends also. Ms. Alice lived next door to us with her six children. She was something else. She was built small on top and exploded on the bottom.

I will always remember Ms. Alice. It was on her front porch where I was playing when she made a statement that influenced me to never have children until I could afford them. Ms. Alice was arguing with her teenage daughter, Sharon and insisting that she do her dishes. Sharon was leaving for a date and told her mother, "I'll do them when I get back. If you don't like it, you can do them your damn self."

Well, Ms. Alice got pissed and started waving her fist around. She always had little white balls hanging from overgrown underarm hair. "Well if you dat goddamn grown, you little bitch, you need to go have yo' own baby so you can get on 'The County' and get your own goddamn place to live."

Even at the age of four, this just sounded wrong to me. Later I repeated the conversation to my mother, "If you don't have a job and you have kids to take care of the government will help you. It's supposed to be until you can get on your feet, but most people get comfortable living off the checks and don't even try to better themselves. They live in government paid housing and with food stamps; they eat high off the hog. Come to think of it they actually eat better then most people who work for a living."

When we went to the grocery store mommy bought a chicken, which was for Monday and Wednesday. On Tuesday we had tacos, Thursday - salmon croquettes. Fridays we went to Stops Hamburgers or the Hot Dog stand across the street. Saturday we had leftovers or went out. Sundays we ate at one of my Grandmother's homes. We changed the menu a bit, but it was not the big thick steaks and seafood I saw Ms. Alice and her company eating.

"Why don't we get on the county? We could have food stamps and get free food, eat crab and shrimp all the time. You could stay at home and play with me and watch T.V. all day like the other ladies."

"They are watching soap operas, I don't watch soaps. Soaps are for folks who don't have a life. Your Daddy and I work, because we don't want to take money from others when we don't need to."

I knew not to interrupt when Mommy started moving her head and hands around when she was talking so I listened quietly.

"Plus, it ain't worth having some county worker coming 'round, all up in your business. You can't have nuthin' nice. Damn social worker be all in your closets and under your bed trying to find irons and jewelry, little luxuries that you can't afford on the pennies they give you. If they find evidence that you got a man coming around, they cut you off, and you better believe these heifers around here tell on you first chance they get."

That was true. I had seen kids running through the projects screaming at the top of their lungs, "The Social Worker's coming, the Social Worker's coming." Men would be jumping out of windows, and folks were running to their neighbor's houses to hide stuff.

"One day we are going to have enough money to move into a house of our own. I took county aide one time. After a month, I told them to keep that damn money. They ask too many degrading questions. How often do you have sex? Do you enjoy it? That ain't none of they damn business. Ain't enough money in the world worth putting up with all that bullshit. If we did get on the county, your daddy would have to move out. Do you want that?"

"No, I don't want that Mommy, but Ms. Alice has a lot of men coming in her house and they still get County."

"Miss Alice has six kids, all with different daddies. Every year she has another baby so she can get an increase on her check. If you notice, those men only show up around the first and the fifteenth, when the money is gone, so are they."

"So they don't really like her, they just come and visit for her money and food?"

"Until she gets another check those kids have to eat wieners, oatmeal, and spam, breakfast, lunch and dinner because she's stupid enough to be cooking steaks for those losers. Humph giving all her money to some man that don't give a rat's ass about her or those kids just to get a little dick...," she looked at me and saw the confused look on my face, "I mean attention. I would rather work and make my own money so that I can feel good about myself. I got a man that works, a man that is with me for more than a little money and he is with me every day, not just for a couple of days out of the month."

Mommy seemed upset. I regretted having said anything about the County. Mommy made sense to me. None of Ms. Alice kids ever had new clothes, they all wore hand me downs. They argued about whose daddy was better even though they were all MIA (missing in action). Nor did they have any good toys. I had to stop taking my toys outside, and they were not allowed inside my house to play because they stole whatever they didn't break.

I had lots of toys, my Uncles, aunts and cousins were always giving me stuff, and when I went to work with my grandmother the people she worked for gave me all the things their children's discards.

Ms. Alice's daughters Brenda and Lisa were my age, they were jealous of my clothes and toys. One day I had finally had enough of them and vowed never to let them get their hands on my stuff again. Mommy went to talk to Ms. Alice when I ran into the house crying.

I had gone into my house for two seconds to use the bathroom, when I returned two of my dolls had disappeared along with my playmates.

Whey Mommy saw my tears she knew what was wrong. "I told you to stop taking them toys outside. Those kids don't have anything decent of their own and what they do have, they don't take care of."

I had seen toys that we gave to them in their back yard smashed to bits, dolls missing heads and limbs.

"If they don't take care of their own stuff what do you think they gone do with yours? They are jealous of what you have, and will steal if you blink an eye. That's why I don't let you bring them in here no more."

She went to talk to Miss Alice and in a few minutes returned with my dolls.

I could hear Brenda and Lisa screaming and crying as the sound of a belt hitting bottoms filled the air through the open windows. Children stood outside listening and laughing.

Miss Alice's voice could be heard with every swing of the belt, "You ....wack.... stupid little bitch...wack, wack... don't you be....wack... taking stuff ....wack, wack, wack.....that don't belong to yo' dumb ass, and if you just have to ... .wack, wack, wack, wack, wack, ...don't get your dumb ass caught ..... wack, wack, wack, wack, wack, ...and have people coming over here embarrassing me."

The wacks went on so long, I was almost sorry that I had told. I had never seen any one get whipped that long. The wacks kept coming even after there was no more crying. I later found out that Brenda had passed out.

The next day when I went outside, the two girls approached with their friends. Their legs and arms were covered with welts. Brenda walked up to me, "Why you tell on us?"

"Because I let you play with my dolls and you stole em."

"You got a whole lot of em, you didn't have to tell. We got whipped because of you. I'm gone beat you up."

"I'm sorry you got whipped, but it ain't my fault, it's yours. If I let you take my stuff, my mother would whip me, so better your butt then mine."

Lisa, the bigger of the two sisters stepped toward me, "I'm gone beat your ass!"

At that moment my mother's voice rang in my head, *"If someone is going to fight you then you might as well get the first lick in and make damn sure that you make it a good one."*

I stood up, ran up to her, and hit her, hard, right in the center of her face. Her hand flew up to try to stop the stream of blood that was spraying from her nose. She saw the blood on her hand and went into hysterics. The other kids ran in the house.

Within seconds Ms. Alice came out, "What the hell is going on out here?"

I pointed at the girl who was now crying and holding on to her mother, "She said she was going to beat me up, so I did what my mother told me and hit her first."

"Is that true?" Ms. Alice said while kneeling down to look at the damage.

"I wasn't going to do it. I just said I was cause I was mad at her cause she so selfish and don't want to share her toys."

"Well I guess you learned a lesson huh? You don't threaten people and tell them you are going to beat them up, cause if they got any sense at all they gonna whup your ass first. She pushed her daughter away. "Get in the house and clean yourself up."

Ms. Alice turned around and winked at me, "Who knew such a little skinny thang could do so much damage." She laughed her way back into the house.

Later Brenda came out. She wanted to be friends again. She was a big bully who terrorized all the kids in the project, but after I decked her big sister, she never tried anything with me. I never brought my toys out anymore, but we found plenty of things to occupy our playtime. We made mud pies, played with cans, tied strings around roaches, and raced them. When they asked if they could play with my toys

I told them that I didn't have any. They knew I was lying, but so what.

I told my Father what happened when he came home, "You did the right thing. Don't ever let anyone bully you. I don't care if you get whipped; at least you get whipped standing up for yourself."

He told me a story about when he was in the Air Force. I loved Daddy's stories. "Me and your mother had started writing to each other."

Now you have to realize my mother is a beautiful woman. I am talking beauty pageant beautiful, and that is exactly what she had sent him, photos of herself in a beauty pageant.

"I had the pictures she sent me taped to the wall next to my bunk. More than a few guys got a kick out of looking at them. One day I went to my bunk and they were gone. I asked around until I found out who had them. There was a gigantic guy who worked in the mess hall. He had taken them. Now at this time, I was all of 150 lbs soaking wet and I'm only 5'10". This guy was huge, he towered over me and had a good three feet on me, and he was at least 300 pounds of pure American muscle.

"Weren't you scared Daddy?"

"Sure I was, but I got my nerve up and went to see the guy. I said, "I want to talk to you. You have something that belongs to me, and I want it back."

The guy turned around and looked at me and started laughing. He could not believe the nerve of this little puny guy getting in his face.

"You got your chest out like you ready to take a beating over those pictures," the giant said poking me in my chest. He poked me so hard I almost fell, but I straightened up, put my shoulders back, and said, "They are mine and I want them back." I put my dukes up and prepared for whatever was about to happen."

"The man laughed and patted me on the head, "You know what? I like you. You got spunk. I'll give you your pictures as soon as I get off duty," Then he turned around and walked away laughing and shaking his head."

"A lot of guys had been standing around waiting to watch me get the snot beat out of me. When it turned out the way it did, they were all surprised and patting me on the back. That night when I got back to my bunk, the pictures were back on the wall."

"Wow," I said my eyes shining with pride for my brave Father.

"You see the moral of the story is that if something is important to you, be prepared to risk your life to keep it. Just like President Kennedy who just died because he was trying to help people, he stood up for his beliefs. Don't matter if you die, if you don't stand up for something, you are going to fall for anything. In some ways that can be worse than being dead."

Burn Baby Burn

The Watts Riots of Los Angeles
Wednesday, August 11, 1965

It was so hot. The car radio said that it was 100 degrees. Most folks sat on their porches trying to catch a breeze. My Father and I had gone out for ice cream after dinner. It was just after 7:00 p.m. when we saw a crowd at 116th and Avalon. They were watch two men and a woman fight with the police. A tow truck driver was attempting to hook up their car but his progress was being impeded by the bottles that the on onlookers were throwing.

My Father saw one of his friends and pulled over, "Hey Buckeye, what's going on?"

"The pigs stopped those two brothers, when the driver could not pass the sobriety test they tried to arrest him. His brother couldn't drive home 'cause he drunk too. The brother ran home to get his mother.

"The driver had been joking around with the cops acting like Richard Pryor doing stand up until his mother showed up and he jumped out of a whole new bag on them."

"Fool had an audience and was showing out, huh?" My Father said.

"Yeah man. His mom's was fussing at him for driving drunk. All of a sudden, he started fighting with the police and talking about, "Get away from me. You're not going to take me to jail! You're going to have to take me the hard way. Don't touch me you white motherfucker. I'll kill you."

The cop called for back up and before any body knew, what was happening the mother and two brothers started fighting the cops. When they busted the mothers lip the crowd starting getting into it."

"Why is that guy in the squad car all beat up?" Daddy asked.

"The cop hit the driver with his baton and drew blood. People started screaming, one pregnant woman spit on a cop and got herself arrested. When her boyfriend tried to pull her out, he ended up in there with her. One cop who didn't have a helmet on got hit with a bottle and started bleeding. That's when the cops started beating every one with their batons." Buckeye said.

It seemed that this community's endurance of police brutality was coming to an end. As the cops drove away, the crowd started throwing bottles and rocks at their cars. A car carrying two White passengers was stopped; they were pulled out of the car. The angry rioters were beating the hell out of them until some of the older residents intervened.

Right before our eyes mobs formed running into White establishments, pulling the owners out into the street and beating them while others looted.

My Father started the car, "We got to get the hell out of here, and Buckeye get in."

"Naw man, I'm going to get me a new television. Why don't you come with me? We can load the stuff into your car."

"No thanks man, I'm taking my daughter home. You know everything that looks free, ain't."

"Suit yourself."

I watched Buckeye run into a store as my Father slowly nosed the car through the crowd wading through people carrying cases of liquor, toilet paper, and cereal across the street.

At home, we turned on the radio. I could not believe what these people were doing. I stood in the window and looked down on people as they overturned cars set barricades made of trashcans to trap the incoming cars on their way to Downey, South Gate, and Lakewood. I watched the hot dog stand burn.

We got in the car to go and check on my Grandmother. My Father told my Mother, "Anna Lee you got to get down. You are too damned light-skinned. They gone think you white and attack us."

Later that night when we got back home my Mother heard something in the back yard and told my Father, "They out there taking our trash cans, you got to go out there and get them back."

My Father looked at her as if she had lost her whole mind, "Woman there are hundreds of people out there fighting and burning down everything they can get there hands on. Why do I want to go out there over some trashcans? Woman you done lost your mind. And keep your ass out the window before they think I'm hiding white folks in here."

The riot made no sense to me. When they ran out of White people to hurt, they started fighting one another over stolen merchandise. They were burning down our neighborhood. Where were we going to shop now?

Daddy planned to sleep in the living room to make sure we would be safe. He took me upstairs and tucked me into bed. As soon as he went back down, I went to my window.

There was a 6'5" Albino man who was always in the projects at one woman or another's house. All you had to do was open your eyes and you could pick out his children peppered through the neighborhood. He staggered into our small patch of backyard with two girls in the crook of his arms. I watched him lean one girls head back and pour liquor straight from a bottle down her throat, then the other. They were teenagers who should not have been out in this chaos.
The girls were struggling in an attempt to get away, but to no avail. He ripped one girl's shorts from the crouch and threw her on the ground and climbed on top of her while he kept his big beefy hand wrapped around the throat of the other girl who lay next to them. He went back and forth from one to the other.

At the time, I did not know what he was doing to them, but I did know that they were being hurt. One of the girls looked up and saw me looking down. She kept her eyes fixed on mine. Something in her eyes begged me not to leave the window. It was as if looking into my eyes helped her endure. Every few moments she would wave to me from over his shoulder.

I wanted to go down and tell my Father to go out and rescue them, but the memory of the Albino in a fight with two men a few weeks before stopped me. When that fight was over the other men were taken away in an ambulance.

I had never seen my Father fight, but I did not think that it would be a good idea to send him out. With his health problems, I could not risk his life.

The other girl screamed and Albinos fist closed tighter around her throat. She passed out and when he went back to her, he kept slapping her and shouting "Wake up," until she moaned and her eyes fluttered open.

When the Albino finished he got up, pulled up his pants, and ran out toward Imperial Highway to help a mob set a car on fire. Two white men had jumped out of their car and ran off in the opposite direction.

The next morning the news said that more than fifty cars were burned. Over 1500 rioters, including men, women and children ran wild in the streets. Thirty-four people were arrested. Thirty-five, including nineteen police officers, had been injured that first night.

The rioters threatened to move out of the Negro communities and attack predominately White districts if the police did not leave. Screams of, "Burn Baby Burn, Kill Whitey," rang out as they set fires to block after block. The only thing that drowned out the chants were the helicopters that hovered over head. The riots spread to San Diego, Pasadena, Pacoima, Monrovia, and Long Beach.

Trucks pulled up in the projects and people unloaded stolen merchandise. They broke into and stripped liquor, convenience, grocery store.

Three thousand national guards were called in to patrol the streets. A curfew was put in effect and they shot people who broke it, no questions asked. By Sunday, things had calmed down.

When it was all over, the statistics were staggering. 34 deaths, that the coroner determined justifiable homicide, and one accidental. 1,032 injured 90 of whom were Los Angeles police officers, 136 firemen, 10 National Guardsmen, 23 people from government agencies and 773 civilians. Of those ruled justifiable homicide, the jury found that death was caused in sixteen instances by officers of the Los Angeles

Police Department and in seven instances by the National Guard. Property damage was estimated at over $40 million dollars.

Helicopters had circled above photographing people with stolen merchandise. They followed them home and recorded the addresses. Old furniture and refrigerators lined the curb waiting for disposal. Kids played in large appliance boxes right in front of their homes.

The police waited until the sanitation trucks had come and taken all the old furniture away. The next morning the police swooped in with convoys of trucks. They went house to house confiscating all merchandise that people did not have receipts for, and some things that they did have receipts for, they said they could not prove it was their receipt. If they could get confirmation from the store, they could reclaim their property. What store? They had burned them all down.

Those trucks left with furniture, electronics, and clothes, cases of food, alcohol, and diapers. Most of the people were left with empty houses and cupboards.

After the riots organizations popped up to help change the hopelessness that had incited the riot. The Son's of Watts policed the neighborhood giving the place a sense of security. Jesse Jackson's operation PUSH was gaining momentum, as were the Black Panthers and the Muslims. Everyone was running around talking "Black Power," and greeting one another with a balled up fist held high.

Breakfast programs and daycare took care of the children. They recruited and trained people for jobs and the opportunity of a better life. A life they could be proud of as they rose up in the world. The reason why black people were so quick to hurt and kill was because they did not value their own dismal lives.

The gangs called a truce and homicides declined. The police didn't like that. They did all kinds of underhanded things to break the truce. They sent in undercover policemen to try to start fights. The gangs were not stupid. They checked the strangers out and found out who they were. When that ploy didn't work, they sent letters that carried threats to rival gangs. They did not get the desired effect.

The train tracks that ran through the projects mysteriously held train cars full of guns and ammunition. They knew that if they left it there the people would break into them, just like they did with the vans that appeared unlocked and full of weapons in hope that they would use them to kill one another.

1976

Six months after the riot, my parents bought a house in Compton in a nice neighborhood, on a quiet, tree-lined street off of Compton and Long Beach Blvd. The whole family helped us move.

We had two bedrooms, a living room with a fireplace, a den, a nice kitchen, one bathroom, a garage, a nice sized front yard, and a huge backyard. We were so happy to be there.

One day I was out in the front yard and a little girl, Shelly, came over and asked if I wanted to play. I was ecstatic to have a friend. We spent the morning on my porch playing with pick up sticks, jacks, and hopscotch. When her mom called her for lunch she said, "I'm going to ask my mom if you can come to lunch 'cause you are my new best friend." She came back, "Come on my mom made us lunch."

I asked my Father if I could go and he said it was all right.

When we walked into the kitchen, her mom was looking in a cabinet. "Hello dear, Shelly tells me that you are her new best friend." When she turned around and looked at me, I swear her jaw dropped and she had the most dumbfounded expression on her face that I had ever seen. I felt something strange about the way she looked at me. I looked down to make sure that I was not dirty or had stepped in poop or something. She pushed Shelly toward the door, "You guys go out in the back, and I'll make you a picnic."

"Can I wash my hands?" I asked

"I'll bring you a towel out to the back yard. You can use the water hose."

"Okay." I always washed my hands before I ate. I didn't think anything when she told me to use the hose. She brought out peanut butter and jelly sandwiches and milk; mine was in a paper cup. "As soon as you two finish eating I need you to come inside Shelly. I need your help with something."

While we were eating Shelly's Father pulled up, "Hey, daddy's home for lunch, maybe he will eat with us." She ran to her Father. I heard them talking before he rounded the corner. He stopped and looked at me with the same strange look that her mother had. He went into the house, there were raised voices, and seconds later her mom came outside, "Shelly you have to come in. Right now."

"Yes mommy."

"Tell your friend goodbye and come on inside."

"You want to play tomorrow?" I asked my new friend

"Sure, we can play dolls tomorrow."

"I got lots of dolls and doll houses."

"Alright, see you tomorrow."

When I got home, I saw that Shelly had left her ball. I went back to return it. When I got by the window, I heard her crying, "But I like her, she's my friend, and I like playing with her."

"Have you lost your mind? That is a nigger? We don't play with niggers. If I catch you playing with her again, I will beat you within an inch of your life, do you understand me young lady?" Her Father shouted.

"No I don't understand, you are prejudice, they talked about this in bible school. If you don't like someone because of their color that makes you prejudice. I don't want to be prejudice."

"You mean prejudice. Honey you have to do as your Father says, we are only looking out for your best interest. You be a good girl, mind us and stay away from her," her mother said.

"I am going to play with her and you can't stop..."

Before Shelly could finish the sentence, her Father grabbed her by her hair and hit her. He was breathing into her face, which had a big red palm print.

Shelly must have felt my presence because she turned and looked right into my eyes. I dropped her ball, turned and ran home, tears blurred my vision, and I was almost hit by a car when I ran into the street.

The only other White kids I had ever played with were the ones where my grandmother cleaned and they were all nice to me. I did not know how to process what I was feeling. For the first time I felt like there was something wrong with me. I went in my room and lay on my bed and cried.

My Father had been working in the back yard and when he came in, he heard me. He came into my room and sat on the bed. "What's wrong?"

"I'm a Nigger." I said between sniffles.

"What happened?" I told him all about it. I could see rage forming like clouds on his face. "They called you a nigger?"

"They didn't know I was at the screen door. They were talking to the little girl I was playing with. They said that if they caught her playing with me they would beat her because I'm a nigger. Her Father hit her in the face."

My Father said, "The world can be an ugly place sometimes. Now that Black people are getting more rights, a lot of White's don't like that," He pulled me onto his lap and held me close.

"What do you mean more rights?"

"Do you know what slavery is?"

I shook my head and waited for him to explain. "There is a continent called Africa and there is another one called Europe. The European people came to America. They wanted to farm here, raise crops like cotton, but they didn't want to work the fields themselves. So someone came up with the bright idea to go and kidnap the Africans because they are really strong people. They put them on ships and brought them here and made them work. They called them slaves."

I had heard that word before from Sally, but I didn't know what it meant.

"They brought them here and sold them to plantations and forced them to pick cotton from sun up to sun down. They called them Niggers. Niggers is short for ignorant. But we are not ignorant anymore. We can read and write. During slavery days if they found out you could read or write they killed you.

If a slave didn't work hard enough or tried to run away and were caught they were punished as an example to the others."

"I would have fought back."

"Yeah, me too," Daddy laughed

"After hundreds of years of Slavery there was a war because the Northern states decided to do away with slavery. There were some other reasons that made them fight but you can learn about them later. The South was forced to stop shipping Africans into the states because due to breeding."

"What is breeding?"

They had a lot a lot of kids. Let's see how I can put this so that you can understand. If your mother was a slave and had a baby the masters, would take her baby and sell it off for money. Because of this the slaves outnumbered the masters."

"You mean they would make Mommy sell me?"

"That's what they did with slaves. When the South didn't want to go along with the North, they had a war and the South lost. Not too long ago we could not go into certain restaurants or drink from water fountains that said 'Whites only.' It was called segregation.

"Segra – what?"

"Segregation. That's over now, thanks to a man named Martin Luther King."

"You mean the man who you listen to on the record player. The one who says, 'I have a dream,' I mimicked the loud voice.

"Yeah baby, that's him. We are supposed to be able to go anywhere we want. There are some people who don't think that is a good idea. They don't think we are as good as them, in their eyes, we are not equal. They would like nothing more than to see us back in slavery, don't you worry, it will never happen."

"I'm glad they don't do slavery anymore."

"Because slavery is over there are ignorant, prejudice people who don't consider us human beings."

When Shelly called her parents prejudice her Daddy hit her in the face."

It is pronounced prejudice. If they don't want their daughter to play with you, then you don't want to be around them anyway, right?"

"I guess. But Daddy I liked her, we had fun playing together. But I think I liked her enough not to want her to get beat for playing with me."

"I'll be right back."

I don't know what my Father said to those people, but when he came back he said, "You don't have to worry about being called a Nigger by them anymore."

One day on the way to The San Fernando Valley, I broached the subject with my Grandmother, "Mother how come we can go out here with these rich White folks and their kids play with me and their parents don't get mad, but where I live parents beat their kids for playing with me?"

"For one thing you don't live in their neighborhood. When I finish cleaning, we go on back to our side of town. Some folks don't want you living in there lily white neighborhoods."

"Sometimes I wish we had never moved. I liked it better in the projects. At least when somebody says 'Nigger' they are the same color as me and I don't feel like I have a tail or something."

"You listen to me little girl, ain't nothing wrong with you. Black people are the most beautiful creation on God's green earth. We come in a rainbow of colors and we don't age fast. Our bodies are built to last. We are the strongest race there is. They keep trying to tear us down, but we just rise up above it all. White folks didn't understand why the slaves sang in the fields while they did back-breaking work that the masters felt they were too good to do themselves."

"Why were they singing?"

"We have our own language. We sing while we work 'cause we know the lord can hear us. What ever happens here in this world just makes us stronger. We know that we are going on home when our time comes, home to be with God where there is no work, no pain, and no prejudice."

"Daddy told me about slavery. We have been reading books about Harriet Tubman and Nat Turner. If I had to be a slave, I would have been like them, fighting to get free. They would have killed me 'cause when they tried to whip me, I would have snatched that whip and turned around and started beating them with it."

She looked at me, "I just bet you would have. We still have to fight to make them treat us like human beings. A lot of people died to get us freedom. You need to read about the civil war and the KKK."

"Mother do you think that what they did was fair?"

"Ain't much in this world fair, but everything that happens is God's will, no matter what happens, he ain't gone put no more on a body than it can bear."

"But they ran up in Africa and kidnapped people to come over here and work like horses."

"Black folks are strong. God wanted us in America. Those people got so full of themselves they didn't see the civil war coming. God had to take them down a peg or two."

"That's when everyone got freedom?"

"In some ways, lots of people are still slaves. Tell your daddy to get you some reading on Juneteenth. In Texas and Louisiana somebody forgot to tell the slaves they were free for two years."

"Why?"

"Cause they could. For the simple reason that they could get away with it."

"Boy they were bold."

One day you are going to do something great. I done seen a vision. That's right; God done already showed me that you are going to make a difference in this world. You're smart and you gone make us all proud, Right?"

"Yep, just like Sojourner Truth and George Washington Carver. There are a lot of famous black people. Did you know that black people invented almost every thing? You can't open your eyes without seeing something that black people invented mixers, peanut butter, light bulbs, mops, and traffic lights."

Mother started naming some things that I didn't know about, "Ironing board, straightening comb, sprinkler, lawn mower, air conditioners, heating furnace, electric lamp, clothes dryer, refrigerator, and just think, we did all that without knowing how to read and write, well at least without letting them know that we knew how to read and write," she laughed.

"You know if it wasn't for us, they would be in big trouble, seems like they would be nicer, and stop calling us names, like Nigger."

"Sticks and stones may break your bones but names can never hurt you. Child you got to realize folks is folks. You got good white folks and bad white folks. You got good black folks and bad black folks. Don't matter what color a person is, it's the color of their heart you got to go by. Some people will hurt you just as soon as look at you. You know most people who are brave enough to stand up for what's right usually get killed."

"I wonder why that is?"

"We lost a great leader in President Kennedy and people mourned him deeply. Look at Malcolm X, after all, he tried to do for people somebody done gone and shot him dead, but you know what, he home now. We are the ones left here to deal with hell on earth. Going home is the best thing that can happen to a body. So you don't ever be afraid of anything or ashamed of your color, no matter what."

Holidays

I loved our new house. The back yard was laden with apricot, plum, fig, persimmon, and pomegranate trees. The avocado tree in the next yard hung into our yard. A grape vine climbed the back fence. Daddy planted citrus trees and spent hours working in the yard and fixing up the house. He put in a covered patio and had two huge oil can barbecue pits set in a wooden stand that he built.

Christmas dinner was hosted in our new house. My Father bought a gigantic flocked tree that went all the way to the ceiling. We decorated with every color glass bulb, lots of shiny silver tinsel, twinkling lights and a gold star on the top that my Father had to climb a ladder to put on. It was the most beautiful thing I had ever seen. The tree we had in the projects was a sad little foil thing missing half its limbs.

The fireplace reflected off of the bulbs and crystals colored the flames. Pinecones on the hearth filled the house with an outdoorsy fragrance that mingled with the aroma of holiday fare. Christmas music vibrated from the stereo cabinet.

Every one came in bearing gifts that were added to the ever-growing stack that surrounded the tree. They bought their signature dishes. We had so much food that we had to put trays on the clothes washer and dryer, every counter space and folding card table held platters and serving bowls. Gumbo, turkey, ham, fried chicken, macaroni and cheese, dirty rice, greens, string beans, potato salad and rolls.

My Father made a lemon pie that was so wonderful and rich that your whole face screwed up from the sweet tartness. A long wooden table covered with a holiday cloth spanned the length of the kitchen wall laden with fragrant apple sweet potato and meringue pies. German chocolate and coconut cake, called my name.

My favorite drink, a carton of pineapple sherbet floating in Hawaiian punch and 7up in a bottomless punch bowl that had to be refilled every half hour because the kids could not get enough of it.

I looked forward to holidays, everybody laughing, hugging, kissing, and dancing. When everyone was full to bursting, we all crammed into the living room and watched as each present was opened one by one. The gifts were oohed and aahed over, while the gifter received affectionate gratitude.

I saved half of my allowance from August to Christmas so I could buy presents. Mommy started shopping for Christmas right after Halloween. She took me to get my dads gift, and he took me to get hers.

I bought my Father his favorite cologne, Russian Leather. I love the way it smells on him. I hugged him all the time just so that I could inhale his scent. I used to think; when I married, I was going to make my husband bathe in that cologne. I also thought, maybe I should just marry my Father. Every little girl falls in love with their Father a little bit.

Now, my mom, she smelled good too. Her Chanel No.5 was intoxicating. Her light brown hair had natural highlights and her eyes changed color with the season. She had one of those bodies that made men stop, stare and whistle. She never paid them no mind, just kept on walking, and swinging her right arm as if she didn't here a thing.

On special occasions she let me dab a little perfume behind my neck and wrist, I felt so pretty. It kind of made up for the time I spent in the kitchen chair with the hot comb, getting pressed and curled into Shirley Temple ringlets.

Daddy made our clothes on special occasions. We were something to see in our coordinating outfits. One year he and my mom had matching gold Nehru jackets and pants. They were sharp as a tack. I was so proud, nothing from any store could compare to the clothes my Daddy made.

When we had a party, cars took up two blocks. All the neighborhood kids were outside showing off their holiday clothes. Mommy gave me a couple of presents on Christmas morning, but we had to wait for Daddy to get up before opening the rest.

I was outside looking at all the other kids ride their new bikes. I was so envious, when I could not take it any more I went inside.

"Kim your daddy needs your help out in the front yard," Mommy said.

When I opened the door and walked out onto the porch Daddy stood holding a beautiful, shiny blue stingray bicycle, with streamers on the handles. "Merry Christmas."

Elementary School

Compton was changing fast, and so was Ralph Waldo Emerson Elementary School. I do believe that within six months of our moving into the neighborhood it seemed every house on the block grew a 'For Sale' sign. I was glad that the prejudice people were moving out. Can you say, "Blockbusting?"

I was outside playing and three White kids stood on the other side of the street, "Hey Nigger, hey jiggaboo." Their parents thought their antics at my expense were funny. They just sat on the porch laughing. I continued to ignore them... until they crossed the street. The first one that jumped in my face got a big surprise when I hit him in the jaw and kicked him in the nuts.

His parents stopped laughing. I had my dukes up waiting for the boy to get up, or for one his friends to try something. The boy's mother ran across the street and pulled the crying boy off the sidewalk. They never crossed the street again.

I loved school and got good grades. My mother dropped me off at school in the morning and afterwards a lady named Ms. Jones waited outside the gate for me. She watched kids until their parents got off work. I looked forward to the homemade cookies she had waiting for us everyday.

I made some black friends at school and we stuck together. The whites called us names at first, but they didn't do it too many times because we whipped their asses when they got out of line. It didn't matter to the principal that they started the mess; we always got in trouble because we finished it. Within a few years, Whites were the minority.

My family stressed how important education was. Good report cards equaled good rewards. Being the Leo that I was, I loved the praise, money, and gifts they garnered.

During the summer when my Father was going to school or working, I stayed with my Aunt Mary, who was

Curley's wife. Their son Poncho was about two years younger than me. We ran around playing on broomstick horses through the sprinklers all day. We had so much fun.

Soon we had another toy to play with. Mary had a baby boy, Christopher. Mary entertained us with the best stories and games. Poncho could not drink regular milk, so while at Mary's I had to drink goat's milk and I hated it.

When Daddy was not working, we fished, sometimes everyday. My Father was my best friend and I loved everything we did together, but fishing was at the top of my list. Nothing tastes like a fish that you caught, scaled and gutted yourself.

In San Pedro, the Tuna Factory opened the drains to discard the parts they don't can and thousands of fish wait to feed. Daddy put five-four prong hooks on three fishing poles. He cast out and reels in really fast while jerking back on the line. This was called snag fishing. When he reeled in I took the fishing pole and laid it down with the fish on it and gave him another, while he snagged I took the fish off the line and put them into the cooler. We caught smelt, blue gill, and croakers.

I preferred fishing off the pier in Long Beach with bait. Because then I could catch some fish. When we got home, we laid out our catch and mommy took pictures of Daddy holding the big ones before we cleaned and bagged them for the freezer. Daddy had a whole photo album of these pictures.

We stocked fish for the Fourth of July celebration that was at our house every year. Everyone showed up with boxes of fireworks that we started se5tting off as soon as the sun went down.

The fish frying and barbecue stank up the whole neighborhood. We danced and ate till the early hours of the morning.

Church

1966

We did not go to church every Sunday. We went on Easter and Christmas Eve. We went to a huge catholic church where you had to kneel down on padded boards every few minutes. The music was slow with no beat coming from a huge organ accompanied by lots of people in robes singing at the front of the church.

I spent most of the time in awe of the beautiful huge stained glass windows that portrayed pictures of Jesus and his followers. I loved how the sun sent prisms of multicolored light through the church. I didn't understand half of what the man in the robe with the pointy hat was talking about.

We didn't read the bible, but I said a prayer every night as my mom watched, "Now I lay me down to sleep, I pray the lord my soul to keep, if I should die before I wake, I pray the lord my soul to take. Bless mommy and daddy, and then I would proceed to name everyone in my family putting off bedtime for a few more precious minutes.

One weekend I stayed with a family member, we are going to call her Esther. That Sunday Esther took me to church. It was different than what I was used to. There were only Black people, not one white person in the whole church. It was a small house that had been turned into a church with only one little stained glass window. There was a band with drums, piano, and guitars and the music made you want to jump up, and dance like the whole congregation was doing. The preacher screamed his sermon and said 'uh huh' or 'yeeeeaaahs' in between every sentence.

The people got all riled up and started speaking in a crazy language that I could not understand. People ran to the front of the church where the preacher would touch them on the forehead, they screamed and fell out on the floor.

I had never seen anything like this and was scared. Esther stood up to go up front. I grabbed onto her and begged her not to go. I guess she saw my fear and sat back down.

Men came with stretchers and lifted the people off the floor and carried them out. My young mind told me that these people had done something wrong, the preachers touch was killing them, and they were going to hell for their sins. I had only seen one other person on a stretcher in my life and the next time I saw them they were in a coffin.

Afterwards the preacher stood on the church steps speaking to everyone as they filed out, I walked past him and when Esther turned around to introduce me, I was no where to be found because I was hiding behind a large lady.

When I saw Esther walk away from the preacher, I appeared at her side. In the car, she asked me, "So did you like Church?"

"No, it was scary and I don't want to go back there again."

She laughed, "It is important to go to church so that god knows that you love him."

"God knows everything so he knows that I love him and if he needs to hear it I will just to go to my mommy's church and tell him."

Back at her house, I sat in the kitchen playing with my Barbie dolls while she prepared dinner. "We are going to have company for dinner and I want everything to be just right. Can you help me?"

"Sure, I cook with my mommy and grandmother all the time, what do you want me to do?"

We measured out every thing to bake a cake and I stirred while she turned her attention back to the macaroni and cheese. I was licking the leftover cake batter with my fingers when the doorbell rang. She used a damp towel to clean my fingers off, "You go and get the door and offer our company a seat."

I ran to the door and opened it. It was the killer preacher from church. "Well hello you must Kim, if you aren't the prettiest little girl I've ever seen," he said while rubbing my cheek.

"Thank you, have a seat in the living room."

I went into the kitchen "The preacher is sitting on the couch," before she could say anything I went into the bathroom through the adjoining door to the bedroom. I turned on the television and climbed on the bed hoping that she would let me stay in here until her company left. No such luck. "Kim what are you doing in here when we have company? Turn that T.V. off and come on out here, get the preacher a glass of lemonade."

I took the preacher his glass and went back in the kitchen. "Kim I got to run to the store."

I got my sweater and ran out the back door and waited for her next to the car. "Oh no baby you have to stay here and keep our guest company, it would be rude to leave him all alone."

I slowly followed her back into the house.

"I'll be right back."

I sat down in a chair across from him with my doll in my hand. I pretended to study her.

"That is a pretty dolly, can I see her?"

I heard the back door close. I did not move or look up for a minute. "God does not like people to be rude or selfish. I know you heard me."

I got up and walked over holding the doll out to him. He grabbed my hand and pulled me to him, picking me up, and putting me on his lap.

"I think you are prettier than the doll."

"Thank you."

For some reason I forgot everything from that moment on. The next morning when I woke up, I put on my clothes. I did not want any breakfast. I just wanted the day to pass and for my parents to come and get me. I could not wait to go home.

When my Father pulled up to get me, I was sitting on the porch waiting. "How was your trip Daddy?"

"It was good, we won a little money."

"Next time you go take me with you, would you please not leave me here again."

"Why what's wrong?"

"I just don't want to stay here anymore. I don't like the church she took me to, it's scary."

"Well we will talk about it later lets get you home."

"My stuff is right here, I'll put it in the car and wait for you while you go and say goodbye."

On the ride home, I felt like I wanted to tell my Father something but I could not think of what it was.

After that weekend, I refused to go to church. I would get to the door and cry, scream and holler. I would take my spanking but I was not going to a church and I refused to pray.

Dinner at Tracton's

That lobster is bigger than yo' head.

Finally, Mommy was dressed and we were ready to go eat. I put the photo album down and went out to my car. I took five hundred dollars and a package of cocaine out of my stash before I climbed into my Father's van that he had fixed up the van with curtains and a small refrigerator. The eight-track tape played Al Green.

I fell asleep on the ride that took a little over an hour with traffic.

"Kim, we almost there," mommy said tapping me on the leg.

We made it just in time for our reservation and were seated immediately. Good thing cause I was hungry as a big dog. When the waitress came we knew what we wanted and put our entrée order. We always had the same thing, Daddy had a cut of prime rib that took up the whole plate, Mommy had shrimp that were the size of normal lobsters, and I had the lobster tail.

I remember the first time we came to Tracton's. I was twelve and we came for my graduation from elementary school. The waitress came rolling the trolley down the aisle. I could not believe my eyes. That lobster was so big, I grabbed my mothers hand and started screaming, "Mommy, Mommy, look Mommy, look."

"Child what is wrong with you?" She said trying to figure out why I was so excited.

Then she saw it, "Oh my God, what in the world, that's not, oh my God it is." She grabbed my Father's hand and started bouncing in her seat. "Clyde will you look at this. Look Clyde, Look."

"Ya'll embarrassing me, quiet down, got all these folks staring at us...."

The waitress stopped the trolley in front of our table. Daddy's eyes almost popped out of his head. "Good googly woogly, what the hell is that?" he yelled. Now people really were staring at us.

"It's your order Sir," the waitress said as she served us.

"Clyde, now you are embarrassing us," my mother hissed.

"Anna look at the size of that thing, how she gone eat that? That lobster tail is bigger than her head."

"Well look at your prime rib, it's half a cow." Mommy said as the waitress placed the platter in front of daddy. The meat took up the entire oversized plate and must have been at least two inches thick.

"Anna we can eat for a week off of this hunk of meat."

"Mommy your shrimp are huge and look at the potatoes."

I started giggling from the memory.

"What are you laughing at?" Mommy asked

"I know what she's laughing at, she's thinking about the first time we came here. We lucky they didn't throw us out. I can't take ya'll no place," Daddy said.

"Clyde you got a lot of nerve, you were the one getting all loud."

Our drinks came and the waitress said she would be right back with our soup. I ignored the fruity hurricane and dug into the warm, buttery bread.

"I hope that helps, your stomach was growling all the way here. I thought we had a bear in the car." Mommy said.

"Dang, you heard my stomach growling while I was asleep?"

"The whole state heard it, we thought it was an earthquake, don't know how you slept with all the noise you were making." Daddy joked.

"I slept through it hoping that you would not come down the hall to carry me back to your room where we all got under the covers and waited to die as a family."

I was referencing the earthquake we experienced shortly after moving into the house. The house felt like it was on skates as it rolled, things falling off of shelves and tables.

Daddy bounced from wall to wall making his way to my room, where I was screaming bloody murder, "Daddy, Daddy. He picked me up and carried me back down the hall and put me in the bed between him and mommy, pulled the covers over our head and waited.

Mommy started cracking up, "I remember that Clyde, What were you thinking?"

"Hell I didn't know what to do, so I did what I did when I got scared growing up. You remember that huh?"

"Oh yeah, that and the time when I was vacuuming and I couldn't get the little green piece of fabric that was peaking under the door, when pulled that door back a lizard was sticking his tongue out at me. I was screaming and hollering while you were asleep in the bed. You jumped out of the bed and closed and locked your door."

"I didn't know what was going on. I needed time to get my gun."

"You left me out there. Had someone been in the house I would have been dead. Oh yeah, and what about the time I had my first allergic reaction."

Mommy was laughing so hard that she had to put her fork down.

Daddy had to pick me up from school, I had a fever, and the nurse had given me aspirin. I had been taking it for years but this time I had a reaction. I didn't start swelling until I was in the car. We stopped at a light and I was making a weird noise because I couldn't breath. Daddy turned around, I was swollen up like a pumpkin. He screamed like a woman and jumped out of the car.

"That wasn't my daughter in that back seat, you looked like a monster. The cops saw me jump out of the car and pulled up to see what the problem was. They told me it was an allergic reaction and we had to get you to the hospital, fast. They turned on their sirens and I followed them. You were alright in the end, you didn't die," Daddy said.

"That ain't the point. You left me in the middle of the street in a running car, while I was having an allergic reaction."

We were laughing and having a good time. The bread stopped my stomach from rumbling. A tureen of rich, thick clam chowder rolled up to the table. It was served in bowls made from bread. No one said a word until the soup was gone, bread, and all. As if on cue, the waitress arrived with salads garnished with olives, parmesan cheese, and a creamy Italian dressing. It doesn't matter how old I get, when I see that big 24 oz lobster tail I still get excited to this day. Conversation flowed throughout the meal. We paced ourselves to save room for dessert.

Tracton's had the best German chocolate cake in the world and they gave you a big ol' Flintstone hunk. I always cut it in half and had the waitress put one piece in a to-go box.

I had a system for eating cake. I ate the cake first saving the rich frosting for last. I was almost through the cake when Daddy started telling jokes. He did this to me every year. I always swore that I was not going to fall for it, but as hard as I tried, I could not stop laughing long enough to stop him from eating my frosting. I think he looked for jokes and saved them up just for this day. He had some new material taken from Robin Harris, Dolomite, and Moms Mobley. He made their jokes sound funnier than when they told them. Even the people at the neighboring tables were holding their sides. Daddy missed his calling; he should have been a comedian.

We took our doggie bags that were exotic animals twisted out of foil and I directed Daddy to the club where I was going to meet Laisyv. When we pulled up to the speakeasy, there was a long line of men standing outside.

"Why are all these men standing outside?" Daddy asked.

"Do you really want to know?" I joked.

"I want to know," Mommy said.

"Well tonight is male exotic dancer night and the men wait out here until the show is over, they have to get here early cause only so many can get in because the place is so packed."

"When is the show over," Mommy asked.

"About eleven."

"That's forty minutes from now, why do they wait so long to get into a club?" Mommy asked.

"Anna, think woman, you got all those women worked up into a frenzy. By the time they let these guys in its easy pickings, man is guaranteed to get lucky."

"Don't let me hear about you coming back here trying to get lucky."

"Ya'll want to come in."

"No we don't want to come in and you shouldn't be going in there either." Mommy said.

I hugged and kissed my parents goodbye.

I hugged the doorman Bubba, "Hey Sparkle what's going on?"

"Just you baby. Is it jumping tonight?"

"You know it is. Hey I got a couple of customers for you, you holding?"

"And you know this. Give me a few minutes. We can take care of the money before I leave."

"Cool."

I went to the club window, "Nessa, what's going on girl? Give me fifty in ones." I handed her a hundred dollar bill.

"You got it Sparkle. Girl you looking good tonight," She counted out my ones and gave me the rest in tens. "Thanks girl," I gave her a ten, "This is for you."

I stopped Gail, the waitress and told her "Bring me three double cognacs VSOP, 7 up back."

"I got you girl,"

"Here's your money,"

"Why don't you keep that and hook me up with a fifty."

"I got you; just give me a few minutes."

The women in the club were going crazy. They were definitely ready for the fireman who was on stage to hose them down. Laisyv was in the middle of a private dance. The dancer had her legs over his shoulders, thighs down hanging upside down while he bit into the crouch of her thin pants. She was stuffing dollar bills inside of his G-string, her braids were hanging down and she was screaming, "Oh my God."

All the other girls at the table were hollering, "Go Thunderbolt, Go Thunderbolt, Go Thunderbolt."

Thunderbolt finally put Laisyv down into her chair and she picked up some money off the table and handed it to him while dabbing her breast and brow with a napkin. She turned around and saw me.

Laisyv introduced everyone. I knew most of them. I was halfway through my first drink when Laisyv looked at me and touched her nose. I got up and headed for the restroom. Laisyv and I went into a stall. Hold this, I pulled the gun out of the pouch behind my neck and took out three packages of coke. I gave one to Laisyv, "This is you." Then I put one package in my purse and from the other I poured some on top of the toilet paper holder. I used a gold straw to snort the crystalline powder. I took two lines and moved over for Laisyv.

"Wow." she said as she rose up holding her nose. "Girl Christian wasn't home when the limo came to pick me up so I had to leave. I sold all the work that was at the house."

"You cool now. Did you say limo? Damn ya'll just gone all out tonight. We need to roll down Sunset and see who we can catch coming out of Carlos and Charlie's."

"Damn, did you see that fine ass dancer, girl he got me wet."

"Hell yeah, girl, I was getting hot just watching him. We can always have him and his boys for a party at my house. Get some real private dancing. See if your girls are down."

"Girl you ain't said nothing but a word. I know they are with it."

I was folding up some dollar bills and separating coke into gram packs, and handing them to her so she could fold them closed. Laisyv and I worked well together, we spent many a day cutting, weighing and bagging up cocaine. I had been selling dope for her man Christian almost three years now.

I met Laisyv working at a toy company and we started hanging out. After she met some of my Uncles, she knew that I was cool and told her husband about me; soon I was bringing him steady clientele on a commission.

I took another blow and passed the straw to Laisyv. "You all set, girlfriend?"

"Oh Yeah, Let's party!"

I walked up to the bar and handed a package to Gail and then went out to the front to serve Bubba.

I sat at the table taking in the environment and my drink. Dancers were on the stage and at various tables throughout the room. They would be doing their finale pretty soon, so if I wanted to have any fun I had to do it now. I took out the fifty dollars in one's and threw half of them on the table, "Let's party girls."

We ran up on the stage, money in hand. These were some foine ass – Adonis sculpted men up in here. I was having a good time, once I ran out of one's I went back to the table. The dancers all climbed on stage to do their finale. We watched with rapt attention. Laisyv and I looked at each other and at the same time said, "Shake it up tonight," and broke out laughing.

As the dancers left the floor, the doors opened and men flooded in.

I was going back to the bathroom when I saw some of my Uncles friends and stopped to speak. Joe Joe whispered in my ear, "You got some blow?" I took his money and went into the bathroom to separate the last package. I came out and hugged Joe Joe, slipping the pack into his pocket.

I was en route to my chair when one of the dancers who looked just as good in his clothes as he did in the G-string grabbed my hand and pulled me to the dance floor. The Gap Band was singing, "You dropped a bomb on me." We danced through two songs before I went back to my table.

I was sitting with my back to the crowd, talking to some of the girls at the table, when their mouths fell open. They were staring at something behind me. "What is wrong with ya'll?"

I felt a tap on my shoulder, "Come dance with me, Kim."

I knew that voice, it still sent chills through me. Without turning around I said, "Why would I want to dance with you Howard?"

"Because I miss you and I still love you," His hot breath in my ear.

"Don't even try it," I stood up and attempted to walk away from him but his strong grip propelled me to the dance floor. A slow song came on and he pulled me into him. I hated the way my heart fluttered. I hated the way my body responded to being so close to him. I hated that the way he smelled made me moist. I hated it so much that I settled into his arms and pretended he had not broken my heart two years ago.

1979

Kim

It was summertime and I was staying with Ann, Martha, and Wendy, on Venice walk and Rose Avenue in an apartment owned by Ann's sugar daddy, who was in Europe for three months.

We sat on the balcony and picked our prey as the crowds walked by. When we spotted a guy that we liked we skated past them in our bikinis and belly chains. It was a game for us. We tracked our dates on a calendar. The one with the least dates had to clean the apartment after our Saturday night parties where we charged for food, liquor, and drugs. We put music speakers out on the balcony and every one partied right on the walkway.

On Sundays, all our friends came over and each of us put twenty dollars in a bowl, the one who garnered the most phone numbers was the winner. It was on one of these Sunday's that I first saw Howard. He was with a group of eight guys and they were all abnormally tall, and fine.

"Kim, check it out. They have got to be ball players," Ann said.

All of us rushed out on the balcony, "Time to go get my man," Martha said. We put on our skates and raced past them so they could get a good view. The guys called out for us but we kept going. After we got a block ahead of them, we turned around and skated back, slowly knowing they were not going to let us get by.

I was talking to a guy named Norman. He had grabbed my arm to stop me. All the while we talked a guy was standing behind him beckoning for me to talk to him. He walked up and insisted on being introduced. Sparkle this

Howard, Howard, Sparkle. Now go on about your business and stop trying to block," Norman said.

That week Norman called me a few times. After a few weeks, we made a lunch date. He was going to come to my job and pick me up for lunch. Ann's man had returned from Europe, and I had moved back to my parents.

I worked at Imperial Mattress Company as a receptionist. The accountant, Sherry, was fast becoming fast friends since we were the only blacks employed there. We started going out to happy hour after work. I spent the night at her apartment in Inglewood a few times because we rarely got any sleep before having to go to work the next morning. It didn't matter how late we stayed out, we always made it to work.

Many days we were the only one's in the office because the boss did not come in but once or twice a week. The salesmen were our in the field most of the day so we snuck catnaps in the showroom.

Norman arrived and I told Sherry, "I'm going to lunch now."

Sherry looked up from her work and went off like a roman candle, "Oh hell no, no you ain't trying to pull this crap." It was a good thing that the other office personnel were already gone to lunch because she was all up in Norman's face reading him up one side and down the other.

"Sherry what's up? You know him?" I asked.

She was too busy waving her finger in his face and cursing to answer me. Then she went to the door opened it and told him, "Leave." He lowered his head and slunk his 7-foot ass out the door.

"Sherry what's going on?"

"Remember Julie, the one who was over my house crying because she just found out that she's pregnant."

I nodded.

"That's the asshole that doesn't want the baby."

So Norman was Sherry's best friend's man. Julie lived right next door to Norman in an apartment building in Inglewood.

One Friday night I was staying over at Sherry's, we picked Julie up to go to Digbys, a club on La Cienaga where I worked on Friday and Saturday nights. The club was owned by Darrel Jordan, he was the sixty-year-old Principal of the Junior High School that I worked at before taking the job at Imperial Mattress Company. I had carte blanche at the club, Darrel paid me to come to the club and bring friends, all we had to do was wear t-shirts that said Digby's Dolls.

Darrel had been my sugar daddy for six months while separated from his wife. He was going through a midlife crisis and bought a red sports car and started doing cocaine as if he was trying to snort up Peru all by himself. He really did look ridiculous in his shiny suits with seven gold chains and medallions around his scrawny wrinkled neck, while telling any one that would listen that he was "A real cool cat."

He was insecure because of his age and lack of height. He compensated with money. No matter what he did for me, I refused to live with him. I had keys to his Wilshire apartment and came and went as I pleased. He had even asked me to marry him. NOT. He put the down payment on a car for me and paid the monthly note.

Darrel could not keep up with the fast lifestyle that came with having an eighteen-year-old girl friend and a club. One night during sex, he had a heart attack. I called 911.

Upon getting out of the hospital he went back to his wife, which was good for me because he was getting on my nerves and I was not about to play nursemaid. The bitch found out about the car that he had gotten me and had it repossessed.

Julie and Norman were having problems since Sherry busted him out about the lunch date. The next week she had gotten an abortion. We were leaving her apartment when Norman and Howard walked outside. Julie must have told them where we were going because they showed up.

Every time I turned around Howard was staring at me. I danced with him a couple of times and he sat at our table and ordered a round of drinks. "I don't know why you wanted to talk to Norman instead of me that day on the beach, but I got you now. I have been thinking about you a lot. I tried to buy your number off of Norman since he couldn't take you out anyway, but he wouldn't give it up. I been going to Venice Beach every Sunday looking for you. I even knocked on the door where I saw you and your friends go into that apartment, but some White guy answered."

"You have gone through some changes trying to get at me. Why?"

"I like you."

"You don't know me."

"I plan to change that. You are going to be mine."

"You are awful sure of yourself."

"I know, that's because I'm a man."

He was right about that, all 7'4'' of him. He had a beautiful caramel sepia tinted skin, which verified he was Black and Cherokee. His Father was at the club and when he introduced me to him, I saw where he got his looks from. His dad was just as fine as he was and though he was a bit older, he was not lacking for attention. His long black ponytail had girls clambering for him.

Howard had a Jehri Curl that went down to the middle of his back. His features were different, exotic. The only thing I didn't like was that he didn't have any lips. He wore a full mustache and beard and when he talked, I noticed he didn't have the full lips that turned me on. He had a very sexy voice, it was deep baritone, and when he talked in my ear, it vibrated through my being.

I looked up and Darrel was calling me. "I have to go talk to my boss, here's my phone number, call me."

"You aren't coming back?"

"No, the club is closing pretty soon."

"Can I wait for you?"

"No." I could feel his eyes boring into me as I walked away.

I told Sherry that I would be in the office. I knew what Darrel wanted. The club would be closing soon and he wanted to get high before he had to go home to his wife. I pulled out a quarter ounce of cocaine from my purse that was in the wall safe and poured the powder on a mirror and separated it into two piles.

I opened the floor safe that was under the desk and removed the paraphernalia. I poured one of the piles into a chemist tube and added baking soda and hot water. I placed the tube in a glass, letting the liquid fizz like alka seltzer until it turned solid.

There was a knock on the door. I turned on the security television. It was Sarita, one of the bartenders. I put the glass and mirror with the drugs into a desk drawer and locked it. I used the remote to turn on the camera for the office, and buzzed her in. She placed the bar and door cash register drawers on the desk.

I started with the money from the door. I ran the stacks through the automated money counter, stacking it on the desk before putting money bands around the thousand dollar stacks. I wrote the amount from the door on one page and the bar on another in the accounting books. I liked to have this done before the club cleared out and Darrel started bringing people into the office. He did not realize that jackers were always hitting nightclubs.

"How you doing girl?" Syrita asked.

"I'm cool. They were working you out there tonight huh?"

"And you know this. Cheap fuckers don't tip worth a damn. I got to let them think I'm gone give up some poon tang to get a tip out of their asses. What's messed up about that is it don't work but one time, when they ask for my number I have to tell them that I am not allowed to date the customers. When they come back, they don't even bother with the bar. I should think about waiting tables. You guys be checking bank out there."

"I just do it to help out when it gets busy. I'm not really a waitress. Trust, the money is good and I do give out my number." I held my hand up for a high five. I clocked two hundred tonight."

"I clocked about four, but believe you me, they worked a bitch."

"Girl, what you complaining for?"

"Cause I'm tired as hell."

"Chile, quite tripping. Give me one of them fifties. I got some pearl that will wake you up."

"That's on like popcorn," Sarita dug into her bra and came out with a roll of money, "Can you make it a G?" She handed me a Benjamin. "I got a date."

"I thought you didn't date the customers?"

"Girl this one is too fine to turn down. This brother is tall and fine, I just know he's packing in the pants. Shoot, even his daddy is fine. I wish I could take both of them home."

"Over 7", beige suit, shag Jheri Curl?"

"Yeah girl, that's him. You checked him out too."

"You could say that. Let me know how it turns out. I'll bring that pack out to you in a few. I got to finish up here, you know Darrel has to get out of here before his wife comes looking for him."

"Girl, when I was outside on my break, I swear I saw her El Dorado roll by."

"For real? Did you tell Darrel?"

"Ain't none of my business. You the one that was getting paid from that cheapskate, not me, but I figured since you sitting up in here I should give you a heads up, don't want to see you get hurt when she comes busting in."

"Thanks for looking out for me girl, that is one big ass woman."

"I got to go put the glasses away so I can get up out of here. I'm gone get me some," she said in a singsong voice.

"Go for it girl, get some for me too."

I put the money in the wall safe after I took out the tips from the credit card receipts for the waitresses and bartenders. I popped the safe door open and put the money and totals inside. I went back to the desk picked up the remote and scanned the cameras until I found Howard. He was standing by the bar talking to his Father who had some woman draped over him. For some reason I felt a pang of jealousy.

I retrieved the glass vial and set up the torch and put fire to the tube until the contents melted into liquid. I put the beaker into a glass with water and ice and set it in the refrigerator. I used a spoon to grind down the powder on the mirror before I used a card to put it into a small baggie. I took two large snorts before locking it in the desk drawer.

I went back out to the club. The house lights were on and people were streaming out. Howard stood at the bar waiting for Sarita to finish up. I went to the back of the bar and poured myself a Gran Marnier. I slipped Sarita's package in between her tip money and handed it to her. I took my drink and went to pay off the waitresses. Howard followed.

"I was hoping you would come back, I was waiting for you."

"You were waiting for me?"

"Yeah, I was."

I looked at him for a long minute, then I looked behind him, "I think Sarita is ready." I said coldly before walking away.

Darrel was surrounded by his over-the-hill-gang. He was talking loud as he did when he drank too much, "Hey baby, Kim, get over here! You know I love that girl right there! I asked her to marry me and she turned me down! That might be a good thing though; it's hard to keep up with these young tenderoni's! You don't watch out they can give you a heart attack!" He was laughing so hard at his own joke that I thought he was going to have another one.

Darrel often embarrassed me by recounting the story of how I almost killed him. They all knew that we were having sex when he had the heart attack. He was proud of it, all ways talking about "When I die, I want to be knee deep in some good pussy," Well the fool had almost got his wish. Always telling his dirty jokes to his friends and acting like some sort of Casanova.

"You got me together?" Darrel said, pulling me too him.

"Yep, you're all set up."

"Alright everybody, you ain't got to go home, but you got to get the hell out of here," he shouted to the stragglers.

After the last person was gone, Darrel and two of his friends, along with me, Sherry and Julie went into the office. "Set it up baby, get the big one out."

I went into a china cabinet that held bowling awards and golf trophies. I took the bottom panel out and removed a Hookah pipe that had six tubes coming out of it. Everyone grabbed pillows and sat around the coffee table. I put the pipe in the center and got the dope out of the refrigerator. I used a razor blade and cut the rock into four big pieces and laid one atop the pipe. Everyone picked up a hose and smoked while Darrel held a torch to the dope.

I was sitting at the desk finishing up the totals and writing out the orders for the next day's alcohol when I noticed something on the camera. A white El Dorado had parked in front of the club. I knew that car! It was Darrel's wife who hated me with a passion.

Now that Darrel was back with her, he had to stay on his P's and Q's. She told him if she caught him with anyone that he would be out on his ass and she would take him to the cleaners.

"Clean up, now! Hurry up, Darrel your wife is here," I sprayed air freshener. Shelly grabbed the pipe and put it away. I opened the desk and took the package of coke out and threw it into the open safe and locked it.

Darrel looked like he was going into shock or something. He was high and had to straighten up quick. "Darrel snap out of it, here drink this," I gave him a glass of Jack Daniels. His wife was using her key to let herself into the club.

"Let's go girls," I picked up the remote and turned off the security monitors so she would not see us going around to the front and getting into our cars. The next day Darrel phoned and told me that when his wife walked in all she saw was him and his buddy's playing cards.

The next week Sarita told me that when Howard got to her house he did not do anything. "You could have told me that you knew Howard instead of letting me take him home for nothing."

"I don't know him. Friday was the first time I ever really spoke to the man." I told her about seeing him at the beach and talking to Norman and how they had come to the club.

"Girl all he did was sit there like a lump on a log asking questions about you. I was so bored I started yawning and told him I was going to bed so he would leave. Shit the only thing I got last night was my beaver."

"What the hell is a beaver?"

"Girl you don't know what a beaver is? Girl it don't give you grief, it don't stand you up, it don't argue, it just does its job, girl it got this thing that goes inside of you and rotates while this other little thing vibrates and beats your clit. Best head I ever had, works every time, on time."

Something was wrong with every guy I talked to that night. I had been thinking about Howard, and they just did not compare. Either their shoes were cheap, or not polished, which was a pet peeve of mine. My Father had told me that a man who wears cheap shoes does not take care of himself, so he sure won't take care of his woman. A man who stepped to me had to be clean and his clothes had to fit like a glove. I could not see myself dealing with someone who wore an ill-fitting suit or fake jewelry.

The guys who passed the attire test asked all the wrong questions trying to find out what I had, or they were too busy talking about what they had. I found that when men talked about their money or possessions it was how they measured themselves. Nine times out of ten they were lying. Were probably renting a showy car and living with their momma.

I did party my butt off though. An hour before the club closed, Howard showed up. He took my arm and led me to the dance floor. I was drunk and high. Anita Ward rocked me, "You can ring my bell ell ell, ring my bell, ding dong ding, ding a ling a ling."

Damn watching Howard move and seeing the imprint on his thigh made me wish he would ring my bell. When the club closed I told him to come back in an hour, I handled my business and got high with Darrel until I saw a Seville pull up front.

We went to breakfast and talked. Lord, I really did not want him to drop me off, but I was not going home with him, I could not give up the panties so easy. He was too fine. I saw how girls flocked around him. He needed someone to tell him no, and that's what I did.

Howard came to the club the next three weekends and took me to breakfast. I always had him drop me off at Sherry's apartment. He started taking me to lunch a couple of times a week and we talked on the phone every night.

Howard was an NBA basketball player until he blew out his knee during his second year. He was currently on worker's compensation and awaiting a settlement from his job at Hughes Aircraft, where something had fallen and displaced his shoulder.

Howard was thirty-six, I was nineteen. He did not do drugs. I liked that. He drank cognac, had two cars, a paycheck, and did not live with his mother. *Hum, what's a girl to do?*

He invited me to Las Vegas for a fight. We stayed at Caesars palace and arrived just in time to change clothes and get to the fight. I loved the excitement, and he loved all the money he won.

After the fight, he stuffed a roll of money into my hand, "I have business to take care of, entertain yourself but don't leave the hotel. You can gamble, catch a show, eat in the restaurants, get a massage, go to the salon, shop, whatever you want, just sign my name, but don't leave the hotel."

No problem. I had a wad of money and I was going to have fun. I went to the room and got my I.D. that boasted I was twenty-two and went to the casino. I found plenty to keep me busy. I sat for hours and watched the myriad of people. I decided to take a chance on the black jack table. It was really the only card game I knew, my Father had taught me.

As a rule, I did not like gambling. I had worked for a bookie in between jobs and saw people lose everything they had and then some. I played for a half hour and came out four hundred to the good. I decided to take my winnings and quit, the fun had worn off the first hand I lost.

I went into a bar where a group was singing Motown oldies. I saw some one of my Uncle's protégé's, Redbird. He beckoned me over, "You holding?"

I took his money and went up to the room came back down and slipped the dope into his jacket pocket and turned to go back to my table.

"Where are you going?" Redbird asked grabbing my arm.

"Check your right pocket."

"Damn girl, you good, ever think about being a professional pick pocket?"

"You sure you still got your wallet?"

The look on his face was panic as he checked his vest pocket.

"Just kidding." I laughed.

"Stay and have a drink with us?"

"Naw that's okay wouldn't want ya'll to get no ideas. Are my Uncle's down here?"

"I saw Cricket at the fight, he had pulled some square."

"Messing with Unc, she ain't gone be square for long."

"The jewelry that broad had on, a pimp could retire," Redbird said.

"I got to go, see you guys later."

Redbird was trying to stop my exit, "Who you down here with? You know your Uncles gon' want to know."

"I think you are the one who wants to know. I'm with a friend, tell my Unc' I'll be around. Where's he staying?

"He's checked in here."

"Cool I'll page him tomorrow."

"See you around girl, you know you need to think about getting with a real player and quit messing with them wanna-bees," Redbird was tracing my spine with his bejeweled hand.

"Didn't I tell ya'll to quit trying to come up with my niece, back off Redbird," Cricket said walking up behind me. "What you doing here Neicy?"

"Hanging out with a friend."

"What kind of friend?"

I patted my purse and said, "A good kind of friend."

"Damn, maybe our broads need to roll with you," Redbird said.

"I don't think so. I ain't sharing, and this ain't no trick."

"Where is he?" Cricket asked.

"He had business, probably somewhere in a card game, he likes to gamble."

"Sounds like you done hooked up with a high roller. My niecey, you do know how to stay down for yo' crown. You got anything with you?"

"What you want?"

"Give me a eight ball," Cricket said.

"Be right back." I went into the bathroom and took a package from the lining of my jacket. I went back to the bar and hugged my Uncle.

"I felt that," Cricket said.

"Dang, I just dipped Redbird and he didn't feel a thing."

"Redbird's so busy trying to feel you, that he's asleep."

"Man she got me, the girl is good, had me looking for my wallet and shit," Redbird said.

Now that my Uncle was here, I could sit down and have a drink. I was very careful not to get out of pocket with my Uncle's friends. Even though they knew that I was not in their aspect of the life, they were always trying to recruit.

While they talked shop, I played my little game. I loved to guess where people were from and what kind of life they lived. You could see it on their faces when their whole life was riding on the next card, or roll of the dice. Some could bet ten or twenty grand on one hand without as much as a blink of an eye. I wondered what it would feel like to have so much money that you could take such a chance.

I was getting tired. I kissed my Uncle good night and went up to the room bathed and climbed into the bed.

I woke up alone. When I returned from breakfast and a massage, the red light on the phone was flashing. Howard had left word that he was in a penthouse game and if I needed him, I could page him. The operator told me, "Those games can go on for days."

I saw evidence of Howard coming to the room to change clothes when I returned from shopping. I hung out with my Uncle and his girls for a few hours. I wandered from hotel to hotel going to the stores and running into friends. It seemed like every body from Los Angeles had come for the fights.

Three days had passed before I finally saw Howard. He had come in without waking me and showered and ordered a champagne breakfast.

I must have kicked the covers off in my sleep. I sensed him standing over me before I opened my eyes. He had a nice smile. He stood there with nothing but a towel around his waist and it was rising in the front like a tent. He placed the back of his hand on my cheek and kissed me, "You hungry?"

"I can eat."

He rolled a cart to the side of the bed. He pulled me forward and placed pillows behind my head. He forked food into my mouth. Sitting in the center of the table surrounded by plates with silver covers, sat a briefcase.

"What's that?" I asked.

Howard opened it and turned it around, it was full of money. He started throwing handfuls of money into the air. I giggled as hundred dollar bills rained down over me, onto the bed.

"I won big," he said as he started kissing me. I pulled the towel and it fell to the floor.

"No shit, Sherlock."

We made love and rolled around on the bed all morning. Howard had a way of flinging me all over the bed as he tried position after position. After round, four hundred dollar bills stuck to our damp bodies.

I fed him and poured champagne straight from the bottle down his throat as he held his head back, I spilled it onto his hairy chest and drank mine from his navel. He told me about his card game. "How often do you gamble like this?"

"I come down here at least once a month. I gamble at some clubs in L.A."

"You like to gamble huh?"

"Doesn't everyone?"

"I don't," I told him all about the bookie joint where I worked when I needed extra money. I had seen women searching for their husbands who had spent the rent money and the owner sometimes had to loan heavy loser's money so that they could feed their kids. It had turned me off of games of chance."

"I'm good at it."

"That ain't all your good at. I massaged his nipples until he rose again. Afterwards we slept in one another's arms through the entire day and half the night, we woke up ordered dinner and watched a movie enjoyed one another again and fell back to sleep.

The next morning we gathered up the money and put it back in the briefcase. "Get dressed, we're going out."

We had a limo courtesy of the hotel. Howard told the driver, "Neiman Marcus." I followed him to the women's department where the sales girl knew his name.

"I want you to take care of her." He walked around looking at clothes, the sales girl searched for a size eight as he made his selections. "I want her to try these on, this, that, that, oh and that over there, this one," he said in his deep voice.

The sales woman gave the clothes to another woman who took me into the dressing room. He came into the dressing room, "I'll be back in a bit, give you time to see if everything fits," he said as he playfully hit me on the behind. He handed the saleswoman a credit card.

When Howard returned he was carrying a silver fox fur jacket. I squealed with delight as he slipped the coat over my shoulders. I stood in the mirror admiring myself. When I put my hands into the pocket, I felt a box. "What's this?"

"I don't know, look, and see."

I took it out and opened the carton, it held a little velvet box. When I opened it, there were two gold bands sitting side by side. I looked up at him confused.

"Marry me?"

"Huh?"

"Marry me?"

I smiled and threw my arms around his neck.

"I'll take that as a yes," he said.

I nodded. The next thing I knew I was standing in a chapel.

When we got back to Inglewood, I didn't need to go home for clothes. Howard had purchased a whole wardrobe for me, underwear, shoes, lingerie, shoes, jewelry, everything I could possibly need, and a lot of things I didn't.

I was in no hurry to tell my parents I had gotten married and I made Howard promise not to say anything. .

I came to regret my marriage within weeks. Howard played around, a lot. Several women called or knocked on the door to tell me they were sleeping with him. "And you are telling me this why?" I asked them before hanging up or closing the door in their face.

Howard had a son, who I never met. I never met any of his family. On holidays, he went to my family's house, stayed awhile before leaving to go to his family's house.

Howard told me that his mother would not let him bring another woman to her house. She was upset because he had not married his son's mother, Francesca.

Francesca was a basketball groupie who had gotten pregnant to trap him. He wasn't even sure the boy was his at first. As the years rolled by the boy grew into an exact replica of his father. He sends money every month. The only time he gets to see him is on holidays at his mom's because Francesca was bitter.

Howard drove his Seville, I drove his Volkswagen. Since Darrel's wife had taken my car, I needed transportation to get to work. Howard was always out gambling. He had not lied when he said he was good at it. He usually came in with a lot of money that he put in a safe under the carpet in the closet floor.

Howard was screwing around so much that he just knew I had to be doing it to. I was working at the toy company, ten minutes away from the apartment. If I was five minutes late getting home, he would accuse me of meeting someone, having an affair, getting engaged and planning my escape. It got so ridiculous that he didn't want me to go anywhere without him. He tried to run off all of my single girlfriends and was plain old overbearing, controlling and insufferable.

I was not happy and I told him so. He did not take me serious when I told him that I was going to get an annulment. One day there was a knock on the door. It was the disillusionment of our marriage, delivered by courier while he thought I was at work.

He signed for it, assuming it was from his attorney concerning his workers compensation settlement. He put it aside for the moment so he could get back in the bed with the flavor of the day. He forgot about the envelope. It was sitting on the table when I came in from work. I put it in the desk drawer. I planned to hold on to it, until I could plan my move.

Every time Howard and I went out, he ended up in a fight. Twice I had to bail him out of jail. We could never just have a good time. If anyone looked at or spoke to me, he wanted to fight them. I guess they were right when they said Indian's could not drink, liquor made him act a zip damn fool.

"You better get a grip fool. I ain't nobody's wife."

"What's this then?" he held up my hand referring to the ring.

"What? This piece of metal? That's just jewelry Howard. It don't mean no more than one of these chains around my neck, or the earrings in my ears. Don't you see that it's on the wrong finger of the wrong hand even? Howard you should really pay more attention to your mail, especially when it comes by courier. Oh, but you were too busy that day. I annulled our wedding two months after we got married. You were acting crazy. I felt it was the right thing to do. You never even opened the envelope because you were to busy screwing around with the girl that came in right before the courier. I changed my work hours so that I could sit down the block and watch all your little whores come and go."

"I have to got to the bathroom," Howard darted out of the room so that he could think of a good lie. As he walked away he mumbled, "You don't know what you are talking about." He knew that was how I had been busting him. I even recited the names of the girls who left the house. They were only too eager to talk to me, hoping that I would leave so that they could step into my shoes.

I followed him and stood outside the bathroom door, "I decided to get the annulment the day of your Baby Mama Drama."

Francesca had climbed over the balcony and let herself in through the sliding glass door of the second floor apartment. That is the day I realized his life was not in order and I refused to stay in this mess.

"Why do you always wait and bring stuff up weeks later instead of when it happens? No, you got to drop little hints and make little remarks for weeks before you come out with it. That is precisely why I be tripping? You be messing with my head," he said pointing his finger in my face.

"No you be messing with your own head. You know what you are doing and you feel guilty, that's why you always think that I'm messing around, 'cause you are."

Howard

Several times Kim had thrown things up in my face. Things I couldn't explain away - a condom wrapper from the garbage, a pair of panties left under her pillow by a devious broad.

One girl, Betty had the nerve to put her earrings in the bedside drawer. She placed the earrings right on top of Kim's daily sinus medicine.

She was waiting outside the next morning and when Kim pulled out of the drive, she knocked on the door. "I left my earrings here, I wouldn't have bothered you but they are gold and emerald tear drop hoops and they really mean a lot to me," Betty said.

I was perturbed and showed it. What if Kim had still been home? I was expecting someone else, that's why I had answered the door wearing a towel. "Let me check."

Without closing the door, I ran into the bedroom looking everywhere. I did not see them. The thought of Kim finding them was distressing. Suddenly I remembered. Kim had been wearing the earrings that morning. When we made love, she had them on. They had gotten in the way when I put my tongue in her ear.

Kim never wore earrings to bed. They had large stones. Diamonds and emeralds paved in gold. That's why she kept looking at me funny. I had a feeling something was not quite right, but at the time, my hard dick would not let me put a finger on it, and all through breakfast, she kept playing with them.

"Damnit," He was busted again. Kim had not said a word. Most women could not sit on something like that for two minutes. Not Kim, she got some perverse payback pleasure from tormenting him. She looked at him some time and just shook her head while laughing.

Kim

The phone rang at one in the morning. At the sound of my 'Hello', they hung up. I looked at Howard, rolled over and went back to sleep.... so he thought. When he heard my breathing slow, he rose and went to the kitchen.

Howard picked up the kitchen extension, "Betty, you ever do that again I will stop messing with you?" He hissed while cupping his hand over the phone and hiding behind the open refrigerator door. "I'll see you in the morning. Just keep it hot for me."

I laid the handset on the bedside table.

When Howard hung up he practically jumped out of his skin when he turned around, and saw me sitting at the table. "Tha, Tha, That was Norman," he stuttered, wondering how long I had been there.

I looked at him for a long moment before rising from the table to make a cup of chamomile tea. He wrapped his arms around me from behind.

"It must have been really important. Maybe you should go and see him, it sounds as if 'he really misses you and can't wait to see you,' I said turning to look into eyes that would not meet mine. He might have been good at playing poker but I knew all of his tells. He blanched at the exact words that the girl had used when she explained why she had called so late. I walked into the living room, sat down and turned on the television.

"Aren't you coming back to bed?"

"I'll be there in a second, you go ahead, 'Honey," another word the girl had used.

When he walked into the bedroom, he jumped at the sound of the magnified Bomp, Bomp, Bomp, Bomp, Bomp that came from the phone that sat off the hook. *Damn busted again.*

Howard

In light of the new developments, Howard canceled his date with Betty. He felt like a child waiting for his whipping. He did not plan on having any company that day, but he ran across a phone number in his jacket pocket.

He dialed the number of the girl he had picked up from a bus stop and given a ride home. Before good sense could kick in, he had extended the invitation. He could not resist a girl who bragged about her sexual prowess.

When he opened the door instead of who he was expecting, there stood Betty talking about her damn earrings. He did not have time to deal with this right now. He had to get rid of her before the other one showed up. When he had looked everywhere possible, he decided to give up. *Forget her and her earrings. Her dumb ass shouldn't have left them behind in the first place.*

That's when he remembered Kim's ears that morning.

When Howard walked back into the living room, it was too late. The other girl had showed up and both women were sitting on the couch talking. The new arrival looked up and said, "The door was open so I just came on in. Betty said you would be out in a moment. We've been getting to know one other."

Howard sat in between them, "I see." He had noticed that they were holding hands. He put his arm around both of them. The towel around his waist came undone.

When Kim came home that evening Howard had forgotten about the earrings and about that morning's ménage a trois.

He was beside himself because she walked in over two hours late. She had not even had the decency to call. She knew better than that. Breezing in all smiles, "Hi, I had to work late," on her way to the kitchen.

She busied herself with dinner, putting steaks she had marinated the night before under the broiler. She popped some potatoes into the microwave and started making a salad. I followed her into the kitchen. The smell of the meat reminded me that I was hungry. Kim could definitely burn, but I was not going to let that stop me from getting to the bottom of where she had been.

I tried to interrogate her, "I called your job Kim, no one answered the phone, and you always answer the phone when you are working late. Why didn't you call?"

"Get a grip Howard. I was helping with inventory in the warehouse, it pays time and a half and I can use the extra money," she pushed me out of the way and opened the refrigerator and started making a salad.

"If you need extra money you can damn well get it from me. I don't want you in any warehouse. I've seen how those guys look at you."

She smiled sweetly "Oh the big man is a wittle jellus, wellus," she said in a baby voice. "O.K. Mr.-tell-my-woman-when-and-where-she-can-work, I need two grand for a down payment so that I can have a low note."

"We have two cars, why do you need another one?"

"No, you have two cars. I want my own, that way if you decide to replace me with miss-call-and-hang-up-if-my-woman-answers-the-phone-fore-day-in-the-morning, I won't be stranded," she shot at me with unveiled venom. "Oh yeah, I'm going out with my girls tonight."

I was just about to voice my objection, when she shut me up by tucking her hair behind her ears. *Betty's earrings*! I choked on my words right along with an olive I had picked out of the salad bowl.

I fell into a chair and pointed to my back while wheezing for air.

Kim raised her eyebrows, "Oh honey, what's the matter? Are you choking?"

When she got up, I thought she was coming to help but she walked to the stove, took out the steaks, and put them next to the potatoes. *Damn is she going to let me die?*" I sat gasping for air almost a full minute before she finally hit me so hard in my back that the olive went flying across the room.

I was still trying to catch my breath when she picked up the keys and walked out the door.

I knew I could not ask her for the earrings. I would have to tell Betty that I did not find them and never see her again. She wasn't worth the aggravation. Any girl that leaves things around when she knows you have a wife is dangerous. If she had, the bad judgment to leave something so expensive, that was her faux pais. *Now what to say to Kim about where they came from? I could tell her they were a gift I had gotten for her.*

I spent the rest of the night going from club to club trying to find Kim. I was afraid that she might sleep with someone to get back at me.

Kim

We went to a new club out in The Valley so Howard could not track me down. When I got back that night, he was fit to be tied. The next day when he left, he took the keys to both cars. That I could deal with, I had two extra sets cut after the first time he pulled this on me. But then things got really crazy, the fool had installed a dead bolt on the apartment door, one that could be locked from the outside. I couldn't get out so he thought.

I climbed over the balcony and down to the first floor apartment where Miss Adams, the older lady who lived below waited to let me through her balcony door. I could not have gotten out without her help, as there was a wrought iron gate that I could not get over because of the spikes.

Miss Adams was a real sweetheart. She called me at work every time a strange woman went up the stairs. And she did not miss a thing. She sat all day in a lounging chair in her living room watching soaps and game shows and listening for footsteps on the hallway stairs. She would tell me what time they got there and when they left.

Sometimes if I was not too busy at work after she called with her alert, I would call Howard and he would pretend to be asleep. I would keep him on the phone as long as possible. When he finally got me off the line, I called back two minutes later. I knew I was messing up his stroke, I also knew he had to answer the phone to ensure I was still at work and not on my way home.

Once I got out of the building, I stayed out until I knew that Howard would be home from his escapades. He would be so pissed off, demanding to know how I got out of the apartment.

"Stop locking me in, there could be a fire one night."

But he kept on doing it. I took his keys one morning while he slept and had copies made to the deadbolt. I gave one to Mrs. Adams so when I called she could let me out.

One night I was going out with Sherry and her sister Sheila. Howard was supposedly at Norman's playing cards around the corner. He had called me a few minutes before I left to make sure I was still home. I heard cards shuffling in the background, but when I passed by Norman's house Howard's car was not there.

I picked up Sherry and her sister. My mother always said, "What you do in the dark, is gonna come out in the light. Karma has a great sense of humor. If you're supposed to know something, it will be put right in your face."

Anyway we were going to ladies night at the Red Onion on Wilshire when for some unknown cosmic reason a few streets before my intended turn, I swear it was as if the car turned the corner all by itself, and there parked in front of a duplex sat Howard's Seville. I stopped the car, "So this is where Norman lives now huh? " NOT."

Sherry looked at me, she didn't know what I was talking about until she followed the lasers that were my eyes, "Ooooooh, that's Howard's car and he's supposed to be at Norman's."

Sheila said, "Honey Boon, let's set the alarm off and see where he comes from and go beat that bitch down."

"What I'm gone fight some girl for, she didn't drive that liar and his dick over here, he drove his damn self."

I thought for a minute. I was hotter than a firecracker. Suddenly I knew what I was going to do. "I should have read the writing on the wall and never moved in with his cheating ass. Sherry I need you to drive this car, please?"

I took the keys to the other car off the ring and got out of the Volkswagen and into his Seville. I drove the car to the Red Onion where I proceeded to flirt with every guy who tried to talk to me. When we left the club the pocket on my parachute pants were chocked so full of numbers that they were falling out as I stumbled to the car. I had drunk so much that there was no way Sherry was going to let me drive. She got behind the wheel of the Volkswagen, and Sheila, the Seville.

We had sat in that club planning my revenge.

We drove to my parent's house and I had Sheila pull the Seville in the back yard, all the way to the back behind the garage where no one could see it unless they were in the kitchen. My parents were in Las Vegas and would not be back until Easter Sunday, which was a week away.

We climbed into the Volkswagen and drove to Stop's twenty-four hour drive-thru on Imperial and Central. The chili tamales were known to soak up alcohol. It was four in the morning by the time we got to Sherry's house. We sat around the coffee table on floor pillows. We shared stories about no good men who had screwed us over while we freebased cocaine and smoked weed.

I decided not to go home that night. We had been there a half hour when the phone rang. Sure enough, it was Howard at 4 in the morning.

Sheila had to hold a pillow over my face or Howard would have heard me cursing his triflin' ass out. Sherry tried not to laugh as she lied and told Howard that I had fallen asleep on her couch. Sheila had her ear to the extension. Every few minutes Sherry would say, "Damn, for real" or "Aah man, that's too bad." When she got tired of listening to him whine, she said, "Well, I'm really sorry to hear that, I'll tell her when she wakes up in the morning because she wasn't feeling too good. She was looking green when we got here; I drove us home and made her lay down. If you want I can wake her up."

Howard knew that I had been having bouts with nausea and told her that was okay and to let me sleep.

When Sherry hung up the phone she said in an exaggerated tone, "Kim guess what? Honey Chile, Norman had to give Howard a ride home, somebody done stole his car. Poor thang. I wonder who could have done it." We burst into laughter.

Suddenly the hurt was too much for me and laughter turned into gulping sobs. I could not understand why Howard was sleeping with everyone else when he had an oversupply of pussy right in his own house. I had a good hard cry. I cried for the love that I had for him that had just died for the last time with this last blow. I cried for every time he told me that he loved me and those women did not mean anything. I cried for his child in my womb that I was going to have to kill.

Howard and I had been together for almost a year when I found myself pregnant. I knew I was not ready to be a mother, and I certainly did not want to be tied to Howard for the rest of my life. He was not a good Father to the child he had and the way he messed around he would soon have a football team of kids running around the city.

"You cannot kill my child, it's a sin. You are my wife! I forbid you to do it! What's your problem? I give you everything you want, and then some. Don't you love me?"

I let the tears fall while Sherry and Sheila held me and listened to everything. I told them about the women that Mrs. Adams called me about almost daily, the phone calls and confrontations from other women. I told them about Francesca, his son's mother, who stood downstairs throwing rocks at the window and how she had climbed over the balcony and tried to attack me, I told them how I had broke my finger knocking her out. How he told me to leave while he took care of this, because she might want to call the cops, how he had tried to intercept her right before she reached me, but not before I bopped her upside the head.

After I heard everything, they had to say about, "What a dog Howard is," and how, "I shouldn't be shit off of no man," I told them, "I'm pregnant."

The tears started afresh.

"I made arrangements to get an abortion twice, but when he was supposed to take me he would get up before daylight and disappear. He even changed the lock so that I couldn't get out and, "Kill his baby" as he put it." Soon we were all holding one another and crying.

Sherry volunteered to take me to have the procedure if that was what I really wanted to do.

The next morning when I got home, Howard was looking like a little boy whose puppy had died. He really loved his Seville. I sat down next to him on the bed and he pulled me into his arms.

"Where's your car? Sherry said you told her it was stolen. Did they get it in front of Normans' house?" I feigned pity.

"Yeah, and you know if they find it my wire rims and Alpine stereo is gone be history." I looked in his face, He was actually crying, the bastard.

Throughout the next week, I asked him more than a few times, "Have the police called yet? Have they found the car?"

"No, not yet."

"Are you sure they stole it from in front of Norman's house and you weren't somewhere else?"

"No, and the funny thing is, I didn't even hear the alarm go off. They must have had a key or something. I wouldn't be surprised if the guy who did the detailing didn't set me up."

"Where is the police report, can I see it?"

"I forgot it at Norman's house."

I took the week off of work. Every time Howard left I took clothes and put them in the front closet so that I could take then down to the car. I would take the clothes to Sherry's house and later to my parent's house and them in my old bedroom closet. I called them in Las Vegas to ask if I could move back home for a while. They did not question me. They just said it was all right.

Every morning I told Howard that I had to get to work early. I sat down the street to wait. Low and behold, it never failed. I watched girls pull up and go to the apartment. Just to mess with his head, one day I went back in. When I put the key in the door, I made a lot of noise. When I got into the apartment, I yelled out, "I forgot my work badge in my other purse."

I could smell the sex and perfume in the air. I walked to the closet and opened it, nothing. I pretended to look in a purse for my badge. "Hum, its not here. Wonder if I dropped it," I looked under the bed, nothing. I went into the bathroom and pretended to use it. I looked in the shower, nothing. I heard footsteps and the sliding door open. I took a moment before coming out. This was it. There was no turning back now.

I walked out of the bathroom, "Why does it smell so funny in here, we need to air this place out.

Before he could deter me, I walked briskly to the balcony door and stepped out. "There's a nice breeze out here."

I could see the panic on his face. I just stood out there for a moment, and then turned as if I was coming back into the house. He breathed a sigh of relief – until I spun around and snatched open the storage closet door. Bingo, there she was, naked as the day she was born. I looked at Howard and walked out the door.

That Thursday night I went to The Speakeasy and the Carolina West nightclubs with Sherry, Sheila, and Julie. Sherry had taken two days off of work and we got as high as we could. When Howard called, she told him, "No Howard she's not here, we went to a club and then she said she was leaving, that was about one in the morning. She ain't home yet?" She could hardly control her laughter.

I went to the apartment and Sherry, Sheila and Julie came up with me, it was six in the morning. "I'm getting a ride with Sherry and after work I'm going to my parent's house. I'm staying the weekend to help Mommy with Easter dinner."

I knew that he would not try to talk to me in front of my friends. When he went into the bedroom, I handed them some of the bags of clothes that I had in the living room closet and they took them down. I went into the bedroom, packed some clothes, and got the few things that were left in the bathroom. He did not notice that I spread out his clothes and mixed in some things that I no longer wanted. So my side of the closet would not appear empty.

I knew that he was going to his parent's house on Easter so I had that covered. "Can we talk?" he asked.

"Not right now, I got to go. I just don't have the energy for this Howard."

"You're not going to work?"

"It's Good Friday, there is no work today."

"Well, where have you been? I called over to Sherry's you were not there."

"You don't have the right to question me anymore Howard. I'll see you later."

"What time is dinner on Sunday?"

"Don't worry about it. Sherry and her family are coming to my parents for Easter dinner so I can ride back with them."

He tried to hug me, but I did not return the gesture. He tried to talk but I interrupted him, "It's okay, let's just skip it, I don't want to talk about it, it didn't happen."

"You don't want me to come to your parents?"

"Naw, that's alright, you should spend the day with your son."

Sherry drove me to the clinic and waited while I had the procedure. Afterward she took me to my parent's house and helped me into their bed, where I laid and watched television.

Sherry would be back later to check on me and bring food. She left a pitcher of water next to the bed along with the prescriptions for pain and antibiotics. It was noon on Friday.

I woke up about 7 p.m. when Sherry, Sheila, and Julie let themselves in. They brought me lobster and enchiladas, my two favorite foods. They fawned over me for a few hours. We watched one of the videos they had rented. They got ready to leave when I started falling asleep from the medication. They would call me in the morning.

When they called, I told them I was fine. I got up, went to the restroom, and changed my pajamas and the sheets because I had soiled them. I ate the leftovers and took more medicine and went back to sleep.

I woke to the sound of my Mother's voice. It seemed like it was coming from far away. I could not shake the thick fog that I was trapped in. I felt like I was floating around on the ceiling watching these horrific events unfold.

"You are burning up. What's going on? Oh My God, what's happening?" she screamed when she pulled back the covers and saw a pool of blood.

Somehow, I was in the car. When I woke, I was in a hospital bed. I tried to move, and could only groan, from the pain. My mother woke. She had been sleeping in a chair next to me. I could tell by the redness in her eyes that she had been crying. I didn't want to look at her. I was not sure what had happened and hoped she did not know about the abortion.

"How you feeling, baby?"

I could not answer, the tears starting flowing down my cheeks. My mother sat on the bed and pulled me into her arms. "Everything is going to be alright; you had a high fever and were hemorrhaging. We got you to the emergency room. You are so fortunate that I came home early. They did a D.N.C. and were able to stop the bleeding." She leaned back so she could look into my eyes, "You were pregnant?"

I nodded.

"Did you try to get an abortion?"

I nodded again. I didn't know whether or not Howard knew about it, so I didn't call him, do you want me to?" I shook my head no.

The doctor came into the room and my mother said, "I'll see you in the morning."

"The abortion was not done properly. They took out one child but left the other. You were carrying twins. We found tissue from the first child while removing the second. You can still have children. You get some rest; we are going to keep you until tomorrow. I am going to give you this shot so you can sleep," The young White doctor said.

My mother picked me up the next day. I was feeling a little weak but for the most part, I was fine. I enjoyed Easter dinner with the family. Sherry and her mother came.

Sherry followed me back to Howard's apartment. I pulled the Seville into the covered parking space. It did not feel like home anymore. I rode with Sherry to her apartment, en route I saw Howard's Volkswagen in front of Norman's house.

I knew Howard wouldn't be home anytime soon.

When we got to Sherry's we called Julie. She was at Norman's playing cards with them. We told her to call us when it looked like Howard was ready to leave. We went over to Laisyv's, picked up some coke, came back, and got high while we waited for Julie's call.

Two hours later the call came. I parked Sherry's car where Howard would not notice it and went into the apartment. While I waited for Howard, I gathered the last of my things and put them in Sherry's trunk.

I was on my way down with another bag when I heard the Volkswagen pull down the drive. I knew that he was going to freak out when he saw the Seville parked in the stall. I heard the beep beep of the Seville's alarm and the engine start and turn off.

When Howard came in, he was confused as to how the car had magically appeared. It was not stripped or anything. "Did the police find the car and bring it here? Did they call and you went and picked it up?" Howard asked.

"What are you talking about Howard?"

"The Seville is in the parking stall, how did it get here?"

"Oh, the Seville, that couldn't be your Seville because I picked that car up over in the Wilshire district, and your Seville was at Norman's, remember?"

He was stunned and did not know what to say. By the time, he thought of something I was heading out the door and halfway down the stairs with the last of my things. He ran down the stairs, grabbed my arm, and pulled me back into the apartment. "You stole my car?"

I just looked at him.

"You made me file a police report and go through all that insurance shit for nothing. You are crazy."

"No I was hurt, but I'm not hurt anymore Howard. Be glad you got your car back in one piece. Remember I have family who I could have gotten to sell that sucker off part by part, so consider your self lucky."

"What's in the bag?"

"Just some stuff, I need a break. I need to think."

"You know I love you, you can't just leave like this. You're pregnant with my kid."

"Yeah, you love me, you love Francesca, you love the naked bitch in the storage closet, and all the other girls that have been running in and out of here. You love pussy and there are enough of them out there to keep you occupied. Don't worry about the kid, I took care of that."

"What do you mean by that?"

"You know what I mean. You thought if you didn't take me to the appointment I couldn't get there without you?"

"You didn't have an abortion? Did you? You were so mad at me that you killed our child?"

"You need to work on your relationship with the child you have before you think about having more kids to mess up. Goodbye Howard."

Howard

"I'm going to let her cool off for a little bit. Yeah, that would be best. When she comes back, I'll get her a real nice gift. Maybe I'll take her back to Las Vegas, we can get married again. I know she was not telling the truth about the abortion stuff. She wouldn't do that. I'll send some flowers to her mom's. I know that's where she is going. Whatever she wants, she wants a car, and I'll get her a car. Some jewelry, I'll go see my friend Harry the fence and get her something nice, he sells real nice jewelry, hot, but nice. I'll get a few pieces and take it to my jeweler and have her something custom made. I better get on top of that if I want to have it done in time," He was speaking aloud.

He napped for a while, when he woke, he noticed something was different. At first, he thought that he was just missing Kim. He turned on the television. By the light of the screen, he noticed that the photos of her family were not on the dresser. Suddenly he could not catch his breath.

He got up and opened Kim's closet, the dresser drawers, he rushed to her drawers in the bathroom, empty. Everything that was hers was gone, as if she had never been there. He sat on the end of the bed with his head in his hands. Then he noticed that the side of his closet was open a bit. He looked into his stash and removed several rubber-banded rolls of money. It appeared to all be there.

He went downstairs, when he needed to think he took a ride in his Seville. He had a lot to think about. Both cars are here. He thought she had left in the Volkswagen, but it was still here. That's when it dawned on him, Kim's last good-bye could very well mean gone.

Kim

When I got back to Sherry's I went into the restroom and shed my last two tears, washed my face, and went back out to join Sherry and Julie around the table. It was party time.

"Sherry this party can go on forever, girlfriend. It's on Howard." I said as I pulled out a roll of hundred dollar bills. I counted it. Then I put both hands on either side of my face and said, "$4800," In my best Jewish accent I said, "What's a girl to do with so much money."

It was months later when Howard discovered that the denominations in the middle of three of his money rolls were not Benjamin's, but in fact ten-dollar bills.

I had enough money to buy myself a car and my Father was going to cosign for me.

Sherry

1978

I was having some financial problems and asked Kim if she wanted to move in with me. It was convenient because driving to Hawthorne every day from Compton was the pits for her.

I was three years older than Kim was and she called me her big sister. She had been spending the night at my place three nights a week anyway, after happy hour she was in no shape to drive. She had dope customers on this side of town. She would not sell to anyone in Compton because her parents knew too many folks who would love to tell them what she was doing.

I had more customers than Kim with my brothers being in the music industry, but she had the bomb hookup. She left weed, cocaine, and pills with me and called to let me know who was coming through, what they wanted and how much money to collect.

She couldn't stay at her parent's house with a beeper going off all times of night, and she sure couldn't be running in and out, so when I offered for her to move in she jumped on it with both feet.

My siblings and their friends were always dropping in. My sister Sheila was two years older than me. I had twin brothers, Fred and Ed who were four years my senior, sang in a popular band, and always had an entourage of musicians with them. .

In the late 70's and early 80's everyone was into freebasing or snorting cocaine, it was a fad. I was dealing and some weeks we had so many people hanging out in my apartment around the clock that we were running on very little sleep. We partied all night either at the apartment or at a club nonstop. The Speakeasy had ladies night on Wednesday's, the

Red Onion on Thursday's, the Marina on Fridays, and there was always the Carolina West which did not close until 9 a.m. on Sunday mornings.

Back to the present at the Speakeasy

1980

Kim

All the time we danced Howard listed the reasons I should come back to him. All I heard coming out of his mouth was how much he had he had taken from me, my love, my body, my children.

Suddenly pain and regret took the place of the nostalgic attraction that I felt two dances ago. It was amazing that within less than six minutes I relived all that hurt. I turned to walk off the floor.

Howard grabbed my arm, "Where are you going?"

He must have seen the frost in my eyes because he go, "Kim can we just talk?"

I held a finger up to his face, and with all the hatred I could muster I hissed, "Stay away from me. You don't get to hurt me again."

I needed to get to the bathroom. I was going to cry and I didn't want anyone, least of all Howard to see me. I was passing the bar where my Uncle Butch and some of his friends stood.

"Hey Neicy, what's up?" Butch said as he hugged me.

I pulled myself away. I had to get to the bathroom before the flood gates opened, "I'll be right back."

Before I could get to the bathroom Howard grabbed my arm and twirled me around, "You don't walk away from me!" His raised voice had that heavy bass and authoritative ring to it, the one that I had always rebelled from. I looked around him at my Uncle who had heard it too.

Butch and his friends approached. "Say Brother, let her go."

"Who the hell are you? You better get out of my face, this is my woman."

Howard turned to me "I saw you hugging on him. You can't do this. I'm not going for it."

Butch had never met Howard. He was in jail while we were together. "Howard I was hugging him because…"

"I don't give a damn why you were hugging him, don't do it again."

Butch stepped up and pulled me from Howard's hands, "She was hugging me because she is my Niece."

Butch turned back to me, "Who is this clown?" You want to talk to him.

"Naw I don't want to talk to him, this clown is history." I turned and went into the bathroom. Laisyv and the other girls had seen the disturbance and were right behind me.

"Girl what is going on?" Laisyv asked.

"You remember I told you about Howard?"

"You mean the one you were married to?"

"Yep, that was Howard."

"Girl he is foine, if you don't want him, I'll take him." Shirley said.

Laisyv and I looked at her. This bitch was always trying to fuck with somebody's man. "I'm sure you will, you can have him."

"Well he's sitting there talking to your Uncle, right now. What do you want to do?"

I took two snorts of blow and told Laisyv, "I'm going to party. He ain't gone mess up my night." I left them in the bathroom and went back to my drinks.

Howard was just getting up. I don't know what Butch said to him but he turned and left without a word.

Butch came over to me, "What did he say?" I asked.

"Don't matter what he said, unless you are thinking of getting back with him, are you?"

"Naw, after everything he put through, I could never be with him again."

Enough of this trippin, come on Unc, let's dance. When we walked off towards the dance floor, I hugged and kissed my Uncle and slipped a package into his pocket.

"I felt that," He said.

"Only because you were expecting it"

We invited some dancers back to my house and climbed into the limousine. We rode down Sunset Boulevard and stopped in front of Carlos and Charlie's where celebrities were pouring out. A couple of the girls got out and were talking to guys. I was drunk and feeling good.... until I saw Alonzo.

"What is this? Men who broke my heart night? "Damn let's go ya'll," I hollered, but I couldn't get down inside the limo's sunroof fast enough. Alonzo saw me.

"If you bitches don't get in this car right now, I am going to leave your asses," Laisyv shouted. She had seen Alonzo and knew I did not want to talk to him.

"Did you hear me? Let's go, Ho," she shouted at Shirley

They must have heard the urgency in her voice because they said good-bye and jumped into the car, Alonzo was banging on the car door. "Kim I need to talk to you. Please Kim, just for a minute."

"Drive off," I screamed at the driver.

"Kim come on, don't be like this."

"Did you hear me say drive?" I yelled.

The limousine pulled off. I could not resist the compulsion to look out the back window. Alonzo stood in the street shaking his head.

"Damn what is going on? That nigga was fine too. You don't want him either. Pass him on to me," Shirley said.

"Shirley, why do you keep talking about taking my leftovers and shit? Don't you think that if I ain't with them, maybe there is a reason, the possibility that something ain't right? Does that not send up a red flag for you? Are you so desperate? Damn, bitch you starting to piss me off."

"Girl, I'm sorry, I was just kidding," Shirley said.

"Just kidding until you can sleep with 'em. Then they gone leave you like all the others, but before they will make sure to leave you a present, you will be pregnant as always. You got three kids and no man." Laisyv said.

"Shirley's voice registered the blow she had just received to her character, "Damn Laisyv, you had to take it there? I thought we were supposed to be out having a good time."

"Shirley you know I love you girl, but sometimes your jokes can be ill-timed," Laisyv said handing her a mirror of blow.

Suddenly the good buzz that I had before disappeared. "Driver please pull the car over," I shouted.

The driver pulled to the curb. I stumbled to a flowerbed in front of an office building and proceeded to throw my guts up. Laisyv brought me a soda and some tissue. She rubbed my back until I finished. I set down on the ledge of the flowerbed.

"You alright girlfriend?"

"Not really."

She held me and I could not stop the tears from falling.

"Laisyv you ever have someone hurt you so bad that you feel like you want to die? You break up with them and swear off relationships forever, but when you close your eyes, you dream about them every night. When you wake up in the middle of the night you find yourself reaching for them and when all discover that the only thing in your empty bed is a pillow all you can do is cry yourself back to sleep. You pick up the phone to call them a million times a day and have to curse yourself out so that you can hang up before you dial their number?"

"Girl you done been through a lot of shit. You know Christian and me go though it. You know damn well I cried myself to sleep many a night. The only difference between you and me is that I got two kids and can't leave my husband because I like the money too much."

"I ain't got kids to think about, when honeymoon and good times are over, I'm gone like the wind." I said taking the soda from her.

"Kim can I say something and you promise not to get mad at me?"

"Of course, girl." Then I thought about, "Well maybe, I don't know maybe you should save it for later because you know way too much about my life and I would like to salvage some of this night. You liable to say that make me go up on top of this building and jump." I laughed.

"I'm gone speak anyway. Alonzo is a fuck up, just like all the rest of these dogs out here. Kim, if you really love him take him back. All he does is talk about how much he misses you whenever he's at the house. Alonzo made a mistake. He is only human and people make mistakes."

"He hurt me Laisyv. He hurt me bad."

She took me in her arms and held me while I cried. "If you ain't love him then he couldn't hurt you, it's better to have some one you can feel something for in your life at least then you know you are alive."

Laisyv had been a wonderful friend from the day I met her.

Laisyv and Christian

Kim

1981

I had just gotten the news, even though this girl was incompetent as hell, after a month on the job the boss, who took long lunches with this little chippy, had the nerve to tell me that he was promoting, not just a step up, she was being promoted over me.

I had been working at this job for two years and several people that I had to train were promoted into a position that should have been mine a long time ago.

To top it all off, working double shifts put me in a different tax bracket. I just knew I was going to get a big fat tax return check when I filed. Instead, I ended up with two hundred dollars. The whole job situation was getting on my nerves and I was preparing to do something about it.

"What's up with you girl? You look tired," Laisyv said.

Laisyv had just started working as a temp in the next department over and we talked on breaks. She was married with two kids living in an apartment in Inglewood.

"Girl, I'm pissed and tired. People keep getting promoted over me, while I get to stay here and work overtime cleaning up their mistakes. It's mentally wearing me out. I work hard and I do good work, but I guess because I'm not White and sucking the bosses shriveled up dick, I don't get to move up. It's damn frustrating Laisyv."

"Here, try one of these black beauties, they will have your eyes open in no time," Laisyv handed me two black pills.

Within an hour, I had the music playing and had flown through my work and was ready to go. I no longer felt like I had not had a proper night's sleep in weeks.

"What are you doing after work?" Sylvia asked.

"Nothing, what's up?"

"You want to get something to eat and come by my house and have a drink?

"Sure, why not? It's Friday night, no work tomorrow, let's do this."

We went to a Mexican restaurant on Hawthorne blvd and had dinner and margaritas before going to Laisyv's house where I met her husband Christian and her two boys, Darnell and Eric.

There were a lot of guys sitting around the living room watching a tape of the Tommy Hearn's fight.

"Kim, do you do coke?" Laisyv asked hesitantly.

"Yeah, girl. Why you looking so nervous, you thought I was gone say no and run back to job and tell your business," I laughed.

"Girl you never know. But when I saw your Uncle dropping you off in that Rolls last week, I figured you must be pretty cool. I took a chance."

"Girl if you only knew. I'm the last person you have to worry about."

Laisyv went to where the guys were sitting and with a plastic card, scooped some coke off a plate. She and I sat at the dining room table talking, snorting, and drinking pina coladas, until three o'clock in the morning.

On my way out the door, I asked Laisyv, "You want to go with me to a birthday party tomorrow night at the Speakeasy?"

"Sure, I don't have anything else going on."

We started hanging out regularly. One night I picked her up on my way to see my Uncle Crickett. His bottom woman, Mika needed some blow. I had to stop and pick it up on the way. Laisyv saw me take the money and give my Uncle the package.

The next Monday, she came to me, "Christian wants to talk with you. Can you come over after work?"

We sat down over dinner and Christian, "What kind of price you getting for your cocaine."

I explained to him that the guy I was buying dope from was becoming unreliable and was tripping lately. He kept raising my price every time I told him that I did not want to sleep with him.

"I can give you a good deal if you want to work with me. I can teach you how to free base and rock up dope. I got some customers that will pay for a pretty girl to sit and cook for them."

"Kool and the gang because the guy I'm dealing with is not taking care of business like he should, last time he gave an ultimatum, said that the next time I showed up at his door I better be ready to take my clothes off."

Things ran smoothly through Christian. Sherry and I were making money hand over fist and splitting everything down the middle. In the beginning, he gave me half ounces at a time and paid me on the other end.

Within two weeks, I was paying for ounces up front and making a larger profit. It was lucrative for all involved.

Before long, Christian and Laisyv came to be like family to me.

Sherry and Kim

Sherry started dating G, a drummer with a popular band. He was at the apartment so much that Kim felt like a third wheel and decided to move.

Kim's Uncle Johnathan's house off of Broadway was vacant so she rented it. He did not want the housesitting empty and if I moved in, I only had to pay three hundred fifty a month. I moved into the big two-bedroom house. My grandmother gave me enough furniture to be comfortable. I painted the walls blue, sewed curtains, and settled in. This was my second time having my very own space and I liked it.

My favorite thing about this house was the bathtub, a big ball and claw tub that called to me every day when I got home from work. Some days I preferred my bubbly hot bath to the clubs.

Sherry's romance did not last but a hot minute. G had moved in when I moved out. People always say that you don't know someone until you live with them. G turned out to be crazy as hell, prone to jealous, rageaholic behavior.

Sherry told him that he was smothering her and she needed her space and independence. He went off. He only had to put his hands on her once to get thrown out on his ass.

Whenever Sherry went out, G stalked her. He showed up at every club and made a scene demanding they get back to together. This got old real fast. She needed him out of her life. She would come home to find G inside the apartment as if he still lived there preparing candle lit dinners and baths with rose petals all over the floor and bed. She would scream, "Vacuum this shit up and get the hell out of my house."

Changing the locks did not discourage G. He broke in through a window or picked the lock. Several times, she woke to find him standing over her bed or laying next to her and he would not leave

Sherry got a restraining order, but that did not deter G. Her brothers told him, "She don't want you and if you don't leave her alone we are going to beat you down." This did not faze him and after they beat him up, he still persisted.

He laid in wait for her brothers outside of a recording studio one night and shot Fred. Ed tackled him and the gun to the ground. The 357 bullet pierced and exited Fred's shoulder. The police arrested G a block away.

He bailed out and went directly to Sherry's. He was enraged when she came home with another guy. He slashed her tires and broke out her car windows. He threw a brick through her living room window to gain entry.

The visitor was coming out of the bathroom when G surprised him. The attack was a vicious one. Sherry rushed to the phone and called the police as the two men struggled. She picked up a lamp and brought it down hard on G's head, knocking him out.

G was taken away and charged with breaking and entering and two counts of assault. He made bail and was back early in the morning. When she opened the door with a gun and started shooting, he ran to a phone booth and kept calling and leaving messages on her answering machine, "Don't you see how much I love you, we are meant to be together, I'll do what ever it takes to be with you.

Sherry was so afraid for her life that she quit her job and gave up the apartment. She packed up her belongings, put her furniture in storage, and moved in with me until she could find another apartment.

Howard had been calling my mother's house trying to find me. She told him not to call anymore. He tried to explain how stressed how important it was that he talk to me.

"I'll tell her but I don't think it's going to matter," My mother said before hanging up.

I was a telecommunications operator at a toy company, which meant that I had access to every area in the building, including the store. Every week I bagged up toys and took them home when I got off. On the 1st and 15th of the month I set up a table in my front yard and sold the toys.

When I wasn't working, I was selling dope and cooking for Christian's customers. Several clients had propositioned me for sex. I declined but hooked them up with my Uncles prostitutes for $200. They came in, I gave them one hundred, kept the other hundred, and they handled their business.

Kim

I did not go to work for a couple of days. I did not call in or return my supervisors call when he called me in a panic. I wanted to be fired so I could collect unemployment. I was tired of working my butt off while everyone was promoted over me.

I had purchased a California government seal stamp from this guy who worked at the hall of records. Shelby liked weed. I sold weed, it worked out just fine. I kept him supplied and he kept supplied with authentic blank birth certificates.

All I had to do was type in the information, smack it with the seal. I accompanied the purchaser to the Department of Motor Vehicles where I paid Sandra who worked behind the counter to make sure their licenses went through without a hitch. Uncle Butch kept me running to the DMV almost every two weeks.

Sherry and I were at The Candy Store, a popular nightclub on the corner of Sunset and Highland. Uncle Butch was throwing a birthday party for one of his girls. I was stylin' in a purple halter-top of raw silk with a matching draped skirt that showed a lot of leg. I had made it myself and it garnered me a lot of compliments. I was twenty years old. Twenty-one was the legal age for the club. I used my fictitious I.D.

We sat at a table nursing Gran Marnier with seven-up backs. I had been on the dance floor nonstop with my Uncles friends, all of whom I had known since I was a little girl. I decided to sit down before I got too sweaty, my top was starting to stick to my small breast.

We were having a good time. Drinks started arriving at our table from admirers. I had to be careful who I accepted a drink from in this crowd. Uncle Butch knew every one there because he had reserved the club that Sunday night and it was closed to the public. I put the business cards of men who I met in my purse. Butch would school me later on what they were about and if knowing them would be to my benefit. He also kept a watchful eye on us. If someone stepped to us that he did not approve of he promptly gave me a sign that meant squash it and I immediately dismissed them.

Some asked what my problem was. I had no qualms about telling them, "My Uncle Butch over there, doesn't seem to think I should be talking to you. You got a problem with that let me know, and I'll call him over, so the two of you can discuss it." Most of them stepped off politely.

One guy, who called himself Kenyatta, sent a bottle of champagne to the table and when Sherry nodded for him to join us, Butch sent me a disapproving look.

"Sorry but, you are going to have to excuse yourself from our table," I said as politely as I could.

"What you saying bitch, I done spent money on this bottle of champagne and you telling me I have to get up?" His tone was menacing.

I picked up the bottle and held it out to him, "You can take it with you and as far as the glass that she drank, she'll be going to the ladies room momentarily, if you like she can bring it back and give it to you."

"Cocky bitch, you must think I'm a sucka. You better ask somebody who you messing with," Kenyatta shouted. I put the bottle on the table and attempted to walk away. He was not to be brushed off so easily. He made the mistake of grabbing my arm and loud talking me.

One of my Uncles friends said, "Man you really don't want to do that."

"Who the hell are you?" Kenyatta's voice was so loud it carried over the music to where Butch and Cricket stood.

Cricket stepped to him and said, "You gonna have to campaign with somebody else playa. She's a square, and she's going to stay that way, this is my family."

"I just spent $200 on a bottle of champagne for these bitches."

"I told him to take it with him."

Butch stepped forward and asked the man who was still holding my wrist, "I don't know you partner, who you here with?"

"Who are you? What difference do it make, who I'm here with?"

Butch picked up the bottle, "Why don't you take this and move on, my brother done already told you this is family. I don't know if you knew it or not but this is a private party, that means I'm like Castro, the dictator up in this piece, and what I say goes."

Kenyatta opened his mouth to say something but before he could utter a word Butch's friend T-bone walked up and pried his hand from my wrist. "Let me talk to you for a minute man."

They walked outside together. It was obvious when they returned that he had been schooled. He searched for Butch and Cricket and apologized. He stopped me as I was leaving the dance floor and shouted his apology over Rick James, Super freak. "Excuse me baby girl, I apologize for anything I may have done to offend you, enjoy the champagne."

"Don't worry about it, enjoy your evening,"

I sat down to dry off. I was just cooling down when I looked up and noticed a guy staring at my legs as if he was in a trance. I had noticed him watching me on the dance floor. I waved my hand to bring him out of it.

His big brown eye's opened wide and he blushed with embarrassment. He flashed a brilliant Billy D. Williams smile. I felt a strong attraction to his energy.

"Hello, my name is Alonzo. I wonder if I could have the pleasure of buying you a drink." His voice was like a warm blanket.

I looked over at Butch and was relieved when he nodded his approval, I thought aloud, "Maybe this is my lucky day." I didn't realize I had spoken aloud.

"Excuse me?"

"Oh nothing. Why don't you dance with me first?"

One of my favorite songs had just started. We were on the dance floor for five songs before the D.J. slowed the music down with Marvin Gaye's, 'Sexual Healing.' He held his hands up, a silent question asking if I would slow dance with him. I moved into his arms, even though I had just met this man I felt so comfortable.

The Lagerfeld cologne he wore was intoxicating and made my senses reel. I remained in Alonzo's arms through the Commodores 'Three times a lady', and 'I like it' by Debarge. I could feel him responding to our closeness. I was glad I did not have a penis, because if I did it would have been on hard as his was getting. I looked at him as if to say, "What's up with you?"

He blushed, "Maybe we should sit."

En route to the table Alonzo gestured to the waitress who was on the other side of the room and pointed to the table. She knew what to do. Brief exchanges of conversation were all we could glean because the music was so loud. We had to lean into each other to be heard, I did not mind one bit.

Alonzo worked in the shoe department at Harris & Frank on Wilshire. I knew from the Rolex he wore and the quality of his attire that he was not living on a salesman's salary.

We discovered that we were both under the birth sign of Leo, five days apart, he was 33 years old. Way too soon for me, Alonzo finished off his drink and handed me his business card, "I am going to have to be leaving now."

I asked him for a pen and wrote my number on a napkin. I was disappointed. He explained that he had an early flight. He was going to his hometown for the Kentucky Derby and his mother's sixtieth birthday. "I'll be sure to call you as soon as I return from Louisville."

I watched Alonzo leave. He detoured to speak to the waitress and gave her some money. A few moments later, she brought fresh drinks, "All the drinks at this table for the remainder of the evening are paid for, compliments of Alonzo."

I asked her, "What's your name?"

"Denise."

"Well, Denise, you should get yourself a drink and take a break at our table while you tell me all about Alonzo?"

"Girl you ain't said nothing but a word. Be right back, I'm about to be off anyway."

By the time Denise finished four long island iced teas, I had the 411 on Mr. Alonzo. Denise and her southern accent could not be stopped once she was on full.

"Alonzo is a booster. Not just some shoplifter girl, a professional. He came to L. A. six months ago and lives right across the hall in my building. I make more money through Alonzo than I do busting my butt at the bank everyday. I'm a teller and I work here on the weekends so I can keep an eye on my old man. Speaking of my old man that's him over there talking to that guy whose perm looks better than half the women's hair up in here. Damn he's fine, if he wasn't a friend of my old man I would have to get me some of that, honey chile, still might have to."

Our eyes followed where her pointing finger. Sherry and I looked at each other and laughed. Sherry raised her eyebrow and said, "Stop," like she often did when something was funny.

I put my hand on Denise's shoulder and leaned in to look the girl in the eye. I knew that she was drunk and I did not want her to miss a word, I kind of liked her and if I was to hook up with Alonzo, I was going to need her. "Girlfriend if you want some of that, I can make it happen, but you better know right now that the guy with the pretty perm, My Uncle, he don't play. He is about his business. Trust me; I'm doing you a favor telling you this."

"He ain't a pimp. He's friends with my man. They do business together."

"Girl, didn't you just hear her say that the man is her Uncle, open your eyes, there's five woman over there waiting on him hand and foot. Chile you better wake up and smell the coffee before you be fetching it to his bed every morning along with yo' quota."

We all laughed at Sherry's humor.

"I guess I better stick to my old man then, huh?" Denise said once she could stop laughing.

"Honey boon, I'm getting drunk mixing this champagne and yac together. I think we need to take a trip to the bathroom and wake up," Sherry said.

We stood up, "Denise you want to go to the bathroom with us?"

"No, I don't need to pee."

"Me neither, I'm going to powder my nose."

"But you ain't wearing no make ...oh, oh yeah girl, sure," Denise said, finally catching on.

We all squeezed into a cubicle in the small bathroom. Butch had given both me and Sherry a vile of cocaine when we arrived. We returned to the table, revived and ready to party. Sherry and I went off to dance to Tina Maries, Square Biz, while Denise talked to her old man.

When we returned to the table, we found Denise sitting with her old man whose name was Luke and Butch. "I need you to hook up some identities for these folks. They are going to need at least six each. Can you do it this week? Butch asked.

"Of course, I can do it tomorrow."

"Tomorrow morning then. Get her number so you can call and tell them where to meet you. I'll call you in the morning and give you details."

After Butch and Luke left the table, Denise started talking again. "I got Alonzo a lot of clientele from this club, he's definitely getting money. He doesn't have a steady woman. We've gone on some double dates. I tried to hook him up with every single girl in the bank where I work, cute sisters too. Honey boon, you think it ever amounted to anything? Not. He never asked one of them for a second date. Every day except for Tuesday he's at work from 10 to 8 except on the weekend, he gets off at 9. He just made manager of the shoe department. Alonzo is going away for a few weeks. He's been shipping boxes of clothes to his mother's in Louisville so he can sell them at Derby. A lot of hustlers go to Derby, to make that money. A lot of rich folks go to the Kentucky Derby and they party hard." She went and got us some more drinks.

A few minutes later she was rambling again, "Alonzo has a couple of kids down there, but he don't like his baby mama, Rita, they don't get a long. I know the bitch and she ain't about shit. She messed around with one of his best friends. He let her bring the kids down for a visit because she kept begging, trying to get back with him. As soon as she got here, she disappeared and didn't come back for a week. He had to hire someone to take care of the kids, so that he could go to work. Anyway, it's obvious he can't stand her, but he loves those kids. When she did come back, he put them all on a bus back home."

I made a mental note to go by Harris and Frank and check out the clothes. If they were as nice as Denise said, Mr. Alonzo and I had some money to make. Between my mother, family, and friends, who were all clothesaholics, we could make bank whether we hooked up or not.

It was Sunday night and Sherry had a job interview in the morning, we said our goodbyes and heading out the door. We both knew she was going to be missing that appointment. I was not going to work. I had other business that would make me more than I would get in a month on that job.

I was in the kitchen rocking up cocaine in a pot of boiling water. Sherry walked into the kitchen laughing. She had changed into her pajamas.

"What's going on with you? Why you laughing."

In a deep voice she said, "Hello Kim, I am so relieved that I got you because the last number on this napkin got wet somehow and I couldn't make it out. I woke up about eight people trying to find the right digit. Any way I almost wish I could cancel this trip, and if it wasn't my Momma's birthday, I would. I love your voice on your message. Well, you have a nice night. I'm really looking forward to seeing you when I get back. I'm asking you to go to dinner with me now, so make sure you put me on your calendar in two weeks. Oh yeah, just in case I'm not the only guy you met tonight, this is Alonzo."

"Girl, what in the hell are you talking about?" I asked.

"I am talking about the message on the answering machine from Alonzo."

I was in such a hurry to hear the message that I dropped the shaker bottle into the boiling water and headed for the bedroom.

"Girl, are you crazy? That's $200 worth of cane you about to mess up." Sherry said as she grabbed the tongs and rescued the bottle.

"You finish it, just keep turning it around, release the pressure, it should be about ready." I said as I rushed into the bedroom.

When Sherry walked into the bedroom, I was listening to the message for the sixth time.

"You got him girl."

"Girl I hope so, we can all get paid. Did you hear girlfriend say that he was a booster, I'll turn my living room into a store every first and fifteenth."

We turned on the television and Sherry set up the backgammon board. On TV was playing "Which way is up," an old Richard Pryor movie.

We got high into the next day and as I predicted Sherry rescheduled her interview. Every few minutes I replayed the phone message. I dreamt of Mr. Alonzo later that day when I finally went to sleep after coming back from the Department of Motor Vehicles to get Denise and Luke's identifications.

Two nights later, I was still dreaming about Alonzo. Through the depths of sleep, I heard the phone ringing, "Hello."

"For some reason I just can't stop thinking about you." I had listened to his message so much that I knew his voice. It was Alonzo.

"I know the feeling. I was just dreaming about you."

"That must be why I had to call, you were sending me a signal, what kind of power you got over me girl?"

"I read somewhere that it's called astral visiting, when you think of or dream about someone and they reach out to you at the same time, it's almost as if you are together."

"O.K. so since we are together what can we do?"

I giggled, "I think we are going to have to wait for you to come back to do the things I been dreaming about."

"Dang girl, you got little Lonzo waking up."

"What can we do about that?"

"Keep talking to me, I love your voice."

Several nights he called about two in the morning. I found myself leaving the clubs early and leaving the late night deals to Sherry so that I could be home for his calls. We talked well into daylight.

Kim

Alonzo's Back

I woke to the phone ringing. Butch needed an ounce. His dealer had gotten busted.

"I'll call you right back."

I dialed Laisyv's number and when Christian answered, I spoke in code.

"Can we take care of some I.D at the same time?" he asked.

"Sure, that means you need to come my way. I'll make them up and tell Sandra when to expect you. You've been to the DMV with me enough times to go on your own."

Butch showed up with his money and while we waited for Christian, we talked about the guys I had met at the Candy Store. "Most of these you can sell dope to. Anything else would be a headache. You are too strong willed, you just ain't gone bend, and you know what they are about. Now when you hook up with the booster you can sell clothes to all these hustlers. Luke says he gets good merchandise. Don't forget about your Unc."

"I got you covered, don't sweat that."

"What's up with Lucas and Denise?"

"Since you hooked them up with the I.D, she's been taping into the big bank accounts. We make up the checks and send folks in to cash 'em. She's a teller so she tells the manager that she verified the checks, we don't write more than two grand on each piece of paper. She takes a cut. Luke drives people to the bank, picks up carbons with bank account information every day at lunchtime, and brings them to me. He gets ten percent of everything. Right now I'm checking the big business accounts to see where we can hit em' up for at least a hundred grand. Maybe I can pull you in on a couple of these because we are going to have this temp agency placing our people at some of the Wilshire companies, that way we got the inside line.

When Christian arrived, he and Butch handled their business. I typed out the birth certificates with the information Christian gave me. They got to talking about some other deals. Christian got into his car and went to meet his people at the DMV.

I got $300 for the dope hook up and 50 for each I.D. After paying Sandra, I had cleared $700 dollars.

"I'm hungry let's get something to eat, I'm buying," I told my Uncle.

We went to a little breakfast spot on Inglewood Avenue called M & M's, they had the best-fried chicken wings and biscuits in town.

"It's nice doing business with you," I told Butch when he dropped me off.

"May we have a long and prosperous relationship," he said mimicking the Godfather.

When I got inside the house, the phone rang. It was Sherry who had left early that morning.

"What's happenin' girl?

"I got the job, I start work Monday."

"Cool."

I told her about my morning as I ran a bath in my claw foot tub. I fell asleep in the tub while reading a Jackie Collins novel.

I woke up, climbed into bed and went back to sleep. When I woke, Sherry had come and gone. She had left a note saying that she was running errands and making deliveries. She had left $200, weighed out two grams of coke, and taken a pound of weed. She also said that we were running low.

I took out the package that Christian had brought for me when he had taken care of butch and started weighing out packages. The phone rang.

"Hey baby, guess where I am," Alonzo said.

"No, you're not" I screamed. I could only hope that he was back in town.

"Yes, I am."

"Alright, what are we going to do?"

"Well, why don't you come over here and then we can go have some dinner, and what ever you want from there."

I took down the directions and dressed. Sherry walked in just as I was leaving.

"Girl, it is on now, I'm going to see Alonzo," I said as I swung her around.

"Have fun, I'm going to happy hour with this guy I met today."

"Be safe."

"Ditto, girl."

I was so excited that I could not get to Wilshire fast enough. I found the address and there was a parking space right outside the older building. I could just tell that it oozed history.

I found Alonzo's apartment and knocked on the door. The door across the hall opened and Denise said, "Alonzo, Kim's here, come on in girl."

We sat with them for a few minutes before going back to Alonzo's apartment. It was one big room with a small kitchen in the corner, a tiny dining room table. On the other end was a couch that looked like a hideaway bed and a coffee table. "Well, I know it don't look like much, but it's comfortable."

He got that right, it was downright tiny. "It's cute," I lied.

"Have a seat, and I'll get myself together. I'm a little jet lagged but I'll be ready in a minute."

"If you're tired I don't want to drag you out. I can go home so you can rest."

"After thinking about you every day that I have been away, I don't think so. How about we order in, I have a bottle of cognac. We can watch T.V."

"That'll work, what are we going to eat?

"Pizza, Chinese, or Thai?" he asked as he whipped out some menus.

"Pizza is good for me."

"Are you a pepperoni and sausage girl?"

"With black olives, mushroom and extra cheese?"

Alonzo picked up the phone and placed the order. He poured drinks and brought them to the coffee table. We talked about his trip and what growing up in Kentucky was like. I told him all about growing up in Compton.

While eating I spied a backgammon board under the table. "Don't even try to act like you know anything about this game," I said pulling it out.

I found him to be a formidable opponent. We played for hours. Alonzo excused himself, went across the hall, and returned with a small package of coke. We snorted some lines and continued playing and talking.

I felt comfortable with him, as if I had known him in another life. We had spent so much time on the phone talking about heartbreaks, travel, clothes, and music.

"I really do feel like I have known you forever," he said.

We talked about me helping him sell clothes. He had quite a bit of inventory in boxes. I looked through them. He had quality merchandise. "I'll make some calls. I can take you to meet some people tomorrow if you are available?"

"I can get off work at six."

"Next week is the first of the month. If you can pull together some inventory we can have a sale at my house."

"You do get busy when you hustle don't you?"

"You didn't know? I'm a hustler, you get the merchandise I can move it."

He leaned in and kissed me, it felt warm and soothing. His hands explored my back in an offer to massage my shoulders. I lay on my stomach while he lit candles. He knew what he was doing. It was so very therapeutic and relaxing. Before I knew it, I had fallen asleep.

I woke in his arms still fully clothed. He had put on some shorts and was not wearing a shirt. I looked at his smooth chest and body without waking him. He stirred and spooned me deeper into himself. I went back to sleep.

The next morning when I woke Alonzo was gone. He left a note with his work number. I phoned, "Please stay there, I'm going to bring you some lunch."

I used the time to make some phone calls about the clothes.

When he arrived, he gave me a burger, fries, and a shake in one bag. After eating, he produced another bag, a big one. I pulled out a silk dress, a wool suit, and a satin blouse. "Can you stay until I get off? Then I can take you out, like I should have done last night."

"First we got to go and make some money, I made some calls, I need dresses, and suits sizes 8 thru 12 in women's and everything you can get your hands on in men's."

"Okay, why don't you start going through these boxes and see what you think will work. I have some more in my trunk that I will bring up. Call me at work and let me know what else you might want, maybe I can get it before I clock out for the night," he said pulling some clothes out of the boxes he had in the kitchen. I'll be back about six thirty,"

"Why don't you help me take this stuff down and meet me at this address," I wrote down the address and directions to Christian's house. "I should be done with my business and meet you there at 8."

When I got home, Sherry and I talked about our dates.

"Some people have called you trying to get hooked up, I wrote the names down."

"Can you handle it, you know all of them? I got some runs to make."

I showed Sherry the clothes. She paid for most of the dresses.

"We should be alright as far as blow goes, but we only have half a pound of weed. If you run out you can re-up. "

"I can handle it, you have fun."

I might not make it home tonight, Christian has some people who need someone to cook for them, and you want to handle it? It's a nice chunk of change?"

"Shit yeah."

"I'll let Christian know, I'm going over there about eight"

After taking care of some of my dealers, I went to Christians and talked to him about Sherry standing in for me.

"If you trust her it's alright with me," he said

He had a customer waiting. I went to meet Sherry and give her the package, the address, and the beeper that I used on Friday and Saturday nights.

Laisyv and I weighed and packaged coke for two hours. At 8', o clock on the dot there was a knock at the door. Christian opened the door and welcomed Alonzo who I had told them about.

Christian played the big brother role, asking a lot of questions.

"Alonzo why don't you bring in any thing else you have in the way of clothes. Here's the money for what you gave me this afternoon. Christian will pay you for the men's clothes. If you have some more women's bring them up."

"All of them?"

Christian and I looked at each other and laughed, simultaneously we said, "All of them."

"Don't you want to look at them first?" Alonzo asked Christian.

"Naw. Just leave them in the car. You and I are going for a ride."

Christian had called his friend who owned a store on Crenshaw. He was always looking for hot clothes.

Laisyv and I went downstairs to get the women's clothes. She liked every outfit. What she couldn't fit she would sell.

When the guys came back, we decided to go out to dinner. Laisyv was wearing one of the outfits. How much for all of these?" she asked Alonzo

"Nothing," Alonzo said.

"Nothing?" Laisyv said.

"I just made six grand between Kim and Christian. You don't owe me a thing."

After dinner, we went back to Christian's and watched a movie that was still in the theaters. Christian had a hook up at the movie studios who gave him videos. We snorted coke and drank cognac.

Around midnight Alonzo and I decided that I would spend the night at his house. I left my car keys with Christian. I would come back and get my car tomorrow.

I wanted Alonzo so bad my body ached. This was going to be my man. He had asked me if we could be exclusive. He said that I was everything he needed in a woman. I did not see a reason to wait.

I was ready to be in a committed relationship. There was no reason for me to hold back. He was perfect. He was attractive, intriguing, dressed nice, treated me good, had a job, and hustled. Now if he could screw we were on like popcorn.

When we walked in the house, his phone was ringing.

When he hung up he said, "I have to go and take care of some business. Will you wait here for me?"

"Where am I going to go? I don't have my car," I kissed him with everything I had. My way of letting him know what he was going to get when he returned.

While he was gone, I ran a tub, got in and fell asleep.

When I woke, Alonzo was standing over me, naked. His desire extended toward me.

He climbed into the tub and washed my body, lingering between my legs with his soapy hands. "Stand up," he said. He spread me wide and my swollen clitoris called to his mouth. When I exploded, he didn't stop, though I screamed that I couldn't take anymore, I found out that I could

Alonzo washed himself and lifted me out like a child. He poured baby oil over my body and rubbed it in until I was dry. I did the same taking in every inch of his smooth physique. I sucked and nibbled him. He was so thick that my mouth could not take all of him.

He stopped me, "You making me feel too good. I've been looking forward to this since I laid eyes on you. I don't want to cum yet."

I could not wait to feel him inside of me. He picked me up and carried me to the folded out bed. My every nerve tingled and I was wet. He played in my well and looking into my eyes licked my juices from his fingers.

He stood up, "Are you ready for me?"

I nodded my head. As he entered, I felt myself stretching. I had never felt so full. I saw his imprint through my stomach. All I could do was move my head from side to side. I couldn't even scream, a low guttural noise came from deep within me.

Warm waves washed over my body over and over again. My back arched to meet him and we collapsed at the same time. Our bodies bathed in sweat. The breeze from the open window swept over us.

We napped, woke, made love again. There was nothing in the universe but our organs, throbbing and pulsing for one another. We showered together and went back to sleep.

I woke alone. Alonzo had gone to work. My body felt as if it had a love hangover. It felt good. I went back to sleep.

I woke to Alonzo kissing my forehead.

"Get up sleepy head before I end up back in bed with you. You must be hungry, let's go out to dinner." It was after five in the evening. I had slept the entire day.

Alonzo laid out a satin pantsuit for me. I got up and dressed. He had gone across the hall and borrowed a hot curler from Denise so I could do my hair.

He took me to a lavish Chinese restaurant called The China Wall on Wilshire Boulevard. We dined on a huge crispy fish, shrimp fried rice, egg rolls and dun dun noodles. We drank plum wine, lots of it we kissed every two minutes.

After dinner, we rode to Christians so I could get my car. We could not keep our hands off one another. Christian and Alonzo got on well. They sat in the living room watching a game. Laisyv and I were in the back room smoking coke.

When we left Inglewood, he followed me to my house. Sherry had a house full of company. Her brothers had just finished recording an album and were celebrating. Music was playing, liquor and dope was flowing.

We laughed, joked, and danced until four in the morning. I grabbed some clothes and followed Alonzo home. It was three days before I made it back home.

While I was at his place, I went to the store and bought food. Every morning I woke early and cooked him breakfast. At noon, I went to his job, took him lunch, and picked up clothes.

Wednesday I had to be at the store at 11 in the morning. There was a delivery scheduled. My Nissan was so full of clothes that I could barely see through the back window. I took all the clothes to my house.

There was a clothing store around the corner on Broadway that was closing. I talked to the manager, purchased some clothes racks, took them back to my house, and started hanging up clothes by size. By Friday, my living room looked like a clothing store.

I stayed at my own house for a few days. I had two sewing orders that I had put off to the last minute. I did not want to get a reputation for being unreliable. These people had been my customers since high school. I also made a shirt for Alonzo.

Saturday we had our first sale. Everyone I knew walked out satisfied with their purchases. My mother came early with her friends to get first pick. Sherry's mom brought people from her church and Julie and her co-workers came by. By five o'clock, I had sold everything.

I got to the store about six, parked next to Alonzo's car, and waited for him to get off. He was happy to see me.

I kissed him and pressed the roll of money into his hand. He looked at it.

"What's this?"

"Fifteen grand."

"Fifteen grand? You sold everything?"

"Everything," I kissed him.

"Damn girl, you sold all those clothes that fast?" He smiled and hugged me.

"Yep, and as soon as you can come up with some more, we need to go through my Uncles. He just took off a big sting and got plenty paper right now."

"Ain't no thang, but a chicken wing, what size he need?"

"Medium, 32 long."

"We can go see your Uncle and then catch a movie and go to the after hours. Oh Yeah, Christian called and invited us to the Marina City Club on Sunday."

"That'll be fun,"

"Why don't you call them back and confirm."

"Sure, baby."

We went by Alonzo's so he could pick up some suits and dresses for my Uncle and his girls. When I called Christian, he told me that Butch had just called him and needed something. He couldn't get away just now and wanted me to make the delivery.

"I got to go out there and take some clothes anyway. I'll pick it up in about a half hour."

We finished up business and went to a movie. Afterwards we went to dinner at Friday's in the Marina. We took Christian his money and hung out until two o'clock then headed for the after hours on Buckingham.

I saw Cricket's custom burgundy van in the parking lot. I knew it was his because he had female gladiators spray-painted on the sides. I approached him at the bar where he was talking with his friends. "Me and you got a bone to pick," Cricket said after we hugged.

"What I do?"

"Don't be rude, who is this?"

"Alonzo this is my Uncle Cricket, Cricket this is Alonzo."

They shook hands and said that they recognized each other from around town.

"Now, back to you Miss. How you gone turn Butch on to the clothes hook-up and not call me. I saw them suits, I want the hook-up, and that blow wasn't bad either."

"Don't be salty Unc, I just been kind of busy with my new man. You looking at the hook-up, I was going to call you tomorrow. I got a proposition for you. Every other Saturday I need you to turn one of your women's houses into a store. We bring the clothes, you let all your colleagues, and their women know that for two hours they can come and shop. We'll cut you in for a percentage that you can collect in blow or merchandise."

"Sounds like a plan, when do we start?"

"Next weekend and you get first pick."

"That's a fly shirt you sporting, got anymore of those around?" Cricket was talking about the black taffeta soldier shirt with tan piping and pearl snaps. It looked really good on Alonzo who was wearing it with tan jeans, cowboy boots, and hat.

"You need to get with me about that one Unc. I made it."

"You made this Niecy? Girl you definitely got your Daddy's skills. I want one Burgundy and one Gray. You know my colors hook me up. How much?"

"A bill each."

"But how much for your Uncle?" Cricket said.

"A bill, I do have to buy the fabric and it ain't cheap, for your friends, it's gonna be two."

He handed me five hundred dollars, "I want four, and I'll pay for the fabric. I need them by the middle of next month."

"I got an idea, how about I hook up coordinating dresses for your girls. I could sketch them out for your approval before I start cutting. You guys could walk in there and turn the place out."

"Now you pimpin' me," Cricket said.

"Hey somebody's gone get paid to make them shine, why not keep it in the family?"

"Let's see what you come up with. Look at you, walking in your Daddy's footsteps." Cricket said.

I blushed and excused myself. I had to answer my pager and visit the restroom. I nodded at Mea who was on the phone as I came out of the restroom. She was Crickett's bottom woman who had had been with him for twenty years.

Cricket turned to me, "You got blow?"

"And you know this man. I got a couple of grams I can part with. If you want some weight call me in the morning, but you have to call me at Alonzo's house."

Alonzo handed Crickett a business cards.

"So it's like that huh? My Neicy is sleeping at your house?" Cricket said giving Alonzo the evil eye.

Alonzo shuffled nervously.

Cricket handed me two Benjamin's. "Brother Man, step into my office and let me talk to you for a minute. I need to find out what your intentions are since you got my niece sleeping at your house and all."

I went out to Alonzo's car to get my stash. I stopped at the bar, got two plates, and handed one to Cricket along with his packages. I could see that they were still deep in conversation so I went to the bar and sat with Mea. I poured some blow on a plate and passed it to her.

"This is just what I needed. I have been working around the clock for the last three days." Mea said as her pager went off. She snorted two lines and went back to the phone. When she finished her conversation, she went to speak with Cricket who whistled and beckoned me over.

"I need you to do me a favor."

"What's up?"

"Mea got a party jumping off. I need you to take her back to the house. She's going to need some weight in that green stuff?"

"Let me check."

I made a call, went back to the table, and asked Alonzo for his car keys. "Mea you ready?" We had to leave now if I was going to meet up with Christian.

"Alonzo is going to kick it with me for awhile. We'll be here after you handle your business."

Christian met me at Fat Burgers on La Cienega with a pound, then on to the workhouse on La Cienega and Franklin. The huge apartment occupied the entire first floor.

"Kim I need you to pick up some girls for me, they are going to be waiting for you on Sunset Boulevard across the street from the Candy Store."

After I dropped the girls off Mea asked me to pick up a food order from Huffs on Hollywood Boulevard, she had already called in the order.

When I returned Mea's party was in full swing. Mexican guys boasted their wealth in the gold, diamonds they sported. They all wore the nicest boots of ostrich and eel skin that I had ever seen."

"While I waited for Mea to pay for me one of the clients approached me, "Como se llama?" He asked my name in Spanish

I sure wasn't going to tell him my real name. My favorite movie was Sparkle so I used that. "Me llama es Sparkle," I said with a smile.

"Tu Hablar espanol?"

"Poquito, just I little that I learned in escuela."

"Mea yo quiro Sparkle."

Mea laughed and handed me my money, "Valentino you can't go with her, she doesn't work."

"I'll pay double," he said in English.

"Sorry, I got to go," I laughed and made a hasty exit.

Mea walked me to the door, "See ya later Sparkle," she laughed

When I got back to the club, Cricket and Alonzo had left word that they would be at Butch's house.

"When I walked in, I could tell that they were all feeling more than a little good.

"Alonzo's aw'ight Neicy, I like him."

"Thank you for your seal of approval, Unc."

Alonzo half stumbled on his way to the car, "Girl, you just wait 'til I get yo' fine ass home."

I looked at him and laughed, "Don't threaten me with a good time."

Tuesday was Alonzo's day off. He had started playing basketball with Christian. They had become fast friends.

The toy company finally fired me. Now I could file for unemployment. I registered with a false I.D. at an employment agency down the street from his job in the Wilshire area. They sent me on temp jobs in the area, which meant we could lunch together everyday. Sometimes lunch meant parking on a secluded dead end street and stealing some love like two teenagers.

Alonzo and I made love every morning before going to work. After work, we met at happy hours and pretended to pick each other up. It was so funny the way people looked at us when we started kissing and feeling each other up.

Sherry had settled in with a new boyfriend and her new job. All the girls got together a couple of times a week to go over finances and catch up. It was so funny; it seemed that we were all in a good place as far as men money went. For the first time in a long time, nobody was singing the man blues.

Kim

Four months I had been seeing Alonzo with not so much as a ripple until we were at his place watching television and cuddling, when the phone rang.

He was visibly upset when he hung up. I walked over and put my hand on his shoulder, "What's wrong?"

"Nothing," Alonzo said briskly shrugging my hand away. I did not know how to react to this. I went to the restroom and when I returned, he looked angry.

"Is there anything I can do to help?"

"I said nothing is wrong, why can't you just leave me alone?" Alonzo shouted.

"Hey, I ain't the one who was on the other end of that phone. But if you want to be left alone, I can do that for you." I stood waiting for him to come to his senses and apologize. Imagine how I felt when he didn't.

"Then why don't you leave me alone?"

I picked up my keys and purse. Through my tears, I walked out of the building to my car. We had never had harsh words before. Well, whatever the problem was he obviously did not want to share it with me. But I'll be damned if I let him think that he can go off on me like that.

I went home and called Sherry and after two minutes of crying my pain, she said "I'll be there in a minute,0 I had called you a few minutes ago and didn't get no answer, girl I got man blues too."

Sherry arrived with a bottle of cognac fifteen minutes later. Within a half, an hour the whole crew was in my living room. She had called in the cavalry. Sheila, June, Shelly and Theresa were there, it seemed that we all had man problems. We passed the pipe and the knowledge. "Girl it must be something with the moon that makes these men go crazy all at the same time."

"Girl, you did the right thing walking out of there. Don't let no nigga' go off on you," Sheila slurred.

"That's right, we are independent women, and we don't have to take no shit," Julie said falling to the right just as Sherry slid a pillow under her.

"We pay our own bills," June said.

"We can hustle just as good as or better than any man. They like busses you miss one, you just get on the next," Theresa blew out a cloud of weed smoke that filled up the room and closed her eyes and lay her head back on the couch.

As if on cue the radio station played Gloria Gaynor's, I will survive song came on. We held our glasses of cognac high in a toast.

"Turn that shit up, turn that shit up," June said running to the radio. We all got up and picked up anything we could to use as a microphone and started singing and dancing around the room. We all fell down exhausted when the song went off.

Sherry looked at me as if she was in deep thought, "But Kim, answer me this, even if ya'll do break up, you are still going to be selling clothes right? I don't mean to be "insensitive" but my wardrobe has been growing along with my bank account since you got this hook up. Don't make me have to deal with Alonzo myself."

Everyone laughed and Spoke their agreement. I threw a pillow at Sherry.

About two o'clock Sherry got a call from a guy who was a blast from the past whom she had been seeing while she stacked enough paper to leave her current boyfriend. He was headed home and invited her to come over and spend some quality time.

"Girl, that was Denny, I'm going to get my bell rang," She stood up and emulated a very sexy semblance of screwing. "Uh, Uh, Uh, Uh."

"Lucky Bitch," I said heading to the bedroom. I brought out a plate of blow so everyone could clear their heads before driving. I didn't want anyone to have an accident. Within an hour, they had all filed out together hugging me and saying things like, "Stay strong, girlfriend. He'll be calling you and apologizing soon enough."

Shelly hugged me on her way out. "That man loves you girl like my Ma Floye always say during sad times, just be still, and wait."

When the door closed, loneliness fell over me like a cloud. I was more than a little drunk. I stumbled into the bedroom. The answering machine was blinking at me. I took a huge hit from the hookah pipe that was full of smoke. Weed was something I rarely did because it either made me silly and laughing like a hyena or sad and crying like a baby.

I turned on the television. Wouldn't you know it? Mahogany with Diana Ross and Billy Dee Williams was on. I took off my clothes, got under the covers, watched the movie, and cried when Billy Dee said, "Success is nothing without someone to share it with."

The light on my answering machine was still blinking at me. I hit the pipe one more time so as to help continue to be strong enough to ignore it. When the movie was over I ran a bath and climbed into my bathtub, "I love my tub. It don't trip out and yell at me," I said to no one.

The water felt like arms comforting me and erasing all my problems. I turned on the radio. They would be playing love songs tonight. I fell asleep.

I woke to the sound of the phone ringing. By the time I made it out of the tub, I had missed the call. I climbed into my bed. "I love my bed. My quilted velvet headboard that I dyed blue, the elaborate carved wood I painted in gold leaf. I love my heavy quilted comforter that I dyed to match the headboard, it's always so nice to me, and it doesn't make me cry." I stumbled to the bed and passed out.

"Bang, Bang, Bang, Bang."

I heard the insistent noise through the fog that was sleep. My eyes were assaulted by bright light shining through the bedroom window. I pulled back the curtain and saw Alonzo.

I got up and unlocked the front door. He walked in and without saying; a word pulled me into his arms. As bad as I tried to hold it back, the floodgates opened and I started to cry.

"Baby I'm so sorry, please forgive me. Please don't be mad, tell me I didn't lose you. Will you let me explain? You know I got kids back in Louisville right?"

I sniffed and nodded.

"That phone call was their mother. She wants to get back together. But I can't stand her. She cheated on me with my best friend. We had been a couple since high school. She hurt me bad, not to mention made a fool of me with all my friends. Everybody knew but me. That's why I could never get serious about anyone else ever since. I never wanted to hurt like that again, but when I met you all that changed.

I looked into his eyes. They were big, brown, watery pools of sincerity, maybe that was just what I wanted to see, but if it got me my man back, I did not care.

"She's threatening to put me in jail for child support, if I don't bring her and the kids out here. I brought them out here before and she took off on us. It was an important week for me on my job. All the corporate big shots were in town. I had to hire someone to take care of the kids so I could go to work. I couldn't even comb my daughter's hair."

He gripped my hands, "Do you know how that feels? When you have a little girl expecting you to take care of her and you can't even comb her hair. I had been sending that greedy bitch money for them every week. She spends it partying with her boyfriends. I started sending the money to my mother so she could make sure the kids got what they needed. Now she's trying to say that I havn't paid support. If they arrest me they will send me back to Kentucky, I don't want to go to jail in Kentucky."

I saw the confusion and anguish on his face. Denise the waitress at the Candy Store had told me some of these things the night I met Alonzo. He had never talked to me about his kids or their mother before. I put my arms around Alonzo and kissed away his tears.

"I'm sorry I got salty with you Kim. I don't know what to do. Then you left and I started feeling really alone. I fell asleep and had a nightmare that I lost you. I tried to call and you didn't answer."

"I called Sherry when I got home, she knew I was upset. She called the crew and everyone came over. The girls came over and we were playing the music really loud."

"I called Christian. You know I don't have any friends that I can really talk to. I guess he sensed from my voice that I was in a bad way because he came right over," Alonzo said.

"He's your friend Alonzo, that's what friends do."

"I talked to him and his advice was that if I loved you, really loved you, I had better go find you and fix things." Alonzo pulled me into his arms. "I know that I love you. I don't want to be with anyone but you. I got in the car and drove over here as fast as I could. I was so scared that you would not want to see me. I was so scared I had lost you. No relationship I have ever had has come close to what we have. I don't ever want to be without you, Kim."

I walked into the bedroom and sat down on the bed. My hand hit my pillow, it was soaking wet. I had been crying in my sleep. "You got so angry, you yelled at me. You never did that before, I got to tell you Alonzo, and I didn't like it. You hurt me. I don't like being hurt. I have been hurt before and I promised I would never care about anyone enough that they could make me feel that way again. Then I met you and everything has been so great, like some kind of fairy tale, but then out of the blue you could just flip on me like that." A tear fell from my eye and Alonzo sat down next to me.

"I'm sorry Kim, I am so sorry. I never want to hurt you. Can we start over? Maybe you can help me figure out what to do?"

"Well let's talk in the morning. I'm really tired, I smoked some weed earlier. I pulled the covers back and climbed into my bed. "You want to stay with me tonight?" I had never invited him to stay here before. I had never invited anyone to stay here and he knew it.

He took off his clothes and climbed into the bed. We spooned into one another and fell asleep; his light snores were the waves on which I slept.

Living Together

The next morning I woke Alonzo with a tray of bacon, eggs, hash browns, French toast, and mimosa's. "I don't think that you look too good today. I think that you should take the day off. What do you think?"

"I think I could do that, I have never taken a sick day before. You look sick too, you better get into the bed with me, and you know what else I think?"

"You doing an awful lot of thinking on an empty stomach ain't you?" I stuffed a piece of bacon in his mouth.

As he chewed he said, "I think we should live together. You should move in with me."

"Alonzo be serious boy, you live in a one-room efficiency. Your clothes don't even fit in your place, plus you pay almost seven hundred a month. I pay four hundred a month for this huge two bedroom house."

"That's all you pay for this house?"

"Yep, it's my Uncle Bumpys house and he would rather rent it to family than have it sitting here empty. I think you should move in here with me. Plus if you were to get mad and tell me to leave you alone again, you would be the one that has to get to stepping because this is my place."

"That's not going to happen," he said with determination.

"Well in that case I think that you should move in here."

"Are you sure?"

"The way I see it, we spend so much time together, it makes good sense. Paying the bills here would be cheaper and we have ten times more room."

Alonzo gave up his lease and for two years, we had a wonderful fairy tale relationship. We never argued. We were soul mates, we laughed, we talked, we loved, our every thought was of one another, and when we would be back together, workdays seemed to drag on before we would get back where we belonged. We fit.

I played a game at least once a week. I decorated the house with themes from different countries, prepared cuisine, and dressed to go along with the décor. For Mexico I, hung piñata's and made myself a colorful tiered skirt. When Alonzo walked in the door, I took his suit jacket and dressed him in a poncho I made and a sombrero hat that I had bought on a trip to Tijuana. I prepared enchiladas, taquitos, tacos, and strong margaritas. I danced to mariachi music for him with castanets.

When I fixed Chinese, we sat on pillows on the floor and I fed him with chopsticks from plates on the coffee table. I wore a kimono and a wig adorned with hair ornaments I had bought at the restaurant on Wilshire where we had our first date. I put on light, almost white makeup and dark eyeliner drawn out to my hairline with bright red lipstick. We drank warm sake and plum wine and listened to oriental music.

On Italian night, I put scarves over the lamps and dressed like the girl in the movie, West Side Story, with a peasant blouse, full skirt and no shoes. I melted candle wax and dripped it over a wine bottle that was encased in red netting. We ate spaghetti or lasagna complete with salad, warm garlic bread and red, red wine.

Alonzo always had a hot bath and dinner waiting for me on Tuesdays. He could burn down home soul food as good as anyone. Neck bones, short ribs, greens and gravy, and under my tutelage, he learned baked macaroni and cheese.

We went to clubs or movies on Friday and Saturday nights. On Sunday's Alonzo always went with me to my family dinners either at my parents or my grandmothers. Holiday's were always a big deal in my family and we never missed the excuse for a big dinner. At least once a month we hosted.

Every night I helped Alonzo take off his support socks, and girdle that he wore to smuggle clothes out of the store. Almost everyday he stole something especially for me.

Since our birthdays were only four days apart, we combined our party. Family and friends filled the house and back yard. We had a huge, double sheet cake, and lots of food.

We started early in the afternoon for family so that around nine family with kids and the old folks were ready to go and the real get down started. We turned up the music and broke out the drugs. Our parties lasted two days.

Alonzo was great with kids. We had my little cousins over one Saturday a month and he would take off early so we could go to the movies or an amusement park. We had so much fun with them. I think that he liked having them around because they reminded him of his own children who he sorely missed. We often spoke of trying to get custody from the mother. The kids were usually with his or Rita's mother. She ran the streets and sometimes did not come to get them for days. We found a lawyer to research his options.

One morning we had just finished making love and he pulled me into his arms staring at me with a weird smile.

"What? Why are you looking at me like that?"

"You and I should have a kid."

"That would be nice, but first you have to handle your business with the kids you already have," I said picking up the framed photo of his children.

"Don't you want children? I mean you are twenty three, most women already have kids."

I turned over. I didn't want him to see the pain I was feeling at that moment.

He turned me back over before I could wipe the tears away.

"What is it? Kim please talk to me."

I told him about the children that I had aborted. He held me while I cried.

Every three months Alonzo went home to visit his children and family.

Take This Job and Shove It

Nine to Five
Dolly Pardon

One day I met Alonzo for lunch. I was so upset that I was crying mad. I had been passed over once again for a promotion on a job where I was doing all the work and training others to allow them to advance over me. The boss was a real bitch who often requested that I work through lunch and stay late without overtime pay. I could not deal with this job anymore.

"Quit," Alonzo, said.

"What do you mean?"

"I mean quit. You've been there for a year and they keep screwing you around. Make them fire you and collect unemployment. You can always find another job. Shoot with all the money we make under the table you don't need to work."

"I like to work. But, maybe I will take a little break and look for another job. If I can get them to fire me or i have an accident on the job maybe I could get unemployment or workers compensation."

I did not go back to work that day, or the next or the one after that. Nor did I call. When I did go back to work things were so backed up, that though my supervisor was upset, she was so glad to see me that she did not say anything about my absence. I worked for a few hours and then told her that I was leaving for the day.

Kim you have not been very unreliable lately, is there a problem that you would like to discuss with me?"

"Yes, there is. I would like to discuss the fact that I have been working here for more than a year, I have trained person after person who you promoted over me, even though I work double shifts cleaning up their mistakes, mistakes that could cost this company clients and money."

"We appreciate all that you do, and you will be rewarded for all of your hard work," The skinny white woman said.

"Frankly I think that you are unfair and racist. I don't feel like my work here is recognized or appreciated. If I don't get a raise, and I mean now, you should just fire me because I will not work where I am not appreciated any longer. I will not be working any more over time without time and a half."

"Well, I am sorry you feel this way. I can see where you may think that you have been looked over and we will rectify the situation. You know that I have always given you stellar reviews and a raise every six months. Look, in a few months you come up for review again, I will make sure you get the promotion you deserve."

"I can't live with that. I want a promotion now. I happen to know that you are planning to promote the girl that I have been training next week."

"She is the CEO's niece. I have no control over that. The order came from upstairs."

"Well I hope that the CEO's niece can do the work, because from this point on I am only doing my job. No where in my job description is anything about training others?"

"You are not being a team player."

"I got up and walked to the door. " I have a doctor's appointment and I have to leave now"

"You havn't been here in three days and now you think you are leaving early. This cannot go on."

"I don't think anything, I am leaving and if you don't like it fire me, why dontcha?"

They did not see me again for a week. I had a doctors excuse so there was no action they could take against me. I worked for a couple of days and took off a couple of days until finally she had no choice but to fire me. Fine by me, I had the hook up at the employment office and could collect another unemployment check.

I had been getting unemployment for almost two years from the toy company. I had taken this job under a phony identity and social security number, and the home address was one of my relatives. I would be getting enough in unemployment to match my salary and I didn't have to get up everyday and go anywhere.

I gathered my things went through the building saying my goodbyes and headed home. On the way, I stopped and got a bottle of champagne and two live lobsters to celebrate.

I enjoyed being off work, I did a lot of sewing and had lunch with Alonzo everyday to pick up the days boost. I also worked at my friend Lee's bookie joint.

Broken Heart

Kim

Alonzo and I were going into our third year together. I loved living with him. Every morning he was my alarm clock, my eyes opened to oral orgasms. He sure did know how to put the zippadeedooda in my day. We woke up making love, and went to bed making love and in between we were best friends until.

I refer to this day as terrible Tuesday. Alonzo and Uncle Willie had just brought me back from Martin Luther King hospital where four impacted wisdom teeth had been extracted. The doctors said that while under the anesthesia I was laughing my head off. I was still laughing as Alonzo and Willie led me to the car.

I stopped laughing when the Novocain started to wear off. I was in serious pain. Alonzo helped me change and climb into bed before he and Willie went to fill my prescription.

I was flipping through channels when the phone rang, "Hello." I got a hang-up, but seconds later, the phone rang again. A woman's voice, "Can I speak to Lonzo."

"Who's calling?" Lots of women called Alonzo to buy clothes so I didn't trip.

"This is his fiancée," the voice on the other end said.

"Excuse me?" I said sitting up in the bed.

"You heard right," the voice said.

"Rita."

"Well Rita he is not here, I'll tell him that you called.

"Do you know who I am?"

Of course I knew who she was, "No but I assume you are going to tell me."

"I'm his kid's mother."

"Alright I'm listening; you obviously have something you want to tell me."

I listened as the woman bragged about all the promises Alonzo had made to her and the children, "Alonzo is only with you because of the money you giving him. As soon as he has enough saved up he is going to send for me and the kids and you will be history."

"I see, and when are you planning to come here?"

"It won't be long."

"Okay if you say so."

"What you trying to say?"

"I ain't saying nothing; I'm just listening to you."

"Well you need to hurry up and give him some more money, I'm tired of waiting."

"Why don't you make your own money? Wouldn't that get you here faster? I mean if I had a man and baby daddy and I wanted to get to him, I would get off my ass and make money instead of waiting for someone else to pay for a ticket. It couldn't be that much. What kind of woman waits for another one to pay her way? Another thing if I am giving him so much money why would he get rid of me for a broke like you."

"Who the hell do you think you are talking to?"

"You said your name is Rita and that you are his kids mother, is that right?"

"What did he tell you about me?"

"Nothing, I didn't even know you existed." I knew this would piss her off.

"Stop lying Bitch. If I thought for one second that you were telling the truth, I would have his ass locked up in a heartbeat. I ain't tripping about the money that the courts ordered him to pay every month because I know that he has to save up to get us a house."

"That might be kind of hard when he is paying all the bills for my house. I know that sends money to his mother for the kids."

"He is supposed to send it to me. His mother doesn't know what these kids need."

"I spoke to his mother. She knows what they need because she keeps them more than you do."

"What did you just say?"

"He told me that his mother and your mother take care of the kids and that you are not in the picture much." I was looking at the shine on my two-carat ring that Alonzo proposed with.

"That is just some bullshit he is saying to keep you happy until he leaves your ass. If you don't believe me, you should do some house cleaning. Alonzo always hides stuff in shoeboxes. I should know, that's where I found the letters from the last broad he was cheating on me with. He was spending all his time and money on her. That was the first time I locked his ass up."

"I don't believe anything you are saying." I did not want to believe her. I could have said a lot of things to strike back at Rita, but I needed more information. If he was saving money to send for them, why would this dumb broad want to bust him out like this? There had to be more to this story. I knew that he had more than enough money if he wanted to move out.

"You are a lying jealous bitch," I said

Rita laughed and told me to get a pencil. She gave me her phone number. "Check that number against your phone bill and you will see that we talk every Tuesday. I send all the letters special delivery to be delivered on Tuesdays. Be home when the postman comes around and you can intercept this weeks. It will be delivered to 152 W. 157th Street."

Unbelievable. This woman had just given me my own address. I hung up and made a beeline to the closet where I started tearing open shoeboxes. I found and read several letters that Alonzo had received from Rita. There were also a few marked, 'return to sender,' that he had written.

She had not been lying, in Alonzo's handwriting the letters clearly stated that he only cohabitated with me so he could stack enough money to send for her and the kids. He said that I paid all the bills. There were also some recent pictures of him with her. I knew they were recent because he was wearing the shirt that I had made him. *"Well I'll just be damned."*

The pain swelled up in my chest with every tear-blurred word. I was having trouble breathing. It was as if someone was smothering me. I never knew disbelief could be so thick. The experience must have been similar to that of old people who heard bad news and dropped dead.

The Novocain had totally worn off. I went into the living room and poured myself a glass of brandy. In the bathroom mirror, I examined my swollen, tear streaked face. *You are a stupid gullible idiot.* I took a big gulp from the brandy bottle before replacing the blood soaked gauze with cotton soaked in Brandy.

I was on my way back to bed when I heard the postman's singing voice. I met him at the front door. There was another letter from Rita, perfumed, with kissy lip prints all over it. I put it in the freezer to harden the glue so I could open and reseal it.

I felt betrayed. I dialed the only person that I knew would be honest with me. When the phone was picked up, I let go of my tears, loudly, "Daddy."

"Alright, what's wrong?"

"Aah, Aah, huhhhhh Ahhhhh."

"O.K. that must be a new language, but I can't understand it. You are going to have to speak English."

"Daddy," I started. "He's cheating on me and he ain't taking care of his kids." I let go with the whole story.

"Well, he couldn't be cheating on you because his dick is not long enough to reach all the way to Kentucky. Now, you remember when Alonzo and I went fishing. You were at work."

"Yeah,"

"He told me about this situation. She has him between a rock and a hard place. I believe that he cares about you. I had to listen to the boy bragging on you for hours. A couple of times I had to remind him that I am your Father. He has given you everything you could possibly want from day one. Remember when you wrecked that woman's Cadillac and didn't have any insurance? The woman threatened to call the police unless you could pay to get her bumper fixed and Alonzo pawned his jewelry to get you out of trouble. The boy had only known you for a few weeks. A man doesn't pawn his jewelry for any old piece of ass."

"Yeah, but daddy he is either lying to me or lying to her."

"He told me that the woman slept with his best friend. No man wants to be with a woman who has made a fool of him, and the whole town knows about it. I think that you should leave this alone."

"She said he's not sending any money to his kids, if that's true, I can't respect that."

"He said he can't send it to her because she good-times the money away. He sends it to his mother, why don't you ask his mother?"

"I have and she said that she buys everything the kids need with the money orders he sends like clockwork every month. I have even sent some for him."

"Didn't you guys talk to an attorney about getting his kids? The man is just trying to stay out of jail. You need to keep enjoying the good life and keep your mouth shut."

I heard the front gate open and Alonzo's car pulled in the drive. "I'll call you back Daddy, Alonzo, and Lil' Willie are back with my medicine, my mouth is killing me."

"Remember what I said, he's a good man and until you know the whole story don't do anything. Remember all those women who came to your mother about me. She always said as long as she is getting treated right, someone else is always going to be envious and try to cause problems. Plus you just got your teeth pulled, you probably still high on the anesthesia, so don't do nothing you might regret. Go to sleep, you hear me?"

"O.K. Daddy." I hung up.

Alonzo and Lil Willie came through the door laughing. Alonzo got me a pitcher of water and gave me two pain pills. "Here baby I got you a shake so that you wouldn't be taking medicine on an empty stomach."

"You comfortable, Sweetheart," Alonzo asked.

"Yeah, I'm comfy, I'm going to sleep." I felt the pain medicine kicking in.

We'll if you'll be all right we are going to meet Christian and play some ball. If you need me just hit me up on my pager." On his days off, he hung out with Christian at the school where he worked as a janitor. A bunch of the guys helped Christian with his work so that they could play basketball in the afternoon.

"You have fun, I'll be fine." He hugged and kissed me before leaving.

How could he be so sweet to me and tell Rita the things that he did in those letters. He was so attentive. We spent just about every waking moment together. We made love twice a day or more. All my friends were envious of our relationship.

My number one rule was never to be with a man I could not trust. I knew for a fact that all the money Alonzo made, we spent. There were days when we had thousands, and days when we were faced with the dilemma of how we could eat off of six dollars.

I did not understand how this woman could think that he was her fiancé when we had been talking to me about marriage, getting his children to come and live with us, and having one of our own. How the hell could he be this woman's fiancé when he had just proposed to me with a two-carat diamond ring?

I tried for three months to forget about the letters and Rita. I talked to Sherry and Laisyv about it. They told me, "As long as he is here and she is there, what is the problem. The witch is in another state, don't worry about it. Girlfriend the man is paying all your bills. He treats you like a queen, you got more clothes than you can wear in a lifetime and he still brings you something almost every day. You need to keep quiet and keep living the good life."

"I heard that," "Here, Here," and "Honey Boons," reverberated through the room.

I knew they were right, but like The Righteous Brothers said, "You've lost that loving feeling." I did not trust Alonzo anymore. It was hard for me to enjoy sex with him; my head just was not into it. I did not even consider it love making anymore. I started making up excuses.

When Alonzo went back home for the Kentucky Derby I asked him if I could go with him. He made up some excuse about spending all his time with his mother and that I would have to stay at a hotel alone because she would not allow a woman who wasn't his wife to sleep in her home.

I asked some of my Uncle's friends who were going to Derby to keep an eye out for Alonzo. When they returned they told me they saw him with Rita, looking all lovey-dovey, they had even taken pictures without him knowing and could not wait to show them to me.

When Alonzo returned he was the one making excuses. He did not even want to sleep in the bed with me for two weeks. Saying he had some kind of rash.

I found a receipt from a doctor's visit that explained it all. Obviously, he had slept with Rita, and caught something. *At least he knew not to bring that shit back to me.*

I started going out with my girlfriends and staying out late, very late, if I came home at all. I did not want to do any of the things that we used to do that defined our relationship as special. After a while, I could not stand being around him. He always asked me what was wrong and if I was seeing someone else. I never answered him.

Finally, I asked him to move out. We had a big argument. "You are torturing me, why are you treating me like this? What happened? You just woke up one day and decided you don't love me anymore? Kim what is going on? Please don't do me like this, you're killing me."

I walked to the closet, took the shoebox down, and handed it to him. "This is why I don't love you anymore, you are either lying to her or you are lying to me. You were with her when you went home for Derby. She called me and told me all about it. I no longer trust you, therefore I can't love you," I threw the pictures of him with Rita on the bed.

"You don't understand. I was trying to keep her from putting me in jail."

"Well, now you don't have to lie to her, you can keep your word and bring her and the kids out here, one big happy family. You got two weeks to move out of here."

I picked up my purse and left. I had put a weeks worth of clothes in my car so I would not have to come home. I stayed with Sherry.

Alonzo moved into an apartment off of Crenshaw in an area called the Jungle. When we did cross paths, I would not talk to him.

Christian was always trying to play the go between in an attempt to get us back together. After a while, Christian gave up and stopped talking about Alonzo altogether. I knew that Alonzo had been going out with some girl that lived in the building next to Christian.

Christian and Laisyv gave a party at the Marina City Club. Alonzo came and when I went outside to have a cigarette he followed me onto the balcony, "Kim, can we talk?"

"No," I tried to walk around him.

He grabbed my arm, threw me against the railing, and put his hand around my throat. "You can't just do a person like this. You are driving me crazy. I even had to go and see a psychiatrist because of you."

I don't think Alonzo fully realized what he was doing. Someone saw what was going on and shouted out to Christian. They grabbed me and pulled me back over the balcony where I had fell over, they pried Alonzo's hands from around my throat. Christian grabbed his arm, hit him with a right cross, and took him into another room.

When Alonzo came out of the room, he walked over to me, "Kim I am sorry, and I didn't mean to hurt you. I'm going to leave now. If you ever need anything or decide you want to talk to me, well, I'll be waiting."

The next day we were getting high, everyone had left by four in the morning. Laisyv and Christian told me to stay in the extra bedroom. We had not made it to sleep. I guess they were waiting until I was good and high to tell me.

Laisyv made Christian do the dirty work. "Rita and Alonzo's kids are on a bus making their way to Los Angeles as we speak."

Alonzo told Christian that he was bringing her out here to let her know that they would not be getting back together and to try to get custody of his kids.

Somewhere in the back of my mind, I had thoughts of getting back with Alonzo. I was lonely and I missed him. No one I met could hold a candle to him. I just could not see myself with anyone else, but with this information, I knew that this was no longer an option. When Rita got here, there was no way she would leave Alonzo, not if she had any sense.

A few days later, my house was broken into. The only thing that was missing were things that Alonzo had left.

I called Uncle Cricket and he came right over. "There was no forced entry, if it was a burglary there would be a lot more stuff missing. Alonzo is trying to mess with your head."

I made a decision, right then and there. Anything concerning men in my life would be about getting paid. I did not want to see another penis unless it had hundred dollar bills hanging off of it.

Kim

Growing up

I had been around the business all my life. As a young girl I watched and listened to everything Cricket's girls did. I didn't realize it but even then, I was in training. I had always been in awe of my Uncle's girls. The fancy clothes, fur coats, diamonds, jewelry, and pretty cars were alluring.

I was twelve when Cricket and his colleagues rented almost every apartment in a building on Highland. I would go with my grandmother to clean and when I was spending time with my Uncle and cousin, we would be with him when he went to "Check his traps."

I gawked as he collected rolls of money that could choke a horse. His women had the best of everything. All I knew was one day, somehow, by hook or by crook; I was going to have money like that.

My Grandmother cleaned the apartments for Cricket and his friends and she paid me to help. A little money for doing what I would have done anyway.

When the girls were not working, I would hang out with them. One day a tour bus pulled up in front of the building. I followed Mea downstairs and she gave me list of apartment numbers to buzz. This was the signal. Within minutes, girls flooded the lobby, wearing fancy nightgowns and lingerie.

Mea greeted the Oriental men as they filed off the bus. She led them into the lobby where they chose girls who took them onto the elevators. I had never seen so many men bowing up and down in my life.

Two hours after the bus left my grandmother set about cleaning. Cricket and some of his friends showed up. He gave me a list of apartment numbers and a paper bag and told me to go to each one and collect the money for him. I was to write the amount from each apartment next to the apartment *number. I was so pleased that he would trust me with such an important job.*

When I came back to Mea's apartment, the bag was so full I couldn't even close it. "Add the money up for me," Cricket said.

Within a few minutes, I gave him the paper that totaled up to 7,500.00. He checked my figures and gave me a 100-dollar bill.

I was thinking about all of this while Cricket was going around checking the windows. His pager went off and he got on the phone. When he got off the phone, he came into the living room where I had poured us both a drink and was grinding some coke on a mirror. I took a couple of snorts and handed him the mirror. I waited until he finished and was picking up his glass to speak my mind, "Cricket I want to get in the game."

He looked at me for a full minute before telling me in no uncertain terms, "I forbid you to even think about getting down like that. My sister would kill me if she knew that I was even talking to you about this," he picked up the mirror and took another blow.

    I'll tell you what I will do for you. You can drive for me."

"What does that pay?"

    "Twenty dollars a stop, you take the girl on the call, wait for her, and bring her back. If I ever hear about you trying to get with a pimp I will make sure you don't work and I will take his women and run him out of town and make sure he don't work in any other."

"I wasn't thinking about getting with a pimp."

"We don't let girls outlaw. We got an international network. If a girl shows up on the street or tries to work for an agency and ain't got no representation, someone is going to break her every time they see her. We make life real hard for outlaws."

"I wouldn't have to be an outlaw if I was working for Mea."

"I know you Niecy. You are going to do what you want no matter what anyone says. I also know that you can spend your own money just as fast as any pimp can. You've been around the game long enough to know what happens to girls when they can't work no more. You have seen first hand what has happened to girls in the business, they get beat up, hurt, and killed. Why would you want to get into that?"

"I'm not stupid Cricket. I know how to protect myself."

"Kim, so did those girls who ended up hurt or worse. You never know who you are dealing with in this game."

"I never know who I'm dealing with anyway."

"Hell you always attract men that lose it, don't think I forget about that crazy ass sugar daddy you had that tried to blow you up in the Porsche that he bought you."

"You did not have to bring that up."

"Yes I did. Listen Niecy, you are smart, you keep good jobs, and you know how to hustle, even if you break up with Alonzo, you can still keep hustling the clothes with him."

"I don't know that I want to be around him. You can always call him and he'll hook you up with clothes if that's what you are worried about."

"It's that bad?"

"Worse, I was at Christian's party at the Marina City Club last weekend and he grabbed me around my throat and damn near threw me from the thirtieth floor balcony. He said that I am making him crazy."

"Why didn't you call and tell me about this?"

"Christian handled it. Alonzo apologized. I really do think that he has lost it. His baby mama and the kids are here, so I guess he is he is a family man now. He told Christian that he is just trying to get his kids but I don't believe anything he says anymore."

"Well you know best as far as that goes, but I don't want you in the business, that is definitely, totally, uncompromisingly out of the question."

I knew better than to argue with Cricket. He was my Uncle and he was right the life was dangerous and no man wanted to see his relative in the game. I had been with him when we found one of his first women, Candy. She had been mutilated and murdered. She was left in a hotel after a trick had cut her breast off and stabbed her thirty two times.

Cricket had told me to wait in the car, but when I saw a woman who was walking by the open room door start screaming I got out to check on Cricket. It was a gruesome sight. We later found out that it was Ted Bundy who had killed her. Yes, the game could be very dangerous.

"Okay, I will settle for driving."

Kim

Driving for dollars

I got twenty dollars for each call that I drove the girls on. I was averaging anywhere from $150.00 to $500.00 a night. Not bad for a little girl from Compton.

All I had to do was pick up the girls, either from Sunset Boulevard or their apartments, take them on the call, wait while they handled their business and then take them home or on their next call. They paid me extra to take them to get food or shopping.

I was making more money than I had working as a secretary for the school district, a receptionist at the Mattress company, Berman liquor imports, or as a telex operator for the toy company, which were just a few of the jobs that I had since graduating from high school in 1977.

One thing Uncle Cricket always told me was to keep a regular job. The only reason that he had ever done time was for tax evasion. No matter what hustle I was involved in I tried to keep a square job. I sold and transported drugs, sold hot clothes, booked horses, but I always kept a job unless I was collecting unemployment, disability, or workers compensation. I did whatever it took to keep my ass covered and I paid my taxes.

I worked during the day and drove for Cricket at night. I slept from 5:00 to 9:00 p.m. and drove until 6:00 a.m. I took catnaps in the car while I waited for the girls. This worked out real well for a few months.

I sewed for the working girls and made costumes for exotic dancers. I kept a sewing machine at Mea's and in between driving, I sewed. I had a passion for designing outfits, and with these girls as clients, I could let my creativity run wild. These girls had good figures and needed clothes to show them off, flashy, eye-catching clothes. I also made silk shirts with matching ties for my Uncles and their friends.

The two women who had been with Cricket the longest were Mea and Kalyn, all the girls were rivals trying to out do one another for his attention, but these two were his top earners. Both of them had a lot of customers and were always having parties at their workhouses.

Sometimes more than one party was going on at a time. Even though Cricket had other women, they did not trust one another not to steal money or customers. They distrusted each other so much that they would rather pass on a party than let their wife-in-laws run it, nor would they trust other pimp's girls.

I talked to Cricket one day when I had to take him some blow, "You are losing a lot of money, and you don't have to be."

"What do you mean, Jelly Bean?" he said playing as if he was going to hit me.

"You need a host. I've watched Mea and Kayla lose work because they can't be in two places at one time."

"I wonder where I could find someone who is qualified to do such an important job. You know they would have to know the game, and they would be dealing with my money, so I would have to be able to trust them. Maybe I should put an ad in the paper?" he said with a mischievous grin on his face. I did not know why my Uncles liked to tease me so.

"Sure you go ahead, I can just picture the ad, 'Needed - someone to go to jail for pimping and pandering.' Nope, for some reason I don't think that will work in The Los Angeles Times." I punched him in the arm.

"I guess you have someone in mind?"

"And you know this."

Mea and Kalyn could train me. Let me know everything about the clients that I need to. I pay the girls when they come out of the room so they can't steal anything. It's a win, win situation, all the way around."

I was on unemployment and was receiving checks from three different jobs under three different names. I was also suing the toy manufacturing company for discrimination and it looked like I was going to win.

I made more money than the girls who went in the rooms with the tricks. They worked on a 60/40 split. Hours were 40 minutes or until the trick got off. I got a hundred dollars an hour to keep coded records of who went in the rooms with whom. I was known as Sparkle, I loved that movie. Aretha Franklin did the sound track and I played it often.

"Never let a trick know your real name, you never know what could happen. You don't want them to be able to track you down," Mea told me.

I paid the girls, answered the phones, and booked outcalls when Mea wasn't available. I got twenty dollars for every successful outcall. The girls also tipped me for giving them the call.

When there was a party, I called in new girls every few hours to keep the clients interested. When the clients walked in the door, they handed me a stack of money usually about 5 to 10 thousand, this way they didn't have to worry about dealing with the money every time someone went into the bedroom.

When the party was over, I went over the books with the client. Most times, they didn't bother and the extra money went to Mea. She always kicked me down a few hundred.

When the clients were drug cartels they brought keys of coke and one girl was paid to sit and grind up and prepare plates of powder for sniffing. They always left the remaining coke and Mea and I split the profits after I sold it.

The Cartels were in town on business and usually were waiting for pages. Sometimes they were there three or four days. Sometimes they paid to go to sleep after they were all sexed out.

I snorted coke to stay alert. After being up for 72 hours, you get a little goofy. I would take all the money I had made, excuse myself for a few minutes go in one of the rooms and lay out my money on the bed and roll around on it. This usually revived me because every twelve hours I would go and count my money. Usually the other parties that Mea or Kalyn had would end and they could come and handle there business while I got some sleep.

I had another friend who was driving the girls on outcalls nights when I was hosting. I had been hosting for a year and every few months Valentino, the guy who I had met that night when I picked up food for Mea came to town.

Valentino always had an entourage of ten or twelve men with him. He remembered me. Every time he saw me, he asked, "Sparkle will you go in the room with me?"

"Valentino you know that I don't work, I am just a host."

"One day" he would say shaking his finger at me. "One day, I am going to get you to go with me."

One day the party had been going for three days and I had just brought in a new shift of girls.

"Sparkle, will you come with me in the room?" Valentino asked.

The men had taken care of their business and would be flying back home to Columbia the next day. They had made good use of their time and had spent over thirty thousand dollars with the girls. Most of them took two or three at time.

"Valentino you ask me this every time, and every time I have to tell you that I don't work?"

"It is because you keep turning me down. It makes me want to be with you even more. Okay the other girls get one hundred to go in the room, I am going to give you three, come on?"

"Nope, can't do it, sorry."

One of the girls who did not know that I was Cricket's niece said, "Girl you are crazy, you should go get that money."

"Okay, how about five hundred?"

Everyone had been sitting around listening to music, watching television, and taking a break. They were pretty much sexed out. Everyone stared at me waiting to see what I would say.

When I still did not move Valentino put down five more hundred. "Now that is one thousand dollars, do you not like me so much that you would turn down one thousand dollars?"

"Valentino it is not that I don't like you, I do. I would marry you if you were not already married. It's just that I don't date."

"Okay Sparkle, how about now." He put ten, one hundred dollar bills on the table, next to the other ten one hundred dollar bills, there was now two thousand dollars on the table. I knew that no girl had ever been in the room with him for more than fifteen minutes. I could go in the room for fifteen minutes. It wasn't like I was a virgin.

"Girl that is two thousand dollars," one of Cricket's women, Star said. Sparkle get yo' money girl."

I looked at the money. Valentino put two more hundred down. Everyone was urging me to take the money.

It looked really good. I stood up and picked up the money, "Okay, come on Valentino."

We went in the room. I helped him take off his clothes. He sat on the bed, "I want to watch you undress."

I took my time and swayed seductively to the radio. I had been to the strip clubs delivering the costumes that I made for the girls so I did what I had seen them do. I guess I was doing all right because he was aroused. When I was finally naked, he pulled me in between his legs and ran his hands over my back and legs turning me around examining every inch of my body. "You are flawless, your body is beautiful."

"Thank you Valentino."

"How old are you."

"I'll be 24 in two weeks."

"You really are new to this business, most girls if they were 23 and looked like you, they would say that they were eighteen."

"Where I come from, in Compton, I am proud to be alive at my age, so why should I lie about it?"

He laughed, "I love the way the way you think. You are so honest. Am I really the first man you have gone with, this way, you know for money?"

"Yep, you sure are. I might be fired after Mea finds out that I have gone with you."

"I would not let that happen, I'll tell her that if she fires you that I won't come back here again," we laughed.

"Don't do that, I don't plan to make a habit of this."

We lay on the bed, "Your shoulders are so tight. Would you like a massage?" I offered.

"Sure."

I turned him over, sat on his back, and started massaging him using the oils in the warmer next to the bed. I knew he was tired and I was hoping he would fall to sleep. His breathing slowed and he started to snore. I rose off of him.

Before I could get all the way off of him, he woke and turned around and grabbed my hips. I realized that this was going to happen. It was over in seconds.

I showered and dressed. When I came out, he was dressed. We walked back into the living room. Every one started clapping and the other girls gathered around me telling me that they had never gotten that much for twenty minutes of work. I put my 40 dollars into the envelope for the house and put twenty one hundred and sixty dollars into my envelope bringing me to a grand total of $9,200.00. After that night, there was no stopping me.

Cricket found out that I was turning tricks. He was livid and did not speak to me for a month. But he did not try and stop me.

Kim

Back to the present

"I wanted you to meet my kids." Alonzo said at my front door.

I did not have the heart to be rude to him in front of his children. I went out with them to eat and when he had brought me back home I combed and braided his daughter's hair.

"Can I see you again?" he asked after putting the kids in the car.

"Not a good idea."

"Whose going to comb my daughters hair."

"I'm sure you can find someone. Ever hear of beauty parlor?"

At the time, he didn't know where Rita was. She had disappeared. He didn't find out until weeks later that she was in jail for passing hot checks.

Christian kept me abreast of what was going on and gave me the out of town number to call Alonzo when I was ready.

Alonzo had taken his children back to Louisville Kentucky on a bus. They were living with his mom. I did not know he was back in town.

This was where my life was the night I saw Alonzo coming out of Carlos and Charlie's. That night when the limo dropped us off at my house there were five cars of people that we had invited to party.

We danced, drank, and snorted coke. I ended up sleeping with one of the exotic dancers. It was an empty act with no satisfaction.

Laisyv and the other girls were ready to leave about six in the morning. The limo driver had slept with Shirley and took them back to Laisyv's to get their cars.

The dancer thought that he was going to stay with me but I told him that he had to leave. He was hurt, "Don't you want my number?"

"Can I see you tomorrow?"

"I have to work."

"Are we going to take this any further than tonight?"

"I'm just getting over a relationship. I'm not in a hurry to get into another one."

"Can I call you sometime?"

I gave him my beeper number."

The next day I woke 12:00 and called Laisyv to take me to my parents to get my car.

Laisyv dropped me off and I went into the house. My parents were on their way out. I had told my aunt that she could drop Keisha and Jay off at my parent's so she and my Uncle Bumby could have a night out. She would not arrive for a couple of hours so rather than drive all the way home I sat on the couch and picked up the photo album that I was looking through before we left for dinner, and went back down memory lane.

Kim

The Blue Bug

Mommy had a blue Volkswagen Bug that we putt-putted around town in. I used to think that she knew magic. We would get to a traffic light and she would snap her fingers and say "change," and like magic, the light would turn green.

My parents took me and my cousin Marvina to the drive-in movie to see 'Herbie, The Love Bug.' The next day Marvina and I were in the back yard all day trying to get the Volkswagen to do tricks.

One day the blue bug really did do a trick. In my heart, I just knew that it had some of Herbie's soul. It was pouring down rain and the streets were flooding. We were on our way home from a store in Lakewood and had to go under a bridge. By the time we realized that the underpass was flooded we could not turn around. People were swimming out of their stalled cars.

The water picked up the Bug and somehow the car just kept going like a little boat. We got to the other side and the car went right on up the hill. It was amazing.

"Mommy, now do you believe that the bug is like Herbie?"

"Yeah baby, I think you are right, it definitely saved us."

Me and my friends were always doing odd jobs to make money, we had a car wash every weekend, we pulled weeds, ironed clothes, walked dogs, anything that could make us a few quarters.

I spent a lot of time in the room behind the garage watching my Father sew. One day I decided I wanted to try, I was going to make a halter top out of some light blue-checkered cotton fabric. I cut a triangle of fabric and attached the top to a choker ring.

I sewed on yellow yarn for hair, button eyes, and nose. I did not think the mouth through very well, I attached red licorice for lips. I sewed it all by hand. I was so cute riding up and down the street on my bike in my new top that I had made all by myself, until…

The hot California sun melted the licorice. I had to take off the sticky top because flies and bees were following me.

The next time I used red fabric for the mouth. All the girls in the neighborhood wanted one. I was trading dolls, board games and IOU's for allowance.

I got so many orders that I knew it would take me a long time to finish if I had to sew by hand – but if I could use the sewing machine I could finish in no time. The regular Singer sewing machine was not threaded and I couldn't figure out how to do it.

Then I noticed that the industrial machine was all threaded and ready to go. It could not be that hard to use. Daddy made it look so easy. What? You stick your fabric under the little foot thingy and then step on the foot peddle. I convinced myself that if he were home he would want me to do this. I had orders to fill just like he did.

When I stepped on the peddle the machine went so fast that it pulled the fabric through with such unexpected force that I could not move my finger in time and sewed right through it, the needle was stuck through my finger nail between the presser foot and the feed.

Once I stopped screaming, I used a screwdriver to turn the knob that would let the needle come out of the machine. After I extricated myself from the machine, I cut the thread and pulled it through my finger. I went into the garage cabinet, got a bottle of alcohol, poured it over my nail, and put on a band aide.

I cleaned the drop of blood off of the machine. Though my finger was throbbing, I was more determined than ever. I was not giving up; this machine was not going to beat me. I got the hang of it and finished a top in a half an hour. By hand, it took me six hours. I finished up six orders in no time.

Then I got an idea, I went into the house and pulled all the money out of my piggy bank with a nail file. I went down the street to Jean's and presented her and her sister Renee with a proposal to invest in my halters.

Jean and her sister Renee emptied their piggy banks and we pooled our money, got on our bikes and rode downtown Compton to Woolworths and bought chokers and fabric. We were in business now.

The next day I made twelve halter-tops, we set up a stand in the front yard and after we sold the first top, we took that money, went to the grocery store, and bought stuff to make lemonade and chocolate chip cookies to sell along with the tops. Jean and Renee manned our table while I sewed more tops. We were charging four dollars a top.

At the end of the day, we had to buy more fabric because we sold out.

The next week daddy was home and had taught me how to thread the singer machine. I sat in my room sewing. One evening the doorbell rang and my Father answered. Two of my friends had come to get their tops. My Father watched the transaction and asked one of the girls if he could see the top. He examined the top, a smile dawning across his face.

The next day he asked me to see one of the tops. There were some minor details that I had left out of the construction – like hemming. The next morning Daddy woke me up, "Meet me in the sewing room in an hour."

I dressed, did my chores and summer homework, ate cereal and went out back.

"If you are going to sew then you might as well learn how to do it right." He gave me a book. "Look through this later tonight. Today we are going to start you off with some stitching. You have to learn how to make long even stitches."

He took a swatch of cheesecloth fabric, ironed it out, made marks a quarter inch apart on the side and top, and told me to start stitching by hand. After I finished the first row he told me he wanted me to make lines all the way across, each stitch needed to be identical.

It took me two hours to finish and when I gave it to him; he looked at it, took a pair of scissor, cut the stitches on each row, pulled the thread out, and ironed it. "Now do it again."

That night I read the sewing book. The next day we went shopping for patterns and fabric. He taught me to read a pattern and to cut out the fabric. He guided me step by step and within an hour, I had made an outfit that looked like it came out of the store. It was at that moment I fell in love with sewing. To be able to transform a piece of fabric into a garment made me feel good.

I sewed a lot of my school, summer clothes every year, and continued to sew for others. By the time, I was in high school I was sewing for my friend's parents. Recycled jeans and Maxi coats were popular and I was spending every evening filling orders. I was president of the modeling club and always threw some of my designs in every show. I also made the best-dressed list.

Camping

The Volkswagen Van

My parents went to the Compton or Rosecran's Drive-in Theatre every Thursday night. It was Mommy's payday. Daddy had a Volkswagen van. They sat in the in the back and I sat in the front behind the steering wheel with the window cracked so that I would not choke on their cigarette smoke.

We always ate what was called the three P's which was actually four P's, broiled pork chops, big sour pickles, pepperoni pizza from the snack bar and home made popcorn out of a big paper grocery sack. Mommy always let me help make the popcorn. We heated oil in a big pot on the stove, added popcorn kernels, and put the lid on. She would keep shaking the pot so the popped Kernels wouldn't burn on the bottom. When it was done, she poured it in a doubled brown paper grocery bag and poured melted butter and salt over it and I would shake the bag. I looked forward to Thursdays with my parents.

We also took our vacations in the van. The day finally came when we were going on a camping trip. It was my eighth birthday present. I was so excited I couldn't stand it. For the last two weeks as soon as I opened my eyes and before I brushed my teeth, I ran to the calendar and marked off a day. We were going to Lake Arrowhead camping and fishing. My cousin's Kara and Ria were going with us.

Daddy had rented a tent, three cots, lamps and a cook stove. We packed our clothes and fishing gear into the blue Volkswagen van, picked up my cousins, and were on our way.

It was slow going rounding the winding road that climbed up the mountain to the lake. The van was a stick shift and did not have much power and the engine was straining. There was a long line of honking cars piling up behind us and we had to pull over at each rest stop in order to let them pass. It seemed like the higher we got the harder the car strained.

"Every body lean forward and help Betsy up the hill," Daddy said. We all did it actually thinking we were helping the poor van.

Finally, we got to the campgrounds. We set up our tent and cots and went exploring. We went back to camp and mommy made a fire as the sun went down. We roasted hot dogs on sticks for dinner. Afterwards we held jiffy pop popcorn over the fire until the top blew up like a silver balloon.

We sat around on logs and told stories and jokes. As usual, Daddy had to tell his favorite joke. No matter how many times I heard it I always burst my sides laughing. He took a long drink of beer and started, "There was a family that had invited the preacher for Sunday dinner. The son was in the kitchen helping his mother and he kept farting. Finally, the mother turned to him and said, "I am not going to have you embarrassing me at the dinner table with all that farting, you take this here pickle and you stick it up your butt."

He went to the restroom, came back, and helped his mother set the table.

"Now the preacher is our special guest so what ever he wants you make sure you give it to him, you understand?"

"Yes, Mama."

The preacher arrived and they all sat down to dinner, there was one breast left, the Father wanted it but so did the preacher so the son gave it to the preacher. There was one roll left and though the mother had her eye on it, she gave it to the preacher. They were all full and set back drinking ice tea.

The preacher undid his belt and the button of his pants and was rubbing his belly, "Boy that sure was a good meal, and you know what would top it of just right, a pickle."

The son went into the kitchen, looked in the pickle jar, and found that it was empty. He came back, gave the preacher a pickle, and sat down. Just as the preacher was taking, the last bite of his pickle there was a loud noise, waaaaaaaaaaamp.

Everyone looked at the little boy and laughed. The preacher through his chuckling said, "Boy that sure was a whopper." The boy laughed and pointed at him, "Yeah and you ate the stopper."

When we finally stopped laughing, we cleaned up and put all the food in the back of the van. My cousins and I went into our tent and changed into our pajamas. Kara and Ria volunteered to take the trash over to the big cans across the road.

Mommy and Daddy went into the van to sleep. We climbed under our blankets on our cots. We used the kerosene lamp for light and Kara read Charlotte's Web aloud until we all were asleep. We turned off the lamp and went to sleep listening to the hoot of an owl.

I woke up about three in the morning, I could tell by the glow in the dark hands on my Betty and Veronica watch that I had saved up and ordered from the back of the comic book. I could not move, it was so cold, I felt frozen. I yelled "Daddy," over and over again. He never came. I guess hypothermia put me back to sleep.

I woke up and my cousins were peeking around our tent, giggling. I got out of my cot to see what was going on. There was a lot of clattering and clanging outside. When I peeked around them, I saw bears at the trashcans. "Momma," I yelled.

They shushed me put their hands over my mouth trying to keep me quiet. They thought it was funny, I was scared. "When we took the trash out we put pancake syrup around the cans to see what animals would come."

"Well you didn't get animals, you got bears."

"Don't tell."

"I ain't got to tell, but I ain't fixin' to get ate up."

I ran to the van and banged on the door. When my Father opened it, he said, "What's wrong with you?"

I couldn't talk, I just pointed.

He looked at what I was pointing at, "Goodgooglywoogly," and he slammed the door on the van. I banged again. "You just going to leave us out here?" I screamed. "Go back in your tent he said, if they come this way I will get rid of them." He said from the front seat of the van.

I ran back to the tent, on the way I saw that the bears were heading up the hill. My cousins were still laughing when I fell back to sleep.

I woke to the smell of bacon sizzling. My cousins were already putting on their clothes. Mommy had gotten water for us to brush our teeth and wash our faces. I went over to the port-a-potty. I opened the door and checked for spiders or snakes before I sat down.

Daddy was talking to a group of men about the freak weather we had last night. "I was listening to the radio this morning and it said the weather had dropped to fifty degrees it's supposed to get up to eighty today." A freckled, red headman said.

The sun was shining and every campsite was alive with breakfast. Mommy made pancakes and bacon on a butane stove. It was really good even with the sand and debris from the trees.

"So what are we going to do this morning?" Daddy asked.

"Let's go swimming," I said.

We all changed into our suits and walked to the pool. There were a few people sitting around on lounge chairs.

My dad dove in and when he hit the water, he let out a loud scream. Some of the onlookers were laughing. He swam to the stairs and got out.

"Daddy, what's the matter?"

"The water is freezing."

"There was a freeze last night so the water is about twenty degrees right now, we have to wait until around noon when the sun has heated it up," a lady said through her laughter.

I stuck my toe in the water, "Maybe we should go fishing, or something else, I don't want to go in there."

We went back to the campground and put on some clothes for fishing. We rented a small motor boat. We were out there for about fifteen minutes when I caught the first fish of the day. It was a nice size, about ten inches long. Daddy kept moving the boat trying to find a good spot. Mommy was at the front of the boat making our salami and cheese sandwiches for lunch.

After we ate, she picked up her pole, "Okay everyone, it is time to catch some fish." We were in a little cove and the sun was getting hot. She baited and dropped her line in. "Ya'll watch me. Here's how you do it. Here fishy, fishy, fishy, here fishy, fishy, fishy, come to mama."

"Anna, do you really think that is going to work?" Daddy said.

In answer, her pole dipped and she reeled in a fish, a small fish, but a fish just the same. She baited up again and started her chant, here fishy, fishy, fishy, here fishy, fishy, fishy.

"Anna, I don't think they are listening," Daddy joked.

Mommy started reeling in her line and low and behold she had another fish, "What makes you say that Clyde?" she laughed.

After the fifth fish Daddy got a little upset, my cousins and I had taken up the chant, I had caught two more, they had caught two each, and he had not caught anything. "Anna switch places with me, I want to catch at least one fish."

They switched places. We were all chanting and catching fish. Daddy still didn't catch anything. He was mad now. Mommy must have caught about twenty little fish by the time we were ready to go back to camp.

"Anna these fish are too little to take back, you need to throw them babies back. If the park ranger came and saw these you would get a ticket."

"You must be out of your mind I'm eating these fish for dinner, I can cook em' up hard and crunch right through them, bones and all."

We were back at the camp cleaning our fish and mine was the biggest one, a man walked up while I was scaling it and said, "That's a nice bass you got there."

"A bass, I didn't know that I had caught a bass, I never caught a bass before. Look Daddy he said that my fish is a bass."

"Yeah, yeah just hurry up and clean it." Daddy was still a little salty because he had not caught anything.

We went back to the pool for a swim. The water had warmed up and felt really good. Back at camp mommy fried up our fish, it was one of the best meals I ever had. I shared my fish with every one else. Mommy was right about the little ones, they were really tasty. Nothing taste like a fish that you have caught, gut and scaled yourself.

Kim

Tomboy

I didn't have the same distractions as my girlfriends who were boy crazy by the time we were in the sixth grade. Not that I did not want to be interested in boys, they were just not interested in me.

I was often mistaken for a boy because I was tall with long skinny legs and knees that looked like doorknobs, big feet, and an afro. I had begged for an afro and one day I was with my Father at the barbershop and when a chair opened up Daddy looked at me and said, "Go ahead."

I couldn't believe he was going to let me get my shoulder length haircut. I jumped into the chair. My mother had spent years cultivating my hair with a jar of Glover's mange that made me smell like a sick dog. It was not that bad because every one else's mom used this old home remedy in their hair.

When my mother saw me, I thought she was going to have a heart attack. "All that work I did to grow your hair and you done went and got it all cut off." She cried every time she looked at me for weeks.

One good thing about being a tomboy was that all the neighborhood boys recognized me as one of them, because I could hold my own in sports. Basketball was my favorite. I ran track for three winning years.

I envied the girls who had breast and hips. I wondered if the boys would ever look at me like that. It was not that I wanted to have sex; I just would like to know that I had the option. I was the girl that the boys asked, "Can you tell your friend that I like her."

I talked to my mother about it and she said, "Don't worry about it, those girls that are developing fast are going to end up fat later, the longer you stay skinny the longer you will have a good body." I guess she should know because my mom turned heads.

I heard my Aunts car pull into the drive way and I put the photo album down and picked up my purse and met the kids at the door. I was ready to go and enjoy some time with my little cousins. We ate at a pizza parlor that had video games on Long Beach Boulevard. Chico's had the best pizza. Then we went to a movie and home.

Surprise

We were on our way home from the movies when the kids spotted a fair in a grocery store parking lot. They rode every kiddy ride in the place and spent a lot of money playing games that the kids would never win because they were rigged. They ate cotton candy, and I bought them candy apples, huge suckers and caramel corn to take home.

The kids fell asleep on the ride home. I had to wake them to guide them to the front door. I steered them to the bed and put the sleeping beauties into their pajamas. They were out like lights. They were getting big, Keisha was five, and Jay was seven.

I took the phone in the living room and phoned Sherry to gossip and plan our new venture. We were going to put our money together and run an ad in the phone book to start an escort service. That was the way it worked in Los Angeles, Hollywood and Beverly Hills. You either ran ads in the phone book or a newspaper called The Hollywood Star. All the agencies networked together and shared information. If a girl gets busted in a sting then the agency owners or who ever is working the phones calls the others to let them know what is going on at that particular hotel.

If a trick tried to get rough or take his money back, his name went on a blacklist that was shared. After you work an ad for a while, you build up a clientele of regulars. I was paying attention and asking questions at the workhouse and after snorting and drinking the girls were very informative.

Mea had built up her business twenty years ago. She was Mexican, but had slanted eyes that made her look oriental and she was really petite. She started off working on Hollywood and Sunset Boulevards. She hit pay dirt when she was picked up one day by a man who was part of a Mexican Cartel. Every time he came to town, he called her. When he came with friends she brought girls from the street, when he dealt with other cartels, he did business with her for entertainment. Within a few years, she had enough regulars that she didn't have to work the streets anymore.

At this point in the game, I was working with two agencies. I had proved that I was reliable. I watched a lot of girls get blackballed. If you stole the agencies customers, the client would try to pay you less, or they would tell the agency that you had back-doored them. When the word went out that you could not be trusted, that was the end of your career in that town. It wasn't worth it.

I wanted to build my own business where I could send girls on calls to find out what the tricks were about. If they wanted sex, I would continue to send someone else, if they did drugs I would go and see them once and pick them up as a drug client. After that, they would deal with me because they could get their girls and dope from the same place.

I knew that after a while once all the clients at the agencies had seen you they would be looking for the next new face. I was still working with Mea but sometimes when there were no parties going on. I knew that just driving and taking dates was not going to get me the money I had gotten used to.

I was learning a lot from the girls who worked at Mea's. Some of them worked on the streets and some worked in the hotels. I like the hotel set-ups better. You go in, sit at the bar and make yourself approachable, in the guys room you asked for his I.D. and plane ticket to verify that he was in fact an out-of-towner. In the 80's you could ask the client if he was a cop, by law, he had to tell you or it would be considered entrapment.

With the telephone or newspaper ad agency, when the person calls in you get their name address and phone number. Then you call the phone company and ask for the listing to verify the address. When you get to there house you ask for a check stub or something verifying what kind of work they did. A badge, or business card, that you could check against their photo I D.

The best customers are cocaine addicts because they spend more time getting high then having sex, unless you have the bad luck to get to them when they have run out of dope that could be hard work. Usually if they had a choice between buying cocaine or sex, they will usually take the cocaine.

I knew how to work my drug customers. I would put their plate somewhere so they knock it over or spill their drink on it. Then they have to buy more. I switched the plate with one that had mostly cut so when they had their accident they were actually buying the same plate of dope.

Sherry and I talked for about an hour. She had been talking to a lawyer friend who so that we could find out all the legal loopholes that we could use to avoid getting busted when we started the agency. We covered all the bases.

I got off the phone and climbed in between the kids. It really felt good having them curled up around me. One day I wanted children of my own. Had Alonzo and I stayed together we might have been pregnant by now. Damn I missed him, I missed him bad.

The next morning the kids and I were watching cartoons in bed. I was about to get up and fix pancakes when there was a knock on the door. Jay ran to the window and looked out. He started jumping up and down, "Its Alonzo, its Alonzo."

I could not believe it; I had dreamed about him all night and had woke during the night crying.

"Open the door Jay."

I stayed under the covers. Alonzo walked through the bedroom door carrying Keisha. He sat on the end of the bed and talked to the kids. They really loved him, everyone in my family did.

My emotions were mixed, I still felt betrayed, but since I knew how bad things had turned out, I felt sorry for him. Looking at him, I knew I still loved him, but I was going to take it slow.

The big problem was he did not know what I was doing now and I did not think he would like that I was a prostitute. I doubted that if he knew he would want to be with me.

I felt pressure between my legs. Well, I could sleep with him, I knew before I confirmed the thought in my mind that before the day was over I would. Had he not come over I had been thinking about calling him. I had not had a decent orgasm since we had been together.

I had dated a few guys but there was not enough interest to go to bed with some and the two that I did sleep with, well let's just say it was a dismal disappointment.

I got up out of the bed in my flannel gown, went into the bathroom, and brushed my teeth. When I came out, he was laying across the bed with the kids watching cartoons.

I sat down. He turned around and looked at me. "Hi."

"Hello, how are you?"

"Sitting here I'm fine. This is the first time I have been fine in eleven months." He scooted next to me. "What are you guys doing today?"

"I was going to fix pancakes, I wasn't sure after that. Maybe go by my grandmothers. Their daddy is picking them up here at four."

"Why don't I take you guys out for breakfast, I've really missed them. I've missed you, and everyone in your family."

"I don't know Alonzo."

The kids who had been listening moaned, "Please let's go to breakfast and have fun with Alonzo?"

I was not aware they had been listening to us. I was going to say yes, but I wanted to be convinced. I also wanted to know why he was here. I would have to find this out after the kids were gone. I could not turn down their pleading faces.

Alonzo's face appeared thin and gaunt, like someone who is ill. I would have to ask about that later too. He had lost weight.

"Spending the day with you guys would really do me a lot of good," he said.

"Okay, okay, okay, let's run a bath and get you guys dressed so we can go," I said as I walked into the bathroom and ran the water.

They jumped up and down on the bed, screaming "yeeeeyyyy," and hugging Alonzo.

We went to the House of Pancakes on Crenshaw, after breakfast, we took the kids to Centinella Park and let them play on the swings. He took a blanket out of his car.

"You know that song, "Stormy Weather?""

"You know I do, why do you ask?"

"Because, since you and I ain't been together, it's raining all the time," he sang.

He could not sing, never could, but he tried so hard I had to give him an E for effort.

I watched the kids play, I was trying to think of a response and then decided to remain silent and let him continue.

"Has Christian told you about everything that happened?"

"He tried, but I always cut him off and changed the channel," I lied. I had hung on to every word.

"Well when a sent for Rita it was so that I could let her know that it was over and try to strike some kind of deal with her to let me have the kids and she could still get a little money here and there. You took things all wrong."

"You know something Alonzo; you still have that same tell."

"What do you mean?"

"It's just like in poker, all players have a tell. Something to let you know what is really going on. And you ain't telling it all. I know that bitch was in love with you since school days, ain't no way that proposal was gone fly. The way she talked, she would rather see you in jail than with another woman. I'm a woman Alonzo, I know how they think. You either gone come correct with the truth, or this, this little outing or whatever you trying to do, can be ovah, right now. I know that you slept with her when you went back for Derby and you got syphilis for your trouble. I know that you were sleeping with her every time you went home."

"I made some mistakes but I didn't know what to do. I was trying to keep her from putting me in jail. I wasn't honest with you because I knew that you wouldn't go along with it. You know you are always saying what goes around comes around and talking about Karma."

"Because it is what I believe in Alonzo. I believed in you and you betrayed me. That hurt. I don't plan to go through that again."

"It ain't like I'm trying to run game on you. I'm straight up about what I am trying to do. I want to get back together with the best thing that ever happened to me. I love you so much more than I have ever felt for anyone but my momma and my daughter. I guess there is Karma because I messed up, and things went terrible. I felt like you must have put some of them voodoo roots on me or something, for things to go as bad as they did."

"I don't use no hoodoo. It is not good to try to manipulate people you love with that kind of magic."

"I know, I was stupid and I'm sorry."

"I don't deal with people I can't trust, if I do you can best believe that I handle them to my advantage. You're lying to me, you want something, and it ain't just old times. Everything come's to light Alonzo, you might as well tell me."

The kids ran over out of breath and I could tell they were tired. I got up, went to the Ice Cream truck, and bought them some juice. We all laid down using one another for pillows. Soon the kids and I fell asleep.

Alonzo woke us after an hour and we went by my grandmother's house. She had prepared a huge dinner as always on Sunday and a lot of the family was there. Everyone was ecstatic to see Alonzo.

We went back to my house in time for my Uncle Bumpy to pick up the kids. Before they left the kids made Alonzo promise to be here the next time they came.

Bumpy told me that he was going to be fixing up the house so that he could sell it. They were happy living out in Chino and would not be coming back. He was going to invest in some property out there. This meant that I was going to have to look for someplace to move.

I helped him get the kids into the car. "You still got time. I want you to keep the place in order so people can walk through and look at the house. You can deal with the realtor for me."

When I walked back inside Alonzo was sitting on the couch. He looked so handsome. I went into the bathroom and took off all my clothes. I got a pair of high heels out of the closet and walked into the living room, Naked.

Unfortunately, Alonzo was asleep. He was snoring like he did when he was exhausted. I didn't have the heart to wake him. I went back into the bedroom and got a pillow and tucked it under his head, removed his shoes and lifted his legs onto the couch and covered him with a blanket. He never woke up.

I went back in the bedroom and called Sherry, I didn't get an answer. I took a bath, put on an oversized t-shirt, and climbed into bed.

I woke to Alonzo biting on my neck. He knew that was my spot. I had not had any good sex since we broke up. I was wet and I wanted him, I closed my eyes and let his mouth make love to me. Before he entered me, I told him that he would have to use a condom. He looked hurt. Hell I didn't care. I wanted sex but I did not want to catch anything.

My body soared like it did when we first got together, but something was missing, I knew that I still cared for him, but I would never be able to love him the same because I would always have that distrust.

I rocked up some coke and we smoked while he talked. I knew it was like truth serum for him. The store where Alonzo worked had closed and he had taken a couple of other jobs in the mall but wasn't able to steal any thing because they had cameras everywhere.

"When Rita went to jail she was hustling with a prostitute named Quima who worked for a guy named Comfort."

I noticed that Alonzo looked kind of uncomfortable, paranoid even. I rolled a joint, lit it, and gave it to him. I went into the living room and fixed him a drink. I also wanted to contemplate what he was telling me.

I knew Comfort. He had hung around with Cricket for years. He showed up at all the players parties. I also knew that Cricket and Butch did not like him. I did not tell Alonzo that I knew him. It had been years since I had seen Comfort, back then I was a skinny little girl. He wouldn't recognize me.

"Anyway I have been hustling with Comfort to get Quima and Rita out of jail, he got a bunch of keys from some Columbians, and as soon as we spring them from jail we can split up the money from the rest of the dope."

"Why do you think this man is going to pay you? Why would he get your woman out?"

"Rita is not my woman. She knows that, she is my children's mother. Comfort said that she was working with his crew when she got popped; it was four of them that went to jail. He says that it's his responsibility to take care of the people on his crew. He's letting me make a little money and I'm staying at his house."

"Boy that's convenient. He got you living in his house, what work are you doing to make this money?"

"Selling a little dope and running some checks. I could use some I.D's?"

"What happened to the ones you had?"

"When Rita disappeared she stole them. Comfort said they used them for some checks."

"So your I.D's are burnt up and you didn't make a dime off of it. The people on Comfort's crew are sitting in jail and he's probably hot as hell. I ain't going to use my connections and get my people burned. Rita and the rest of them will get tired of being locked down and start talking. Everybody is going to go down. You living in his house and hanging paper, you are going too."

"It ain't like that."

"Let me think about it," I didn't want him to know that I was picking him for information on my Uncle's enemy.

"So I see your Uncle put a for sale sign out, what are you going to do?"

"I'm going to stay here until the house sells and then move."

"You know we could get a place together, or Comfort would let you stay with me. I got my own room and bathroom."

"Alonzo I'm not sure that we are getting back together. Even if we did, I wouldn't stay at that house. You don't know when the feds are going to break that door in."

"I really want to get back together with you."

"Let's take it slow."

"You still running dope for Christian?"

"Why?"

"Why don't you help me sell this stuff that I'm running?"

"You mean help you sell the stuff that Comfort is running? Nope, no thank you. I got a good deal with Christian, he's like a brother to me, and I ain't going to stab him in the back to help you get your babies mama out of jail. So if that's why you came you have wasted your time. Meanwhile I got to get ready to go to work."

"That's not why I came, I told you I love you and miss you. My life has been going down the toilet since I did you wrong. I figure if I can make it right maybe my life will come back together somehow."

I wasn't going to work that night, but I now that I knew why he had come I wanted him to leave. He needed I.D. and someone to help him move product. I got up and ran my bath.

"What work?" He asked.

"I drive for Cricket," I didn't want Alonzo to know that I was doing more than driving.

He got dressed and I walked him to the door. We kissed and I gave him my pager number.

"When am I going to see you again?"

"I'm usually off during the day most of the time. Page me if I'm not working I'll call you back."

I lay in the tub getting high while I thought about our conversation.

Snakes in the Grass

I kept getting high for two hours before I decided to sleep. Dope always made me think more clearly and I had a lot of thinking to do.

I lay in the bed most of the day and into the evening. I called Christian's to see if he was going home after work. I would meet him there. I needed to re-up and I needed to talk to him. I decided to work from my pager that night unless I needed to host. Mondays were usually slow.

I told Christian about Alonzo's conversation.

"I guess that's why he ain't been through here lately."

"I guess so, but I'm going to talk to Cricket about Comfort. I think Alonzo is being taken for a ride. Sounds like Comfort is pimping him to me."

"Well you got good street sense. Go with your first mind and stay away from there. If his woman got popped with checks, that's federal."

"Yeah, he asked me to get him some I.D's. I told him that I would think about it. I ain't going to do it though. I got enough business with you and Butch, and I ain't going to bring that kind of heat down on us."

"That's smart."

I called Mea and told her that I really needed to talk to Cricket.

"He's coming by later, you alright? You seem worried about something."

I told Mea about Alonzo and Comfort.

"Your Uncle doesn't like Comfort. They fell out a few years back. Comfort is a snake. When his girls go to jail, he doesn't get them out. He doesn't pimp his girls, he lets the dope do it. I used to work with his bottom woman Quima."

"She went to jail for hanging paper, with Alonzo's babies mama. Alonzo is supposed to be working with Comfort to help get them out."

"That ain't going to happen, Comfort might get Quima out, but Alonzo's girl is going to be in there. Sounds to me like Comfort's pimping Alonzo."

Boy did that statement ring familiar, "That's what I was thinking."

I took two girls on calls then I went on one my self for another agency before going to Mea's to drop off some drugs and money. When I returned Cricket was there. "What's going on Neicy?"

I repeated the news to him. He told me everything about Comfort, "He spends more time getting high and sleeping with his girls then he does letting them work. We fell out when I knocked him for two of his broads. He didn't want to go by the code. You know if a broad chooses someone else when he gets served he's supposed to take it like a man. He got salty and tried to set me up with the cops."

"Dang, he took it there."

"Mea had another house back then; the police were going to raid it. One of the cops who I pay off let me know what was up. Buy the time they came in the place was empty; we had got a truck and moved everything. It was business as usual, just at another spot."

"Did you let him know that you knew what he did?"

"No, but we ain't been cool since. He ain't no real pimp. He got one stomp down ho. He makes most of his money through robberies and hanging paper.

"He's selling dope now."

"I heard something about he had a package. You wouldn't happen to know where he got it."

"Columbians."

"They ain't to be played with. If he don't pay them off, him and every one around him is going to come up dead. If he has, Alonzo around you can bet he's using him. Niecy if you care anything about the man, get him away from Comfort."

I told him about what happened with Rita and that Alonzo wasn't working at the store anymore. "He is just flunkyin' for Comfort from what I could see. I ain't going to help him get that broad out of jail. He got to do that himself.

Plus Bumpy is going to sell the house. I'm going to have to move pretty soon."

"You can stay at the house in Balboa, you ain't hardly ever home anyway. You can bring Alonzo with you if you need to," he laughed.

"I don't know yet. Alonzo doesn't know that I am working, all he knows is that I'm driving for you, and I want to keep it that way."

"While you are figuring out what you are going to do, I want you to find out what Comfort is up to for me."

"Don't you think he might have a problem with me being your niece?"

"All that will do is make him try to get at you. Look, if Alonzo got any sense he won't like that, that's how we pull him up out of there. Tell him that Comfort hit on you, trust me, once he finds out that you are my kin, you won't be lying. Alonzo would be to mad and jealous to stay, he ain't stupid; eventually he'll figure out that Comfort is using him. Also when you are around there buy a gram of dope, if those Columbians need to find him and their product, I want to be able to help."

"I'm not trying to be hanging out at that house; they probably got heat with his crew sitting in jail."

"It ain't like you got to move in. You being their a couple times ain't gone get you heat. Just don't leave there and go get know identities or go anywhere that could cause anyone else a problem."

This was a conundrum for me, I was selling dope, fake identification and working escort. Being around Alonzo could bring me attention that I did not want. But if Comfort was putting Alonzo in a position to get, hurt I was going to have to decide whether I had enough feelings for him to not want him dead or in jail.

I started putting a plan together. I would let Christian take care of the identifications for himself and Butch for a while. I would get two keys from Christian so that I would not have to go by there for a couple of weeks. That way if I got tails dealing with Alonzo it would not fall back on anyone else. It would not take me long. I figured a month at the most.

I would take off of work at the house for a while. It was time for a vacation anyway.

Alonzo

What the fuck am I doing here? Alonzo thought aloud as he took the Ak-47 and the brief case full of drugs out of the building. Comfort was stripping three White men of their wallets and jewelry after he had tied them up.

When he came out, he headed for his Rolls Royce. "I'll see you at the house," he told Alonzo.

Alonzo pulled down the alley and without pausing for ongoing traffic pulled out. He looked in the rear view mirror. It was just his luck that a police car was making a U-turn.

One of the victims had gotten loose and pressed the alarm at the antique store. The dispatcher announced the robbery just as Alonzo pulled into view.

Alonzo stepped on the gas in an attempt to outrun them, but realized they would be calling for back up and roadblocks. He pulled into an underground parking lot just as the security gate was closing.

He jumped out of the car grabbing the briefcase. He did not have time to get the gun out of the trunk. His heart raced as he heard the gate opening and a police car radio. He hid behind a garbage can next to a door that lead into the building. Someone came out and he got to the door just in time to catch it before it closed. He walked down the street to a restaurant and went in to use the phone.

He called Comforts car phone. "Man the police got my car."

"Did they get everything in it?"

"Naw, I got the briefcase, but they got the gun that was in the trunk."

"We gone have to get you lawyered up. We can say your car was stolen. Where you at?"

"On Beverly and Rodeo Drive."

"I'm turning around, stay out of site until you see my car."

Kim

I made a couple of dates with Alonzo over the next two weeks but had to cancel because of work. I was kind of relieved to be able to put off getting involved with Comfort.

Butch was having a birthday party at The Speakeasy. I called and invited Alonzo. "I don't have a car."

"What happened to your car?"

"It's a long story. I don't want to talk about it on the phone."

"What if I pick you up?"

"That'll work."

Alonzo sounded depressed. I was worried about him. I had decided that I wanted to at least help him get away from Comfort.

The night of the party, I picked him up at a nice condominium in Ladera Heights. I sat in the living room waiting for Alonzo to finish dressing.

The front door opened and Comfort walked in. "Damn you're cute, who are you?"

"I'm Alonzo's friend."

Comfort walked over to shake my hand, pulled me up off the couch, and spun me around. "Damn you got a nice figure. You need to forget about Alonzo and hang with me."

"Thank you for the offer, but I think I am going to roll with Alonzo tonight."

"You know this is my house right? I'm Comfort."

"Yeah, he told me."

"Where are you guys going tonight?"

"A birthday party."

"Where is it? I like to party."

"It's at a club in Hollywood, Carlos, and Charlie's."

Comfort went upstairs and when Alonzo came down, he was following him. "Why did you say the party was at Carlos and Charlie's when it's at the Speakeasy?"

"Because I don't know you, and the party is private."

"Who is this party for? They got bank to have a private party and close down the Speakeasy on a Sunday night?"

"A friend."

Alonzo didn't realize that I did not want Comfort to go with us, and I didn't want him to know who my Uncles were just yet. "It's for her Uncle Butch; you want to roll with us?"

"Butch? Butch? He wears his hair in a press and curl, you talking about Cricket's brother?" Comfort lit up.

"Yeah, you know him?" Alonzo said.

I could have killed Alonzo.

"Cricket and Butch are your Uncles?"

"Yeah, why?"

"You kind of mean, huh?"

"Like I said, I don't know you, and all of my Uncles friends are not my friends."

"Don't worry, me and your Uncles go way back."

"Kim you ain't got to act like that. He's alright," Alonzo said.

"If he's alright then why did he ask me to forget about you and hang with him tonight?"

"I was just kidding with you. Alonzo is my main man."

"Yeah but if you know my Uncles that don't mean much, do it?"

"Oh, I see you know the rules of the game," Comfort said.

"Yeah, I do, but I don't play the game." I walked over to the door, "Alonzo I'll be in the car."

A few minutes later Alonzo got in the car and I pulled off. When I looked at him, he was looking at me sideways. "Why you gotta' act like that with Comfort? I told you he's helping me out."

"He's helping you out huh? What do you think would have happened if I took him up on his offer to forget about you and hang with him tonight? Comfort helping you out ain't got shit to do with me, remember that. I ain't gone be nice to him, he's a pimp, and my Uncles taught me not to be nice to pimps unless I want to pay them."

"He was just jiving around with you."

"Alonzo, pimps don't jive around. To him, I ain't nothing but another potential payday. Don't get it confused. I don't play with pimps. That's how you get caught in a cross."

"You don't have to worry about Comfort."

"How do you know? And another thing My Uncle's have enemies. I don't tell every body that I am related to them for that reason. Please don't do that again. If he didn't know about this party then he wasn't invited. Every big time player in town knows about it. Don't you think there must be a reason for that?"

"I see what you are saying, but I'm telling you he's alright."

"What happened to your car?"

"The police took it."

I pulled the car over, I had to hear this. "Why?"

"They were trying to pull me over and I tried to outrun them. I pulled into an underground lot and hid behind a garbage can. They towed it in."

"Why did you do that?"

"I was leaving the scene of a crime, and there was something in the car that shouldn't have been."

"What kind of crime Alonzo?"

"A robbery," he was not looking at me.

"What was in the car?"

"A gun."

"Why didn't you take them with you? You could have said someone stole the car. You do know that you are going to have a warrant now. And you can't get your car back if it was used in a crime."

"Comfort is going to get his attorney on it. I'll get out of it. I called the police and reported the car stolen."

"For your sake I hope that gun ain't got no bodies on it."

"What do you mean by that?"

"I hope that the gun was not used in any other crimes that could result in you and your fingerprints going to jail for something you did not do. You didn't kill anyone did you?"

"No we just left some white guys in Beverly Hills at some antique store tied up."

"Beverly Hills, an antique store, you do realize that you are dealing with some big time people. You better hope they don't track you down.

I looked at Alonzo like the fool that he was. *Man I don't know that I should be rolling with this idiot.*

The party was jamming. Christian and Laisyv were there. We set at their table. I gave Butch an eight ball package of coke for his birthday. Alonzo and I danced the night away. About twelve o'clock Comfort came in with a girl on his arm. Butch and Cricket were sitting at the table next to us. "Who invited the snitch?" Butch said.

I turned to see who he was talking about. I got up and went to talk to them, "Alonzo didn't know what he was doing. He knows that I'm your niece too."

"Damn, I guess that means we cain't toss his ass out of here." Cricket said.

"Don't worry Niecy, it's cool, you need to school your man though, if he tells the wrong person who you are related to the both of you could have a problem."

"He tried to hit on me, when I was waiting for Alonzo."

"I knew that would happen. That's a good thing, that way you can get that info for me."

"Yeah I guess so. I told Alonzo in front of him, he sad he was just kidding around."

"What did Alonzo say?" Cricket asked

"Alonzo is sleep to him."

"Fool better wake up," Butch said.

"Alonzo has a case, the police got his car, and it had a gun in it. He thinks Comfort is going to get him a lawyer."

"When was this?" Butch asked

"About a week ago,"

"He ain't going to do nothing for that boy. He's in some deep shit and he better figure out how to handle his own business."

Alonzo and I went to the dance floor. I saw Comfort standing next to my Uncles table. Cricket was smiling a lot. Not a sincere smile, the one he used with people he didn't like.

After the party, I said bye to everyone and took Alonzo back to Comfort's. He was drunk and high. "Don't leave. Stay with me, we have the house all to ourselves. Comfort isn't coming home. He'll probably spend the night with Nia. We can go up have a drink, get high, what ever you want to do. We can make love; curl up in each other's arms. I don't sleep good without you. I need a good nights sleep Kim."

I was tired and horny. "You sure he ain't coming home?"

"It don't matter if he does, I got my own room and bathroom."

We went upstairs. "What do you want to do?" Alonzo asked while hugging me.

"Actually I'm tired, how about we shower and get in the bed."

"Okay, if that's what you want that's what we will do."

After the shower Alonzo massaged oil into my body, I was so relaxed that I fell asleep. I woke to an earth shattering orgasm, Alonzo's head between my legs. My body jerked and shook and he held me still and kept going, all I could do was scream out in ecstasy. I was on that same roller coaster that only he could take me on.

We had always been very vocal in our lovemaking. We were so loud that we had not heard Comfort come in. The next morning we sat eating breakfast in the kitchen. Comfort came down. The way he looked at me made me uncomfortable. Nia came down; she was looking at me the same way.

"Why do you guys keep staring at me?" I asked.

Alonzo had noticed it too. "What's up with you guys?"

"How the hell do you get off like that after getting high all night?" Comfort asked.

"What are you talking about?" Alonzo asked.

"We heard you guys last night. All night," Nia said.

"Man I tried all night long and couldn't get off. What is it that you do that makes him get off over and over?" Comfort said looking at me.

"Alonzo has never had any problem performing with me," I said.

"I know for a fact that Alonzo ha s been with people and couldn't do anything. What's so special about you?"

"I love her. I didn't even like those people." Alonzo said.

"We love each other, but I can't get him hard when he's high," Nia said.

"Maybe you shouldn't get high when you plan to have sex," I said getting up from the table. "I'm going to get dressed." I did not like the conversation.

"That was weird huh?" Alonzo said walking up behind me in the bathroom.

"Hell yeah, what did they do listen to us all night?"

"Comfort has been in that room with two or three girls sometime and he never gets off."

"And I want to know about this, why?"

"What are you doing today?" Alonzo asked.

"I'm going home and clean up the house. The realtor is bringing some people through this week and I don't want anything out of place. I am going to stay at my grandmother's for a few days."

"Will you call me?"

"Yeah, I miss being with you. What do you plan to do Alonzo? You can't just keep working for Comfort. You need to work for yourself. You know you can't depend on others. Go find another store so we can start selling clothes again."

"As soon as we get these people out of jail, I'll do that."

"What are you going to do about your own legal problems?"

"Get with the lawyer and see what can be done,"

I kissed him and left. Comfort and Nia were sitting in the living room watching Scarface. They were still looking at me crazy.

Back to work

I went home and cleaned. I loosened two boards in the closet under my shoeboxes, so that I could put my paraphernalia and drugs into a metal safe that I picked up on the way home.

I told the realtor to show the house Monday through Saturday evening. I did not want her to show the house on Sundays.

I had most Sundays off and if it didn't look busy, I took the night off. I called Mea and she was taking the night off. All the partying the night before had her worn out. I checked out with the two agencies that I worked for.

Shelly and I went out to dinner to catch up. "Sounds like you might want to step off from Alonzo for a minute. You know he is going to jail."

"I'm going to get him an I.D. If he does get popped for something as long as he bails out before they run prints he should be all right. He ain't gone get his car back."

"Damn, he was such a good hustler. Doesn't he see that he's being used?"

"I can't just tell him, he got to figure it out for his damn self. Any way he doesn't know that I'm turning tricks. I don't know how he is going to take it."

"Don't tell him, I don't see any reason for him to know. When he starts making money again you can quit."

"Girl I got a list of regulars that I ain't giving up, I ain't even got to sex them, and they pay well. I could train someone else to go for me and take a cut but I'm addicted to trick money," I laughed.

"Yeah, me too. As long as I can I'm gone get that paper."

"Sherry had been with me on a few calls. We had built up a clientele of dope customers through the Hollywood Star.

I spent the night at Shelly's. The next day my pager went off, it was Mea. They had three cartels in town. She was going to work two of them combined and I had to go to a hotel and work the other one. Mea was running out of girls, I told her that I had five friends that I had been working who were tried and true. She told me to call them.

They all met me in the parking lot of the Beverly hotel. I went into the lobby and called up to the room. Three men in turbans came down to escort us up.

There was a sheik from Arabia. He looked as if he was not even of legal age. He liked me. He was interested in Black American music. I went down to my car to get all the music tapes I had. For six hours, I taught him the words to "Rappers Delight" and all the current dances.

They all wore traditional attire from their home and when we left, he gave me some beautiful fabric as a gift. I could not wait to start sketching some designs.

I worked for a week straight running parties. In between, I went on a call for another agency. Heidi had paged me while I was working and I told her that I would be tied up for a while.

When I got free, I called her back and went on the call. There were several girls there. It was a football team that we were entertaining. There was a girl there that I did not know, her name was Quima.

Kim

Love changes

I went home bone tired on Sunday Night. I lay in my tub for more than two hours before crawling between the sheets. I always changed my bed before I left so that when I came home I could get into a nice crisp bed.

I dreamed of Alonzo. He was being tortured by Comfort. I tried to free him but I could not get the nails out of his hands that held him to a wall. Comfort laughed and laughed at my efforts. When I turned to shoot him, he held his arms out, "Come on, and be with me. You can't help Alonzo. The boy is worthless. He isn't the kind of man who can deal with a woman like you."

I woke up to the phone ringing. I let the machine pick it up, I turned up the volume. I had three messages that I had slept through. It was Christian. I picked up.

"Boy I just got home a couple of hours ago, I been working for a week straight. I got's to get some sleep,"

"Kim wake up,"

"What's up, I just got home a couple of hours ago."

"Alonzo is in jail. His bail is forty grand."

"What happened?"

"He had filled out an application to get a job and when they ran him, he had a warrant for his arrest. They called him back for a second interview on Saturday morning and the police were waiting for him. They got him for suspicion of a robbery in Beverly Hills. The gun that they found in his car had his prints all over it and the bullets. Even though he said the car was stolen he still going to get the gun charge. The gun was used in something else where someone was shot in the leg. I had my lawyer go up there for his arraignment. I have been trying to page you all night."

"I left my pager in the car. When I got home, I had a lot of messages. It was the operator trying to put through a collect call but I didn't know who it was."

"Alonzo said that he has some money in his mattress. He said that you would know where, and that there are a couple of keys of coke in his hiding place in the bathroom. Do you want to get him out?"

"I got to get him out Christian. Alonzo ain't never done no real time. I'm going to see if I can get his money and then I'll call you back. Will you buy the keys?"

"Yeah, come over here as soon as you get it so we can go see the bondsman."

"Thanks Christian, I know you didn't have to do this."

"You my little sister, I know you still love him, I'll do whatever I can."

I knew that Alonzo had reported his car stolen. He said that he had his face covered so the people they robbed shouldn't be able to identify him. I remembered my dream. For some reason I had a feeling that someone snitched on him. I called Cricket and told him what was up.

"You got the bail?"

"I think so. I have to go get his stash from Comforts house."

"Be careful and call me after you get it. I got a bondsman who will take fifty percent without collateral."

"That'll work, thanks Unc."

I took down the address for the bondsman, got up, and dressed. When I got to Comforts, his Rolls Royce was sitting in front of the house. I rang the doorbell. "I was taken aback when one of the girls from the call I had done for the other agency answered the door. That is when the name clicked in my head, "Quima." This was who Alonzo was talking about getting out of jail.

I didn't have time to worry about this now. "Is Comfort here?"

"What's up Sparkle? How you doing girl? You getting with my man?"

"It ain't like that. I need to get some clothes I left in Alonzo's room. He's in jail, he's my man."

"You the one he been bragging about, huh? Girl do he know that you working?"

"Quima I really need to get my stuff and talk to Comfort. So if you don't mind."

"Comforts in the shower, I'll go tell him that you are here."

I went into the bedroom and closed the door. I got the money out of the mattress and the two keys of coke out from under the board in the bathroom cabinet. I put them in a sports bag that was in the closet, I was zipping it closed when the door opened. I looked up. The girl standing in the doorway was Rita. I recognized her from the pictures.

"So you're Kim, huh?"

"Yeah, I'm Kim. Did you know that Alonzo is in jail?"

"Yeah I knew. I'm the one who told the police who he was. I was still in jail and Quima was out, she told me what happened so I dealt my way out. Better him than me."

Comfort was standing behind Rita and overheard everything she said. He grabbed a handful of her hair and started beating her. "Snitch ass bitch." I could hear his fist hitting bone and her jaw cracked. She fell to the ground and he started kicking her. "I'll kill your ass." She passed out.

Comfort turned and looked at me. "Where's Alonzo?"

"He's in County. He tried to call you but couldn't get an answer."

"How much is his bail?"

"Sixty Grand," I lied.

"I thought he was with you or something. You don't think he talked do you?"

"If he talked he would be out and I wouldn't be trying to bail him, would I? Everybody don't give up others so they can walk," I looked down at Rita who was moaning.

"I see what you mean. Hold on let me see how much I got. I damn near tapped myself out getting Quima out of jail."

Quima walked out of the room, "I heard that you and Alonzo be getting busy up in here, you must have platinum in your pussy girl, all the tricks at Heidi's love Sparkle."

"What are you talking about Quima? Who the hell is Sparkle?" Comfort asked.

"You don't know? Oh, I forget you call her Kim. This is Sparkle. I met her at Heidi's Saturday. Girl be getting paper too. She had tricks waiting in line to go in the room with her after the host came out bragging about her."

"Damn, maybe we should let Alonzo stay where he is. You want to get with me Sparkle. Alonzo don't know what to do with a woman like you."

He sounded just like in my nightmare. Those were the exact same words.

I looked at the money in is his hand. "Is that to help get my man out of jail?"

"I guess you in love huh? Here's thirty G's, Alonzo said that you can move caine. If you need some more money you can work one of these packages."

"I think I got what I need, thanks. I stepped around him. "I got to go meet Cricket's bondsman's."

Quima walked me to the door, "Look Comfort has been curious about you. After you handle your business why don't you come back and party with us."

"No thanks, I don't party with pimps, and I don't turn Black men. It's too much work if you know what I mean."

"Well, you can party with me then," She backed me up against the wall, ran her hand over my breast, and tried to kiss me. I pushed her aside, "I don't kiss tricks," I opened the door and walked to my car.

I went to Christian's. On the ride over there, I knew that I was going to have to tell Alonzo I had been working. I was reasonably sure that I would not get the chance to tell him myself if Quima and Comfort had anything to do with it.

I didn't know how things were going to go down.

Rita

Rita had turned the ringer off on Comfort's phones when she arrived. She knew that Alonzo was going to be calling as soon as they finished questioning him. The deal she made was that as soon as Alonzo was in their custody they would let her out.

Rita accepted a ride offered from a nice detective to Quima's upon her release. She did not have a clue that he was investigating her fraud case. He knew she was working with a ring and when he checked, the address and Quima's info came up he felt like he had caught the brass ring. He would let them stay on the street for a few days before rearresting them for some other checks that had come through with their prints on them. He also wanted to find out who the ringleader was.

When Rita arrived, Quima and Comfort were getting high and invited her to join there little party. She had been with them before, Comfort couldn't get it up, and Quima was insatiable.

She had considered choosing Comfort for her man since her boyfriend who worked for Comfort was in jail and was not going to be getting out anytime soon. The problem was Quima was his bottom woman, and she could never compete with that money getting broad. Though she smiled in the woman's face, she hated her because she was light skinned.

She knew that Alonzo was going to try to send her back to Kentucky. From the moment she arrived, she could tell that he was pining for Kim. He told her that he had only brought her out here so that he could talk to her about custody of the kids. He was talking about giving her a couple of hundred a month just to stay away. Forget that, she wasn't going to sell her kids, not for two hundred a month anyway.

When she ran into Quima at a nightclub, it was on. She didn't even bother to go back to Alonzo and the kids. She started hustling with Quima and went home with her. She made enough money to buy clothes from a booster and started sleeping with one of Comfort's henchmen.

A month passed and Alonzo had not heard anything from Rita until Comfort called to say that she was in jail. Alonzo had taken down Comfort's number and went to work.

Alonzo took the kids to see Kim. He thought that maybe she would see the kids, feel sorry for him, and take her back, but it was evident that she was still hurt and angry.

Alonzo booked tickets on the Greyhound bus and took a week off work to take the kids back home to live with his mother. When he got back to California, he called Comfort. They met at the after hours on Buckingham.

His job was only going to last another month and he was stealing everything he could get his hands on. He was selling clothes through Comfort and his friends. When his job was over, he couldn't find another that had the advantages to keep him in the boosting business.

Alonzo considered purchasing clothes and selling them. He had a hook up at store in the Valley. He rode out there and found that the guy he needed to see had been fired for stealing.

When Comfort met Alonzo, he saw someone he could use. He said all the right things to reel Alonzo in.

Over the last couple of days, Comfort had wondered why he had not heard from Alonzo, but figured that he was knee deep in him some Kim.

It dawned on Comfort that the phone had not rung in a couple of days. As a matter of fact if had not rang since Rita had shown up. He went to the phone, the ringer and answering machine were turned off. "Quima did you know that this phone was turned off?"

"Daddy you know I wouldn't do no shit like that."

"So that scandalous Rita did it huh? What I want to know is how did that bitch find out about the robbery?"

"I might have said something to her about it when she called," Quima said moving out of arms reach.

"Bitch you on the penitentiary phone telling my business?" He lunged at her, she tried to run, but he caught her by her leg and beat her with a belt that he pulled out of his pants. Quima was half-oriental and half black so her bruises would stop her from working for at least a week.

Comfort didn't trust Rita. If he threw her out, she would snitch on him, if she had not already. He walked over to where she was curled up on the floor holding her jaw. He stomped her hard in the ribs with his size 14 foot. He walked back in the room, dragged Quima out by her hair, tossed her on top of Rita, closed, and locked his bedroom door.

He had to think of what to do. He went in the bathroom and started smoking so that he could think. He blew out so much smoke that he could not see himself in the mirror. As his face came into view so did the answer as to what he would do with Rita. He got his best ideas in this bathroom mirror.

He picked up the phone and dialed, "Hey man this you?

"Yeah, I know it's you, this is me." Comfort never used names when he called this guy. "Can you use some black merchandise?"

He talked to the man for a few minutes. "I'm sending her to you in a cab."

"He went into the other room where Rita was nursing her face. She was dark so the bruises didn't show as bad. It was obvious that her jaw and nose were broke and she was holding her side.

"Bitch, Quima can't work because she got her ass kicked for talking to you. I got a high dollar trick, wants a Black girl. Get dressed."

She was too scared to do anything but pull herself together. She heard the phone ring.

Comfort picked up the phone and accepted the collect call, "Man that silly baby mama of yours turned off the damn phone. You ain't gone believe this, man she snitched on you. She called here, Quima told her about your car, and she gave you up to get herself out. If she would have waited a couple of days I would have bonded her out."

Alonzo couldn't believe his ears. Rita had snitched him out. "Man get that bitch out of there, if I see her I might kill her. Can you bail me out? I'm up in here fighting for my manhood."

"Man yo' Ho just left here with some money to get you out. She's on her way to the bondsman right now."

"Who are you talking about?" Alonzo said confused.

"I'm talking about Sparkle," Comfort was loving this, he had a feeling that Alonzo didn't know that Kim was tricking."

"Who the hell is Sparkle?"

"Kim nigga! Don't you know what yo' own woman is doing? She worked a party with Quima last weekend. Quima said she had tricks waiting in line for her. You got a money maker man."

"Kim ain't turning tricks, she drives for her Uncle."

"Man, Quima ain't gon' lie to me. Why you tripping Nigga. You got a broad that obviously cares about you, she trying to get the money to raise you up. What's your problem with her making money? You need to start charging her ass up, she cain't be outlawing. If you ain't gone charge her, I will."

Alonzo couldn't believe it. The thought of Kim turning tricks made him want to throw up. "Man I got to get off the line. I'll see you when I get out."

Alonzo hung up the phone, went to the steel toilet in the corner of the room, and threw up.

Taking out the Trash

Comfort got dressed, took another blast, and went to see if Rita was ready to go. He decided putting her in a cab would be a bad idea. Who knows when she might decide to cause him problems? He did not need to have some taxi driver testifying that he had picked her up from his house.

"Bitch, you ready to go?" Comfort said opening the bedroom door.

Damn she looked fucked up. Her jaw and nose were swollen and she was holding her side and wincing with every step. *Too goddamn bad, this snitch had to get the hell out of his house.*

He took her in the bathroom and gave her a package of dope. He straightened out her nose. Here try to take a blow it will make you feel better. He watched her try to snort without much success. He dropped a rock on the pipe, lit it, and held it up to her mouth, "Hit this so we can get up out of here." As soon as she blew the smoke out, he made her hit it again before she could mellow out, three times before he said, "Let's go."

All the way to there destination Comfort questioned her about how she dealt herself out of jail. What she had said to the law and how she got to his house. She swore that she had just wanted to make Kim mad because she did not like her. She swore she had not snitched on anyone and that a friend that she made in jail had bailed her because she said that she would get with her man, but when she got free, she hitchhiked back to him. She talked about how she wanted to be his woman. He quizzed her over and over again. Though her story never changed, he still did not believe anything she said.

When he pulled up to the back of a warehouse, he dialed the phone in his Rolls, "Hey, I'm here motherfucker, come get this bitch."

When the back door opened, he told her, "Go on."

He did not have an ounce of remorse for Rita. She could not be trusted. He was doing Alonzo and himself a favor. The first time she got mad at him, she would turn on everybody.

Rita slowly made her way to the door where the man stood waiting for her. Something did not feel right. If she had not been in so much pain, she would have turned and ran.

Rita was led to a back room of a warehouse. She knew she was in trouble, but she didn't know how much.

Akhab made movies that were bought by people with unusual appetites. Sodomy, children, bestiality, sadomasochism, and wet works (murders.) He was going to have to put a bag over this girl's broken face. His clientele would not care what her face looked like, some prefer the battered look. He would book her through out the next month, depending on how much she cooperated and how well she held up, this would determine what he would do with her after that. He would either sell her to someone in another state, or make a movie of her gruesome death.

Kim

Springing Alonzo

When I got to Christians house I called Cricket and told him I was on my way. "Come on I'll take you," Christian volunteered.

"Guess what, Comfort gave me thirty grand, and I have Alonzo's ten. With Cricket's bondsman that will get Alonzo out. Here take this suitcase; it's got Alonzo's two keys in it. You can give it to him when you see him."

"You aren't going to pick him up?"

"I can't. The bondsman will give him a ride home, unless you want to get him. Mea has a party jumping off so we can drop my car off there, then go meet the bondsman, after that you can take me back to work."

"Does you not wanting to pick him up have anything to do with the fact that he knows you're working?"

"Damn, he knows already?"

"He called right before you got here. He's upset. He feels like you are playing him, and that you made him look like a fool."

"How the hell am I making him look like a fool? I have seen him three times since we broke up. I ain't even said that I was back with him officially. What does he have to be mad about? Man, don't make me mess around and leave his ass locked up."

"How did Comfort find out anyway?" Christian asked.

"I did a party with his bottom woman Quima last week. I didn't know who she was until I rang the doorbell today. She hurried up and let Comfort know that I was working. Rita was there too, bragging on how she set Alonzo up so she could get out of jail. She was obviously freaking with them. She should have kept her mouth shut because Comfort heard her say that she snitched and laid into her ass. I don't know if it was for my benefit or if he really didn't know that Alonzo was in jail."

"So she put Alonzo in jail, got out and went to freak with them. Damn, they be partying like that?"

"Cricket says Comfort spends so much time freaking with his girls that they don't have time to work. Of course, he offered to leave Alonzo in jail if I wanted to get with him. On my way out his woman told me that Comfort has been wanting to get with me since he heard Alonzo and me one night."

"What's that about?"

"It seems that his soldier has trouble saluting. Alonzo says that he has two or three girls in the room and never gets off. Too much dope and liquor."

"When I used to get high, it was hard for me to get off sometime, but I could always get up. It kind of dulled it for me after awhile. It seems like he would realize that the chemicals are affecting his libido and leave it alone."

"Hell his woman thinks I have platinum in my pants, she asked me to come back and party with them. I told her that wasn't going to happen. She backed me up against a wall, grabbed my breast, and tried to kiss me. I pushed her away, "Come back and party with me.""

"Damn can I get front row seats for that show?"

"Like I told her, that ain't gonna happen."

Alonzo

"Hey man, thanks for picking me up."

"Ain't no thang, I'm glad to help?"

"Damn man, what the hell happened to you?" Christian said looking at Alonzo's black eye and scraped knuckles.

"You know they got to try you up in there."

"You still got your manhood? You didn't get punked up in there did you?" Christian laughed.

"If I would have been raped, I wouldn't be looking like this. Man I never stopped swinging," Alonzo laughed. "Why didn't Kim come?"

"I could tell you that she had to work like she told me, but if you want my opinion she didn't come because of what Comfort and his woman told you. And I told her that you were tripping about it."

"Man that's fucked up, everybody knows what she's doing but me. How long she been hooking?"

"About six months after you guys broke up. She was hurt man, she said; let me see how did she put it? "I don't want to see another dick unless it got hundred dollar bills hanging off of it."

"Then when I first went over there, she was doing it. I know I haven't seen her but a few times, but she could have told me. She should have let me decide whether I wanted to deal with a Ho."

"That "Ho" came to your rescue as soon as she found out you were locked up, Nigga."

"Comfort gave her the money didn't he?"

"Kim had the money to get you out within ten minutes of me calling her. If Comfort had not given her the money, you still would have been free. That motherfucker let you sit in jail for two days. She got your ass out in two hours. You need to think about who really has your back. Comfort was too busy freaking with your baby mama."

"Rita disconnected the phones, he didn't know I was in jail until Kim told him, the same time he found out she was a Ho."

"Well Kim never snitched on you. She stands behind her people. And another thing motherfucker, don't forget that's my sister you calling a whore. Shit all these bitches out here running around giving up pussy out of both panty legs, if they had any sense they would be charging."

"But she's fucking other men."

"That's your fault asshole. When you broke her heart, she decided to go to work. She's not sleeping with other men. She's turning tricks and getting paid, and getting paid well. Who are you to judge her? You know Alonzo, I know for a fact that she never stopped loving you, you know how I know? Because she told me to keep working with you after ya'll broke up. If it wasn't for her telling me to keep dealing with yo' ass, you and me would have broke up too, Nigga."

"Damn, I didn't know that."

"I'm gone tell you some more shit you don't' know, I know that you asked her to sell Comforts dope instead of mine. We supposed to be boys and you trying to pull my best worker out from under me. If you're selling dope for Comfort, you should have had enough money to get your own ass out of jail. He's trying to tell Kim that she needs to pay him the money back that he gave her to get you out. He also asked her if she wanted to leave you in jail and get with him. His woman asked her to freak with them. That's the kind of friend Comfort is to you."

"I know he likes her. Ever since he found out that, she was Cricket's niece it's like he's been obsessing over her. Damn I got to deal with all this shit, and I got this charge hanging over my head. Thanks for sending your lawyer for me man."

"It ain't no thang; I'm still your brother. Where are we going?"

"Man I need a drink and a blow. I don't really want to go to that house just yet. I think Rita is still there. I want to wait until that bitch is on a bus back home because if I see her I really will have murder beef."

"Let's go to my house, Kim left your package there."

"She didn't sell it?"

"Naw, Cricket's bondsman only needed fifty percent so what Comfort gave her was enough. You make sure you talk to Comfort about repaying it if that's what you have to do. I don't want him trying to charge Kim up."

"Naw, it ain't gone be none of that."

Kim

1972

I was at my parent's house looking through the photo albums. I needed to be around people who loved me and I needed to think about a time when I was not a "Ho," as Alonzo had so eloquently put it. I had been avoiding Alonzo for two weeks since he got out of jail.

The only thing that I could compare the pain of Alonzo calling me a "Ho" is the way I felt when my second boyfriend tried to sleep with my best friend.

But I have to tell you about my first boyfriend before I can get into that.

My first boyfriend was Terrell Dunley. I was thirteen, flat chested, bony with legs so thin my knees looked like doorknobs. I was often mistaken for a boy in my Levi's jeans, high top converse tennis shoes, and afro.

I was tired of fighting my way home every day because I did not want to join a gang. I didn't like the things they did and sure wasn't going to get gang banged into one.

Sometimes I won the fights, but that didn't matter because I would rather fight these girls than my Father who if he were to find out I had joined a gang would beat me more than they ever could.

I went into my mother's make up to cover up the bruises. I held frozen steaks to my face to keep the swelling down. I rubbed my bruised eyes with a frozen spoon until the color came back and the swelling went down. I did not want my parents to know about the fights because it would only upset them. Besides there was really nothing they could do. At these times, I wished I had siblings I could run to.

Jean and I had been friends since we were six years old. They were the second black family to move on our block. Jean and her sister attended catholic school.

It was August during summer vacation. I was helping Jean hook up with Allen, a guy she had been talking to over the phone when she misdialed one day and he struck up a conversation. After a few months, Jean finally got up the nerve to meet him face to face.

Allen brought Terrell with him, a nineteen year old. Jean had lied to Allen about her age. She said she was 16; she was 13 just like me. She knew my parents were not home so she gave Allen my address. We sat on the front porch discussing how much trouble I would be in if my Dad came home.

Jean and Allen went in the back yard to "talk."

Terrell was not cute by any standards. I felt awkward sitting with him at first, but once he started talking I found him entertaining and funny. After that day, we started talking on the phone during the day when my parents were not home.

When school started, I often walked out of the gate to find Terrell waiting outside of Roosevelt Jr. High to give me a ride home. Magically once the girls who I was having the fights with were now befriending me when they saw me with Terrell. I found out why, he was the leader of the U.S. chapter of a gang that held down the Wilson park area.

Terrell fixed up old cars into low-riders. He also raced and hopped them. Big money and pink slips were on the line at the street races, which were held late at night on blocked off roads. He often won.

Terrell taught me how to work the hydraulic lifts so that we could run a con. He would tell people he was going to let his little brother hop against them. I looked like a boy so they thought they had an easy win. I always won and he kicked me down a few hundred dollars.

Terrell always had more than one car that he was working on. His yard was full of Chevy's, Cadillac's, and Mustangs. He was a real artist with cars. He bought antique cars and within a week, the hunk a junks would be running like tops and the pearlescent paint would shine like new money, along with reupholstered and refurbished interior, topped off with spoke rims.

Some days I would pick up a car from Terrell and me and my home girls ditched school. We rolled all over Compton, Watts, and Los Angeles. One day we were sitting at a light. Allen's sister, Latrelle was in her boyfriend's car and we were hitting switches against each other.

I looked to the left and saw my Father's van. I stepped on the gas and ran the light trying to get out of dodge before he could see me. First of all, I was not old enough to be driving, second I was supposed to be at school. My Father didn't play that. I would have been dead if he busted me.

I kept my grades up only because my Father made me do homework for two hours when I got home whether I had any or not. He would assign me pages from his old Trade Tech books. I went to school on Monday to find out what the test for the week was on and came back on Friday to take it. I got and turned in all the homework assignments through my friends. As far as attendance went, my girlfriend was messing with the principal so nothing showed up on our report cards.

I was making a lot of money hustling with Terrell and it wasn't about sex because I was not ready for that. I was not allowed to date or go to parties so I lied about spending the night with friends to get out. I did most of my hanging out during school hours and went home everyday as if I was coming from school because even if my parents weren't there, they would be calling home to make sure I was.

I got tired of hearing about sex from all my friends and decided to try it with Terrell. He had asked me a few times and I liked him. Actually, he was the only boy who had ever shown any interest in me.

I always felt awkward around my friends because they were developing, I felt left behind. They all told me that if I got rid of my cherry I would start getting some curves, that's when theirs had developed. Some of them had started blossoming really young. Later I found out that those girls were being molested by older men, which also explained why they liked sex so much.

The day I planned to rid my self of my virginity my parents were out for the day and I invited Terrell over. When I saw his penis, erect I looked down at my small hole and then back at him, "That telephone pole is never going to fit inside of me; I would like you to leave now."

Terrell laughed, but he said he understood and left. I decided to try again the next week. When it was over, I didn't see what the big deal was. The next time he performed oral sex, I liked that better. It was pleasant enough, but I still had no clue what an orgasm was. I did not see any reason to be dishonest about how I felt. He tried and tried, every time he asked 'Well?" I shook my head. I just figured I was not made right or something.

I ran away from home one weekend because I had given a ditchers party and someone snitched. The principal and police showed up outside. I knew I was going to be in big trouble so I grabbed some clothes and money and jumped the back fence along with everyone else.

I spent the night at with my friend Beverly's. Her eighteen-year-old brother, Bennie was having a garage party. Terrell came and we discoed, U. S stomped, break-danced and pop locked to The Commodores, Parliament, The Ohio players, and Con-funk-shun until four in the morning.

We were drinking mad dog 20 20 and silver satin with packages of Kool-Aid to kill the taste. I experimented with PCP for the first time that night. I did not handle it well, the room started to spin and I threw up. I went in the house, lay down, and went to sleep.

It was weird the effect that weed and PCP had on me, my friends loved it. The first time I smoked weed was in a vacant house behind the school with some friends. When I got to class, I started laughing and could not stop. Then I fell asleep. I was sent to the counselor's office. He was not going to do anything because he liked to look at naked girls.

I woke to pressure on top of me. When I realized I was not dreaming I started fighting realizing that Bennie was on top of me. I think he enjoyed me hitting him because it was over as quickly as it started.

The next day I called Terrell and when he picked me up, he told me that my parents had contacted the police who had spoken to my friends at school, which led them to him. I needed to go home or they would put him in jail for messing with a minor.

I told Terrell what happened with Bennie. Dark clouds gathered on his face. He stopped the car. When I found the nerve to look at him tears were falling from his eyes. I thought he was mad at me until he spoke, "I knew Bennie liked you. He asked me about you and I let him know that you were my woman. I would have never left you there if I thought he was crazy enough to try some shit like this. You should have used that knife I gave you on his ass. That's alright I'll handle this." I had never seen him so upset before.

He took me home where my whole family was waiting for me. He came inside with me, and my family drilled him. They did not like him, but they knew that would not stop me from seeing him.

The next time I saw Bennie he was in a wheel chair and when he saw me coming down the street, he crossed to the other side. He even avoided looking at me. Terrell had taken care of it.

Kim

The Youth Program

My Father took me to the police station and told them I was incorrigible and he could not handle me. I tried my best not to cry as the lady jailer came around to take me away. My mother hugged me and cried.

I was put in a brick cell that was painted green. When the door closed, it was the loudest clang I had ever heard in my life. I was alone in the cell. I did what I always did when I wanted to escape my surroundings, I went to sleep.

I woke to the sound of a key in the lock, the heavy door opened. A lady came in and offered me a candy bar and a soda. I sat up. She sat on the bottom bunk next to me. "I am Sergeant Wickett; I would like you to tell me why you are here."

"My parents are strict. I want to hang out and go to parties, date, and stuff. They don't think I'm old enough, so I ditch school. I ran away because I gave a party and someone snitched, the principal showed up with the police. I grabbed some clothes and ran out the back door and over the fence with everyone else. I knew I was going to be in trouble so I figured I might as well make the best of a bad situation. There were three parties I wanted to go to this weekend, so I ran."

"Do you feel like you are old enough to be going to parties and ditching school?"

"This is Compton lady. Every one is older than their age and doing more than their parents think they should."

"Your parents are responsible for you. You don't attend school they can get in trouble. Don't you think to get a good education is important to ensure your future? You can't get a job if you don't graduate. To don't you plan to go to college?"

"I do alright in school. I'm going to graduate, one way, or another."

"How is that going to happen with you ditching school?"

"I get good grades."

"How do you manage that?"

"I've always liked to read and my Father makes me study even if I don't have homework, I enjoy studying. I go to school and find out what the test are on Mondays, study in the evenings and make sure that I take the test and turn in any homework. My teachers like me because I don't cause trouble. You know how it is here in Compton, as long as you don't shoot the teacher they are going to pass you."

She doubled over laughing, "I'm laughing, but it really isn't funny. The way you put it though, you are something else.' She composed herself and looked at me real serious like. You are smart Kim. You have never been in trouble. You need to go to school everyday and do something with your life. What do you want to be when you grow up?

"Well, I like to sew. I make a lot of my clothes; maybe I'd like to be a tailor like my Father. He wants me to be a secretary, I type pretty good."

"You have all this talent, it's a shame you are wasting it. It really pisses me off when I see kids like you throwing your life away," she stood up, "I'll be back in a few."

"A few" passed and she did not return. I went back to sleep.

I wasn't sure how long it was, but the clanging door woke me up. A woman came in wearing a bloody shirt.

"Hey," she said.

"Hey," I said not really wanting to get into a conversation with her. What if she hadn't gotten all the anger out of her system? I did not want to be killed.

"How old are you?"

"Thirteen," I said timidly.

"What the hell are you doing in here? You should be in school."

"My Father says that I'm incorrigible and he doesn't want to deal with me anymore."

"You don't look like a bad kid."

"Uhm, do you know that you're covered in blood?"

"Yeah, I guess I am." She looked at me and laughed. Aw baby girl, you don't have to be afraid of me. I don't have any cause to hurt you."

"Why are you here?"

"I stabbed my boyfriend. Caught him molesting my daughter and it seemed like the right thing to do at the time."

"Why did they lock you up, he's the on that should be in here."

"Oh he will be, if he lives. They had to take him to the hospital. They took my daughter too, said they needed to do something called a rape kit."

"How old is your daughter?"

"My baby is sixteen. She's a beautiful girl. Her Father died in the war when she was three. I hadn't gone out with anyone in over twelve years. But then Henry came along and swept me off my feet. I was so starved for male attention that I wanted to believe he was 'The One.' He sat me down from my job, took us out of the apartments on Santa Fe Avenue, and moved us into a nice house. He always gave us money for shopping, took us on trips. I really, really thought that God had answered my prayers and sent me a man who I could grow old with," She started to cry.

I felt bad for this woman. All she had done was protect her kid. Too bad all mothers didn't have her conviction for their children's welfare. I held her as she cried.

I thought of my friend Sarah whose Mother threw her daughter out in the street rather than stop her boyfriend's abuse. If Sarah's Mother had of listened to her she would not have had to run around staying from pillar to post.

Sarah and I had been friends since elementary school and before her parents separated when the father caught his wife in bed with another man, packed up, and left.

Not a week later, the other man had moved in. By the end of the week, he was raping Sarah while her mother worked. He threatened to kill her and her parents if she said anything. She told her mother that she was not comfortable being alone in the house with her boyfriend. Her mother thought Sarah was fabricating a story so that the boyfriend would leave and her Father would come back home.

Eventually Sarah could not take it any more and decided to tell her mother everything in spite of the threats. Her mother told her, "Get your funky ass out of my house. I can't trust you around my man. You probably been trying to get him in the bed all this time while I been at work you little whore!"

Sarah and I gathered her clothes into a pillowcase and since it was Friday, she spent the weekend at my house. I told my parents that her folks were going away for the weekend and would not be back until late Sunday.

Sandra's mom worked nights during the week and Sarah could stay there for a few nights. At school, we recruited our friends and made a schedule so Sarah would always have somewhere to sleep. It worked out well. Twelve of us shared our clothes and money with Sarah so she wouldn't have to live on the streets.

Soon Sarah realized that she had not menstruated and she was getting sick every morning. She went to her mother and told her that she may be pregnant. Her mother took her to the clinic where the doctor confirmed the pregnancy.

When her mother went to the clinic restroom Sarah was questioned. She told the truth. When her mother came back into the examining room, the doctor told her that he was bound by his oath to call the police and report the rape.

"What makes you think that she was raped?"

"Her stepfather is grown. Sarah is a minor. That is statutory rape."

"That is a lie. Sarah tells them the truth. When she remained silent, her mother dragged her out of the building before the police arrived. She did not care if her boyfriend had done this, she did not want him to go to jail. He made a mistake, the same one her own Father had made when she was seven years old and she lived through it. It was no big deal.

She told Sarah, "Tell them it was your boyfriend who knocked you up." Sarah would not agree to do it even after she was beaten, she would not change her story.

Her daughter was not lying, but she just did not want to put her man out. She was going to arrange for Sarah to stay with her sister.

When the boyfriend walked up to the door detectives pulled up and arrested him. The neighbor saw the police take the man away. She also heard what they charged him with and wasted no time calling Sarah's Father who she had been dating and keeping informed on his wife's antics.

When Sarah's Father stormed into the house, he flew at Sarah's mother with both fists. When he left, he took Sarah with him. He went to a bail bondsman and arranged the release of the boyfriend anonymously.

Sarah was in the car when the man exited the jail and her Father followed him. The boyfriend had gotten almost home when he stepped out to cross the street. Sarah's Father mowed him down like grass with his car. He got out, picked him up, and threw him in the trunk. He dropped Sarah at his apartment. When he came back, he told her never to speak of what happened to anyone.

At least Sarah got closure. She said that something about seeing her abuser hurt made her feel better about the whole thing. Sarah's parents decided the best thing to do for their daughter was to get back together.

Sarah's mother took her for an abortion. She didn't want anything to overshadow her reunion. It was a kitchen butcher who punctured Sarah's uterine wall. She was in the hospital for a long time. Some friends and I went to see her. She told us that she would never be able to have kids.

I got some tissue and gave it to the woman. "You are a very brave woman who did nothing but take care of and protect her child. I wish all moms were like you."

The outer cell door opened and an officer called my name, "Come with me."

I followed her to an office and Sergeant Wickett sat behind a desk with the phone to her ear. She motioned for me to take a seat. "Thanks Marion I'll give them the information and they will be calling you sometime today."

"Well Kim, do you think that you can stay in school and not give your parents any more headaches if we let you go home?"

"I don't think my parents want me back."

"What they don't want back is the problems you have

been causing them. I spoke to your Father and he can't and should not have to put up with you ditching school. Do you know that your parents can be fined or worse, incarcerated if you don't go?

"No I didn't know that."

"If you don't go to school and continue to have truant parties in their home you are going to be in big trouble. You will be monitored. You are a smart girl I called the school and spoke with your counselor you are very bright, too bright to be wasting your life like this. Also, what is this I'm hearing about a nineteen-year-old boyfriend?

"I've been seeing him since last year. I love him."

"Girl you don't have a clue what love is. Just make sure you don't get pregnant and ruin your life."

"Okay."

"You do know that he can be put in jail for statutory rape. You are a minor and he is not. He is using you, you do know that don't you?"

"We are using each other."

She looked at me, "Well I just hope what you are using him for is worth all this trouble" Her phone bussed and she picked it up, "We'll be out in a second."

"Your Father is here for you. I am recommending counseling for you. You will call this woman and set up an appointment. Call her as soon as you get home. I spoke with her and she knows that I want you in her office ASAP."

She walked around her desk and gave me a piece of paper and her card. She hugged me, "If you ever need to talk feel free to call me. "

She walked me up front, where my Father stood. He walked up and hugged me. I started to cry. I was happy to be going home.

"Sir, can I speak to you for a minute."

They went into her office while I signed some papers to be released.

On the ride home my Father asked, "Well you had your first night in jail, how was it?"

"I didn't like it."

"What are you going to do now?'

"I'm going to school so I don't have to go back."

"Alright."

I went to the counselor, Ms. Marshall the next day and had to report every week for the next couple of months. After that, she had my parent's come in. After talking to my Father, Ms. Marshall told him, that he was too strict and ordered him to come in for counseling. He was not happy about that.

Ms. Marshall dealt with all kind of delinquents and in comparison, I was an angel. My parents lightened up a bit and let me start hanging out for a couple of hours after school. After a while and by the suggestion of the counselor they allowed me to see Terrell.

I was ordered to participate in a youth program that was supposed to help at-risk children. If the parents knew the criminal education their kids were getting at this place, they would have burned it to the ground.

The guys who founded the youth program were ex-cons who were making amends for their sins against society by reaching out and helping youth so that they would not end up in jail.

The government gave them a grant and a two-story apartment building. In many ways, they were doing good for the community by offering good training programs. The kids had to keep their school grades up to stay in the program. Tutoring was available so you had no excuse for failing any studies. Kids from ages 12 to 17 could take martial arts, arts and crafts, modern African dance, auto mechanics, and carpentry. Once the month our modern African dance troupe performed at schools. We participated in local parades.

I was one of the lead dancers and performed with a snake around my neck. The snake had been devenomed but no one in the crowd knew that. Nights before performances the dance troupe, martial arts and stomp studies spent the night at the youth program.

This was convenient for the directors and counselors who were sleeping with the female youth they were saving. If you weren't hooked up with a counselor you could have the boyfriend that your parents didn't approve of spend the evening with you.

There was always liquor and weed provided by the counselors. Long lines of new counselors were employed by the program because the state required that they employ ex-cons and this was a win-win because it helped them satisfy the conditions of their parole.

They had classes on birth control so there were very few accidents and if someone did get pregnant, they could opt for the local doctor who gave them confidential abortions and birth control pills.

All youth participated in the summer and holiday jobs program. I do mean jobs plural. They connected with stores and restaurants in the area who were eager to have the government pay half the salaries for employing us.

The kids were given anywhere from two to five identification cards. We had a job for each name. The money that the government paid to the establishment was split with the kids who did not physically work there. You had one job that you really went to for 6 hours a day. The program director cashed each paycheck for five dollars. Four of my five checks were split with the director, giving me about $250.00 a week to take home. Not bad for a teenager working a summer job. I brought all my friends into the program for summer jobs and the dance troupe.

The program also had a driving program and had gotten funding for used cars that were used to teach auto mechanics and drivers education. After we got our licenses, we advance to making more money by delivering cocaine, china white, PCP, and weed to consumers.

We also provided insurance robberies. Storeowners paid for us to rob their store. After the insurance paid them off, the owner restocked the store with the merchandise that waited in storage at the center.

We also set up car accidents. People who were in drivers training ran into the people that wanted to get a payday from the auto insurance company. They got a new car if it was done right. After the accident, we all went to doctors who kept us in therapy for months to work up a good case. In the end, everyone received a big fat check.

We learned so many life lessons in the youth program.

Boyfriend Number Two

Terrell was allowed to visit with me at home and on the weekends we were went to the movies and on dates.

The Compton drive-in theater was the spot. Everyone from school hung out on Saturday nights. It was the era of the blaxpoitation movie. Shaft, Which way is up, Super fly, Dolomite, The Mack, Cleopatra Jones, Foxy Brown, Coffee, Jim Kelly karate movies. It didn't matter if you didn't have a car. You could jump in some ones trunk and ride in or sit on the back fence or in a tree.

For $2.50, you could see three movies from the comfort of the backseat of your car while you made out. In between the movies, everyone put their radios on the same station and we danced until the next movie started.

I was in my first year of high school. The tenth grade was a very profitable year for me. I sold joints of weed and PCP that Terrell supplied me with.

I never kept anything in my locker because sometimes they did searches with K-9 dogs. Right before lunch was over Terrell or his sister met me at the back gate to pick up any left over drugs and the money minus my cut.

Over summer vacation, I had morphed into a brick house. I no longer had a flat-chest. I had a nice figure and carried it well on my tall frame.

I was walking down the hall and this guy said, "It must be jelly 'cause jam don't shake like that." It was the middle of the year and Elvin had transferred in from Las Vegas. He was in the eleventh grade, tall, handsome and in one month had moved from the varsity to the senior basketball team and he was 'foine.' All the girls were trying to talk to him because they knew he was going to one day be a superstar ball player.

All I could do was giggle as I speeded up to my girlfriends. "Girl do you know who that is?" Cheryl asked.

"No, I don't," I lied.

"Girl he is only the best ball player that Dominguez has seen."

At lunch, I got my food and was making my way to my friends when I felt someone propelling in a different direction. It was Elvin. I found myself sitting at the table with the senior basketball team! "You are going to have lunch with me and my friends today."

I was in love. From that moment, I knew that I wanted to be with Elvin Emberly. He invited me to the movies on Friday. Now, how would I explain to Terrell that I was moving on?

Since the principal had called the police at my Junior high school prom and they had come, dragged Terrell out, and beat the hell out of him with Billy clubs, I felt like maybe something was wrong with me having a man who was twenty-one when I was only fifteen.

Terrell had just gone to court and was awarded a large settlement for police brutality. My Father had gone to the jail and taken pictures of Terrell's wounds. He was layed up in bed for a few days and had twenty stitches in his head.

I broke up with Terrell after school at the hamburger stand. He was pretty nice about it, "I knew it was going to happen one day," he said. "You know that if you ever need me I'm here for you. If he treats you bad you let me know, me and the crew will kick his ass," He kissed me and we walked to his car.

I kept selling drugs for him. We were making good money, why give that up. I also picked up cars from him when I needed to under the one contingency that no guys ride in his cars. He had gone from boyfriend to big brother.

Elvin and I spent a lot of time together. We went to all the parties and I did not miss any of his basketball games. My parents liked him because he was closer to my age.

Since Elvin was on the senior basketball team, he was definitely going to prom and asked me to be his date. There weren't many sophomores who got this privilege. My Father said that he was going to make my gown.

One night my parents were going to a dance. I invited Elvin over though I wasn't allowed to have male company when my parents were out. We had fallen asleep watching television and woke to the sound of my parents van pulling down the driveway.

Elvin scrambled for the front door. When I opened the front door there were a lot of cars parking along the street. Once again, my parents had brought the dance home with them.

I waved Elvin down the hall and into my closet. Within minutes, the whole house was vibrating to the Temptations, Gladys Night and the Pips, O J Simpson, and James Brown.

"You ain't gone be able to get out of here no time soon. When they party it can go on all night."

I threw a couple of pillows and a blanket into the closet. "Get comfortable." I went out and got us some chips, dip, fruit, and soda. No one would be coming into my room. My mom had kissed me goodnight and they assumed I was asleep. I sat next to the closet and we ate and laughed about our predicament.

I got into my bed and fell asleep forgetting all about Elvin.

The next morning Mommy was walking down the hallway when she heard something in my room. She had just looked in on me so she knew I was sleep.

"Hey, wake up!"

I opened my eyes, "The party over?"

"I thought so? Everybody that we knew has left."

"What do you mean?"

"I mean who is in that closet?"

"Nobody, what are you talking about?" I turned over and saw a gun in my Mother's hand.

"Mommy, why do you have a gun?"

Elvin had on some big platform shoes and had been moving around in his sleep kicking the walls and mommy had heard him.

I had forgotten all about Elvin in the closet. I was scared and in big trouble. I could kiss the prom and my life goodbye.

"Who is in the closet?"

"Uhm," I was going to have to face the music. I was trying to figure out how to explain this.

"Well, if you don't know who is in there, and then I am going to unload this motherfuckin' gun into that closet because somebody needs killing?"

"Mommy wait!"

"What?" she sat on the bed.

"Elvin come out the closet," I said.

Elvin backed all six foot, three inches of himself out of the closet with his hands up. Had he made one wrong move my Mother would have blasted him into the next world.

When she recognized him she said, I'm glad I didn't shoot. "Boy, do you know that you could have got yo' ass killed up in here? What the hell are you doing in there anyway?" She turned and looked at me, "Now what do you think your Father will do if I go and wake him up?"

"He was here when you guys came home. I know you told me I couldn't have company, but when we tried to get him out the front door, all those people were walking up, and I didn't know what to do."

I could tell that though she wanted to laugh she was mad as hell. "Elvin you take your tail on home. I bet your brother is worried to death about you. When you get there you tell them what happened here, and I want them to come over here this evening. We are going to discuss this."

"Yes Ma'am," Elvin said, never raising his eyes to look at her.

I was on pins and needles all day. My Father had tied one on and they were still in the bed at noon. I fixed breakfast for them and cleaned up the glasses and bottles from the party. I washed the dishes and vacuumed hoping that it would help my case. I knew my Father was going to be mad and cancel the prom.

I could not take it any more. I fixed their plates, took television trays, and cracked the door. Mommy looked up.

"I fixed breakfast for you guys, pancakes, bacon, eggs, grits, and orange juice."

"Bring it in. Your daddy is still sleeping. Just leave it next to the bed."

"I cleaned up for you, did the dishes, and vacuumed."

"Thank you, but you are still in trouble."

I called Elvin. His brother thought it was funny. "You think you are going to get to go to the prom?"

"I don't know, doubt it."

That evening when daddy got up, mommy made me tell him what happened. Of course, he was pissed. He didn't say anything until Elvin and his brother and sister-in-law arrived. He stressed the point that Elvin could have been killed. Then they sent Elvin and me to the den while they decided our fate.

I was allowed to go to the prom but I was on punishment for a month, no phone, and no dates.

Elvin went to Las Vegas that summer to visit his Father. We wrote to each other and talked on the phone. When he returned we were still going hot and heavy, until….

One of my best friends Nezia called me. We had been friends since elementary school, "Kim you aren't going to believe this."

"What girl?"

"Elvin asked me out."

"What?" I had to have heard wrong.

"Elvin asked me out."

"He asked you out?"

"Yep."

"What did he say?"

"He walked up to me and gave me his number and asked me to go out with him on Friday night."

"I just got off the phone with him, he's at home. I'm going to three-way a call and listen while you talk to him."

"Okay."

"Hello," Elvin's five-year-old nephew answered.

"Nezia spoke. " May I speak to Elvin?"

"Who is this?"

"This is Nezia."

Elvin came to the phone, "I knew you would call me."

"You did huh, so what were you asking me today?" Nezia said.

"I want to take you to the drive-in Friday night."

"Why?"

"Cause I like you, always have."

"What about your girlfriend? Did you forget that she happens to be my best friend?" Nezia said.

"What about her? We don't have to tell her," Elvin said.

"I think it's too late for that," Nezia said.

"What do you mean?" Elvin said.

"What she means is that I'm on the phone Elvin. Did you really think that my best friend would go out with you and not tell me?"

"I was just asking her because Earl wanted to see what she would say." Elvin explained.

"I haven't been going out with Earl in months, so that's a lie." Nezia said.

"Girl, I know, don't even sweat it. I'm going to hang up on him now. Elvin since you want to go out with other people feel free and I will too."

I hung up on Elvin and talked with Nezia, "Girl men are all dogs," she said.

"Yeah I know, but I kinda loved that one."

"What are you going to do?"

"I guess I'm going to go out with that guy I met at Compton High last week."

"You mean the one you met when we did the fashion show? I thought you told him that you had a boyfriend?"

My phone indicated that another call was coming in. I knew it was Elvin so I did not answer. "He gave me his phone number anyway. He wants me to make him a recycled Levi maxi coat."

"He's cute."

"Yeah he is. I'm looking at Michael Davis's number right now. I'm going to call him."

"I'll see you tomorrow."

"Cool, let's do our shopping trip on Saturday?"

"Sure, we can catch the bus to Cerritos Mall after we get our checks from the youth program."

The next day was Thursday and Elvin sent me a message to meet him at lunchtime. I did not go. I went to sell drugs at the bleachers and stayed there. I came out of Spanish class and he was waiting for me. I walked right past him.

"We need to talk," he said.

"No we don't," I kept on walking to my next class. After school, I rode home with one of my twelfth grade girlfriends who had a car.

I bought an answering machine so I could screen my calls. On Friday when I got out of school, I had Terrell pick me up. I talked to him about what had happened. He wanted to beat Elvin up, but I told him not to.

Nezia and I went shopping at the Cerritos mall that Saturday. We had both saved our money from our summer jobs at the youth program. We had been planning this shopping spree for a long time. We wanted to wait until after the back to school rush so that we could get the new winter clothes.

I was president of the modeling club, I sewed most of my clothes, and if I bought something I wanted it to be unique, something no one else in school was wearing.

We were going to have a real spending spree on all the money we had saved from working that summer. We bought everything that would put us on the best-dressed list for the eleventh grade. We bought matching blue suede skirts, high heels and leather jackets. We had so many bags that we had to stop shopping, or we would not have been able to carry everything home.

We couldn't wait for Monday to come so we could wear our outfits. We vowed not to tell anyone where we got them. We went to a movie and it let out just before the sun was going down.

We were waiting for the bus to go home when we noticed a helicopter circling us. We started joking "That ghetto bird (helicopter) keeps on flying around you Nezia. What you done stole? The police are coming to take you to jail," I laughed.

"I didn't steal anything," Nezia said.

Suddenly three police cars pulled up burning rubber surrounding us. They jumped out of there cars with guns pulled, "Put your hands on the car," a cop yelled into a bullhorn.

We looked at each other and complied. Nezia asked me "Did you do something? I know I didn't." The police searched us as if we were men.

"Isn't a women supposed to be searching me?" I asked the policeman who had one hand between my legs and the other on my breast. I knew he was getting his rocks off.

"Shut up you Black bitch you need to stick to shoplifting in your own neighborhood."

"I ain't stole shit; you just want to feel on me you pervert."

"Your ass is going to jail, you had better shut up. You are making it worse on yourself."

"No you are making it bad on yourself because you are molesting me. I'm not stupid. You ain't supposed to be touching me."

Another officer called the police man over. They had checked our bags. Each bag had a receipt for every purchase.

Another officer came over to us, "Someone went into The Robinsons department store, and stole merchandise. All we knew was that they were black. That's why we detained you."

"That doesn't' explain how you guys treated us. We didn't steal anything," Nezia said.

"How did you get the money to pay for all this stuff? You spent quite a bit of money?"

"We saved our money from our summer jobs and our parents matched it for school clothes," I said.

"Why can't you shop in your own neighborhood? Why do you have to come out here?" the officer who had felt me up asked.

"Because we can, it's a free country," Nezia said.

They got in their cars and left. The ride home was a quiet one. We were both reflecting on what we had just experienced. I had a whole new respect for racial profiling, prejudice and Dr. Martin Luther King.

That night I had a date with Michael. He was tall, chocolate, and attractive. He had his own car, an electric blue pearl, convertible Chevy low rider complete with hydraulics. Elvin had to borrow his brother's car to go anywhere.

Michael was taking me to dinner and a party. The phone rang and I answered it thinking it was him. It was Elvin. "I want to come get you so we can talk."

"Sorry can't do it," The doorbell rang. "I have to go, my date is here."

"What do you mean your date? I don't want you going out with anybody else."

"That's just too bad now, isn't it?" I hung up the phone.

I had a good time with Michael, he was funny and attentive. His friends were all right, except for some jealous girl who he had dated and dumped.

When he pulled into my driveway to drop me off I saw headlights come on at the end of the block, as it neared I recognized Elvin's brother's El Dorado, Cadillac. He sped up in front of the house blocking the driveway and jumped out of the car.

"Go home Elvin. We are over."

Elvin flew at Michael. Michael pulled out a gun, "You sure you want to fuck with me? She told you to go home. She ain't with you no more."

I went in the house, "Daddy Elvin is outside trying to fight with Michael."

Michael lowered the gun when Daddy approached. Elvin was standing there glaring. Daddy approached Elvin, "Come on son move your car, I want to talk to you." Daddy got in on the passenger side. Elvin backed up and Michael went on his way.

Elvin was crying, "Why is she dogging me out like this?"

"You don't know?" Daddy laughed. "It may have something to do with you trying to screw her best friend. Give her time and maybe she'll come around. You can't play with women like this. I don't know what you were thinking asking Nezia out, but you messed up. Don't come around here unless she invites you, do you understand me?" Daddy got out of the car.

Elvin rolled down the window, "Will you talk to her for me?"

"What can I say? You messed up. I don't know that I want someone around my daughter who would do what you did. She has her own mind and I can't make it up for her. Go home son."

Monday Michael picked me up from school. He had the top down on his car and was parked right next to the school bus. Elvin had gotten on my bus in an attempt to corner me. When I got into Michael's car, I leaned over and kissed him in full view of everyone.

I could hear the guys on the bus ribbing Elvin about losing his woman. I looked up, they were pointing at me. I looked into Elvin's eyes and got satisfaction from the pain I saw there.

Later Elvin moved to the Crenshaw area with his sister. He called me every now and then. We even went out a couple of times but it was never the same. That summer he went back to Las Vegas to live with his Father.

Michael and I did not last long. I knew he was going out with other girls from gossip I heard from friends who went to Compton High. It didn't bother me because I was dating others too.

I don't want to pay the piper

After Christian and I paid the bondsman to get Alonzo out of jail, I had him drop me off at the workhouse. I went inside, dropped some dope off to Mea, and told her I didn't feel well and went home. I was not in the mood to work.

I called the realtor to make sure that she did not plan to bring anyone to see the house. I turned on the television, cooked up some cocaine, and got high. I called Sherry and told her to come hang out after work. We smoked and talked.

"Alonzo knows that I'm working."

"What? How does he know? You told him?"

"I didn't tell Alonzo anything. I haven't talked to him yet. Comfort and his woman told him."

I told her all about Alonzo going to jail and what happened when I went to Comforts and my conversation with Christian.

"What are you going to do?"

"I'm going to keep on making my money. Forget him. Who is he to call me a Whore?"

"That's right girl. You gots to do you."

My phone rang I let the answering machine pick it up. It was Alonzo, he left a message, and "Kim I need to talk to you and this is Alonzo."

A few minutes later, it rang again. When I heard Laisyv's voice, I picked up. "Girl what is going on, Alonzo is over here drunk as hell tripping out because he can't find you."

"I don't want to talk to him now. Can you come over?"

"Let me fix the boys dinner and I'll be right there, are you alright?"

"Not really, we'll talk when you get here. Can you pick up something to drink?"

"Sure."

When Laisyv arrived, we lounged around on my bed getting high and drinking. I repeated the story to her. She could not believe what Alonzo had said after about me after I had gotten him out of jail.

"Girl if I was you I would pull his bond."

"That is a good idea, huh?"

We laughed every time the phone rang. Alonzo had stopped leaving messages after the tenth call. I turned my pager off because now he was blowing it up every ten minutes.

Laisyv and Sherry left about midnight. I turned the ringer off the phone and the answering machine down so it would not wake me.

The next day I woke about noon, ran a tub and soaked for an hour. I checked all my messages. Mea had called; there was a party that night. I needed to be at work by five.

I worked for a week straight without going home. Alonzo had been blowing my pager up, but I ignored his pages. He had even come to the workhouse while I was out on a call. He showed up at the door. Mea called Cricket who paged him and let him know not to show up at the workhouse unannounced.

I was requested by a client that I did not know with another agency. When I arrived, Quima was there. The client wanted to see a two-girl show.

"Why did you ask for me?" I asked the trick who I had never dated before.

"Actually Quima told me about you. She knows I like a good show."

Quima walked up to me and handed me four hundred dollars, "I collected your fee for you."

"I see."

Quima untied the belt on my wrap around dress and pulled it off my arms. She knelt down and unzipped my zebra hair boots. I stepped out of them and stood there in my matching underwear. She ran her hands over my body and sucked on my nipples. "Doesn't she have a beautiful body, Stanley?"

"Oh, yes."

"How do you get your skin so soft? Quima asked leading me to the bed."

"I put baby oil on while I'm still wet from the tub and let it soak in before I dry off."

"I'm going to have to try that."

Stanley lay on the bed and put my hand on his penis. Quima started the show. Most of the time when doing shows the girls put their finger over the clit and licked on that. The client could not tell the difference. Not Quima, she was going for the real and she was good at it. I tried to stay disconnected, but couldn't, my body respond to her and to my anguish I came. Stanley exploded in my hand at the same time.

I went into the restroom to freshen up and there was a knock on the door. Quima came in and took a pack of blow out of her purse and took a blow then offered it to me. I declined.

"You want to come home with me?"

"I got to work. My pager has gone off twice since I've been here."

"You know Alonzo has been looking for you, every time he walks through the door he asks if you called. I didn't know that he was in the dark about you working. I never would have said anything."

I continued getting dressed. I wanted to get away from her lying ass. I left the call and on the drive back to the workhouse realized I was hungry. I had not eaten anything all day but a bowl of cereal. I had about an hour before my favorite pizza restaurant on Hollywood Boulevard would be closing.

I parked my car in the restaurants rear parking lot. Walking in the back door my pager went off. I used the phone in the restroom. Mea wanted me to pick up some girls who were working on Hollywood Boulevard. I told her where I was and to have them meet me. She asked me to bring her salad and pasta.

I finished my salad while I waited for my pizza. Three girls came in, slid into the booth, and ordered food. We started talking about tricks.

A woman came in and sat in the booth behind us.

Martika was bragging about her new sugar daddy. He had gotten her an apartment in Brentwood and paid it up for a year. Next week he was getting her a car. He wanted her to be exclusive.

The woman turned around and looked at us. I noticed that she was wearing gloves when she picked up her drink. I thought it was strange, but went back to listening to the girls talk.

"If you got it going on like that why are you still working the street?" I asked.

"Girlfriend I still got a quota. I thought my man would let me stop working since my allowance from this trick is more than I make through the agencies and street combined. Boy was I stupid to think I was going to be able to kick back. He told me if I was gone get lazy he would pull me out of the spot and take the car to the chop shop."

Princess choked on her root beer, "Girl I know I ain't supposed to be speaking on your business, but if I had a trick playing Captain Sav-A-Ho I would have to choose me a new man. What happens if the trick finds out that you are still working? He's paying you not to keep hitting the bricks."

"You right Bitch; you are out of line talking about my business. A real man ain't going to let a hooker take a vacation." Martika said in a huff.

We all ate our food in silence. I had the rest of my food boxed up and paid the waiter for my order and Mea's.

"Ya'll ready to go get busy?"

"Let me go to the restroom," Harriet said.

"Martika was freshening up her makeup, "Sparkle you got any powder?"

"I can hook you up when we get to the house." I was not going to serve her in the restaurant. I had seen her take a blow in public like it was legal.

The gloved woman got up and took her plate, silverware, and glass to the counter where it was immediately removed and taken to the kitchen. She paid her check. Her clothes and necklace screamed expensive. She walked back to her table and left a tip before approaching our table, "Good evening girls."

"We looked at one another to see if anyone knew this woman. I said "Hello," and started to get up but she did not move.

"Can we help you? We were just leaving."

"Martika, Dear?"

Martika looked confused, "Do I know you?"

"Not exactly sweetheart, we have a mutual acquaintance. I have been listening to you talk about my husband. I don't like sharing, especially when the money that he is paying you belongs to me." The Gloved lady said.

People at the surrounding tables turned around to give their full attention to the scene that was unfolding.

"I don't know what the fuck you are talking about," Martika said.

I noticed that the woman had a cloth napkin covering her hand. Then I noticed her hand rising. By the time, I realized what was happening Martika's brains were splattered on the wall.

People were screaming and running out of the restaurant, the other two girls that were returning from the restroom ran out the back door.

"That should teach you to be more discriminate about whose husband you take up with." She dropped a roll of money on the table, "This should cover her funeral," she turned and walked out as cool as you please.

I was frozen. I could not believe that the woman had just walked up and blew this girls brains out.

I snapped out of my trance when I saw the owner picking up the phone. I heard a police siren, picked up the money, and got up from the table. I walked out the back door, the two girls followed me. We drove past the woman who was sitting around the corner in her Mercedes crying.

I didn't go back to the restaurant for months and when I did, I phoned in my order and had someone else pick it up for me.

When we got to the workhouse, we told Mea what happened. She called Cricket and he contacted Martika's man to give him the bad news.

I took a shower and changed clothes. I had to get good and coked up to focus on work. I kept seeing Martika's vacant eyes. The other two girls were so shaken up that Mea told them to go home.

I often had nightmares where the murder played over and over in my head but it was my vacant eyes instead of Martika's.

Alonzo

Alonzo called Butch and Cricket trying to get them to make me call him. Butch told him to come over to his apartment. Alonzo started whining about me working and after let him air his opinion Butch schooled him, "Boy women have been playing tricks from the beginning of time. My niece comes from a long line of hustlers. She got game in her, born and bred. Whatever hustle she is down with you can be sure she is going to come out on top. Why you tripping abut her taking money from motherfucka's who want to give it to her?"

"I want her to get back with me. I don't want my woman turning tricks. I love her." Alonzo said.

"I guess if you can make a call like that you must be planning to take care of her. That girl made nine grand in one week. Do you really think that she is going to turn that down? From what I understand, you ain't selling clothes. You working for Comfort who ain't fixing to pay you shit. You hot as a firecracker and got legal fee's to pay if you plan to stay out of jail. What can you do for my niece except take her down in your fallout?"

Cricket showed up. Butch filled him in, "This nigga tripping because he wants Kim to square up and be broke with him."

"Naw, he don't want her to square up, he wants to let Comfort pimp her just like he is pimping him. You need to wake up and smell the game that is being run on you young blood," Cricket said.

"I love Kim, why should she be laying down with other men? If a man loves his woman he ain't gone let her do no shit like that?" Alonzo said.

"Man you don't know what you talking about. You think I don't love Mea and Kalyn. Tried and true bitches that have been down with me for decades got all my heart."

"I'm not saying nothing against you that's how you get down. I can't roll like that," Alonzo said.

"Then you don't want to be with Kim, What you think? She ain't no different then the woman you met a few years ago. You fucked up, so you really can't be trying to call no shots. You need her more than she needs you, she already walked away from you once, don't make her sorry that she was there for you when you really needed someone. She is an unforgiving Leo when she feels betrayed." Cricket said.

"I can't be no pimp," Alonzo said.

"Nigga what do you think you was doing when you were with her and she was selling clothes and dope. You were living off that income she was bringing in. You said yourself you had never had a woman who hustled like her. When you got a woman who is down for her crown like Niecy you don't ask questions or think about what she is doing to get her money. You just keep her head straight by treating her right. Hell, her customers are paying her for her time, a motherfucker that just wants to get off don't pay two bills an hour. When she is with you she ain't getting paid so that must be where she wants to be," Cricket said

"You are her safe port after the storm. That shit you talking is why she ain't called you back. If you want to be in her life, you have to get your shit right and respect her for that money she is getting. Hell she took off of work because she was tripping about you calling her a ho. What makes you think you can judge her? Hell Comfort is pimping you like a ho?" Butch said.

"You are either going to jail or underground. You have got to fall of the radar. Who do you think is going to get you credentials to be able to do that? We are only talking to you because whatever happened to break you guys up wasn't the end. Niecy still cares about you. We are just trying to hip you to the facts. And make no mistake if you do anything to make her stop caring about you then we are going to cut you loose too," Cricket said.

"I just want to be with her like before," Alonzo said a tear falling from his eye.

"But things ain't gone never be like they were before. You broke her heart and she got in the business. She is hooked on making that paper and is damn good at it. You either need to get ready to accept her for who she is or move on," Cricket said.

They told him all about Comfort and the people he had used who were in jail behind him. He did nothing to help anyone but himself. They told him about how he tried to set up Mea. They also said that if he thought he had a chance of getting with Kim, he would not hesitate. He had already sent Quima after her.

Alonzo got back in the rental car that he had paid Christian to get for him. On the way, he passed by the workhouse and saw Kim's car out front. He parked and wrote her a note.

Dear Kim

Please call me because I am going crazy with out you. I know you still love me and I don't care what you are doing, I still love you

I will be waiting for you,

Love Alonzo

He put the note on her windshield and went back to Comforts.

Kim

I got home about two in the morning on Sunday. I was so ready to get in my bed. I made 15 grand that week hosting three parties and was worn out. I told everyone that I was taking off three days. I would have loved to sleep the day away but I had to go to my grandmother's. It was her birthday and the family had planned a special day.

On Tuesday, she and I were going fishing. I stopped at the Crenshaw swap meet and bought her a nice suit and a necklace. I put three thousand dollars in the pocket of the suit. I went by the drug store and bought paper, boxes and bows to wrap everything up.

When I got to the house, I had to park on the next block because so many cars were there. Everyone loved my Grandmother and they all wanted to make her day special.

After eating and talking, we cut the cake and my Grandmother opened all her gifts. It took her more than an hour to open them. I insisted that she try on her knew outfit that I had bought her. When she put her hand in the pocket and pulled out the money, she smiled.

I was talking to Bumpy about the house. He had a buyer. I would be moving out in a month. Mea was listening and told me that I could stay at the house with them in Balboa. They would be moving to Woodland Hills soon. My Grandmother was going to move with them and my aunt JoAnn was going to stay in this house.

Butch and Cricket had gone outside. They came in the house, Butch grabbed me by the arm, and they led me outside. Cricket opened the back door of his Rolls Royce, "Close your eyes, and get in."

"What is going on?"

"Just do what he said," Butch said putting his hands over my eyes.

"When I got in the car and opened my eyes Alonzo was sitting there with flowers and a box of candy."

"Hi."

"Hello."

"I remembered your Grandmothers birthday, I brought her a gift."

"You mean my Uncles didn't invite you?" I knew they had.

Alonzo looked out the window and turned back to me, "Maybe they did but I would have come anyway. I always liked your family."

He looked me in my eyes and took my hand. "Kim I miss you, I can't deal with being away from you anymore. This is torture. I don't care what you are doing. I love you."

"That's not what I heard. I don't want to be with someone who calls me a Ho."

"I was just shocked and angry that I had to find out the way I did. Plus when I get back to working, you can quit. You don't like doing it do you?"

"It's a job just like any other, do you get off when you sell a pair a shoes or a gram of dope. I deal with tricks, turn my body off, and use my mind to get paid and move on to the next job. I don't work much, most of the time I am hosting parties. I got a list of regulars that I don't have to sleep with to get mine. But I don't have to explain shit to you. You can't take care of me. You can't even take care of you. What do you plan to do with yourself? The way it looks you going to jail?"

"I gave Christian's lawyer a down payment. He can put the trial off for a while and in the meantime I'll get a job using a different name."

"I thought Comfort was supposed to be getting you a lawyer?"

"I don't know that I can depend on him. He didn't pay the people he got the dope from. If he don't come up with their money, well you know how cartel's work. I don't have to tell you."

"So is that why you want to get with me because you need papers?"

"You know better than that?"

We sat and talked for a while. I was not convinced that his heart was in the right place. "I guess you better go and give my Grandmother her gift. Everyone is getting ready to go home."

My Grandmother was happy to see Alonzo. She always liked him. She invited him to go fishing with us on Tuesday. I did not want Alonzo to go home with me because I felt that he had still not come to terms with what I was doing. I told him that I had something to do and I would see him on Tuesday.

"Hold on a minute, let's go somewhere and have a drink." I didn't say anything and when he turned around talking to my cousin, I went to my car and went home without saying good-bye to anyone.

Fishing was fun. We met at my Grandmother's and headed down to the canals where we caught tons of African perch. Afterwards we went to my grandmothers, cleaned, and fried up the fish.

My Grandmother was packing and preparing for the move to Crickets in the Valley where she cooked and cleaned and took care of the kids.

I went home and Alonzo followed me. I had a lot of drug customers to take care of. I weighed everything out and he rode with me on my drops. I had several people dealing for me since I was not always available.

Alonzo spent the night. I started packing up the storage boxes. I was going to let a friend who was moving into her first apartment have the furniture I didn't want. My bed was going to Cricket's.

Christian and Laisyv had an extra room I could use when I wanted to stay in town. I could always stay at my Grandmothers with Jo Ann when I wanted to.

Alonzo kept trying to convince me to stay with him at Comforts or to get an apartment together. I was really waiting to see if he was going to get himself out the situation he was in with the law.

I took Alonzo to get I. D. He was going to need it. Wednesday evening I had to go back to work. While I was getting dressed, the phone rang,

"Hey girl this is Shalei."

Shalei and I had been friends since Junior High School. We had not talked in a couple of years, hearing her voice felt really good.

"What's going on girl? How you doing? You know I went by that last place you had and they said you moved."

"I'm good, renting a house in Long Beach. I got your number from your Mother. I ran into her at the store."

"What have you been doing?"

"I been working and taking care of my daughter. You know my Mom died."

"No, I didn't know Tina died, what happened?"

"Cancer girl."

"Girl, I am so sorry to hear that. You know I loved Tina. She was one of my best customers. She always needed a new outfit for all the parties and dances she went to."

"Yeah, Mommy did like to party. I got that picture of her in that yellow dress you made for her on my mantel. What have you been up to?"

"Girl, I'll tell you that when I see you. What are you doing?"

"I ain't doing anything. What's up?"

"Give me an address, I'll come through."

She gave me the address. I called in to the agencies and let them know that I would be on at nine o' clock. I put some clothes in the car and rode to Long Beach to see my friend.

Shalei

Shalei and I had some good times hanging out together during High School and Junior College. We hung out with older guys. We brought all our friends to their parties. These men were always trying to hook up with younger girls and we were just the ones to take their money. There were about ten of us who hung out together all the time.

When I got to her house, Shalei broke out the yearbook. Boy did that bring back old times. I looked at the picture of me on the homecoming court. I remembered taking that picture. We had to go to Century City to take the picture in front of the fountain.

After taking the picture, some of us walked around the shopping center. We met an old drunk white man who liked young black girls. We were going to take him back to his room and rob him. A few minutes after we got in his room the house detectives opened the door and took us down to the security office. We called Deborah, a friend of ours who we said was out guardian to come and get us. I was so glad I did not have to call my parents.

Homecoming night was a trip too. My Father had made me a beautiful blue dress and jacket. It was halftime and we were in the middle of the field standing on the podium. The whole court was very impressive; the girls in their beautiful gowns and the guys who usually wore Khaki's and Levi's were doing their Tuxedos proud. My friend Sandra won homecoming Queen.

The court had to sit on the front of Cadillac's and ride around the track. It felt pretty good up there with everyone clapping and screaming for us, until...

Suddenly there were gunshots. There was an on-going feud between Compton and Dominguez High Schools. Every year they ended up shooting and ruining what should have been a great life long memory.

I slid off the car and ran for the fence. I jumped on the wire fence hitting it high enough that I could reach over and flip myself. Everyone said all they saw was blue dress fanning over the fence. No one got shot that night.

We laughed about the report cards that I stole working in the office at fifth period in high school. I took packages of cards and stamped them with the teachers duplicate stamps that were kept in the office and sold them.

Shalei and I drank peach wine while reminiscing. We replayed the events of our classmate's funerals. We talked about everyone who was locked up in jail. We talked about the long ride we had to take every morning to get downtown Los Angeles to our jobs at the Bank of America and how they ended up firing me after six months, Shalei worked there for two years.

One time we had hitchhiked all the way to the Kool Jazz Festival. Shalei, Adrienne, Shelia, Donna, Deborah, Michelle, and I hit every hotel party.
We found out where Shelai's boyfriend Roger was staying and went to his hotel. People were partying though out the halls. We walked into the suite and found Roger with some girl all over him. Shelai noticed that he was actually trying to stop the girl from sitting on his lap.

Shelai said, "I know that bitch. That's his old girlfriend Stella, she been trying to get with him every since him and his wife broke up."

"Handle your business girl. I'm down with you if anything jumps off."

Shelai cleared her throat and Roger jumped up knocking Stella to the floor.

"Hey baby, I'm so glad you are here," Roger said getting up and hugging her.

"I bet you are. What's going on?" Shelai was staring at Stella.

"Hey Shelai. How you doing girl? I was just playing around with Roger."

"Yeah, I see that, you need to stop," Shelai said.

I started giggling, Shelai looked at me, and I jumped in the air and said, "Snake." I walked away laughing.

We were busting our sides over that one as I poured some blow out on a card. I took a sniff and offered the package to Shelai.

"Naw girl, I can't. I got to work tomorrow and if I get started, I might not want to stop. It would be just my luck I go in and they decide to piss test me for drugs. I can't afford to come up dirty."

I put the pack away. I could see why Shelai quit. She had a good man, nice home, a beautiful baby, and a job she liked.

We talked about the party we had at my place in the Pendleton Apartments in South Gate. It was my first apartment. I was going to Compton College and had moved out of my parent's house to stay with my friend Donna and her family. I was dating an older guy named Chucky who I had met through Deborah.

I was getting a grant every month because my Father was a disabled veteran. The first year I kept my grades up but then in the second year I was tired of school. I went to Norwalk College for a while and took a class in Court Reporting. When they took me to sit in on a court case, I realized that this was the job for me. I was boring.

I was selling PCP, cocaine and weed supplied by Chucky. My grandmother had given me a couch, a dining room table, and a bed. My place was the hangout spot that summer. After school, everyone hung out at the pool in front of my door.

The second week that I was in my place I woke up to a man standing over me masturbating. I sensed and smelled him before I actually saw him. I pulled the gun I kept under my pillow, shot him in the kneecap, and ran outside where neighbors who had heard the gunshot were peaking out of their doors, "There is a man in my bedroom. I woke up and he was standing over me."
Three men dragged the intruder out of my place and held him until the police came and took him away. The cops didn't even ask about his gunshot wound.

I had a huge party. People were dancing all along the upstairs ledge and in the pool. Shelai and the girls had gotten together and we charged people five dollars to get in. We sold food, drinks, and dope.

Roger was in my bedroom rolling joints. Shelai and I had just walked into the apartment and Katrina told Shelai, "Girl you better go check on your man."

"What's up?" I asked."

"Just go check on your man," Katrina said in an irritated voice.

We cracked the door and peaked in. One of our friends from high school, Trixy was standing there with her bathing suit top off, "I know you want some, come on Roger let's do this."

"Roger was trying to get all his things off the bed. He would not even look at her. When he attempted to stand up Trixy stood in front of him with her hand down the front of her swimsuit bottom.

"Excuse me, I'm going back outside to my girl," Roger said.

Shelai threw the door open, "He said move, obviously he don't want none of you."

"Trixy you need to get your ass out of here," I said.

Trixy put herself together, turned her nose up, and left.

"Let me kick her ass Cous!" Katrina said.

"Girl don't even bother. Can't no broad take a man who don't want to be taken," Shelai said.

"We made a lot of money at that party." I laughed.

"I know, by the time we were going to have the next one you had moved. It was like you just fell off the planet."

"I know girl, sorry about that. I had some problems and needed to get ghost, I didn't want to cause any of my friend's problems. Trust me girl, the best thing I could have done at that time was to sky up.

Of course, Shelai had to bring up one of the most embarrassing times in my life. One Friday we were riding around in Shelai's red convertible mustang, we bought two bottles of peach wine and found ourselves in Hollywood. We were running out of wine and stopped at a store to pick up another bottle. Two Armenian guys were trying to talk us into going to their home in Beverly Hills.

One of them said, "I love your lips, I really love your lips," I opened my mouth to say "Thank You" and he stuck his finger in my mouth.

I looked down. I could not believe this man had put his nasty hand in my mouth. I knocked it out and turned to Shelai saying, "Let's go."

Shelai was laughing so hard that she had to hold on to a parking meter so she would not fall down. I was pissed and embarrassed. I walked off.

One day we were sitting in the Carolina West parking lot. The Carolina West was a club out by the airport that stayed open until the late morning hours. It was six in the morning and we were coming back from my sugar daddy Darrell's Penthouse where we had been partying and getting high all night.

A friend from school, Beaman saw us and came over. "What are you guys doing sitting out here? Why don't you come in?"

"We came to pick up my cousin. She said her date left her and she needed a ride home. We been waiting out here forever, can you go tell them to page her for me?"

"Yeah I can do that. What's her name? "Vaniga."

"Vaniga?"

"Yeah Vaniga Douchae' is her name."

"Alright, I'll tell them."

"We sat in the using our long fingernails to snort blow with our finger nails when we heard the loud speaker say, Vaniga Douche' your cousin is waiting for you outside. Vaniga Douche' your cousin is waiting for you outside. We laughed all the way to my parent's house.

The next time we saw Beaman he said, "I'm pissed with you guys. Why you do me like that? Had me paging Vinegar Douche. Everybody in that place was laughing at me."

My pager went off. It was almost 10.00 p.m. and I knew Shelai had to work in the morning. I used her phone and prepared to leave.

"I want to kiss the baby."

"Girl don't you wake that girl up."

"I won't, I just want to take another peek. She is so beautiful."

I looked at her beautiful little girl. She was one year old and the prettiest thing. At that moment, I was proud and a little bit envious of Shelai.

Would I ever the things that she did in my life.

Kim

Chucky and Deena

When I left Shelai's I was going to stop by my Mom's but kept going down Long Beach Boulevard. I passed by what used to be Chucky's store. Shelai told me that he had died in prison. Boy did that place bring back memories.

I was seventeen and had just graduated from High School when I met Chucky. He owned several liquor stores and a couple of grocery stores. He drove a Harley motorcycle on the weekends. We rode around to all the motorcycle clubhouses. He also took me on a run to Salton Sea. There were motorcycles in a long line roaring down the highway as far as the eye could see. The party lasted three days. We partied, fished, and slept in a camper.

During the week, Chucky drove a Cadillac Brougham that he let me use. . I was still living at my parent's house. One day he came to pick me up, my Mother looked at the forty-year-old man and stood behind the door shaking her head trying in an attempt to stop me from going out that door with him.

I drove Chucky's car home one day. My Father said, "Ain't enough leg in the world to pay for that car if you wreck it."

Chucky was eccentric, generous and a lot of fun. I had met him through Deborah. He was her sugar daddy while her husband Claude was in jail.

Chucky was also married. But his wife, Deena did not mind him having girlfriends. She even came and picked me up sometimes and took me shopping and to parties.

One day Deena picked me up in her Rolls Royce, took me to Rodeo drive, and picked out a really expensive dress and shoes for me before taking me to her mansion in Pasadena. The place was so big that you could be in there for a week and never run into anyone.

When I walked in, I saw a lot of people running around setting up for a party. I later found out that it was Chucky's going away party.

One of the living room walls was covered with a huge newspaper article; the front page had been blown up into wallpaper. Right in the center was a younger Chucky and a lot of other guys in handcuffs posing for the picture. The headline said "Biggest Drug Bust in the History of Long Beach. I read the article. It seemed that Chucky was bringing shipments of China White when he and his crew were busted.

I spent the last few weeks before his incarnation with Deena and Chucky going to beautiful clubs and fantastic restaurants where I ate things I could not even pronounce.

A few weeks after the party Chucky went to jail, he was in a Colorado prison for a year. I wrote to him once a week and talked to him over the phone.
His letters were followed by Chicago money orders that Deena sent me. He said I should not want for anything. Deena bought a house close to the prison so could visit him. From time to time, she came back to California and picked me up to stay with her in the mansion.

Upon his release, Chucky and Deena came to get me. We drove to the airport and flew to San Francisco for lunch. I had never been on a plane before. Needless to say, I was impressed.

Deena and I shopped and hung out on the pier while Chucky took care of his business. That same night we flew back to Los Angeles. I got so drunk and high that I passed out. I spent two weeks with them at the mansion.

Chucky and Deena were not demanding as far as sex went. Chucky had been speed balling (injecting coke and heroin) for so long that he couldn't really get an erection.

Of course, Chucky had ideas of how he was going to make money off of me. When he and Deena had first gotten together he was a pimp and one of her clients introduced him to the drug game. Chucky quickly moved to the top rung in the drug game. He was making so much money that Deena quit and after twenty years together he married her.

My parents did not like me staying away for days at a time and they did not like me to come in late. They told me if I could not be home by two in the morning, I should just stay out. I had moved in with a friend but when her brother tried to rape me, I called Chucky. He came, got my things and me, and took me back to the mansion.

I told Chucky, I have to get back to Compton so I can go to school. Classes are starting in a couple of weeks."

"Where are you going to stay?"

"I guess I'll go back to my parent's house."

"Why don't you get your own place?" Chucky asked

"Because I can't afford it."

The next day we got in the Rolls and Chucky and Deena rode to an area that I had never been to in South Gate. Chucky went inside and after a few minutes he came out and got in the car.

A man came out of the office and got into a golf cart. We followed him. Deena was grinning from ear to ear. We pulled into an apartment complex and got out. The man gave Chucky some keys and he walked to a door in the building. He turned and handed me the keys, "Open your door."

"What?"

"Open the door to your apartment," Deena said.

I was so happy I screamed. I moved in the next day. The rent was paid for six months. The next week Chucky gave me a Toyota. I was concentrating on College and selling dope for Chucky. My friends were into weed, PCP, and cocaine.

I had met Chucky at his store so we could go out to dinner one day. We got into the car that was kept in the garage connected to the back of the store. He hit the remote that controlled the door. He was backing out when suddenly his door flew open and someone jerked him out of the car.

Before I knew, what was going on two men had Chucky in front of the car beating him. I saw one of the men pull a knife out of his pocket. I could not sit there and let them kill him. I reached into the glove compartment and got Chucky's gun.

Just as the man who was holding Chucky by his hair prepared to cut his throat I shot him. The look on his face was one I will never forget. He looked down at his chest, then up at me, and said one word, "Shit," before he fell down on his face. There was a gaping hole in his back. The other man ran away.

I looked at Chucky who was covered in blood. Some guys came running out of the store and helped Chucky up. "Get rid of him and clean this up," Chucky shouted.

Chucky was having difficulty walking. He grabbed my arm and took the gun that I was still holding straight out in front of me. I was not aiming at anything; my arm just would not go down. He pushed me into the passenger seat before getting behind the wheel.

He drove to one of his Compton houses and led me inside. I felt like I was sleep walking. He sat me on the couch. I think I was in shock. The look on the man's face kept running through my mind.

Chucky sat next to me after he took off his clothes and wiped away some of the blood. He had a towel wrapped around his waist. He was covered in purple and blue bruises and had a cut on his forehead.

He took my hand, "You saved my life Kim. You did the right thing. When they finished me off they would have killed you too."

"When I did not say anything he shook me, "Baby, are you alright?"

I turned and looked at him, "I killed him huh?"

"Yeah, but that is a good thing, trust me."

"Who was he Chucky?"

"He was someone I had a little problem with. You know how it is in this business; a person is bound to pick up a few enemies. You don't have anything to worry about."

"They were trying to kill you and I killed a man, now I'm going to jail. How can you say don't worry about it?"

"Kim you are not going anywhere. People get killed in Compton everyday, no one gives a damn. They are going to dump the body in the Canal and no one is going to think twice about him."

"So I'm not going to jail?"

"You are not going to jail," he stood up and poured me a snifter of cognac. Here drink this, you're still shaking."

I took a sip and put the glass on the coffee table. He hugged me. "I love you, Baby."

"That's just because I saved your ass," I joked.

I went into the bathroom and found peroxide and bandages to tend to his forehead. I ran him a bath and put in Epsom salt so he could soak his bruises. When he got into the tub, I handed him his drink.

"The safe is behind the picture in the bedroom, 11-15-22 is the combination. Get us some blow."

I got the safe open and could not believe my eyes. It was packed with stacks of bills. I picked one up and looked at it. It was all hundreds. I did not know if having the combination to this safe was a good thing. If someone were to rob him, he would suspect me. I took out a half-ounce bag of dope and returned to the bathroom.

"Go and get me the baby jar and baking soda out of the kitchen. While you are in there put a pot of water on the stove to boil. I brought him everything he asked for. He did his mixing, poured it into the bottle with hot water from the tap, and gave it to me. "When that turns solid put it in the hot water until it melts."

"I'm hungry can we order pizza?"

"Sure baby."

I took the jar into the kitchen and turned off the stove. He could fix the dope when he got out of the tub. I did not want to mess up anything. I placed the order for pizza, salad, and sodas. He always ate pizza when he was to busy to go out at the store. He only trusted one guy to handle and deliver his order. I called Jess at Chico's and placed the order.

I turned on the television to the news. I did not see anything about a murder. Maybe Chucky was right, no one did care about the man who I shot because there was nothing on the news. I guess the whole ordeal took a toll on me because when I felt stressed I always wanted to sleep.

When I woke, Chucky was opening the door with a gun in his hand. I was alarmed until I saw Jess holding the pizza.

"You were sleeping hard girl, come on lets eat." Chucky said.

I washed my face, opened one of the new toothbrushes in the medicine cabinet, and brushed my teeth. Chucky talked while we ate, "You know an old gangster told me that you never know when a woman is truly yours until she kills someone for you."

"You believe that?"

He looked at me with a thoughtful look on his face, "Yeah, I do now."

After we ate, he rocked up the cocaine. He had kicked his speedballing habit while he was in jail.

. "Take off your clothes."

We had sex and for the first time since I had been with him, he actually got hard. Every other time he was flaccid, frustrated and never got off.

"That's another thing that the old player told me. When a woman saves your life it makes your dick get hard."

"Maybe it's because you are not slamming dope into your arm anymore?"

It was a great two years with Chucky. I had my own place, could do whatever I wanted and always had money from selling drugs to everyone in the Pendleton Apartments.

Chucky was getting crazy and paranoid. He would pick me up and drive around for hours before going home swearing that someone was following him.

"Why would you pick me up if you think someone is following you?"

One day we were meeting Deena and some other girls at a dinner club. I was wearing a white oriental dress and silver sandals. When we walked up to the table one of the girls looked up and said, "Who is this Bitch, ain't he got enough pussy around this table already? He got to bring another Ho up in here?"

She must have been new because Chucky did not allow his women to play these games. His wife was the only one who could say something about Chucky's activities and she rarely did. The girl kept making flippant remarks and looking at me sideways. She said she had to go to the restroom. When she came back, she stood over me and said, "Move Bitch I want to sit next to my man."

Deena looked at Chucky and said, "I told you she was going to be trouble and that I don't like her. Handle your headache."

Chucky looked at the girl, "Go back to your chair, sit down and shut up."

"What, this Bitch supposed to be something special. You can't just treat me any kind of way Chucky."

"What did I just tell you?" Chucky said his eyes clouding over.

We were in a very nice Wilshire restaurant and the white people were staring at the scene.

"I ain't a dog that you can tell to sit and roll over and play dead nigga," she responded.

Chucky stood up and I guess she must have seen something in his eyes because she turned and stomped to her seat and flounced down.

The waitress came and I ordered a red fruity alcoholic drink. The waitress asked me how old I was. I told her I was twenty-one.

"Can you prove that?"

"That little baby Bitch ain't no twenty one," My new rival said.

I pulled out my fake I.D. that Chucky had gotten me and handed it to the waitress. I stared square in this broad's eye. "Leave me the fuck alone."

She was about two minutes away from getting her ass kicked. If Chucky did not do it, I would.

Chucky called the waitress over and whispered something in her ear. "Right away sir," the waitress went to the reception desk and picked up the phone.

When the waitress brought my drink, she brought refills for the other ladies, everyone except my nemesis.

"Where the hell is my drink at?"

The waitress looked at Chucky and he shook his head, indicating that she should not go and get her one. The waitress tipped away.

The broad had the nerve to say something foul and throw a roll at me knocking my drink into my lap. I started to get up but Chucky pulled me back down into my chair. He grabbed the girl by her hair and led her outside where a cab was pulling up. He opened the back door of the cab punched her in the face and threw her inside. He walked back into the restaurant and sat down. He looked at me, "You alright?"

"Yeah, just a little wet and my new dress is ruined."

"Naw you're not alright, but you would never say so. That's why I love you." He leaned over and kissed me. "Deena, take her across the street to that store and get her something to wear."

The salesgirl was about to lock the door, but Deena flashed some money and asked to speak to the manager. I got a really nice pants suit. When we came back, I took my seat and the waitress brought me a plate with two huge lobster tails. Chucky knew that lobster was my favorite.

Weeks later Chucky's behavior had deteriorated even more. He was acting really crazy, and was back to shooting up dope along with constantly smoking. He always felt like someone was watching him and sometimes when I was around him I had a feeling I was being watched too. I even started writing down license plate numbers and checking them when a car looked too familiar. The numbers started matching the ones on my pad.

"Chucky you got heat on you. I think you should slow down for awhile."

"Bitch, what do you know? You can't tell me what to do."

I calmed him down and showed him the license numbers I had on the pad and pointed out the cars that were tailing us.

Later that day Chucky stopped Deena, who was on her way out the door to make a delivery. I am going to follow baby girl's instincts and cool out for awhile."

Later that day he changed his mind and told Deena to make the delivery.

She said, "No."

The look that he flashed at her was a warning that he was getting mad.

Deena said, "I don't give a fuck if you are mad. I ain't catching a case for you. Make your own damn delivery."

When he left to go make the delivery himself she talked to me, "Kim if you got any sense you will get out from under Chucky now, he is about to go crazy. This is how he acted before he got busted before and before he got shot. You already know that someone is trying to kill him. If you are with him when they try, again they are going to kill you too. If he is under investigation you are will wind up in jail right along with him."

"Why are you still here?"

"I'm not here for long. I am about to get a divorce and take off with Tooth sweet. He has made more money than he can spend in twenty lifetimes and he is getting out of the game, he loves me. Chucky has more money than he needs but he is going to end up spending it all on lawyers again."

"Why do you think he is just going to let you walk away and with his friend? Girl you might want to rethink this?"

"He really doesn't have a choice. I know too much for him to go South on me."

"I hope you are right."

Two weeks later, I visited Deena in the hospital. She was in traction, Chucky had beaten her. He had beat her bad and they did not know how long it would be before she would be out of her full body cast, or if she would ever walk again.

She told me that Tooth sweet was dead. She knew Chucky had killed him. When she said his body was found in the Canal, I knew that Chucky had done it too.

I always had a lot of company at my apartment. Most of my friends were still in Community College and lived at home with their parents. They could get high at my place and be comfortable. That was why I had steady clientele. Every few months my friends and I gave a big party at my place.

At the last party Chucky showed up drunk. He walked into the house and I was kissing a friend who had just arrived, nothing special or intimate just a peck. Chucky had seen me kiss people a hundred times before and it never bothered him.

Suddenly Chucky pulled out his gun and started hitting the boy upside the head. Then he went outside and started firing the gun in the air. Everyone ran. He pulled some money out of his pocket, stuffed it in the guys pocket, and helped him up, "Get the fuck out of here. Go get stitched up, nothing personal."

I pictured myself in the hospital looking like Deena. If I ran, he would shoot me. I sat on the couch and snorted two big lines of coke, downed a glass of vodka and lit a joint. I figured if I was good and high I would not feel the pain when he hit me.

After the theatrics Chucky sat down on the couch put his arm around me and kissed me long and hard. He looked into my eyes. I know he must have seen my fear. He laughed, "I love you, and I just felt like spending some time alone with you, nothing for you to be concerned about. I'm not mad at you." Then he wobbled into the bedroom and passed out.

I wanted out. I could not deal with Chucky anymore. His psychotic episodes had come to be too much for me. I did not want to be a part of his little family anymore. Enough was enough.

I was tired of trying to predict his eccentric moods. I found another place to live way on the other side of town. I started moving things out that Chucky wouldn't notice. I bought new furniture and started decorating my new place.

It took me two weeks to get up the courage to tell Chucky I was leaving him. I convinced myself that he would not trip because I was not his wife. He could find a hundred of me any day of the week. Lately I had been feeling like a showpiece, no more significant than the rope chain and eagle he wore around his neck. Something to be picked up and worn when it was convenient and when it wasn't, left sitting wherever until he was ready to wear me again. He had other women. No biggee.

I went to Chucky's store on Long Beach Boulevard and waited for him. When he came in, he was with another girl. This didn't bother me at all, matter of fact I was hoping it would make things easier.

I smiled politely when he introduced me to the girl. "Chucky can I speak to you for a minute?"

He told the girl to go out in the store and get him some ice and cognac.

I handed him the keys to the apartment. "I want to be on my own."

He pulled me into his lap and put the keys back in my hand. He grabbed a fistful of my hair and kissed me hard. "I will be coming to the apartment in a couple of hours, you better be there."

I got up to leave, and he stopped me. "What is your problem?"

"Chucky I still care about you, but this is not the life for me. I want to focus on getting a degree and live a normal life. I don't want to end up in jail or have my throat cut. I have a feeling that if I don't get out now, that's what will happen to me. Plus you got other women you don't need me."

"Are you getting jealous on me?"

"Chucky you would never be happy with just one woman. One day I want a normal relationship and some kids."

"What if we got married?"

"Chucky I am not ready to get married."

I tried to explain how sometimes I felt uncomfortable around him.

"I have never put a hand on you. Hell you never gave me a reason to. Kim you understand me, I can relax when I'm with you. You need more money or something?"

"No, I can take care of myself. I got some money saved up."

"He kept arguing and I saw that his blessings were not forthcoming. The girl walked in with his drink.

"I'll see you Chucky," I said and walked out to the car.

I knew that I was not going to be at the apartment later. I went by my cousin's chop shop and got new license plates for the car.

I went to my new apartment. I was trying to figure out if I should just go buy a new car and leave this one at one of

Chucky's' stores. I did not want him to think that I had taken something from him.

I did not have to think long. I opened my door the next morning and there was a note on the door,

Kim

I know where you live. You moved without my permission. Do not leave this house for any reason. I will be by this afternoon. Do not leave or you will be sorry. Love, Your Daddy, Chucky."

I stared at it for a long time.

I was stunned. How the fuck did, he find me so fast. I had moved to the other side of town. I was going to a different school and the apartment was under another name. I had given a junky some blow to rent it for me.

I was not stupid enough to sit and wait. I called Cricket. He told me to meet him in Hollywood. I packed a few things and put them in the car. I decided to go back in and get my stash of drugs just in case.

I got out of the car and as I ran back inside, I slammed the car door. BOOM the car exploded, the force sent me flying forward onto my face. I could not get up. I just sat and watched the car burn. I was scared to go back into the apartment. I walked to the hamburger stand on the corner and phoned my Uncle.

I realized that there were not many people on this earth as crazy as Chucky but there were a few, they were in my family.

About 45 minutes later, my Uncles pulled up to the hamburger stand, where I sat waiting. There were six cars, two of my Uncles and two of my gangbanging cousins in their low-riders with their friends. There was a truck following them.

We went to my apartment and moved all my furniture while some of my cousin's friends stood guard with guns just hoping they would have a reason to shoot someone. My cousin had made some calls. I gave then the address to one of Chucky's storage warehouses where they kept liquor and dope. I also knew the code to get in because Chucky had sent me there several times to retrieve things for him.

After they put my furniture in my grandmother's garage they used the truck to rob the warehouse, then they set it on fire.

I called a friend who lived down the street from the warehouse. "Girl guess what, Chucky's warehouse is on fire," I could hear sirens in the background.

"Damn, what happened?"

"All I know is that somebody said they saw some guys leaving and then bang the place went up like a firecracker. He must have pissed somebody off."

"Girl you know Chucky, he probably crossed the wrong person. I'll call you later."

Cricket told me to dial Chucky's number. I called him at the Long Beach store. When he got on the phone, I handed it to Cricket.

"Is a fire for a fire enough? Or will this be going any further? Kim is not going to be with you and that is all there is to it."

He listened for a minute.

I'm glad to hear it," Cricket hung up the phone.

That was the last time I heard anything from Chucky. Now he was dead. I wondered how he died, but then again I didn't want to know.

Kim

Dealing

I was working my butt off. Sherry and I had put ads in the Hollywood Star newspaper. We hired someone to answer the calls and dispatch the girls. I was working at Mea's and selling dope, brokering fake I.D's and sewing.

I had started taking off Monday and Tuesdays. I had moved out to Cricket's and kept clothes at Christians and Sherry's where I stayed on the first and fifteenth which was my busiest time for drug sales.

I was introduced to a guy named Ron by a girl whom I had been friends with since elementary school. Jackie and I had always gotten into trouble together. When we arrived at Ron's apartment, my pimp radar went off. I was very careful about what I said to Ron.

We were getting high, Ron ran out of dope, and I offered to sell him some. Ron would soon become a regular customer. I went out there with Sherry to deliver one day and the guy that I had a problem with at Butch's party was sitting there with three other guys.

"Girl you are so fine. I liked you the first time I saw you." Kenyatta said.

"Why are you thinking about me, I'm not getting with no pimp?"

"Yeah, I know all that. But I just want to kick it with you one time so I can stop thinking about you."

"I can't help you with that." I looked at Sherry, "I'll be right back, and we can leave after I handle this business."

Kenyatta hemmed me up in the hall and tried to press himself against me. I pushed him away. "Just let me see you naked," he said pulling out his penis."

I knocked on the door where I knew Ron was. "Ron can we take care of this business so I can get out of here?"

The door opened. "Yeah let me get an eight ball." Ron looked over my shoulder and saw Kenyatta standing there with his dick in his hand, "Something wrong?"

"Yeah, your friend won't back off."

I pulled out the package. I put a dollar bill on his triple beam scale to check the accuracy, adjusted it, and poured the dope onto the plate. Ron came back in followed by my friends.

He started talking to the new girl we had brought with us. Sherry had pulled this girl in to work for our agency. I did not know her or trust her. I had a feeling that she was underage.

"I'm gone need you to rock this up for me."

I went in the kitchen to get the supplies I would need. Kenyatta blocked my way. "You need to move." He followed me into the crowded room. I went back out to the kitchen to finish rocking the dope. He followed me.

"I just want to get to know you, what if we go to a movie or something?"

"Kenyatta you are a pimp, I don't get out of pocket with pimps. I am not going to pay; therefore I am of no use to you."

"Sometimes a man just wants someone that he can have a little fun with," He moved closer, "You know what I mean?"

"Yeah I know what you mean, but I ain't no party girl."

I walked past him and went to give Ron his product and collect my money. Kenyatta sat down next to me and put his hand on my leg. I rolled my eyes and stood up, "Ron I'm leaving. Hit me up if you need anything else."

Sherry stood up. Ron whispered in the new girl's ear and held the pipe up to her mouth. She took the hit and leaned back.

I new this girl was not going to be able to work for me. She put dope before business. I looked at Sherry and saw that she was thinking the same thing.

One of the other guys wanted to buy a gram. I weighed it out for him and collected my money. I looked at the girl. "You coming or staying here?"

She got up and followed me into the hallway. "He asked me to stay. He said he would pay for my time."

I warned her, "Be careful. You do know you are dealing with pimps. You need to get your money up front and you are going to have to give me a cut. Matter of fact, you need to go get my money now and give me my percentage. "

I knew that before the night was over she would be someone's girl and they would never pay me.

Ron walked out and gave me eighty dollars.

"Why didn't you tell me that Butch and Cricket are your Uncles?" Ron asked.

"What difference does it make? Is it a problem?" I said defensively. I new that Kenyatta had told him who I was.

"Ain't no thang."

The next morning I was asleep at Christians. I had only been asleep about three hours when my pager went off. It was Cricket's number followed by 911. I called him back. I was not prepared to hear him yelling at me, "What the fuck you doing getting out of pocket with Ron and Kenyatta?"

"What are you talking about Cricket?" I sat up in an attempt to clear the sleep from my brain.

"You and your friends were over at Ron's freaking for dope last night. Every player in town knows about it."

"I don't know what they know cause I ain't did shit but get paid. But since you are questioning me about some rumors hold on a second.

I clicked over so that I could three-way Ron into this conversation. "Ron, somebody told my Uncle that I was over there freaking, what's up with that?"

"I don't know who would have said some shit like that. You didn't do nothing. Now this other freak is a whole nuther story," Ron laughed.

"She still there?" I asked.

"Yeah, she's here. She's home now, Bitch done chose."

"I don't give a damn about that, congratulations on coming up with her. We got ourselves another problem. You need to tell my Uncle that I was not up in your house sexing nobody."

"You can have him call me," Ron said.

"Man, I'm on the line," Cricket said.

"What's going on Cricket? How's the life treating you?" Ron said his voice animated.

"Looks like you got the best hand playa. Yeah man, I had to get down on my Niece cause Donatello been in the after hours saying that she was at your spot getting out of pocket. What's really going on, nigga. I know you gone tell me the gospel?"

"Man your niece is about her business. She come up in here and broke everybody. I know I spent eight hundred with her. You know it was some playa's up in here trying to get at her but she was straight up down for her crown, told them she was not looking to pay nobody and she just needed to handle hers and get up and out."

"So Donatello was lying?"

"He was just salty 'cause she wasn't trying to hear his rap, Nigga even offered to trick with her but she shut him down. That crazy ass Kenyatta was sweating her so tough that the best thing she could do was leave and that's exactly what she did. When I had to call her back, she didn't even want to come up because he was still here. I didn't know she was your family. Kenyatta sat up in here blitzed talking about her all night. Naw man your niece didn't do anything that could be considered out of pocket."

"Alright dude. Thanks for clearing that up, I'll see you in traffic."

I disconnected Ron, "Well, what you got to say now?"

"Aw'ight, Aw'ight, I should have known you know the rules. But you know I had to check it out."

"Yeah, alright but next time ask me before you start hollering, I didn't know what was going on."

"Why you didn't bring that broad around me if the Bitch was looking to choose."

"I took her over there to see how she would handle herself. I didn't like what I saw. I don't think she chose Ron, she chose the dope."

"Oh, one of them kind."

"Yeah, you know I ain't gone bring nobody around that I don't know."

My pager went off, it was Ron. "I'll talk to you later Unc, got to go serve Ron again. He done already spent 1200 since yesterday. I guess the party ain't over."

"Handle your business."

"Alright, love you."

"Love you too, Oh and niecy?"

"Yeah,"

"I'm proud of you."

It felt good to hear him say that.

I called Ron and got up to put a package together. I had to wake up Christian because I had sold out. My pager went off again, it was Alonzo. We talked for a minute. I told him that I had to ride out to The Valley. I asked if he wanted to ride with me.

I picked him up on my way to Ron's. This time I went upstairs and took him with me. When we got off the elevator, you could smell cocaine and weed wafting down the hall. I knocked on the door, Kenyatta opened it. He was not wearing a shirt. "She's here," he hollered out while rubbing on the front of his pants."

He did not see Alonzo standing to the side of the door. He turned around and disappeared into the hall leaving the front door open. Alonzo stood by the bar talking to two men he knew from the after hours.

Kenyatta walked back in and handed me some money, "Come on we can go in the bathroom and you can give me that package."

"Alonzo can you go in the bathroom with him and give him his package."

I had told Alonzo about what happened with Kenyatta and how uncomfortable I was around him. That is why he had the dope in his pocket. He looked at me like I had lost my mind, "I ain't going in the bathroom with no nigga, and here you go pardna. Who dis, ain't I seen you up in the after hours?"

"Yeah I hang out sometime."

"You that booster ain't you?"

"Man I bought some of your clothes. You had em in the trunk of your car. What you doing with bbbaby?" Kenyatta had developed a cocaine stutter and was sweating profusely.

"He's my man," I said sensing that Alonzo did not know what he should say.

"Say what, that's why you wouldn't give a nigga no play. Man you got a money maker there." He put his hand out for some skin and Alonzo responded.

Ron and the girl walked out. They were both high as a kite. Ron knew Alonzo. They spoke; Ron kept looking at me like he was expecting me to do something.

"What's up?" I asked

"My thang I ordered? I know you didn't come to visit."

"Kenyatta has your package."

"No he don't. That must be his pack 'cause this is my money right here?"

"Ain't no thang, let me run down stairs."

"I'll go get it," Alonzo said.

"So what you doing with that square motherfucka?" Kenyatta said as soon as he thought Alonzo was out of earshot.

"She's with me because she wants to be." Alonzo said. He had come back in to get my keys and overheard Kenyatta ragging on him.

"Man you don't know what to do with this. You need to let a real pimp take care of honey."

"Fuck you and step off my woman."

"I'll get it myself," I did not want to be alone with this asshole.

I came back, took Ron's money, and gave him his package.

He invited Alonzo and me into the bedroom. He loaded the pipe and gave it to Alonzo. Alonzo took a hit. After a few minutes, he started looking very nervous. He had never acted this way when we got high before. I declined the pipe and touched Alonzo's hand, "You ready to go?"

"Hold up, let me finish my drink."

His drink was in the living room. "Let me go and get it for you then," I said sarcastically.

"You can't leave yet, I need you to rock up this package for me," Ron said.

I took the dope and went in the kitchen. Kenyatta came in and gave me his dope, "I need you to cook this for me too." He was standing way too close.

"I charge extra for that. Can you back up off me?"

"I got you, what you doing with that lame? You need to get rid of that zero and get with a hero."

I did not acknowledge his last statement. He walked away and went back in the room where Alonzo was getting high. "Man let me hit that?" he said looking at Alonzo.

"Shit ain't mine, this is Ron's party."

"I ain't talking about the dope."

"If you ain't talking about the dope, then what the hell are you talking about?"

"I'm talking about your woman."

"Nigga, you saying you want to trick with my woman?"

"Yeah, I know you ain't gone turn down no money."

"Man, she don't get down like that."

"Man, I'm gone give you two hundred dollars, my money is green."

I walked in and overheard the last statement. I reached in my pocket and turned my pager off and on so that it would beep. "Alonzo I have to go. Now."

Alonzo got up and we walked into the living room.

"Where you got to go?"

"I want to leave. I have handled my business. Ain't no reason for me to stay here, I don't hang out with pimps."

"You ain't got to trip. They know I'm your man."

"I'm leaving, are you coming with me?"

"I guess so."

I was not happy. I felt like he wanted to stay and get high. I also did not like the way he was acting like a paranoid junkie. I called Ron to come and lock the door.

"Why does every pimp want to sleep with you?" he said walking behind me to the elevator.

"That ain't nuthin but game, a way to pull a woman out of pocket. Alonzo I don't date black men. And if I did, I would not date pimps. They think that you are going to fall in love with their dick and get with them."

"He wanted to pay you."

"What are you saying? Why are you telling me this?"

"I was just telling you what the man told me."

We got in the car, I was really tired. I wanted to go to sleep. When we got back to Comforts, I pulled up and waited for him to get out.

"Why don't you come in?"

"I'm tired Alonzo, I got to get some sleep."

"Come and sleep with me. Ain't nobody home?"

It would be nice to sleep with him curled up against me. I went in took a shower and climbed into the bed.

"Before you go to sleep can you rock this up for me," he said handing me a package.

I did not want to do it, but I did. I took one hit, got into the bed, smoked a joint, and fell asleep. Every now and then, I would hear the bedroom door open. Alonzo was going through the house in the grips of his paranoia. I did not trust paranoid people. I had people pull guns on me and trip out when they got that way.

When Alonzo came back in, I asked him, "What's wrong with you?"

"What do you mean?" he could not speak clearly.

Alonzo you know how people get paranoid and trip out sometimes? The way you are tripping is making me uncomfortable. I'm going home."

"Naw baby, don't do that. I'll just lay down next to you. Everything is all right. Sometimes being in this house makes me trip."

"Well if it makes you trip and you live here, how am I suppose to be comfortable?"

"I see what you mean. Come on lets just get some sleep."

He got in the bed with me and pulled me to him. I fell back to sleep. When I woke six hours later, he was at it again. I got up, went into the bathroom, and used a towel to brush my teeth. I was hungry. "You want to go get something to eat."

"Naw, not really, why don't we order some Chinese."

"Naw, I'll just pick something up on my way to work."

"You leaving?"

"Yep, got to go get that paper."

"So how's tricks?" he said with a strange look on his face."

I looked at him, "Alonzo tricks are just that, tricks. It's not something I want to discuss with you."

"Well if you are going to be telling people that I am your man, maybe we should talk about this."

"If it is going to be a problem then I won't do it again. I just felt uncomfortable in there with Kenyatta."

"Didn't he trip out on you and Sherry at the Candy Store that night I met you."

"Yeah, that was him."

"That man is obsessed with you."

"That's his problem."

"So you are just going to be an outlaw."

"What?" I didn't like the way this conversation was going. I got up and started putting my clothes on.

"You're not going to answer me huh?"

"I got to go Alonzo. I'll call you tomorrow."

Tomorrow came and went; actually, two weeks came and went before I talked to Alonzo again.

I found out that he was serving Ron. He had gotten Ron's number from Comfort and went over there with a package. All it took was one hit to get Ron on a roll. I felt like he was stealing from me. I discussed it with Christian.

"Don't take him around anymore of your customers," Christian and Laisyv said.

"No shit," I replied.

Kim

The Valley

I moved out of the house and got my cousins to load up my furniture and take it out to Cricket's. He would be moving soon to another place in Woodland Hills. So I put most of my things in the garage so that I would not have to do this twice.

I liked the San Fernando Valley it had a different feel to it. I liked waking up every morning and taking a swim in the huge pool in the back yard. I spent a lot of time helping pack up the house and though I was only there a few weeks, I was going to miss it. The new place did not have a swimming pool.

Mea and I spent days at a time working and when I was off I stayed at Laisyv's, mostly sleeping. When I got a little time I hung out with Sherry and visited my parents.

I took care of my dealers twice a week and things were going pretty smooth. I talked to Alonzo on the phone but had not seen him in person in three weeks. I was at Laisyv's asleep and when I woke, he was sitting in a chair looking at me.

"What are you doing?"

"I was hanging out with Christian and he told me you were here. I wanted to see you but didn't want to wake you up."

"Okay."

"You hungry? Want to go get something to eat?"

"Sure, I'll get dressed, give me a minute."

I would have rather gone back to sleep, but I showered and dressed.

We went to The Sizzler and while we waited for our orders Alonzo asked, "Are you avoiding me?"

"I have mixed feelings about you. You aren't the guy I was with a year ago. I figure you need time to get yourself together."

"I can't get myself together without you."

"Why is that? I got you some I.D. What else you need?"

"I want us to be together. Like before."

"You don't have your own place, you are not working, not for yourself anyway, and I don't have a lot of spare time."

"You act like you enjoy turning tricks."

"I do, I like the money and the game."

"What if I want to be with you everyday? Live with you."

"You can't afford a place, how is that going to happen?"

"You can."

"So what you are saying is that I am supposed to take care of you?"

Alonzo was thinking that she owed it to him. In his mind all, the bullshit Comfort had told him made sense.

Alonzo the week before...

Comfort had come home from the afterhours and called Alonzo downstairs at four in the morning.

"What's going on? Alonzo asked.

"I just came from the afterhours every body is talking about you and your woman."

"What do you mean?"

"All that shit that went down at Ron's. Kenyatta said that he even offered to pay her two hundred and you turned it down."

"Kim don't date black men, and she sure doesn't date pimps."

"I know another thing she sure don't do, she don't pay you. She got everybody thinking that you are her man when actually the Bitch is an outlaw. You getting punked nigga and if you ain't gone step up and pimp like a man then I am going to step in and charge The Ho."

"She is just hustling a little bit, she ain't no Ho."

"Man you better open your eyes and get your money."

"I don't fuck with her about what she is doing. Her Uncles told me that is the fastest way to run her off."

"Off course they are going to tell you that shit because they are her Uncles. Cricket and Butch know that they are going against the game letting her turn tricks and she ain't paying no man. I wouldn't give a fuck if it was my own damn daughter, if a Bitch is up in this game she needs to be paying. You letting her make a sucker out of you. I didn't tell them pimps at the club that you were just fronting, but you don't get your shit together and I will let them know that you perpetrating."

"What I'm supposed to do, take fifty percent of her money or something."

"Nigga, what the fuck you talking about? A pimp gets 100 percent of everything. If you her man when she is selling pussy, time or dope that is yours. All of it."

She did tell people that he was her man that night. What did she think he was stupid or something?

Back at the Sizzler...

"What's wrong with you taking care of us? You know I love you and I am behind you 100 percent."

What's wrong is that I don't want or need a pimp. I know this game. I grew up watching my Uncles pimp women and when those women could not make them money anymore they were turned out with nothing. I don't want a man who doesn't have anything to bring to the table. Our relationship worked before because you were working and hustling just like me. We took care of each other. We were both making money."

"Hell, I can sell the dope. You can't just use my name and not be with me."

"Alonzo unless you get that case taken care of you ain't even gone be with you. You are going to be in jail. I ain't fixing to work my ass off and pay your attorney fees. You got to do that for yourself. And as far as using your name, you volunteered to do that shit. Don't think I don't know that you were serving Ron. He called me last week because he said that instead of you dropping the dope off and leaving, you hang around smoking and tripping. That ain't how business is done. You are more interested in getting high then getting money."

"Hell the nigga would call me back every few hours, so I just stayed to sell him more."

"You don't see anything wrong with you back-dooring me on a customer?"

"Girl ain't no exclusive dope customers."

"Yeah okay, I won't be taking you around any more of my people so you can go back to them and sell Comforts dope."

"I could sell yours."

"No you can't. That is my business. You are hotter than a firecracker right now. I don't need you taking your heat to my people. Maybe after you get this court shit together, but for now, no. It ain't gone happen and I will let Ron and them know that you are not my man so you don't think I'm using you."

"You can't be an outlaw."

"Who told you that shit? Comfort? I know plenty of girls turning tricks that ain't paying nobody, and before I'm forced to pay someone, I'll quit the game. I don't want a man who wants to be with me because of the money I make."

''Look Kim, maybe I came at you the wrong the way, I'm sorry and as far as Ron goes I was trying to get the money to take care of my lawyer because Comfort ain't doing shit. I kept two keys off of that job and told him that they were left in the car."

"So actually you are selling your own shit and he doesn't know about it?"

"Yeah, Comfort has partied away all that shipment he got from the Columbians and he hasn't paid them."

"Wow that's not a good thing."

"Kim I need to get away from there. I have let Comfort get me a case and I realize it's just like you said, he ain't going to help me. I see now that he's been using me all the time. The lawyer needs ten grand just to put the case off while he tries to figure out an angle."

"You should be able to get that out of those two bricks."

"I am close. You know Kim I swear I think that either you put some Voodoo on me or karma is coming after my ass. Every since I hurt you my life has gone down hill, I think that if I don't fix things with you my life is never going to be straight."

I laughed, "Voodoo is a religious thing, Hoodoo is the bad one, and I don't mess with hoodoo. It comes back on you. I didn't put any roots on you. My grandmother always says what goes around comes around. The way you put things now I can accept and understand what you are doing; maybe I can even help you, but don't come at me again talking about me paying you."

"I'm sorry I'm just feeling trapped. You can use my name all you want and I'll back you up."

I knew he meant what he was saying, now. I was glad that he was waking up to what Comfort was really about, "I can hook you up with some of my L. A. customers. The bookie that I use to work for, Lee is opening an afterhours and is going to need someone to serve dope. You get yourself some weed to go along with that blow and you will have the spot covered. I'll talk to him. I got a few others out this way. I can buy a key off of you so that you can pay your lawyer."

"You still love me, don't you?" He was smiling from ear to ear.

"I ain't said all that now," I joked.

"I know you. You could put someone in there selling your own stuff and giving up customers is giving up money, so you must still care about me."

"I do, but I am not going to let you break my heart again."

Our food arrived and we talked about friends and family while we ate.

I dropped him off so he could get his car and went to work. I was so busy that I almost missed the bank to get the money to buy the package from Alonzo. When I got there, he was sitting in the living room with Comfort and Quima. I made a big production of giving him twenty grand in front of them.

"Now that's how you handle your business," Comfort said giving Alonzo a high five.

I gave Alonzo a list of customers, "They are expecting your call."

I gave him a pager and wrote the number down for him. It was linked to my pager so I would know when and where he had to deliver to my customers. He was on trial. I had to know if he could be trusted.

"I'm going to take half of this key, the other half you serve the people that hit you up on that pager. When you drop off, they pay you the money for the previous package. That is my money. Use this pager for the people on the list I gave you, that is your money. You need to meet with Lee next week. Here is his number we can split that money. Make sure you call him."

"Right on time as always. You are all about the business."

"Ain't nothing changed about me when it comes to making money? Please don't get high with any of these people, keep it on the up and up."

"Yeah I know."

I went back to work and later that night I checked the pagers to see who had paged Alonzo.

I had a customer who was a White girl with a Black body. I had given Theona half off on an eight ball to enlist her help. She was to call Alonzo for a delivery and try to seduce him. I returned her call, "Hey Theona what happened. " Girl I could tell he wanted it, but he didn't bite. I answered the door butt-ass naked and had two other girls sitting on the couch. He was sweating bullets and had a hard on when he left but he didn't do anything but ask for his money and leave."

"He didn't do anything?"

"Girl, I think he was sitting there with his eyes closed so he couldn't see the other girls who started putting on a show for him. They kept asking him to join in but he took his cash, gave me the dope and left."

"Thanks Theona. I appreciate it."

"You got it girl."

I was happy that Alonzo had not folded.

Kim

Fight

Alonzo passed all the tests. I had told the customers to offer him a hit or a blow and he turned them down every time. My money was correct and in two weeks, the dope was gone. He had paid his attorney and was looking for a place of his own.

I went by Comforts to pick up my money one evening and found Alonzo high as hell and acting strange. Comfort and Quima invited us to go with them to eat. I said I had just eaten.

He was high and looking at me with malice. "What's wrong with you?" I asked.

"I feel like you are pimping me."

"Did I say that shit when I was running around selling clothes for you? You don't like what we are doing then we can squash this right now. Give me my money and I will be out."

He took a hit on the pipe and shook his head.

"Why are you shaking your head like that?"

"I'm shaking my head in answer to your question, NO!"

"What you mean, No? Are you saying you ain't gone give me my money?"

" No, I am going to take it and get a place and you are going to live with me."

"No, I'm not. I'm going to keep staying with my Uncle."

"So you think you are just going to keep coming by here breaking me like I'm some Whore."

"You asked me for help, remember? You're high Alonzo, I'll see you later."

He jumped in front of me, "You ain't going no fucking where."

I pushed him out of my way and he grabbed my arm and slapped me… he actually put his hand up and slapped me. I could not believe he had done that. I started swinging and before I knew it, we were fighting like two people in the street.

"You punk bitch, what the fuck makes you think you can put your hands on me?" I screamed.

"You really think I'm a punk don't you. You don't respect me. You think you can run me around like your little errand boy and say anything you want to me and I'm just going to take it." He hit me again, this time with his fist, busting my lip.

I picked up a lamp and threw it at him, opening a gash on the side of his head.

I stood over him, "Where the fuck is my money? Give me my damn money; I don't ever have to see your crazy ass again."

He pulled my leg and I fell. He jumped on top of me pinning my arms down with his knees hitting me in the face with his fist. I blacked out for a few seconds. When I woke, he was smoking dope with his back to me.

"Crazy ass."

I went into the bathroom closed the door and tried to pull my clothes together, my blouse was torn. I looked under the sink and took my money out of his stash.

I walked right past him and opened the bedroom door. Comfort and Quima were standing in the hallway. I stormed past them and opened the front door and left.

Every bone in my body and face ached. I looked in the mirror, I looked a mess, my lip was swollen and busted, my eye was turning purple, and my jaw was puffing up.

I got on the freeway and headed to Woodland Hills. I did not have a key to the new house and when my grandmother opened the door, she gasped. "What happened?"

She ran into the kitchen getting ice, antiseptic and pain pills. I went up to my room took off my clothes and assessed the black and blue spots all over my body. I climbed into bed.

My grandmother worked on my bruises while I told her what happened. She told me that she left both of my

Grandfathers because they had hit her. "If they put their hands on you once, they will do it again."

When I went to sleep, she called Cricket and told him what happened.

Kim

I couldn't work for four days. I spent my time going to the movies with my grandmother and catching up on my sewing.

I called everyone that I had hooked Alonzo up with and told them not to call him for dope. I made arrangements for Sherry to pick up a package from Christian to serve them. I told Lee that I had someone else to work his club and for him let Alonzo go and why.

Alonzo had been blowing up my pager but I would not answer him. I was through with his ass.

I was barbecuing steaks when Cricket and Mea came in one evening. They had been gone for five days. I put two more steaks on the grill.

"I heard you had a fight," Cricket said.

"Alonzo hit me."

"Yeah, but why did he hit you?"

"I don't know, he was high and talking crazy."

"When mother told me that he hit you I went and had a talk with Alonzo. He was really messed up. I had to take him to get some butterflies on his cut. You hit him upside the head with a lamp. You know you could have killed him."

"He hit me. Out of the blue he just hit me and told me he wasn't going to give me my money what was I supposed to do?"

"He slapped you, but that ain't no big deal, he didn't hit you until you called him a 'Punk Bitch.' You can not call a man a 'Punk Bitch.' Not a real man anyway, and especially one as insecure as Alonzo."

"He can't just hit me and tell me he is taking my money either."

"You have had the man running around taking care of your business like he is your Bitch."

"I was trying to help him get the money to pay his attorney by buying his stash and giving him some customers.

How is that running him? I could have easily made that money and put it in my own pocket."

"You are telling people that he is your man, if he is your man why don't you treat him like one?"

"Look he has to get his own shit together. I can't do that for him."

"You know he needs to get out of that house. He told you that."

"And you expect me to do what? I didn't tell him to move in there."

"If you ever want him to get back to the man he used to be, you need to help him or leave him alone altogether."

"I'll leave him alone then."

"I don't think that's what you want to do. You cut the man off. You got him kicked out of the after hours and told all his customers not to deal with him."

"They were my customers, my people I was just giving him a handout and this is how he thanks me? I said pointing to my face.

"You are emasculating him."

"I don't know what that means but if it hurts him then that's alright with me."

"Niecy this is not you. You are not evil. It wouldn't hurt for you to have a man. You know you can control Alonzo. At least you know what he is about. If you get with someone else, they are going to call the shots. I got people looking upside my head because I'm cosigning you being an outlaw. Do the right thing; you know you care about him."

"I don't like being hit. I am not going to get my ass kicked and just take it."

"Let that go, you can move him in here until you find a place. If you don't help him, and I do mean quick, like today. He is going to die."

"Die? What are you talking about?"

"The Columbians are here. They are going after Comfort. Everybody in that house is going down. Comfort didn't pay for the dope."

"Shit," was all I could say as I went up the stairs to dress.

Kim

Shot

I went upstairs and changed clothes; I knew what I was going to do. I just didn't want to admit it to myself aloud. I asked my cousin to finish up the last two steaks on the grill.

I dialed Alonzo's number, "Hey, it's me."

"I'm sorry."

"Alright."

"Will you please talk to me?"

"I guess I can do that, but I want you to know that if you hit me again I will shoot you."

"Understood."

"I'll be there in an hour."

When I got there, he held me for a long time. It felt good. When we sat, I could see that he was not high.

"Your Uncle came by."

"Yeah, I know."

"I want to be with you. You are all I think about. I'll get a job if you want me to."

"You can't make enough money to get out of this mess with a job. You got to find one where you can hustle."

"Yeah, you're right."

"Why don't you come and stay at the house with me for a few days. Mea is taking off for a week and her, Cricket are going on vacation, and I'm going to take some time off too. "

"Really?"

"Yeah,"

"When?"

"Right now."

"Okay, come up with me while I pack some clothes."

Alonzo was almost ready to go when we heard gunshots downstairs. We looked at one another. He picked up his gun and I followed him to the stairs. Bullets were coming through the front door.

I ran into the bedroom, grabbed Alonzo's duffel bag, and threw it out the window so we could have something soft to break the fall. "Come on, it's the Columbians." I said.

Alonzo ran into the bathroom, grabbed a paper bag, and followed me out the window. I went out onto the roof of the patio and jumped down into the back yard. I got up and as I ran towards the fence, I heard a gunshot before Alonzo jumped. I saw blood spray from his upper leg before he fell from the ledge. I went back to help him and felt something bite into my shoulder.

I picked up his gun and shot towards the window while I made my way to Alonzo and helped him up and out the back gate. I left him in the alley behind a garbage can and made my way around to the front of the house where I had parked my car two doors down. I did not see anyone following me so I got in. When I put my hand on the wheel, I realized I was bleeding. I saw the Columbians come out of the house. I leaned down in my seat hoping they would not see me. They were carrying things from the house. There were seven of them. They got into three cars and drove off.

I drove around to the alley, stopped by the garbage bin, and helped Alonzo into the car. "They are gone."

"Are you sure?"

"Yeah I saw them come out and drive away."

"Go in the backyard and get that paper bag."

I went into the backyard hoping that they had not come back or left someone there. I retrieved the bag put it in his suitcase and put it in my hatchback under the mat.

I drove to the hospital holding my arm. When I finally arrived, Alonzo was passed out. I went into the emergency room dripping blood down my hand. I found a nurse, "My boyfriend is in the car. He's been shot."

I followed the gurney out and they got Alonzo out of the car and rushed him inside. I went to the phone and called Christian to tell him what happened. Suddenly I felt weak and dizzy. I couldn't stand on my own two legs. I dropped the phone. A male nurse caught me before I hit the floor. He noticed that my sleeve was soaked with blood.

When I woke, my Grandmother was sitting next to my bed. "You were lucky, they said the bullet went straight through, it left some stuff in there that they had to clean out but you are going to be okay."

Christian and Laisyv walked into the room. "There she is," Christian said. "I'm glad you gone be alright."

My head cleared and the pain in my shoulder shot through me. I remembered what had happened. "Where is Alonzo?"

"He's going to be alright. He's in recovery right now. They shot him in the thigh, he was lucky, another half inch to the right and he would have lost his... well you know," Laisyv said.

The doctor came in, "Well you are one lucky lady. The bullet went through your upper arm and came out the back without affecting the bone or any major veins. We irrigated and removed two pieces of shrapnel. You are going to be just fine. I am going to give you something for pain and something to sleep.
If you are feeling alright and there is no sign of infection we will release you tomorrow morning."

"Thank you."

"Well, visiting hours are over so we are going to go, you get some rest," my Grandmother said.

"I can pick you up tomorrow. Call me when they release you," Christian said.

"Are you going to come home tomorrow?" My grandmother asked.

"I'm going to stay down here so I can check on Alonzo. I'll call you tomorrow."

Everyone kissed me and left. The nurse came in with a shot and a pill and I fell asleep.

Comfort

Comfort and Quima turned the corner on the street where they lived. There were police cars lined up in front. He kept going.

"What the fuck is going on?"

"The door was hanging off the hinges, did you see that?"

"You got to go find out what's happening. I'll drop you off on the corner. Call me as soon as you know what's up."

Quima did not want to go into the house but she knew she didn't have a choice. She was hoping it was not a raid. If they got into the safe and found all the identifications, checks, and drugs, she would be going to jail. She hesitated getting out of the car.

"Bitch, what is your problem, gets the fuck out and find out what happened."

"What if they got in the safe?"

"They need a warrant for that and ain't nothing in the safe. I moved everything to Nia's. You ain't got shit to worry about."

When Quima approached the house, a policeman stopped her. "Do you live here?"

"What happened to my house?"

"Come with me," he put his hand on her elbow and led her through the debris. "Please don't disturb or touch anything, we are still marking the bullets and dusting for finger prints."

"What happened?" She had seen hundreds of bullet casings outside the front door. The double front doors were splintered with bullet holes.

"The detective can answer your questions." He led her to a man in a cheap suit.

"And you are?" The detective said.

"I am Quima Chen and this is my house."

"I am Detective Sorello; I had the misfortune to draw this case. Do you know who did this?"

She looked around her beautiful home. The piano shaped mirrored coffee table was smashed to bits. Bullet holes riddled the walls. The big screen television was smashed in. All the china was pulled out of the cabinet and broken. Everything was trashed.

"Ms. Chen do you know who was home when this happened? We found blood on the ledge outside of the upstairs bedroom window and more by the fence in the backyard. Someone was hurt here."

"We have a friend staying with us, his name is Alonzo."

"We tested the blood, there were two types. Any idea of who the other type could belong to."

"No, he has company sometime. I haven't been home all day. Did they trash upstairs too."

"Pretty much. They punched holes in the waterbed in the master bedroom. We found several shells in the other bedroom next to the window and on the ledge."

The detective escorted Quima upstairs. Mirrors were shattered; the waterbed was a big puddle. In the bathroom bottles of perfume were smashed all over the floor. In lipstick on the mirror was some sort of sign. "Do you know what this is Ms. Chen?"

"No," Quima said.

"It is the sign of a Columbian hit squad. We have seen these several times. You have problems with Columbians. You need to be honest with me because every time we see this, well lets just say they always get who they come for."

"I don't know anything about this."

The detective picked up a picture. Is this your husband?" He was looking at a picture of her and Comfort.

"My boyfriend."

"Where is he? We need to talk with him?"

"I don't know. I need to call him," she said picking up the phone and dialing the car phone.

When Comfort picked up she looked at the detective, "I got the answering service." She spoke as if she was talking to an answering service. "I need to leave a message for Comfort, the house has been shot up, and the detective says some Columbian hit men did it. They trashed the house. The police said they found blood in the back yard. They think that two people were hurt. Please come home as soon as you can. Thank you."

"I'll be there in a minute," Comfort said.

Comfort knew that Quima was letting him know that he could go to the house. The Columbians had done a number on his place. Better the place than him. He knew they were looking for him. He had been warned when he didn't make the third payment. The second payment had been short. He was going to have to leave town for a while. He wondered if Alonzo was alive.

When he walked into the kitchen, a policeman was talking to the detective. "We have two people suffering from gunshot wounds at the Centinella hospital. One is a male, Alonzo Woods. He was shot in the thigh and is just going into the recovery room. The other is Kim, I forgot the last name, and she was shot in the arm, but is going to be alright."

"I'll talk to them first thing in the morning."

Oh shit, he had to go and see Alonzo first thing in the morning. He was relieved that they were not dead.

"Oh, glad you are here Mr.? The detective said.

"Comfort."

"What is your real name?"

"Dexter Danion."

"I am the detective on this case, here is my card. I am hoping that you can shed some light on why the Columbians want to kill you."

"Why do you say it was Columbians?"

"Because they left their calling card in your bathroom. We have seen this before and when these guys have a target they don't give up until the job is done. Consider this the phone call before the real visit. You are going to need police protection but in order for us to provide you with that, you are going to have to be straight with me. Why do I feel that this is drug related?"

"Naw, it's about a loan. I don't even know the guys name; I met him while I was on holiday in The Caymans. I ran up a gambling debt at the Casino and couldn't settle the IOU. Also, his girlfriend left the island with me. He sent a message he wanted her back, I put her on a plane, guess that wasn't enough."

"You are trying to tell me all this was over some broad. I hope she was good in the sack."

Comfort didn't answer that. He turned and went up the stairs where Quima was crying over her house. "Pack some clothes. Pack like you may not be coming back for awhile."

"Where are we going?"

"Just do what I said Bitch!" Comfort was preoccupied with trying to get out of town so that he would not end up a puddle like his waterbed.

Meanwhile one of the policemen had left and gone to a phone booth to contact the Columbians. He had been given ten grand and promised another ten when he led them to Comfort. "He's at the house."

The Columbians waited down the street for four hours. Quima and Comfort came out and put suitcases in the trunk of the Rolls Royce.

Comfort called a friend and told him that when the cops were done with the house he should come and clean up. It would be a few days because the cops said it was a crime scene.

Quima called the hospital and found out that Alonzo was still in recovery. She told him that he was her brother-in-law. She asked about Kim and got her room number.

"Mr. Danion you are making a big mistake. You can't go it alone with these guys. They are killers."

"Thank you for your concern; I have your business card right here." He patted his breast pocket. "I have to think about this and I'll call you."

He and Quima got into his green, gold plated Rolls Royce. They headed for the hospital with three cars of armed men following him for protection. He needed them until he could get out of town. They went to the hospital where he told the nurse he wanted to see his brother Alonzo Woods. She told him that he was in recovery and could not have visitors. Comfort gave her a hundred dollar bill.

"Lonzo, Alonzo wake up, its Comfort."

Alonzo was pumped up with morphine and was groggy. "Motherfucker you didn't pay those people. They could have killed my woman and me. You ain't shit."

"Hey man, you know I didn't know that was going to go down like that. You're my brother, I love you."

"Alonzo opened his eyes. His head cleared a little and he looked down at his leg where the pain radiated. He looked up and saw Comfort. "Hey man, how you doing?"

"How am I doing, you the one laid up in the hospital, man you was just talking out of your head."

"I'm fucked up man. They say I am going to have to go through a lot of therapy to walk again. They said it was really close to my dick. Man I'd rather be dead than lose my dick." Alonzo laughed.

"I know you would with that woman you got, but you gone be alright man. Look I got to lay low for a while; the house is all fucked up. It's not safe for you to stay there."

"No shit, Nigga. Kim got me out of there. I thought she had left me in the alley but she got me out of there."

"Man, she's a straight up, stomp down ride or die broad. Make sure you treat her right, she's the kind of woman have a nigga's back through thick and thin, you are a lucky motherfucker to have her. Only one or two of them come through in a lifetime."

"Yeah you right about that." Alonzo was nodding in and out of consciousness.

"I'm going away for awhile, I'll be in Jamaica. I got you a ticket waiting at the airport under your name. You don't need a passport to go there, just a birth certificate. I'll be at this resort he said handing him a brochure. I'm going to find a house down there. I'll leave word where I am. Let me know when you are ready to come."

"Naw man, I'm going to stay here with my woman."

"Bring her with you."

"I'm looking at got months of rehab. I want to walk again man."

"Well I left you an envelope at the desk. There is some money in it. What ever you do watch your back man."

"Yeah I will."

They shook hands and Comfort walked to the elevator.

When Comfort came down in the elevator Quima and one of the henchmen went to get the car.

Quima pointed the car towards the hospital entrance. When she stepped on the gas, the car blew up. The Columbians screeched up to the entrance and four men got out spraying bullets into everyone in the entryway.

Comfort looked up and saw the lights on the ceiling, they started to fade, and everything went black.

Kim

Leaving the Hospital

I dreamed about the Columbian's who shot up Comforts house. I heard the shots ripping the front doors apart and saw hundreds of bullets flying through the house. In my dream, Alonzo and I did not make it out of the second floor window and through the backyard. I saw myself lying in a coffin beside Alonzo and next to us was another coffin with Comfort and Quima.

I woke disoriented and looked around the hospital; it took me a second to realize I was not in a coffin. I had survived the shooting and was in the hospital. Then it all came back to me. I had to go find Alonzo and see how he was doing. I called the nurse, "I need to check on my boyfriend Alonzo Woods."

"The doctor will be coming to see you in a minute, he will probably order your I. V. removed then you can move around."

I tried to sit up but pain shot through my shoulder. "Ouch."

"Hurts huh? Let me get you a pain shot." When she returned, she checked my bandage where I had been shot in the shoulder. "Looks good. You are one blessed lady."

"I don't know about all that."

"You sound like you don't believe in God's grace," she said while injecting the pain medicine into the I.V.

I shrugged my shoulders, "Do you know where Alonzo Woods is?" I changed the subject. I could tell that she was one of those people who once they got started on religion would never stop. I was not going to get into a conversation about God whom I stopped believing in long ago. I stayed out of his house and he stayed out of mine.

The nurse could tell that I was dismissing her question, "I'll find out for you."

The doctor came in and after examining my wound told me, I could be released. I called Christian to come get me. After the nurse took the I.V. out, I signed some papers, dressed in the clothes Laisyv had left me and went to find Alonzo. I walked past a policeman who was sitting outside my door. He followed me.

There was a cop standing outside his hospital room. I stood inside the door listening to the detectives interrogate him, "We know you were at the house when you got shot. We matched the blood, not only yours but your girlfriends, who we are going to talk to next."

"You can talk to me right now. I don't know how much help I can be. I was picking Alonzo up; we were going to spend a few days together at my house. When we heard gunshots downstairs, we climbed out the window and someone shot Alonzo before he could jump off the patio roof. They shot me when I was trying to get out of the gate. I went back for Alonzo and hid him in the alley. I went to get my car and drove us to the hospital. I did not see who was shooting."

"Do you know that Quima and Comfort along with several of their friends were killed right in front of this hospital last night?"

Alonzo and I looked at one another. *That's why I dreamed they were dead.*

"How were they killed?" Alonzo asked.

"Quima was blown up by a remote bomb under the Rolls Royce. A few seconds Comfort and his friends were gunned down along with a lot of innocent people. They blew too many holes in them to count. There was nothing that could be done to save them," The detective said.

"I'm so sorry Alonzo. I know they were your friends," I said.

"Mr. Woods you need to be honest with us so we can help you. We offered the same help to your friend Comfort, he declined, and well, you see how things turned out for him. Was this drug related?" the detective asked.

"Naw, Comfort borrowed some money from a guy in the Islands and brought some girl home with him. They threatened him, said they would kill him if the girl didn't come back. He put her on a plane. I don't who the guy was," Alonzo repeated the story that Comfort had told him when he visited last night.

"Whoever 'they is' sent hitters from Colombia. We have had several killings where they leave their 'mark.' It's a dagger through a heart with a C in the middle. They want people to know their handy work. We need to put you under protective custody Mr. Woods."

"I don't need protection, they weren't after me," Alonzo said.

"Well they shot you. They may assume that you can identify them. You really don't have a say in this. We are going to keep officers at your door. The doctor said you are going to be here for a while. Make no mistake Mr. Woods, you and Ms. Harold are lucky to be alive, and if you are smart you will work with us and keep it that way."

"Why don't I feel lucky?" Alonzo said.

The nurse came in, "Mr. Woods needs his rest. I'm sorry but you are going to have to go now."

She signaled for me to remain.

"I thought you had left me behind that trash can. Thanks for saving my life," Alonzo said.

"If that's what you thought you don't know me at all Alonzo?"

"I know you, but when you are bleeding to death with a hole in your body you think some crazy things. I love you Kim."

"How are you feeling?"

"I hurt in places I didn't even know I had."

"That's why I'm here to give you your cocktail," the nurse said. She pushed the dope into the intravenous tube. "He's going to get drowsy soon and he needs his rest so take about five more minutes and then let him get some sleep," the nurse patted me on my arm.

"Okay, thank you so much." I said.

"Look I want to get Christian and some guys to box up your things and get them out of that house, you alright with that?"

"I don't know where I'm going to stay, you got that bag right?"

"It's in your luggage."

"There's some money and dope in there. I'm going to be in here for a few weeks. I don't have anywhere to go when I leave. I'm going to need therapy. They are calling it a crime of violence so Medicaid is going to cover the hospital bill."

"You have somewhere to go Alonzo."

"I do?"

"Yeah, Crickett told me to come get you. He heard about the Columbians and knew they had a hit out on Comfort."

"So you didn't come get me because you wanted to be with me?"

"I came to get you because Crickett said if I loved you I should get you out of there and bring you to his house where I'm staying in Woodland Hills. I don't want to see you dead."

"So you still love me?"

"I love who I know that you can be. I will never be with a man who is not about his business. You had to wake up on your own and see that Comfort was using you. You know how to hustle, but I don't want you to think you are pimping me. If we are going to build a life together, we have to do just that, build it together.

"That's all I want."

"And I am not some broad that you need to hit."

"Kim I was not comfortable in that house, it was making me crazy. I will never touch you that way again, I promise, I tried to call and apologize, and you wouldn't talk to me. I guess I was a little out of my head when I hit you, but damn you went crazy on me to. I needed stitches for that lamp you hit me with. Girl you are dangerous, I know better now."

Alonzo's eyes drooped.

"Baby I'm going to get out of here and let you rest. I've been released. I'll be at Christians until you get out. I'll come see you everyday. Rest and get better."

Christian stopped in to see Alonzo and we left. On the way out of the hospital, we saw crime scene tape and chalk outlines where the bodies had fallen outside the sliding doors.

"Man it was all over the news. They have some video cameras out here and they caught all of them falling to the ground. They didn't even get a picture of the people who did this. So much for Comfort," Christian said.

"We need to find my car so I can get some things out. Then we have to find someone to drive my car from the hospital. I can't move my arm to shift just yet. I'm just glad someone parked it when I passed out. The keys were in my property when I woke up. I'm praying they didn't search it."

We found the car and the suitcase was in the trunk where I had left where. My stash box was untouched. Christian took me to the Slauson Swap Meet to get some clothes because I was not going back to Woodland Hills for a few days.

"You know someone with a truck so we can get Alonzo's clothes?"

"I'll handle it. You all right to go with us? You know everything that is his and I don't want anything stolen," Christian said.

"Yeah I can handle it. I just need to fill this prescription for pain pills."

"What they give you?"

"Vicodin."

"I got a whole jar of those at the house."

"Cool."

"Comfort must have been planning to leave town. The news said he had plane tickets on him when he was killed."

I wonder if he was able to get his stash out with the cops crawling all over his house. He stopped to tell Alonzo what lie to tell the cops before he left."

"You think the police might still be there?"

"I don't think so. It doesn't take that much time for them to do what they need to do."

Christian made a few phone calls when we got to the house. Within an hour, six guys showed up to help us get Alonzo's things. It took an hour to get everything loaded into the truck. I took everything to my friend's house where she let me use her extra room for storage.

The next week Alonzo was moved to a regular hospital room and underwent tendon surgery. I visited everyday and took him food. When I could not go, my Grandmother went.

Two weeks later, he was discharged on crutches.

Alonzo

"I am so glad to be getting out of this hospital. Kim you just don't know," Alonzo said

"I'm glad you are too, all this driving out here everyday to see you been messing up my flow."

"I want to thank you for doing it."

"So anything you need to do? What kind of pain pills they prescribe you?"

"Vicodin."

"I got about two hundred of them, so you are cool"

"I know one thing I would like to do."

"What's that?"

"You know the fish market on Crenshaw you turned me on to? I have a taste for some shrimp and snapper and some of those hot pickles."

"That sounds good,"

Kim pointed the car in the direction of A & J Fish Market where you selected your fish and they fried it up for you in seasoned cornmeal. She helped me get up on my crutches to get inside the restaurant. We were lucky there was an empty booth. It was lunchtime and this place kept a good crowd especially on Fridays. Most religious people eat fish on Friday.

I ate until I thought I would burst. When we got on the freeway, I realized how great fresh air really is. If I never smelled another hospital, it would be too soon. Kim took Pacific Coast Highway and went through a canyon. She pulled into the driveway of a three-story house. This was nice.

Kim's Grandmother met us at the door. She had come to see me a few times in the hospital always bringing something good to eat. She reminded me of my Mother. I had grown to love this woman over the years since I had been with Kim. Even while we were broke up for nine months, I would visit her Grandmother.

"Hey Mother," That's what she told me to call her. It seemed that every one called her Mama or Mother.

"Hey you. Glad to see you up and around, we better get you upstairs so you can get comfortable."

Mother and Kim helped me maneuver up two flights of stairs to the third floor. From what I saw, the house was beautifully furnished. Kim took one of my jogging suits out of a huge walk in closet where I noticed my clothes hanging.

Kim's bedroom furniture dominated the room. My television was set up across from the king size bed. She helped me change and get into bed. Mother opened the curtains and sliding glass door that led to the balcony, which wrapped around the house letting in a nice breeze. I was going to like it here.

"You hungry Alonzo?"

"He better not be. He just ate two whole orders from A & J. I brought home some fish and stopped at the Rib Joint and got four slabs and a pound of sausage, some baked beans, and potato salad, so you don't' have to worry about cooking today. I'll go get it out of the car," Kim walked out.

"So, are you comfortable?" Mother asked me.

"I'm a lot better now that I'm out of that hospital."

"You want the television on? I'm going to go pick the kids up from school."

"That would be nice. Thank you Mother."

"The food is downstairs Mother," Kim said meeting her on the landing.

"I'm going to go pick the kids up from school."

"You want me to go for you?"

"Yeah, if you want to," Mother said.

"I can do that. Alonzo I'll be back in a bit, you need anything just let Mother know."

"Can you get me a bottle of Hennessy while you are out? And before you go I could use a couple of pain pills."

When Kim left, the phone rang. I moved to pick it up but Mother ran in and got it before I could get to the other side of the bed.

"Hello. She's not here right now. Okay I'll tell her that you called."

I wanted to ask Mother who it was but thought better of it. Though I had said that I was all right with Kim turning tricks I still felt a bit uncomfortable about it.

When Kim returned, she returned the call. I pretended to be asleep.

"Hey Hank what's going on, I got your message. What time? I'll be there. Yep it's still three hundred an hour."

"You going out?" I asked when she hung up the phone.

"Naw, that's for tomorrow night. I'll stay here with you tonight."

"What does he want that he pays three hundred an hour for?"

"Alonzo I did feel comfortable talking to you about work."

"Why not?"

"Because when I'm home I don't want to think about tricks."

"Why can't you just tell me one time so I don't have to wonder?"

"I do whatever it takes to get my money. Most of my regulars don't want sex, most of them want to buy dope and talk, and if they do want intercourse, I tease them first so that they get off really quick. "

"You got any weird dates."

"All I have are weird dates. They pay more."

"Do you get off with them?"

"No, I turn my mind off and do my work."

"You are going to tell me that you never got off while your were working?"

"Once, with Quima."

"So you do a lot of those shows?"

"Every man's fantasy is to be with more than one woman. Yes, I do a lot of them, but most working girls place their finger and lick that. The trick doesn't know the difference. Quima did it for real and she was good at it."

"When was this?"

"Right after you got out of jail. I went on a call and she had requested me."

"That freak and Comfort wanted you bad. What if I want to see you with another woman?"

"So now you are a trick?"

"Naw, but it would be kind of fun to watch."

"I'm sure you have done three ways before, we can explore that later, right now you have to focus on getting better."

"You know it's been a while."

"Yeah I know, but the whole house is up now, can you hold off until later?"

"Of course."

Kim

I had my own phone line in the bedroom and only a few people had the number. When I returned from picking up the kids Mother told me, "Hank called and you're lucky I got to the phone before Alonzo did."

"He don't need to be answering my phone."

"I agree," she said.

When I went upstairs to return the call Alonzo was pretending to be asleep. I had lived with him for two years and knew when he was playing possum.

I really did not like when he asked me questions about work. It gave me a weird feeling. After returning the call and our conversation, I turned the ringer off and left my pager downstairs.

I moved two of the lounge chairs on the balcony down by my room so that we could sit and watch the sun go down. It was a beautiful night. When it turned chilly, we went inside and watched television drank cognac and snorted coke.

After my cousins went to bed, I ran a bath for Alonzo. I helped him into the tub, bathed him, and helped him into bed. I gave him a pain pill and ran myself a bath. I fell asleep in the tub. It had been a long day.

"Kim, Kim you sleep in there?"

"I'll be right out," I said wishing that I could linger for just a while longer.

"I'm waiting for you."

I oiled myself down and perfumed up. When I got into the bed, I could tell that Alonzo was waiting for me by his erection.

"You are going to have to get on top."

"That works for me."

I traced my tongue across his chest, blew on his sensitive nipples that immediately hardened from the cold ice in my mouth coupled with the mouthwash I had just used, he started moan.

He pulled me astride him and up to his mouth. I held onto the headboard. I had to bite a pillow so that no one could hear me cry out in ecstasy.

I took a condom out of the drawer next to the bed. His back arched and he exploded and throbbed against my tongue within seconds. He made a loud guttural noise that came from some place deep within.

After he caught his breath, "Dang girl, I know that was quick but you known that I ain't had none in a while. Give me a little time and I'll be ready again, I know this must be disappointing to you."

"It's alright, take your time, it's not like I'm going anywhere. More important I don't want you to strain yourself. You know you are still recuperating. You look uncomfortable is your leg hurting?"

"A little bit, you know how your muscles tense when you climax?"

"Yeah,"

"It's hurting because I think I used the tendons that they operated on."

"Let me get you another pain pill, you want another drink."

"Naw, just a glass of water."

I got up, put on a robe, and got him a glass of ice water from downstairs. My pager was beeping but I ignored it and went back upstairs.

I put the movie, An Officer and A Gentlemen, with Louis Gossett Jr. into the VCR that I had purchased. Since I knew that Alonzo was going to be laid up for awhile, I figured it would keep him entertained. I bought a box of movies out the back door of a video store.

I lay down next to Alonzo and he took me into his arms. We were asleep before Richard Gere met the leading lady.

Alonzo

Recuperated

"Mom I'm doing fine, Kim works a lot but there are other people here that help me with whatever I need. Don't you worry about me? No, I have not heard anything from Rita but I wouldn't be surprised if she is somewhere writing bad checks or boosting. It seems like she would call to check on the kids or something, but face it ma, she was never going to get the mother of the year award anyway. Kim's Grandmother takes me to therapy most days. Sometimes one of her Uncles takes me. I'm getting a lot better. I can walk without crutches now. I have to use a cane sometimes. Getting up and down three flights of stairs is hard though."

Crickett tapped on the door and stuck his head inside from the balcony, "Hey Alonzo, why don't you bring some extra clothes with you and you can roll with me after I take you to therapy," Crickett said.

"Man that would be alright. I'm going stir crazy sitting around all day."

"You sure you can move around? I'm gone be rolling probably through the night. Can you hang?"

"Yeah man. It's time I got back out in the street."

After therapy, Crickett met with a realtor at a building that he was thinking of renting and turning into a nightclub. "What you think Lonzo?

"Man this'll work. Put some booths in, a D.J. booth in the corner and over here you already got a bar. It has a kitchen too, you know people get hungry when they be partying, and you could sell food."

"I got to check on a liquor and restaurant license." Crickett said.

Crickett signed the lease. Then we drove into Hollywood. Mea was just finishing a three-day party so Crickett went by to pick up his money.

"Kim is sleeping in the back bedroom, you can go on in," Mea said.

I only got to see Kim on Monday and Tuesdays when she took off. We tried to catch a movie or go out to dinner if she was not too tired. Sometimes she slept through to Wednesday and had to go back to work that night.

"Hey baby."

Kim woke with a start, "Boy you scared me, what are you doing here?"

"I'm rolling with Crickett, you look tired."

"I've been working three days straight with no sleep. Lie down and hold me for a minute. How you feeling?"

"No more crutches, I'm doing pretty good, should be back to my old self pretty soon."

"That's good. What time is it?"

"One."

"At night?"

"Afternoon."

"I've only been sleep about an hour. Hey, can you take this envelope home for me?" she said reaching under the bed and pulling a thick manila envelope out.

"Sure. Crickett signed a lease on a building that he is going to turn into a nightclub. I'm going to help him get it together."

"That's good. Where is it?"

"In The Valley on Sepulveda. I saw a nice apartment building on the same street. Maybe we can check it out when you come home."

"That's a good idea, I can't keep biting on pillows so no one can here me scream."

I laughed and pulled her into my arms, within seconds she was asleep. I lay there holding her. I don't know how long I had been asleep when Crickett shook my shoulder. I got out of the bed without waking Kim and followed him out of the apartment.

"We gone let them get some sleep. Later on they can meet us at the afterhours if ain't nothing jumped off."

"That's cool. Kim looked wiped out."

"Man when you working for seventy two hours straight, you get tired. Nineteen grand don't make itself, that's hard work."

"That's what they made?"

"That's what Mea made. Now I got to go see what Kalyn clocked, then go check these other two."

"How many women you got?"

"Seven and a couple of maybes"

"What you mean maybes?

"They may be mine and they may not. I'll know when see how much money they got. They are turnouts, new to the game. Sometimes they're just trying to make enough money to go home. You never know who is going to stick and stay."

"How do you deal with all these different women?"

Crickett laughed, "Man pimping ain't easy, but most of these women been in the game for a while. They know how to take care of their business and when they handle it, right they get a few days a month with me. Shit, this is easy compared to back in the day when I had thirty-one women. Shoot, if it was a short month somebody didn't get their day. They worked their asses off trying to stay at the top of the list. Only the top earners got time, and the ones that didn't make enough had to see me the next month."

"Man, I don't know about this. Kim won't talk to me about work. I find myself spending a lot of time wondering what and who she is doing."

"You are gone drive yourself crazy. One thing about Kim, she gets money like a white girl because she knows how to use her personality. Most bitches just know how to lie down fuck and suck, flat backers we call them. Kim knows how to work a trick for time and more money, plus she slanging too, the girl is a true player."

"She is one hell of a hustler."

"She got it honest. She grew up watching her family."

I spent the rest of the day going from house to house watching Crickett collect money. Not just a couple of hundred but thousands from each girl. Kalyn said something to piss him off and he hit her in the mouth. She ran after him as he walked to the car begging him not to be mad at her. That would never happen with Kim.

Eight o'clock we were sitting in the Shark Club on Sunset. There were several pimps in the club and after having dinner, we joined them at the bar. They were all campaigning for the strays in the club.

I watched them closely trying to absorb everything they said and did. I had to be able to hold my own around them. A white girl walked up to me and asked me to buy her a drink. I could feel the men at the bar looking at me to see what I would do. I almost thought the guys were setting me up. Before I followed her to the dance floor, she had bought me two drinks.

"That's how you work it. She might be your number two," Crickett said to me as I passed him on my way back to my seat.

"Man my leg wouldn't let me stay on the floor long, plus that bitch was hurting my eyes with her no dancing ass."

"Man who gives a fuck if the bitch can dance? All I want to know is if she can pay me, and if she can't, do she want to find out how she can, "Cash Money said.

"Yeah but she ain't got no ass," Alonzo said.

"Boy you looking at the wrong thing. I could give a fuck what she do or don't got. I'll take a pig in a wig as long as it brings me my money. That bitch is bleached blonde with blue eyes. Ain't no trick gone turn her down? Shit I got a bitch two hundred and fifty pounds, ugly as a sin, bucked teeth, bug eyes, can't screw to save her life but give that ho a bottle of peroxide and she pays off like a fixed slot machine. Check it, I got a black girl, fine as hell, curves in all the right places, beautiful face, you tell a trick on the phone about her he's ready to eat her up until you say she's Black. The American White boy dream is blonde hair and blue eyes. Other than that pussy ain't got no face."

"Yeah you right," Alonzo, said soaking up the knowledge.

Crickett got up to go talk to three women sitting alone at a table.

Cash Money slid up next to Alonzo, "Let me pull your coat young blood. I'm gone tell you something that Crickett ain't gone hip you to seeing as how you with his niece and all, but in this game you got to hurry up and come up with another broad so you can put that 'Only' you got in check. See she think she running shit, you got to give her some competition. Especially since she was an outlaw for so long, you got to break her down and build her back up, make her think she can't open her eyes without you."

"Why I want to do all that? Kim gets money."

"Yeah but you never know how long a ho is gone be around. You got to put foot to her ass and grind everything you can out of her for as long as you can. I know you a little fresh to the game, but I like you young blood. I'll pull your collar whenever you need some advice just call me," Cash Money gave me his card.

Crickett walked up with the three girls and Cash Money started trying to talk to one of them. The girl that I had danced with stood next to me. She ordered drinks for Crickett, her girlfriends and me.

At last call for alcohol Crickett invited the girls to follow us to the after hours club. They were all too happy to go.

We walked out to the parking lot and when we got into the car, I offered Crickett a package of blow. Right when he was about to take a snort one of the girls walked up to his window. He did not try to hide what he was doing. He handed the pack to me and popped the door locks, "You want a blow?"

"Oh yes, party favors," the silly broad couldn't get in the van fast enough. A few seconds later, the other two pulled up next to us and she opened the door and beckoned them in. They snorted and actually passed the blow between themselves instead of handing it back."

"Let's go," Crickett turned around putting his hand out for the package. They reluctantly handed it over but did not move to get out. He started the car. "We're going on Santa Barbara follow me."

"Why don't we just ride with you," Mary said rubbing his arm.

Crickett turned and looked at her, "Get in your car and follow me."

As we drove, Crickett looked at me, "You alright man?"

"Leg just bothering me a bit, another blow I'll be alright."

"You look like you thinking about something."

"Kind of wondering what Kim is going to say when she sees me with this White girl."

"Kim is down, she ain't gone say nothing. What was Cash Money talking about? Naw don't tell me, let me tell you. He was gone hip you to the game. Help you out, right?"

"How you know that?"

"I didn't want Kim to get in the game, but she did. A lot of playa's looked at me sideways when they found out my niece was an outlaw. Cash Money was one of them. He got some White bitches and though they check more money for him, he likes black women. He's been in the game for a long time. Half my broads I got from other players. Broad get mad and decide to choose someone else a pimp got to suck it up, it's all part of the game. Playa's is always trying to get ho's out of pocket so they can charge them. If they decide they like him, better than you a pimp is minus one Ho. That's all there is to it.

"So that's what he's up to?"

"Yep, Cash Money is trying to help alright, help himself to your woman. I turned him out to the game. I was in a club one day and he came up to me and told me that he had some girls and didn't know what to do with 'em. I took him under my wing, he was my protégé, and because of that, he feels like Kim should have got with him. Be careful."

"I see."

"Kim is with you because she loves you, not because she needs a pimp. She worked for months and I didn't even know it, she can go below the radar and no one would know what she's doing. As far as you coming up with a broad, she wouldn't care, as long as you keep treating her right. Don't play games with her, you don't have to, and she'll bring you more broads than you can handle. Just remember she pulled you in. A pimp is only as strong as his Bottom Woman."

Kim

I woke up after midnight. My pager had been blowing up. When I turned it off of silent, I had missed twelve pages. I had been asleep for eleven hours and could have slept for eleven more if I didn't have to go pick up, cut, package, and deliver drugs. It was Saturday night and I had to meet Christian to re-up and take care of my dealers and Lee.

I dressed and knocked on Mea's door, "You can hit me up on my pager if you need me."

"Crickett and Alonzo said that we should meet them at the after hours on Santa Barbara around three."

"I'll see what's up. If I ain't busy I'll be there."

I finished my runs and made it to the club about four a.m.

Mea and Kalyn were sitting at a table alone. Crickett and Alonzo were at a table with three white girls. I sat with Mea, "What's up with the snow bunnies?"

"They met them at the Shark Club and brought them here."

"They asked us to meet them here so that we could sit by ourselves while they deal with some square bitches," I said pouring blow on a plate and putting it in front of Mea.

"Kim, do not start tripping and acting like some jealous square, you know your man got to come up if he is going to hang in this family," Kalyn said.

"I ain't signed up for all this wife- in-law shit."

"Girl you know if he is hanging out with your Uncle he is going to come up with another girl eventually, you better get used to it," Mea said.

"Well he don't need me here to do this, I'll see you guys later."

"Sit your butt down and act like the pro that you are," Mea said. "Ain't no room for jealousy in this game you brought him into it and he is trying to adapt."

"Sparkle, let me holla at you," Crickett called from the table.

Alonzo moved closer to the white girl that was sitting inside the booth so that I could sit down. He leaned over to kiss me and I turned my head, "What's up?"

"Crickett introduced me to the three white girls, "This is Mary, Mellissa, and Meredith."

I gave the girls a plastic grin. I had an immediate dislike for them, especially the one who was fondling my man's dick through his pants under the table.

"What you holding?" Crickett asked.

"What you want?"

"Give me a quarter ounce."

I went into the bathroom and took the package out of the pocket that was sewed into the nap of my hair weave. I combed my hair, touched up my lipstick, made my way to the bar to order drinks for Mea and Kalyn, and got some plates for Crickett.

"Hey baby why don't you let me take care of those drinks for you?"

I smiled at the guy to my right. I could feel Alonzo's eyes burning into my back.

"You a pimp?"

"Hell no! I got a mother who taught me to respect women. I get my money other ways baby girl. I don't like sharing my woman, not even for money, especially not one as fine as you."

I noticed him looking at the dope in my hand. "So what do you want in exchange for these drinks?"

"Sit with me for a minute, maybe share a blow."

"Why don't you just buy a blow from me and I'll give you my number so you can page me when you need some more. I'm with some people tonight."

"What if I just want to page you to get to know you?" he said resting his hand on my lower spine.

"That ain't gone happen in one night playa, I'm complicated," I laughed.

"Okay, give me a gram?"

I poured a gram out of Crickett's package, took his money, and gave him my card.

I told the bartender to send the drinks over to the table when Alonzo walked up behind me. "Hey man, how you doing? I'm Alonzo."

The men shook hands, "I'm Sincere."

"What you doing?" Alonzo said turning to me.

"I'm taking care of my business. Why?"

"Come here."

"Let me go give this to Crickett."

When I put the plate on the table, the three M's starting bouncing around like care bears or something. I knew it, a bunch of party bitches looking for a high. They didn't know that they were going to get more than a high messing with my Uncle. I watched them with amusement as they stared at Crickett's hand as he separated the powder into lines. "I reached under my weave and pulled out a paper package. " Here, I owe you another gram."

I wasn't going to charge Crickett for this package since I was staying in his house. I watched the girl's reaction to the drugs. Yeah they were fiends all right.

"That looks like some really good cocaine. Can we buy some from you?" the girl who was sitting next to me asked. I looked at her and got up from the table without saying anything. I rolled my eyes at my Uncle.

"Hold up baby girl. You can give me your money and I'll hook you up," Crickett told her.

I did not know this bitch and was not going to serve her anything. Sometimes I wished that I had a penis so that I could pimp dumb girls.

I took my time getting back to Alonzo. I walked by him and out the front door.

"Why were you talking to that guy?"

"Because it's what I do. How do you think I met most of my drug customers? And why are you questioning me?"

"You know how it is up in here. They see you getting out of pocket they are going to think they can step to you."

"Boy please, I have been coming to this club since I was seventeen. I think I know how to keep people in check. Don't you have some little bleach blonde with bad roots waiting for you? You should have paged me and told me not to come. I put work off to come down here, matter of fact I'm going to get back to it."

"What are you tripping about? Mea is here so what work you got?"

"Alonzo I have my own book of tricks. What? You think I only work for Mea. A person in this business has to do her own thing. I work for other agencies too. You don't need me here. You let that bitch sit there with her hand in your crouch like you some kind of trick. If you are trying to come up with her don't lead with sex, because if you do all your going to get in your hand is a wet dick."

"How you gone be jealous? Like you said this is work."

"I'm not jealous; I just don't want you to act like no Buster. But I guess you got your own way of handling business and I'm gon' let you get back to it. Don't forget to get yo' money "main," I said walking away.

He grabbed my arm twirled me around and kissed me.

"What do you want me to do? I'm hanging out with your Uncle. If I don't play the game, I'm going to look like a punk. Plus I can make things easier for you, if I can come up with a couple of broads you can quit working yourself."

"Oh, so you gone retire me, huh?" I laughed as I massaged his neck.

"What's wrong with that? I love you and it ain't no secret that I get a stone in my stomach over you working. Let me work with you. I know you don't want a man who isn't doing anything but waiting for you to pay the bills. Why don't you come back to the table with me and feel this bitch out? Help me reel her in. You know you are going to have to tighten me up on this pimpin' game."

"You ain't got to work that hard. The dope is going to reel her in like a fish."

"I didn't bring a lot with me, hell I only brought a couple of hundred dollars, and hanging out with your Uncle can get expensive. I paid for dinner since he is letting me stay in his house and all, I'm about tapped out."

"Can you walk with me to my car? If you were running short of cash why didn't you take some money out of the envelope I gave you?"

"I didn't know if you wanted me to do that, you know what happened last time I tried to do something with your money, we ended up fighting."

"Silly, this ain't like that. You could have paged me and I would have told you it was alright."

"I'm not trying to overstep my bounds with you. It's like you told that guy, you complicated," we laughed.

In the car, we started kissing. I did miss Alonzo. Some people were walking by so we broke apart.

"What's in that envelope anyway?"

"Twenty G's."

"That's what you made this week?"

"No, that's what I made in two days hosting a party and selling dope," I said opening my stash box.

"Damn girl, you ain't left no pussy for me."

"What can you give away a million times and still have it?"

He looked at me and started laughing, "Pussy." He looked out the window, "So you worked a lot this week?"

"No more than usual. Could we please not go there?"

"Crickett said that it's harder for a Black girl in this business, but you make money like a White girl."

"Okay and your point is?"

"Well if we took a white girl and you taught her everything you know we could make a killing. I was with your Uncle while he was checking his traps today; he is making money hand over fist."

"So you plan to get some white girls and you want me to train these bitches to make more money than me?" The irritation in my voice was evident.

"We'll talk about it later."

"Next week two of my dealers are going to be out of pocket, they are going to the Jazz Festival in San Diego. Think you could help me out and handle their customers?"

"Your drugs or mine?"

I kissed him, "Ours."

"I like that. You want to go get a room?"

"Boy, you just gone leave that girl in there with all those vultures? You need to handle your business, there's a party jumping off about noon tomorrow so I can't disappear. I may not make it home this week, there's a lot going on with the holidays and all."

"I thought we were going to look for an apartment next week."

"You're getting around now, why don't we get Willie to take you to look for a car, and then you can find us a place."

"Speak of the devil and up he jumps," Alonzo said just as some one knocked on the window.

I turned to see my Uncles Willie and Butch with their ladies. I opened my door and got out, "Hey, how you guys doing?" we hugged.

"Hell-a-good, I got money in my pocket, my two gold mines with me, all I need is some blow." Willie said.

"What you need?"

"You got a half ounce?" Willie said.

I reached into my stash and handed him a package, "This is a whole, pay me for the rest later, that way you ain't got to call me again before day in the morning."

"Aw'ight, I'll take care of the rest later," he said handing me six hundred.

"I know you will."

"See you in the club Neicy," Butch said.

I gave Alonzo a package. "Your girl asked me if she could buy some blow from me. I don't serve folks I don't know, especially if they White. Here's two-gram packs and a half ounce, do your thang, don't get ganked. I know how you southern boys are when it comes to White girls."

"Man it ain't even like that. And I ain't from the South, I'm from the Midwest."

"Whatever you say but technically Kentucky is a southern state? I didn't know you were so sensitive about your origins."

"It is bordered by states that are considered Midwestern, I'll give you sensitive, come here," he put his hand under my dress.

I was immediately wet.

"Why don't I go get the keys to the van from Crickett?"

"I am not fixing to nothing in my Uncles van. If don't nothing jump off by the time we are ready to leave you can come with me to the workhouse. Damn you got me horny now."

"We can go take care of that right now."

"Naw, you got business to handle and if I know my Uncle he put this broad in your face as a test to see how you are going to handle yourself. If you don't cut the mustard you know you out of here."

"Kim you know I don't know nothin' about pimping. You got to help me. I know how important your family is to you, if they don't like me I don't have a chance."

Back in the club, my Uncles had pulled three tables together. Meredith was smiling her ass off at Willie. She was not smiling at him so much as the pack of dope he was filling plates from. He passed one to each of his women and Butch.

I put my hand on Alonzo's arm to stop him so that we could observe, "Look at her, now she's smiling and flirting with Willie because he has that sack."

"Bitch is cheesing ain't she? After awhile we should pull her to a booth and see what's really going on in her head."

"May I make a suggestion Pimp Daddy Lonzo?" I said in a baby voice.

"I don't like how that sounds, but what is it?"

"Why don't we sit down on this end and see what she does?"

"Okay, I'm going to get us some plates and drinks."

"Alright, but remember, pimpin' ain't easy," I used the high voice again.

"Stop that," he said laughing as he walked away.

I sat at the end of the table. Several others joined my Uncle's party. They put money on the table so they could blow. Within an hour, Willie paid me the remaining money for the package.

I watched the three musketeers. They did not have a clue what they had gotten themselves into. This was the part of the evening where The Playa's would show their hand. The three silly girls had been fed dope and drinks for a couple of hours and were good and primed. They looked frustrated as no one passed them a plate. Several times they reached thinking the plate was coming their way but were passed over again and again.

When Alonzo came back, he put a plate on the table. He started to pull out the package of dope but I took it from him and sat it in my lap, "Hold up a minute."

I narrated what was happening down at the other end. "They are being separated for the kill," Crickett indicated that Butch should pull Melissa; he was going to deal with Mary. Butch passed his plate to Melissa, "When you finish taking a couple of lines bring that plate around here and pull up a chair," Butch said.

Melissa moved to sit next to Butch and Crickett was talking in Mary's ear.

Meredith looked up and saw Alonzo at the far end of the table with me. She did not move.

"Maybe she doesn't know that it's okay to come down here since you're sitting with me."

"That's bullshit; all the men down there have women sitting with them. Those girls ain't thinking about nothing but getting high."

"I'll go get her."

"Alonzo do not get up and walk over there, you do, and you are going to look like an all day sucker."

"Then what do we do? You going to get her?"

I looked at him thinking, *Boy he has a lot to learn.* "Drink your drink, where does she live? What does she do for a living?" I asked Alonzo.

"Don't know, didn't ask her yet."

A few minutes passed, "I'll call her now, watch this."

I waited until I saw her look down to our end and put the plates on the table and made a big production of pouring the blow on two plates. Like magic, she appeared at Alonzo's side.

"I thought you had left me Alonzo," Meredith said

"Abracadabra," I said laughing.

"Like magic," he said. He looked at her, "Naw just handling some business. Have a seat." he pulled the chair between us.

"So Sparkle, do you come here a lot?"

I could tell that she was feeling me out, "I've been coming here since I was about eighteen."

"You don't look much older than that now."

"I'm twenty two, how old are you?"

"Twenty three, I'll be twenty four next month.

"That makes you a Cancer?" I said.

"Yeah how did you know that?"

"I know my astrological signs, plus one of my best friend's birthdays is next month."

"What sign are you?"

"Alonzo and I are both Leos, our birthdays are five days apart."

Alonzo took a blow and the bartender called him, before Meredith could ask any more questions he said, "Hey, do me a favor and go get those drinks on that tray, it should be six cognacs, and four sodas."

"Do I need to pay for them?"

"That would be nice, and don't forget the ice," he said.

She rummaged around in her purse, pulled out a hundred dollar bill, and sat her purse on the chair.

Kalyn was on her way to the bar, "Kalyn," I called her over.

"What's up?"

"Stand right there and take a blow," I said handing her a plate.

I went into Meredith's purse she had three one hundred dollar bills in her wallet, I took two of them and handed them to Alonzo. I looked at her license and repeated the number aloud several times so I could remember it long enough to go write it down. I would have Butch run her. I closed her purse just as she turned back to us with the tray.

When Meredith came back, she put the tray on the table. I poured a splash of soda into a cognac added some ice and placed it in front of Alonzo. I took a blow from the plate and passed it to him. He took a blow and gave the plate to Meredith and she snorted several lines, she had no cocaine etiquette.

"Most people take a snort in each nose and then pass the plate back to the person who gave it to them, especially if they ain't paying for it," Alonzo said.

"Oh, I'm sorry. I can buy some?"

"Look when you are with me and you want something then you talk to me about it. Don't try to buy anything off of people you don't know," Alonzo said moving the plate from in front of her.

"I'll be right back, going to the restroom," I said.

"Oh I'll go with you," Meredith jumped up and followed me.

I went into the stall and wrote down her license number on a napkin. When I came out, she went in; while I washed my hands, she started asking me questions.

"So Sparkle, you said you have been coming here a long time, is this where you deal your drugs?"

I did not like her line of questioning so I walked out of the restroom. Willie's woman Tanisha was walking in and Meredith was repeating the question.

Tanisha walked out and called me, "Sparkle, what the fuck is she in there talking about?"

"Nosy bitch keeps trying to ask me about dope."

"All of them are fiends."

"Yeah I know but that's how they are going to get turned out."

"Mellissa doesn't know who I am, or what to think of me but she gon' find out."

"You think they are going to bite?"

"They already bit, they just got to take the next step or take their ass's home."

"Pimpin' ain't easy," Tanisha, said laughing.

"With girls like that, you right. They gonna go for the dope instead of the money if they ain't checked."

"No shit,"

I was on my way back to the table when Cash Money stepped in my path, "Hey Sparkle, how's it going?"

"Just fine, anymore questions you can ask my man," I said sidestepping him.

I sat down and told Alonzo about Meredith talking in the bathroom and Tanisha walking in and her asking questions from the stall not knowing who could have been listening."

"She might be more trouble than she's worth."

"She's going to need a lot of reprogramming that's for damn sure."

"So we shouldn't just run her off?"

"Hell no, she has a gold card and lives in Brentwood."

"How you know all that?"

"Didn't you see me go in her purse?"

"Look at this," he was looking behind me.

I turned around to see Kenyatta hemming Meredith up. I got up, walked right up to Meredith, took her by the hand, and led her back to the table, Kenyatta on our heels.

"What the hell is this?" Kenyatta said.

"She's here with Alonzo."

"She didn't tell me that when I was talking to her? Come here snowflake," Kenyatta reached for her.

"What's up Kenyatta, maybe she didn't tell you, but I'm telling you, she's here with me. Right baby?" Alonzo said putting his arm around her.

"Right," Meredith said her voice showing how nervous she was.

"Ya'll go on back to the table," Alonzo said.

He and Kenyatta stood talking, after a few minutes Kenyatta gave Alonzo some money and he gave him a gram pack of blow.

The club was on full at six in the morning. I was feeling good and wished I could just leave with my man but for some reason I knew we needed to stay. I was determined to help Alonzo come up with this girl.

I picked up my drink, "Is your drink okay, you need more ice?" I asked Meredith.

"No, it's okay, thank you."

I pushed a plate of blow in front of her, "Here."

Meredith put her drink down, picked up the plate, took two snorts, and placed the plate in front of me.

I pushed it back, "Keep it. I can blow from this one."

"Thank you,"

Alonzo sat down and put his arm around Meredith, "You got to be careful who you talk to in here."

"Okay, he just started talking to me. I didn't want to be rude. Actually, I was relieved when Sparkle came to get me. Thanks Sparkle."

"We can talk about that later, dang this place is getting packed, guess it's quitting time."

"All these people work the graveyard shift somewhere? Meredith asked.

Alonzo and I looked at one another and started laughing.

"What's so funny?" she asked

"These people don't work traditional jobs."

"Well, what do they do?"

"They hustle, one way or another," he said.

"Are you two related?" she asked.

"No, why you ask that?" he said.

"Well, I was just wondering what your relationship is."

I giggled, "He's my boss."

"Oh really, what kind of business do you have Alonzo?"

"I'm an entrepreneur."

"Of what?"

"Whatever it takes, what do you do?"

"I work in a store on Rodeo Drive. I used to work at my Dad's car lot but I wrecked too many cars and he fired me."

Mary and Mellissa walked up to our table, "Meredith can we speak to you?" Mary stood over her.

I could tell by the look on the girls faces that they knew that Crickett and Butch were pimps and wanted to warn their friend.

"Excuse me," Meredith said and followed them to a corner in front of the restroom.

I got up and took the long way around to the restroom so I could eavesdrop on their conversation.

"I'm ready to go. I don't want any part of this," Mellissa said.

"I don't want to leave. It's not like they are going to try to make us perform prostitution tonight," Mary said.

"Alonzo is a business man," Meredith said.

"Yeah and you are about to be one of the products he distributes," Mellissa said.

"Well it might not be so bad. I bet we can make a lot of money and it's not like we can't use it," Mary said.

"I can't believe you are actually considering this. We need to get out of here now, when someone tells you who they are, believe them," Meredith said

"I vote we stay," Mellissa said."

"Me too," Mary said.

"I'll take a cab home," Meredith said.

"Do you know where we are? Do cabs even come out here?" Meredith asked.

"I don't understand why you guys want to stay. I am trying to be the voice of reason here," Mellissa said.

"We'll just stay a little while longer and if you are too uncomfortable we can leave," Mary said.

"They know," I told Alonzo when I got back to the table seconds before Meredith.

She sat down and took a blow and a drink. "Can I ask you something Alonzo?" she said rubbing his leg under the table. This time Alonzo removed her hand and put it on top of the table.

Before he could answer her their was shouting and we turned our attention to the booth where Valentine had pushed his woman on the floor and was holding her by a fistful of hair while slapping her, "Bitch this all the money you got and you think you can come in here like you done clocked out. You got a quota and I expect you to get my money, I ain't no rest haven for ho's."

The girl scrambled to her feet and ran out the door crying.

It never failed, it seemed like every night one of the pimps had to knock his woman around, or it just would not be complete.

"What did you want to ask me?" Alonzo said.

"Oh, well Mary and Mellissa said that your friends are pimps," Meredith said

"And?" he said.

"Sparkle what exactly do you do for Alonzo?" Meredith said

"What ever is necessary?"

"Well I know you sell drugs, is that all you do?"

"No, I turn tricks, sell clothes, hang paper, whatever financial opportunity presents it self."

"So you are a pimp," she said looking at Alonzo.

"Yep, is that a problem?"

"Oh no. Well not as long as that's not what you want me to do."

"So what are you saying? You just want to sit around and rub on his dick and have a little fun?" I said.

"No that's not what I'm saying at all, I like Alonzo." She stuttered

"What do you like me for? You gone take me home to daddy. I think you like the dope more than you do me?"

"That's not true, that is just unfair," she said.

"You think life is fair, huh? You came here with me, I showed you a good time, now that you know who I am, and what I am, you need to make a decision.

Sparkle likes me too and she does what ever it takes to help me build something. You think I'm just supposed to have her working and you can be with me and don't contribute. It don't go like that. I think that you should take this number and call me if you decide you want to get with the program," he said.

"Well what would I do? I can sell drugs," she said.

"I think you would consume more than you sold, plus that's a position that you have to earn. You want to be with me you got to work your way up to the top from the bottom," he said

"Well, how do I do that?"

"Are you saying that you want to be with me? If so I am going to need a choosing fee, at least a grand for starters," he said.

"I have to know what you expect of me first."

"If you like me the way you say you do it shouldn't make a difference," he said.

"I would have to think about it."

"Yeah you do that, come on baby lets dance," he said taking my hand.

I followed him to the dance floor, when I looked over at Meredith she seemed to be deep in thought.

"What's she doing?"

"Just sitting there."

"She ain't blowing?"

"Nope, when the music goes off you go sit with Crickett, let me talk to her. I know she's got a lot of questions in her head."

I sat down at the table and picked up my drink, "You alright?"

"This is a bit overwhelming."

I took a blow and pushed the plate in front of her, "You can have this. Go ahead; I can imagine this is a lot for you to take in."

"How long have you been a prostitute?"

"I prefer the term call girl, about a year and a half."

"Oh you don't work on the street corners?"

"No, I work in a house and I go to clients homes, not to say I haven't been to the streets but I seem to do better this way."

"Oh, aren't you scared of getting hurt?"

"I'm careful. I don't get too high around a client so I can stay alert. Most of them are pretty cool regulars but you are dealing with human nature and you never know when they can snap, but that hasn't happened to me."

"So it's not like you are seeing people that no one knows about?"

"That's right."

"How much do you make?"

"It varies anywhere from one to twenty grand a week."

"What is the percentage that you give to Alonzo?"

I looked at her sideways, "All of it."

"All of it? You don't keep anything for yourself?"

"Why have a man if I have to do that, he gets me everything I want and need and what I keep he knows nothing about."

"Don't you feel weird sleeping with all those different men?"

"Would you have slept with Alonzo tonight, given the chance?"

"Probably."

"You probably sleep with more men than I do and you don't have anything to show for it the next day."

"What do you mean?"

"Most of my clients pay for time, if they just wanted to get off they could go on the street and pay twenty dollars, just for me to walk in the door is two hundred.

"So all you have to do is talk?"

"No I'm not saying that, I play my tricks for time, talk to them, get a dialogue going, you make more money that way. When it does come time to sleep with them, tease them, get 'em worked up, that way it's over before it really begins."

"Does Alonzo beat you? You know like that other guy just did to that girl, if you don't make enough money?"

"No, I've never given him reason to. He knows I do the best I can, but you would never have that problem.

"Why is that?"

"Because, you are the American dream. Blonde hair, blue eyes, you are what every trick wants. Maybe you could come to the workhouse tomorrow and see how things work."

"That would help me make a decision," she said.

My pager went off and I stood up and gestured for Alonzo to sit with her.

I walked over and talked to Crickett and Mea about having her come to the workhouse and they agreed. I used the phone and arranged to meet a drug customer down the street in ten minutes. I went back to the table where Alonzo was still talking to Meredith.

"Baby I got to make a run and I'm kind of tired so I will see you when I see you." I said.

"Hold on, I'm going with you," he said.

"Am I going with you two?"

"No you are going home and think about what you want to do," he said

"Give me a bill Alonzo."

"He gave me one of the hundreds that I had taken from Meredith and I folded it into an envelope. I took a blow off of the plate I had given to her and poured the dope into the envelope, "You want another blow baby?" I asked picking up the other plate.

"Naw,   I'm   cool;"   he   said
I poured the remainder from that plate into the bill and handed it to Meredith, she said, "Oh, thanks."

I gave her a card with the address to the workhouse written on the back, "Be here at two in the afternoon."

We got up and went to say our goodbyes. Meredith sat down next to Mary.

"We out of here. See you guys later," I said to everyone.

"Hold up, we're going too," Crickett said.

They all stood up, Mary asked Crickett, "Are we going with you?"

"Naw, baby girl you guys need to go think about what you want to do. Come on we'll walk you to your car."

Alonzo

Damn, Kim is amazing. She talked Meredith into going to the workhouse and I am sure before the night is over she will have turned a trick.

When Crickett and I left the workhouse it was noon, Kim and Mea were getting ready for a party. At the house I took some pain pills, ate a big breakfast of grits, eggs, bacon, sausage and biscuits that Mother prepared. It was one of those meals that put you right to sleep.

"Hey Alonzo, get up man we got to go handle our business. The party's over. Them new girls worked today let's go check our traps and see if these bitches plan to pay us," Crickett said.

"They actually showed up?"

"Yep."

When we got to the workhouse Mary and Meredith were there sitting on the floor by the coffee table snorting coke. Their eyes looked like deer caught in headlights. Mary was stuttering.

"She makes any money?" I asked Kim.

"Sixty dollars, Bitch went in the room one time and that was with me, she ain't do shit but make excuses. I had to go ahead and finish the trick off because he was getting frustrated with her bullshit, the only way I got her to suck his dick was to put blow on it."

"Are you fucking serious?"

"All the other girls that were here made at least seven hundred. There were ten guys, even Mary made five hundred, she gets high and horney and has too much fun with the tricks.

Melissa started crying and Butch picked her up. She works in a bank so he is going to take her that route. All your girl wants to do is get high and talk.

Tricks don't go in the room to talk, if they wanted to do that they would stay in the living room. She also asks way too many questions, she makes the customers nervous."

"What you gone do now?"

"I'm tired baby I been working for twelve hours, I want to get something to eat and go home and sleep."

"Why don't we go somewhere to eat and you can tell her everything that she did wrong while I'm there with you."

"I really don't think she will remember anything I tell her as high as she is right now."

"Oh, she'll hear you alright," I said getting up and walking over to Meredith, "Come on we fixing to go get something to eat."

"But I didn't get paid yet."

"Let's go." Alonzo said firmly.

Meredith picked up the plate to take another blow. I took it from her and handed it to Crickett. "You've had more than enough, we are leaving now."

"I'm going to get the car," Kim said.

"You go with her," I told Meredith.

I talked to Mea and Crickett. It seemed that this girl was going to have to be trained from the ground up. She had turned down several of the guys who wanted to go in the room with her and when she did finally go in it was with Kim. She messed up royally because when the trick came out of the room he told the others in Spanish not to waste their time with her.

Mea said she sat there smiling and talking ninety miles a minute. She did not realize that they were talking about her and laughing at her. She was a new face, she should have cleaned up, but her stupidity and inept actions made them suspicious. Mea wanted to send her home but was afraid that Mary would not stay without her friend, it being her first time and all.

Mea said that she would line up some outcalls where there wasn't any dope and see how she did.

Crickett told me to charge her every time I saw her, break her for all the money she has. I watched Mary give him five hundred dollars.

When I got into the car I turned around and looked at Meredith and shook my head."

"Is there a problem Alonzo?" Meredith asked.

"Why did you stay if you didn't plan on working?"

"I did work, tell him Sparkle. I went into the room with you and that guy. I did work Alonzo."

"She went in the room with me and a guy but I ended up doing all the work and with her talking non-stop it made it harder for me, instead of focusing on finishing the trick she kept stopping to blow and talk which made him go down. She actually stopped working to take a blow and started asking the man questions about his wife and kids. No trick wants to talk about his family when he is with someone else. You should have made two hundred off of that trick but I am only going to give you one, since I had to do most of the work. Forty goes to the house," Kim said and handed her sixty dollars.

"Well that's not fair," Meredith said.

"You know you could have gone in there alone. I feel like you took advantage of me and you turned down a lot of guys," Kim said

"I did the best I could. Those other guys were not attractive to me."

"You ain't supposed to worry about how they look. What do you think this is the prom or some shit?" I said.

"I can't enjoy sex when I am not physically attracted. Some of those guys were abhorrent to me."

"You ain't supposed to enjoy sex with a trick. You are supposed to handle your business and get on to the next one. And getting high while you are with a client is something you should not do. You have to stay alert around these men. You don't know which one of them will flip out on you. You let them talk, you comment, make them think you are interested in the subject, but you let them talk as much as possible because that gives you a repoire with them, that way they will want to see you again and not just for sex.

"This is no different than selling clothes in that store where you work, only you are selling yourself, remember that. If this is not something that you want to do just let me know, ain't no hard feelings," I said.

"Can't I just keep working with Sparkle? I'm okay when she is in the room."

"She don't have time to hold your hand, she got her own agenda."

"Well I could do the foreplay and she could finish them up."

"You think you got something that she don't? Why should she have to do that? She ain't doing nothing that you can't do. Don't waste my time or yours. Sparkle let's just go to Fat Burger's on La Cienega and get some burgers and take this girl back to her car." I wanted to get rid of this girl ASAP.

She said she had not drove, so I put her in a cab and told her I would call her. I didn't call her or answer her pages for a few days. Crickett said let her think that I didn't want her.

The next week I bought a car and found a nice apartment for me and Kim on Sepulveda, I liked The Valley. Willie and some of his friends helped me move. Kim had been working for a week straight, when she finally came home I met her at Crickett's and she followed me to the apartment. She liked it.

I worked on the club with Crickett everyday getting it ready for the opening. Kim slept for three days straight. She decided to take a week off. She made a satin comforter with a rainbow down the center and curtains to match for the bedroom and started crocheting an afghan for the couch. We shopped for plants and pictures, and bought a lot of pottery that she painted and glazed herself. She had real skills when it came to arts and crafts.

   Kim was so happy making things and cooking, she had turned our little apartment into a home in no time. We bought a bunch of meat, barbecued on the balcony, and invited her family over. It was just like old times.

Kim

My Uncle Willie had two girls working for him, a Black girl, Jackie and a Puerto Rican, Tanisha. For months, Mea had been shuffling his girls and me at the house trying to keep my working a secret from the family.

We were all losing money. Several clients asked Jackie if they knew Sparkle and wanted to see both of us at the same time. Finally, I had to go to Willie and tell him that I was Sparkle.

"You're Sparkle. The one all the tricks been talking about? Why didn't you tell me?"

"Because I don't want the family to know and you can't tell them. It's hard for Mea to keep trying to set up work where we don't run in to each other. Me and Crickett talked about it and decided I should tell you."

Willie was three years younger then me. My grandmother had him when she was fifty-five. We had spent a lot of time together growing up, and our adventures had gotten our butts beat more than a few times.

I think I was about twelve when one morning we road our bikes all the way from Normandie and Imperial up to Crenshaw. We would have gotten away with it had we not stopped by my Aunts house. She called Mother who was waiting for us with a belt when we walked in the door.

"I'll keep your secret," Willie said. That was about four months ago, during the time I was broke up with Alonzo. Life was so much easier with Willie knowing, that way Jackie, Tanisha and I could all work together.

At the first barbecue at our new apartment, Mary told Alonzo that Meredith was going crazy because he wouldn't call her back. She had gone on a couple of calls with Mary and was ready to work. Alonzo went to see her the next night and she gave him a thousand dollars, which meant that she was now his woman.

It also meant he would be sleeping with her. I made him swear to use a condom. Meredith had wrecked her car and did not have transportation. Alonzo had to have another surgery on his leg and would not be able to drive for a few weeks. He hired my Grandfather to drive her around.

Mr. Willie was my Grandmother's second husband and Willie's Father. Though they were divorced, he still hung around in hopes of getting my Grandmother back and was a permanent fixture at all the family events.

Boy did Mr. Willie love him some me. He was the one who taught me to walk at seven months, he would put a can of beer in the floor, and if I walked to it, I could have it. I was walking in no time.

The first night Mr. Willie drove her on an outcall Alonzo rode with them. The next day my Grandfather told me that, they were damn near fucking in the backseat and he did not appreciate Alonzo doing that in front of him. He told me that Alonzo had said some things that made him feel like he was putting her above me, like she was better than me because she was White. I told him, "Alonzo is just doing what pimps do," but I could tell by the way he looked that there was truth to his words.

"Humph, I ain't never seen no pimp acting like no love stuck teenage school boy in public." Mr. Willie said.

That night Meredith went upstairs, came down crying with no money within fifteen minutes, and told Alonzo some story about the guy looking just like her Father's friend who raped her when she was a teenager and she just couldn't do it.

Alonzo went for her story. It seemed like every call she went on there was a problem. After a week, she had made no money and every client had sent her home because she acted as if they were trying to rape her. The workhouse clients came out of the room complaining.

"Alonzo what's really going on? This girl has not given you any money, it seems like when she is paged half the time she doesn't answer or can't take the call, and you are right there with her. If you just want to be boyfriend and girlfriend you should stop acting like you are pimpin' her when you ain't getting paid."

"She's a turn out; I got to take it slow with her."

"Mary was a turn out too, she's making paper. Even Mellissa has made money-hanging paper for Butch at the bank. Meredith either needs to shit or get off the pot, you keep babying her ass and spending all your time with her for free you ain't gone never get paid. Why should she pay you? And another thing, she is sitting up in the workhouse talking about what you do with her to the other girls."

"I'll step it up, will that make you happy?"

"You ain't got to make me happy, everybody knows that she ain't paying like she should, you are the one looking soft."

I climbed into bed and Alonzo tried to pull me to him. I opened the bedside drawer, took out a condom, and handed it to him.

"What's this for?"

"You, if you planning on touching me."

"We stopped using these. I though we were going to try and have a baby? Why we got to start using them again."

"Because you have been with Meredith without protection. Do you really think that I am going to let you up in me raw?"

"Man the condom broke a couple of times. I didn't just go up in her without one."

"Regardless, you ended up inside of her without protection. I don't care how or why, all I know is you did, oh and we can't kiss anymore either."

"Why not?"

"How did she put it, "You give the best head that she has ever had in her entire life.""

Alonzo could not look me in my eye.

"Matter of fact I am really tired and just want to go to sleep," I said putting the condom back and rolling over.

I woke up and Alonzo was inside of me. I did not feel turned on like I had before. I reached down to make sure he was wearing a condom. He was.

I felt as if I was with a trick and could not get excited. I felt the way I did when I broke up with him before and I knew why. I had no trust for him anymore.
\

Crickett

I had opened the club and it was proving to be more trouble than it was worth. Some cops told me that if I did not turn it into a Country Western club they would make certain that I never got the liquor and restaurant licenses that I needed to make the place a success.

I was forced to rent the place out for private parties every weekend. One of my friends would fill out the rental forms for legal reasons and we could sell liquor and food. All the Los Angeles pimps and hookers came out. Squares that wondered in were prey.

Every weekend the police came through to make sure the papers were in order. I paid them off but others came with their hands out. My dream of being a legal business owner was going down the drain.

Mea opened a beauty supply store and Kaylen opened a day spa, where women came and got their nails done, facials and massages. Not one of the businesses were making a profit.

Alonzo spent a lot of time hanging out with the other pimps and they were feeding him a bunch of crap about how he didn't have Kim under control. They gave him ideas of what he should do to make her more subservient. They should have been telling him how to get Meredith in check.

I tried to help Alonzo but was beginning to see that he was a lost cause. He was beginning to believe the hype that he was a pimp. Kim was not the kind of woman that you had to be down on.

If Alonzo did not wake up soon he was going to lose Kim. I knew my Niecy and she was showing signs of tiring of him. No matter how much I liked Alonzo, I loved my niece more and he was disrespecting her by keeping Meredith around when she was not taking care of business.

Mea would not work Meredith at the house anymore because she drew nothing but complaints. I had even told Alonzo that he should just let her go because she was not paying him like she should and was a dope fiend. He did not listen to me. He though he could make her fall in love. I told him, "The way you start is the way you finish."

There was this Suzy Choosey bitch named Jenny that kept calling me and wanted to meet. She had been with almost every pimp in town and now she wanted to get with me. Every time she called, I asked her if she had a choosing fee. When she said she did not, I hung up.

Kim

It's Over

Alonzo wanted me to take Meredith to see my regular clients and I refused. "Why would I piss off my clients by sending them someone who everybody says can't handle her business. As soon as she takes a blow, it's like turning on a chatterbox. I worked long and hard cultivating my book and I am not going to let you or that ding bat mess things up for me."

"Well if you trained her right maybe she could make some money."

"I held that girls hand through I don't know how many dates. It ain't like she's a virgin. Game is to be sold, not told and I don't have time to babysit. You can't get no money out of her, let her go. Hell the bitch done lost her square job and when she had it, she wouldn't steal shit. Hell let her work with Butch, at least then you can get something out of her except a nut."

"You know that Mellissa just went to jail working with Butch and unless she turns state evidence she is going to do some time, at the very least have a record. Why would I sign Meredith up for that, which would be stupid? Look here, you are my woman, and you are going to do what I tell you. Start taking her on your calls. I ain't got time for your jealous bullshit; now that Mellissa is gone and Meredith ain't got no job, they can't afford that Brentwood apartment. She may have to move in here with us."

"You's a lie! Boy who in the hell do you think you are talking to? You been listening to them pimps too long if you think you are going to talk to me like that and tell me some shit like that. I ain't taking that bitch around the corner, and bring her ass up in this house and I swear it will be you and her living here cause I will be out, out of this place and out of your life. You disrespect me like that and we over, I promise on every person I love. I ain't worried about a Ho' who can't come up with her rent and you shouldn't be either."

Alonzo grabbed my arm, "Why don't you just put a damn dress on me. You brought me into this bullshit, I done came up with a bitch that is finer than all them other girls up in that house and if you would just help her we could be knee deep in money, but no, you on some other shit."

"Naw, nigger you the one on some other shit, if you ain't got no damn money out of her in six months how fine is she. Maybe you should put her fine ass somewhere she can model. Why don't you take her fine ass somewhere and see how fast she can get you what you need to survive. Since the bitch is so fine, you and her should do well. You are through wasting my time and money on that bitch."

"I don't spend no money on her."

"Alonzo, time is money, cocaine is money. If you bring her into my house, I am going to feel violated. This is the only place where I don't have to think about the life, the tricks, the dope fiends, and the police. I can come in here close that door and forget about every thing on the other side of it, don't you think I deserve to have a place where I can get my head together and sew, decorate and cook? You bring her in here I will leave and I cannot impress on you enough how you not hearing me wil devastate our relationship."

"You know they told me that I needed to break you and they are right because you act like you are the pimp in this relationship."

"No, I act like I grew up watching people get pimped and if you think that you can run that pimp crap shit on me you are sadly mistaken, you can't tear me down Alonzo what game could you possibly come up with that I ain't heard or seen in my life time?"

"I'm in the life now, you are going to respect me and treat me like a man."

"I thought that was what I have doing. Alonzo I been getting money one way or another all my life without anyone's foot in my ass. I got with you way before any of this shit ever jumped off and I fell in love with you. You hurt me and it took a lot for me to get back with you. I don't need a pimp Alonzo. So if that's what you want to be now, you can't do it with me."

"What do you think I am supposed to do just be your bitch?"

"You need to get it right with that White girl. Maybe if you stop shoveling dope up her nose she can make some progress. Alonzo you need to realize that I don't need fixing, I ain't broke."

I grabbed some things and got in my car and left. I was so upset that I was not thinking straight. I knew my relationship with Alonzo had just about run its course and it hurt. It hurt so bad that I had to pull over and cry.

After I got myself, together I stopped at a gas station and the pump was not working right. I was so frustrated that I started kicking it.

A man appeared at my side, "Let me."

I had forgotten to lift the handle. Boy did I feel stupid.

"How are you tonight?"

"I'm fine and you?"

"Great, on my way to a lonely dinner, unless you would consider joining me, we could go to any restaurant you want."

"Thank you for the offer but I'm late as it is, got to meet some people in Los Angeles. But here's my pager number, call me sometime."

"I'll do that," he said.

He called me several times over the next two weeks. I returned his calls and listened to him talk about how much he missed his wife who had just passed.

After the fourth call, I asked him, "Are you a cop?"

"No, why do you ask me that?"

"Maybe I can help you with your lonely nights."

"What do you mean?"

"Well I need money and it sounds like you need companionship, fair exchange ain't no robbery."

"How much money are we talking about?"

"How much can you give me to come and visit you tomorrow night?"

"Two hundred good? I don't make a whole lot of money.

He gave me his address so that I could check him out. We set a time to meet at a restaurant.

The next evening after dinner, he asked me, "What will two hundred more dollars get me."

"Give it to me and we will see. I never named a sex act or incriminated myself in anyway. I was riding with him to his house when the police pulled us over. He was doing a poor job of acting like he was part of this setup. He was definitely a cop. I had asked him that over the phone and he had denied. I also had it on tape so I knew my lawyer would throw this out on entrapment.

As I was, being put into the squad car one of Crickett's friends sat across the street watching.

I was pissed, it was Friday night, and who knew how long it would take them to let me bail out. It was my first arrest for prostitution so hopefully within a couple of hours I would be back in the world.

They did not book me in like they should have. I knew this because I had been arrested for book making when I was nineteen and had spent the night in jail as a juvenile, so I knew that they were supposed to take my fingerprints and give me a phone call.

They put two detectives and I in a little room that I had seen in Crickett's club walked in.

"So, Sparkle is it?"

This was some serious bullshit; I had been set up like a board game. I told the trick my name was Brianna, why were they calling me Sparkle.

"So, how long have you been in this business?"

"What are you a social worker? Why don't you just book me so I can bail out?"

"We have some questions that you are going to answer before we even think about letting you out of here."

"I have nothing to say."

The detective took my purse and turned it over emptying the contents. They were not going to find anything, I knew better than to carry anything on first time calls, No dope, no gun, and no beeper. Everything was in the lock box of my car.

"We know that you have had dealings with a Melvin Broussard Jr. AKA Crickett. We want to know about his operation and what is really going on at that club."

"Why would I know anything about his business?"

"We have seen you around him and his girlfriends. You know something, and your boyfriend whose identification is just too clean is always with him and his friends. Make it easy on yourself and tell us how big this prostitution and drug ring is?"

"I don't know what you are talking about and I did not proposition this guy tonight he said he was lonely and wanted a dinner companion. I told him I had a couple of bills that needed paying and he said he would give me the money. I don't know anything about prostitution."

"Did you know that Crickett was incarcerated in the early seventies for tax evasion, they were trying to get him for pimping and pandering, but none of his girls would step up and turn states evidence? They ran psychological test on him and said that his I.Q. was off the chart," the fat detective said.

"You see Sparkle these guys hypnotize and brainwash girls like you to get what they want. You are being used, let us help you, let us help all of those poor girls in that club, we know that ninety percent of those guys at the parties are pimps, help us stop this abuse," the skinny detective said.

These fools had done so much homework, yet they did not have a clue that they were talking about my family.

"How much is my bail?'

"You aren't in the system yet, it's the weekend, and we can hold you indefinitely. We need to run your prints through NCIC."

"What's that?"

The National Crime Information Center and see what we come up with, unless of course you decide to help us out, then we can let you walk right out of here.

I lay my head back against the wall and did not say another word.

Crickett

"Damn, Kim and I have not been getting along lately, she's not stupid. Meredith is not making enough money to justify me risking our relationship, but I get so much respect from the other players having this White girl by my side. I don't know what to do. I've tried to stop Meredith from blowing so much because she can't handle her self-proper when she's high. I even hit her when she came out of a call with no money high as hell," Alonzo confided to Crickett.

"If you let things keep going like they are Kim and every one else is going to lose respect for you. Hell, I've already lost respect for you. Kim told me you tried to gorilla her into taking the girl on calls with her. You better recognize that Kim was running on auto pilot when she got back with you,"

"Man I don't know what to do, I can't let her just talk to me any kind of way and Meredith only gets money when she is working with Kim. The other guys said that I have to put my foot down, but what if she calls the cops on me, you know I got a warrant because I didn't go back to court on that case."

"Kim doesn't need you. You can listen to them other pimps if you want to but trust me they will be the first one's in line trying to come up with Kim when you piss her off enough that she fires you. I told you before, you let Kim do what she do and be her safe place. You can't force your hand with a woman like her, she would be a damn fool to take that broad to her clientele, and all her clients buy blow and time from her, why does she need that girl tagging along."

"How else am I gone get the bitch up to speed?"

"She needs to be building her own book. Cut the bitch off, her and Mary are fixing to get thrown out of that apartment because Mellissa's Father is the one that rented it and she is in jail, once he gets her out he is going to get her as far away from L.A. as possible."

"Damn where they supposed to go, Kim already said don't bring nobody up in her house?"

"She got that right man, she works hard. You think Mea would want to come home and have Kalyn up in our house. You don't want to do that."

My pager went off; I picked up the phone and dialed the number on the display. "Who dis?"

"Man this is Suicide." He had gotten his moniker because three of his bitches had committed suicide.

"What up Playa?"

"Man I got bad news, I just saw the cops take your niece Sparkle away outside of Tracton's on Ventura."

"Thanks for the heads up." I hung up the phone.

I looked at Alonzo and he could tell by my expression that something was wrong."

"What's up man? You look worried," Alonzo said.

"Kim is in jail, Suicide saw them putting her into a police car on Ventura Boulevard."

Crickett called Mea to see if Kim had called her. He called his attorney and gave him her name so he could find out what he could. He called a couple of cops that were in his pocket and asked them to see what they could find out.

"Shit, the last time I spoke to Kim we had an argument. I had hooked Meredith up with another service working with Cash Money's women. She told me I was stupid and should just give the bitch to Cash Money because he was going to pull her anyway. The other girls were going to suck her in or get mad enough at her no trick turning ass to beat it. I told Kim it was her fault I had to send her out with Cash Money's woman since she refused to take her under her wing.

You know what her answer was, "I'll quit the business before I have to work that damn hard."

"I don't understand why you want to hold onto a bitch that is causing you more problems than she is worth. I got to find out what is really going on with my niecy. If it's just a straight up prostitution she should be out in a couple of hours, my lawyer, or these cops need to let me know what's up."

"I want her out of jail. That is no place for Kim, she shouldn't be there man," Alonzo was close to tears.

"Man she gone be alright, look at it as paying your taxes. Toughen up nigger, we'll hear from her soon."

Twenty minutes later the cops called me back and told me it was the detectives that had been pressuring me about the club who had her picked up. They were leaning on Kim trying to get her to talk about me. I wasn't worried. I knew my niece was stand up and would never tell them anything.

Kim

Monday afternoon I walked out of the jail and hailed a cab. I was lucky my car had not been towed out of the restaurant parking lot.

I went to the apartment and when I lay on the bed, I smelled perfume, it was my perfume, but the bed should not have smelled like anything but a dryer sheet or Alonzo's cologne because I had changed the bed right before leaving on Friday night to meet the trick at Tracton's.

I pulled back the comforter that I had spent three days making for my man and me to sleep under. The comforter for my apartment, my place where I could forget about all the things I had done to make money. I found an earring between the sheets along with cum stains and bleached blonde hairs with dark roots that could only belong to Meredith.

"This bastard done bought this girl in my apartment and in my bed?" I said aloud. I could not believe this shit. Why would he bring her here after I told him how I felt? I guess this meant that he had made his choice. This did not feel like my place anymore and he was not my man anymore.

I had a few hours before I had to be in Wilshire. The client was paying me fifteen hundred dollars to go out to dinner and bring in the New Year with him.

I went into the bathroom and prepared to shower, my razor had blonde hairs in it, my toothbrush was wet, my curling iron was on top of the sink, and the top was off of my cologne. My makeup was all over the sink. Trifling bitch could not even clean up behind herself.

After I showered and did my hair and face, I packed up all the toiletries and makeup that she had not used. I did not want anything that girl had touched.

I went into the closet looking forward to wearing this beautiful outfit I had made out of a blue metallic fabric and silver lace. It was one of the nicest things I had ever made, a short three tiered skirt with a form fitting button down blouse with puffy sleeves and silver lace strategically placed on the front to give a peek a boo effect. I just knew I would get a lot of orders for this one. I had made three outfits for the holidays. I had five orders for the one that I had worn on Christmas.

"Motherfucker," I screamed. My dress was not there. I looked in the hamper and found two of my creations. One had a red wine stain on it and the other was torn. What I saw next was just nasty. My underwear that I had just washed was in the hamper, "What kind of bitch wears another woman's panties?"

I opened the safe, eight hundred dollars and an ounce of blow was gone. There should have been more money in the safe, if he sold the drugs the money for it should have been here.

I always paid Christian for the drugs he gave me off the top. I had been dealing for him for five years and the reason we had a good relationship was because I always paid him before counting my profit.

I picked up the phone and called Crickett, "Can I move back in with you until I find another place?"

"Hey, you're out of jail?"

"Yeah they just turned me loose a little while ago."

"I got to find another place to live, can I move back in?"

"What's going on? Why did they keep you so long? Did you have blow on you when they busted you?"

"No I didn't, those same detectives that tried to get you to turn the club were sweating me about you. They wanted me to set you and the other criminals who frequent that establishment up. They said that you are extorting and abusing women. I told them I didn't know anything about you, they don't know that we are related. I just shut my mouth and set it out."

"Alonzo was really worried about you?"

"He wasn't too goddamn worried. The bastard had that bitch up in my bed. On top of that, she wore the new outfits I just made and ruined them. Money and dope is missing, if the dope is gone there should be money in the safe. Lately he is always short because him and his girl are snorting like ninety going north. I'm through with him."

"Does he know this?"

"He will when he comes in here and all my shit is gone."

"You sure you want to do this?"

"I ain't fixing to be with no nigger that pampers some no-money-getting-dope-fiend bitch because she is White, fuck that. And you know how I feel about the clothes that I make, he done crossed the line."

"Yeah, I know how you are about your clothes, I remember that day Tanisha borrowed one of your outfits, you told her she could wear anything except for the stuff that you made, she didn't know the difference and you went off. You know you can stay here, Niecy. You know he ain't been handling that broad, none of the agencies will fuck with her anymore. If he had any sense he would have sent her to the street and not let her ass come in until she made some real money then she would appreciate the agencies and handle her business."

"Maybe he shouldn't have her."

"Is that what you want?"

"That's exactly what I want and when I see that bitch if she is wearing my clothes I'm gone cut that shit off of her ass."

"You know they gone be at the club tonight."

"I can't get there until after one, I got a mission."

"You're working on New Years eve?"

"A trick is gone drop fifteen hundred dollars for me to eat dinner and be there with him when the ball drops, hell yeah I'm working on New Years Eve. Do me a big favor; don't tell Alonzo that I'm out of jail."

"Don't have the police coming up in the spot tonight, I know you can get crazy, you got that from your momma."

"I'll try to keep the riot down to a dull roar," we laughed.

"Can you ask Mother to call the mattress store and have them deliver me a king size mattress, box spring and frame and give her the money and I'll give it back to you tonight, I need some sheets and a comforter too."

"Done. You gone be alright Niecy?"

"I'm hurt but it ain't the first time, I'll get over it."

"Keep your head up, I'll see you tonight."

Kim

Happy Fucked up New Year

I left my client about one a.m. and it took me an hour to get back to the Valley. I walked in the club and there was Meredith in my blue metallic outfit. It was about to get rowdy up in here.

"I hope you have some clothes in the car," I told her walking up to the table where she and Alonzo sat with Cash Money and his women.

"Hey baby you're out, I was worried about you," Alonzo said getting up smiling and moving toward me with his arms out.

I held up my hand to stop him, "Don't even try it. You let this bitch wear my clothes, you fucked her in my bed while I was sitting in jail, I can't fuckin' believe your sorry ass," I yelled.

"Sit down and stop hollering," Alonzo said with clouds forming in his eyes.

I took the plate of coke that he and Meredith were sniffing from and dumped it in his drink, "Fuck you, I ain't sitting with you, I ain't doing shit with you ever again. Turn the camera off, shut out the lights, it's a wrap." I screamed.

The people on the dance floor stopped dancing and the D. J. stopped the music, all eyes were on us.

"I said sit down," Alonzo said getting up in my face.

"And I said fuck you and the horse you rode in on. Don't even try that perpetrating shit with me you weak ass buster."

The other pimps were making comments and laughing. Alonzo turned and looked at them then he turned around and backhanded me hard enough to knock me to the floor. As soon as the stars in my head cleared, I saw Butch approaching and indicated for him to go back to his table.

Alonzo was being urged on by the instigating pimps and was feeling his oats, "This bitch done lost her rabid ass mind, had to knock some sense into her ass," He laughed

A waitress was walking by with a bottle of champagne in an ice bucket. I stood up and grabbed the full bottle by the neck. I heard my grandmother scream, "No don't do it," as she dropped a platter of fried chicken on her way out of the kitchen but it was too late, there was no time for any one to warn Alonzo. I swung with all my might and hit him in the back of the head. He fell like a sack of potatoes. I prepared to hit him again but he was unconscious and blood was spreading from his Jheri Curl onto the floor.

Meredith jumped up out of her seat, "Don't you hit him, you can't do that," she said running toward me.

"Naw bitch, what you can't do is wear clothes that I made," I hit Meredith in the throat with a quick jab using my knuckles and she fell to the floor gasping. I reached into my bodice and pulled out my blade snapping it open with my thumb and index finger. I stood over her, grabbed my blouse at the neck, and ran the knife straight down the front of the top and the skirt. Then I flipped her over and did the same down the back leaving her exposed in my underwear, I thought about cutting that off her too but Crickett pulled me up.

"Stop it, the police just walked in," he hissed in my ear.

I closed the blade, slid it under a booth, and stood up. Mary ran to help Meredith up. Alonzo groaned and his eyes opened. Some of the guys helped him into a booth. Blood ran down his neck, my grandmother brought him a plastic bag filled with ice.

"What's going on here?" the detectives that had questioned me asked Alonzo.

"I slipped and fell," he answered.

"What happened to her? She slipped and fell out of her clothes?" The other detective laughed.

"She hit me and...," Meredith said.

"Ain't nobody hit you? Your drunken ass started tearing your clothes off and fell," Kalyn said.

Tanisha sat down next to Meredith, "Shut the fuck up or I will fuck you up."

One of Cash Money's women went out to the car, got some clothes for Meredith, and took her to the bathroom.

Crickett went outside and talked to the Detectives. The last two parties the police had come in, demanded everyone's identification, and ran them for wants and warrants.

"So Crickett, if you cooperate with us we can stop dropping in on your establishment like this." The dumpy detective said.

"You know we could run everyone in just for fun," The other said.

The club was not worth all this unwanted attention, "My lease is expiring next month, I'm not going to renew it," Crickett said.

"That's a wise decision," they said and patted him on the back and walked to their car.

Alonzo

"I can't believe she hit me like that. Do you think she was trying to kill me?" I said talking to Johnny in the hospital room where they kept me over night for observation.

"If she wanted you dead, trust me I have seen my cousin get mad and go off. You would be in the morgue instead of leaving this room."

"I had to get fifteen stitches to close up the wound. She could have at least hit me with an empty bottle. I probably shouldn't have hit her though."

"No you shouldn't have. I know a little something about pimping growing up watching Crickett. When my mom was his bottom woman, he never disrespected her. All his women have their own space and their own clothes and they don't have to share with wife-in-laws."

"So your mother worked for Crickett? I thought he was a square back then."

"Actually my mom is the one who turned him out. She got extra special treatment and he never had to beat her because she always handled her business. Crickett adopted me and when my mom got sick he paid her bills until she passed.

"Damn, I bet Kim is really mad at me."

"I know my cousin, she handles her business just like my mom did and you hurt her over some bullshit White girl."

"Man the way she was talking to me in front of all those players was humiliating, I had to do something."

"You should have pulled her to the side to talk."

"I guess I should apologize,"

"You can try, but I don't think it's going to make much difference."

"So she's leaving me again?"

"Man I ain't getting into all that, you ready to go?"

I had a really bad feeling in the pit of my stomach all the way home. Johnny dropped me off at the club and I got in my car and drove the few blocks to the apartment.

My heart sank when I opened the door. All the pictures of Kim's family were gone. I went into the bedroom and for a moment I thought that she was still there because of all the makeup and toiletries were left on the sink, then I remembered that Kim always put her things away after using them, this was Meredith's mess.

I walked into the bedroom, the bed was still there, but the headboard was gone. Kim's closet was standing open and her clothes were gone, the safe was empty. I sat down on the bed, how had I fucked up and lost Kim again? I knew that she was gone for good this time unless I could make her see how sorry I was. What if she didn't want me back, what was I to do now? I had a warrant out for my arrest from the bust with Comfort. She was the only one who had been in my corner and I fucked that up. I felt all kinds of stupid right now.

I had got all caught up in the game. I was a fraud. I had made myself look like an asshole. If Johnny knew, that Meredith wasn't making any money than every one did. I was a fool and every one knew it. I picked up the phone to call Kim. I heard a key in the front door. I dropped the phone and ran into the living room. I would get down on my knees and beg her to take me back. I would swear never to deal with another woman, I would let Meredith go, she couldn't hold a candle to Kim in bed anyway, whatever she wanted I would do to get her back.

When the door opened, it was her Uncle Willie. "Hey man Kim forgot a couple of things in the kitchen and asked me to pick them up for her."

"Where is she? I have to talk with her."

"Man, you might as well move on, I know her she ain't coming back this time. I was surprised she came back last time, she ain't keen on the second time around so I really don't think you will get a third."

"If I could just talk to her, let her know how sorry I am, I love her."

"Man she don't want to see you, she told you not to bring that girl in here and you did it anyway, and then you put the girl in her designs. You could have given that girl anything out of that closet that was store bought but Kim is really upset about you letting that girl wear those outfits and you knew that she made them for the holidays to wear herself, why would you do that. "

"I made a mistake, she has to see me, talk to her for me man."

"I don't want to talk to her for you. You fucked her over. You ain't no pimp; you dogged my niece over a bitch that you been wasting time and money on. She would not have cared one bit about you having another woman if that woman was pulling her weight. My women live with me in the same house and they work together, but I don't let one do all the work and give both of them my time, if a bitch ain't paying then she needs to get on. You think we don't know that you been giving that girl money to give to you in front of us. That bitch can't hold water. She gets around the other girls and tells them everything."

"I thought that if I gave her some time she would get with the program."

"Man leave Kim alone. You can only make things worse by trying to see her now."

"But I have to see her, I know I fucked up but I love her."

"Oh now you love her? You love her so much that you hit her in front of everyone when you knew you were in the wrong."

"Everyone else hits their women."

"Actually no they don't, especially when they are in the wrong. I'm telling you man back off, the only reason that you are still breathing is because the cops walked in before Kim could kill you and trust me she has the heart to do it. I have seen her fuck up nigga's bigger than you."

"I know she can get crazy."

"You don't know this but when you hit her she called me and Butch off because we were going to fuck you up." Willie said as he went under the cupboard, got the triple beam and air scales, put them into a box, and opened the front door, "Take care of yourself."

It could not be that cut and dried. I rode over to Crickett's house. Mr. Willie answered the door a scowl replaced the warm greeting that he usually had for me.

"Mr. Willie I need to talk to Kim."

"She don't want to talk to you, and I am glad she don't, you don't deserve her. You didn't love her like you should have. You're just like all them other ignorant niggers who get involved with White girls thinking that they are all big and bad cause they got one on their arm. Well, how stupid do you feel now?"

"I made a mistake Mr. Willie."

"You sure did and Kim will not be making one by getting back with you. I stopped liking you when you kept making out with that girl in the back seat of my car. That's my grand daughter you disrespected fool," he slammed the door in my face.

My head was killing me, I just wanted to go home climb into bed and wake up from this nightmare. I paged Meredith and did not get an answer. I slept all night, woke up and took two pain pills and went back to sleep.

Kim

When Johnny came back to the club after taking Alonzo to the hospital, he told me that they were keeping him over night. Meredith sat at the table with Cash Money and his women. T hey kept feeding her blow and drinks and when everyone got ready to leave she left with them.

I asked My Uncles if they would help me get my stuff out of the apartment. Their friends all volunteered to help. We loaded my headboard into Crickett's van and my clothes into the cars. Willie took my sewing machine and pictures to his place for the time being. In forty-five minutes, there was no sign that I had ever lived in that apartment.

I went back to check one last time after everyone had left. I looked around the apartment that was no longer mine I sat down at the dining room table with my head in my hands and I cried. Why did I always end up with men who screwed me over? Then I got mad.

I went to the hamper and pulled out my two dresses and underwear that Meredith had worn. I turned on the gas fireplace and threw them in along with the pages of the photo albums that documented our relationship. As they burned away so did my feelings for Alonzo. When there was nothing left but ashes, I turned the fire off and walked out the front door for the last time.

I dropped my things off at Crickett's and drove out to the Marina City Club to meet Christian and Laisyv. They were having a New Years day brunch and I had promised to help. Christian took one look at my black eye and asked, "Where that motherfucker at?"

"I'm right behind you man," several of his friends said.

"Don't worry about it. But if he shows up here please don't let him in."

"He won't even get by the gate, and if he does he sure won't get by me, I promise," Christian said hugging me like the big brother he had come to be over the years.

I was in the kitchen with Laisyv and some of her friends who did not know that I was in the life so I could only manage to tell her bits and pieces while we made mimosas. This was not answering her questions fast enough so she took me into one of the bedrooms.

"I can't believe his ass. I'm glad you busted him upside the head. You are not going to get back with him this time are you?"

"No way. I have had enough pain from him to last me a lifetime. I don't think I am going to get emotionally involved with anyone ever again."

"Don't give up on men, somewhere there is a man for you."

"I'm not sure that I have the strength to deal with all it takes to find out."

Later that day everyone was gathered around watching the football game when Laisyv screamed, "Christian," the alarm in her voice made everyone put the drugs under the couch and run to her aid.

It was Alonzo, "Man you ain't welcome here, go," Christian said pushing him out the door.

"Man I just need to talk to her, it was a big misunderstanding."

"Her black eye is not a misunderstanding. I talked to her Uncle. He called because he was worried that she wasn't home when they woke up. He told me what you did. You ain't no man Alonzo, you are a punk for hitting her like that," he slammed the door in his face.

Alonzo stood outside calling my name for a good five minutes before security came to take him away.

We partied the night away and in the morning when everyone was gone Christian, Laisyv, and I went down to the Jacuzzi, and I brought Christian up to speed on everything that had happened.

Back in the suite, I paid him what I owed him and explained that Alonzo and Meredith were sucking up all the profits and I had to take money out of my stash to make it up.

Business would be back to normal, with the one person I knew I could depend on, me

When I got back to Crickett's I went up to my room that was all made up thanks to my Grandmother. I slept for two days and when I woke, I knew I had to go on with my life, put the pain aside and keep on keeping on.

Alonzo Alone

It seemed like every day got worse than the one before. It was just like when Kim and I broke up before and my life went down the toilet, I wondered if she had put some kind of Hoodoo/Voodoo on me. She did tell me that everyone who had ever hurt or took advantage of her got theirs back without her having to do a thing. What goes around comes around. Karma is a motherfucker.

When I got back to the apartment after Christian would not let me into his party I tried to call Meredith and got a disconnected number at her apartment. I paged her several times and she never answered.

Cash Money called and asked me to meet him at his apartment. I had nothing else to do, so I poured myself a drink and measured out the last of the blow I had into gram packages and headed to Hollywood.

When I pulled up in front of Cash Money's apartment building, he pulled up next to me. "I'll meet you in the lobby; I had to drop them girls off on sunset."

Most of Cash Money's women worked the street. They were hard-core-stomp-down-do- whatever-they- had- to- do- to- get- his- money- women. They stole, used knock drops, and flat backed until they met their quota.

Cash Money opened the lobby door for me with a smirk on his face. In the elevator he said, "Thanks for coming man; we needed to talk face to face."

When we walked into the apartment I asked, "What's going on?"

"I needed to serve you and since we have gotten pretty cool I wanted to give you the respect of doing it in person," he said handing me a glass of cognac.

The first thing that went through my mind was that Kim had gotten with him.

"Your girl Meredith done chose me."

It was a relief that he came up with Meredith, not Kim. "Good luck with that man," I laughed.

"It got nothing to do with luck. Just got to pimp hard on A Ho, let her know who is really running thangs. She been working all day on the track. I gave her a three hour break and took her right back out. I had to start her out on the rough end. She said something about she couldn't be a streetwalker. By the time I finished putting foot to her ass she couldn't wait to get out of here and go get my money."

"Oh god, this just keeps getting better. I tried to work Meredith in houses and on outcalls and don't get nothing but pennies. You put her on a corner and the bitch gets busy. Well I guess you are the man, I don't think I'm cut out for this game."

"Every body can't stomach it. If I was you, I would focus on Sparkle. She gets damn good money and works with out a nigger having to touch her. Alonzo you were wrong for hitting her like you did last night. You got a lot of cleaning up to do." Cash money knew damn well that Kim was through with Alonzo. He had helped her load her things into the car last night.

"Yeah, well I don't know if that is possible. She packed her stuff and left. Won't even talk to me."

"You need to catch her where she will have to talk to you. Let her cool off for a minute then send her some flowers."

"I wish it was that easy."

On my way home, I rode down Sunset Boulevard and low and behold, there was Meredith waving at the cars that went by. I watched her get into one.

I went down to Carlos and Charlie's and had a few drinks at the bar. A couple of girls tried to talk to me but I was just not interested. I was more than a little toasted when I got into my car. I prayed that I would make home.

I took the canyon road and halfway through the car made a noise and came to a stop. I pulled the hood up. I do not know why I did because I know nothing about cars.

A guy stopped to help. While he was under the hood he said that I had broke the block. I would need to have the car towed. He called a friend of his who had a tow truck and gave me a ride home.

The next day I realized that I did not have the guys number or the tow truck drivers. Damn, Damn, Damn. Well he knew where I lived because he had come up and listened to my woes and me while we drank and snorted. I called every wrecker in the phone book and could not find the one that had towed my car.

I did give them my business card, all I could do was wait and see if they called.

I decided to take a swim and when I came back upstairs, there was an eviction notice on the door. I went to the office and they told me that I would have to fill out an application in order to stay in the apartment because Kim had taken her name off the lease.

That girl was going to destroy me just like she had before. I beeped her and put 911 in. I called her at Crickett's and left a message, not that I thought anyone would give it to her. They said she was asleep every time I called. Two weeks passed and I had not heard from Kim.

The people had fixed my car and I needed seven hundred dollars to get it back. All I had was about two thousand to my name and the car note was due.

I moved out of the apartment and moved in with a guy that I knew in the old Wilshire building where I used to live. I had to get out of here soon because I could not afford to live with someone who snorted up all the dope I had to sell and kept wearing my clothes even though they were two sizes too small for him.

I wanted Kim back and I was going to get her. I followed her one night. I sat outside of the workhouse where I found her car and when she left, I followed her on her rounds until I felt like I could get her alone.

She went to the after hours on Buckingham. I used my key, got into the back seat of her car, and waited. When she got into the car, I put my hand over her mouth and my arm across her throat to stop her from running away from me. "Don't scream it's me, just listen to me. I will never deal with another woman again. I want us to get married. You can stop hooking and we go back to how we were before in the beginning. I'm going to move my hand now."

"When I moved my arm she opened her car door and jumped out, "Alonzo leave me the fuck alone. Get out of my car."

I got angry. The look in her eye told me that she was not going to consider what I was talking about. I felt hopeless. I saw red. I jumped out and grabbed her before she could get to that little pocket under her weave. I do believe she would have shot me. I hit her hard and she fell down unconscious. I pushed her into the passenger seat of her car.

Valentine pulled into the parking lot. I jumped into the back seat so they would not see me. Kim started moving around and I picked up a scarf that was on the seat and wrapped it around my hands I was trying to hold it over her mouth and did not realize when it slipped down to her neck. She used her foot to blow the horn.

Valentine came over and I locked both doors. She was struggling and swinging her arms and legs. I did not know that I was strangling her. Valentine took out a gun and shot into the back window where I was and knocked the glass out and unlocked the door.

Crickett

Butch and I were sitting in the club. Kim had just delivered some blow to us and left. Valentine's woman, Satin Doll came running to our table, "You have to help her he's trying to kill her out there." She screamed.

"Trying to kill who?" I grabbed Satin Dolls hand to stop her from jumping up and down.

"Sparkle, he's trying to kill Sparkle."

Butch and I ran outside, we heard a shot and when we got to the parking lot saw that Valentine had shot through the window and unlocked the door. He was trying to loosen Alonzo's hands that were holding onto a scarf that was wrapped around Kim's neck. She was turning colors and her eyes were bulging out.

"Motherfucker let her go," I said and hit Alonzo in the head. It was as if he had lost his mind and could not hear us.

Butch used his knife to cut the scarf, pulled Kim out of the car, and started slapping her out of her faint.

I pulled Alonzo out and stuck my gun in his mouth. "We told you to leave her alone. You got two days to get out of town. You need to go back to Kentucky. If anyone in my family sees you, again I swear you are a dead man.

Kim came too. She jumped up and kicked Alonzo in the balls. He pulled his knees to his chest. I pulled Kim away and we all went into the club. Before we got to the door she turned around and gave me her purse, "You have to get the stuff out of the compartment. If he has keys to the car he can take my money and dope."

I went back, got her stuff out of the car, stepped over Alonzo, and headed inside. I sat down at the table with Kim, Butch, and Valentine, "What happened?"

She gave me the details of how he was in the back of her car when she got in. I pulled her to another table so that I could talk to her alone.

"I want you to make me a promise."

"What?" she said holding a towel with ice to the side of her face and neck?

"I want you to promise me that you will be out of the game by the time you are thirty. In the meantime, be careful who you get with. It seems that you always attract men who want to kill you. I hate to think what would have happened if Valentine had not come along when he did. You could be dead right now."

"Thanks for helping me."

"I think that maybe you should take a break until we know he has left town."

"I don't want to hide out. I'm not scared of him."

"If you had any sense you would be. I am sending you out of town. It is just for a few days. Kalyn has a client in Carmel who needs someone for three days. Kalyn had mentioned me finding someone else to go for her. You are that person. You will still be working and getting paid."

"I got a choice?"

"Nope, you are leaving in the morning and another thing. When you get back, I want you to think about getting a square job. You know you need taxes to cover your ass."

"I was thinking about that. My unemployment from the last job is about to run out."

"Look Niecy I am getting out of this business. I would like to see you out too, maybe married with some kids. I am looking for a business that will sustain me in the lifestyle that we have become accustomed to. This business ain't what it used to be and it ain't gone get no better with all this dope. Girls are working for the dope more than for their men now.

"I'll think about getting out. Don't know about the marriage and kid's thing though."

I put my arms around my Niece, "I love you, we gone get ready to get out of here in a few minutes, Butch can drive your car to Kalyn's and put it in her garage tonight. I'll get the window fixed while you are gone. We'll go to the house so you can some rest and pack. I'll take you to the airport in the morning. Love you Niecy."

"I love you too Unc."

The End ...
Of the First Twenty Three years

The beginning of the next

Kim

I returned from Carmel feeling revived. I had spent three days with a celebrity client who we are going to call Bill. During the day, I walked along the beach, swam, and read while he worked.

Carmel was a beautiful little town with lots of quaint shops where Bill had accounts and I could sign his name for anything I wanted. I got clothes, knick-knacks, and an extra suitcase to bring everything back.

After Bill watched himself on his evening telecast, we dined at restaurants on amazing fresh seafood. Afterwards we walked around to bars where he had a few cocktails that brought the freak out in him. After he got good and buzzed we headed back to the house where we snorted coke while I helped him dawn his disguise which included a padded bra, blouse, women's pants, wig and make up. When he was satisfied with his façade, we went to the rough side of town to hunt for his prey.

Bill liked young straight men so that he could be their first homosexual experience. I had contacted the local male escort agency and when we stopped at a bar, I would sneak off, call the owner, and let her know where to send the male prostitute who was on stand by.

The escort had my description, which was not hard because there were not many unknown blacks in Carmel. The escort would try to hit on me using a code word. I would invite them to join us and Bill would seduce them.

The last night that I was to be in town, I could not get an answer at the agency. I would have to find someone for Bill on my own. That night I discovered realized that a lot of guys if offered enough money will gladly climb the fence to the other side.

Bill needed a girl like me along just in case someone tried to harm him. I got five grand a day plus tips for three days of helping him fulfill his fantasies. It was my first time seeing two men together, but I put my professional hat on and played cheerleader from the sidelines.

It was not my taste - old, wrinkled, sagging skin with age spots up against young hard-bodied muscular men. I probably would not have been so revolted if it were two young men, but this fossil did not have no business being with these boys, well not boys, but compared to his fifty-eight year old ass they were babies.

I guess it was no different when I was with old men. I had been with men seventy and eighty years old. The only difference was I could look at the ceiling or the doorknob, anything not to focus on what I was doing. I was a robot doing what I had to do to get to the next payday.

Most of my regular clients liked cocaine, which meant that they were preoccupied with the drug instead of focusing on me. They wanted company more than physical contact. Many wanted sex, but I knew how to get a man worked up so that he would explode before I had to saddle up or soon after.

I also gave the best two finger blow jobs and if I could get the guy into the right position he would get my fist and never know that he was not in my vagina. I learned all this from my Uncle's girls.

I got my hustlin' honest. You see growing up with pimps, drug dealers, bank forgers and every other type of gangster in my family I was destined to pick up the tricks of the trade.

When my plane landed at LAX, I took a cab to Kalyn's and she took me to the auto shop to pick up my car. The window that had been broken out when my Uncle's were trying to save me from being choked to death by my Ex had been replaced.

I talked to my Uncle Crickett and he told me that he and two of my uncles along with some of my cousins had put Alonzo - my ex, on a bus back to his hometown, Louisville, Kentucky.

I fought back the desire to cry. As much as I loved Alonzo, even through his betrayal, I knew that I could never be happy with a man who could treat me the way he had.

I called my mother and found out that he had not left without getting revenge. The bastard had called my parents, who had been beeping me for the last two days and told them I was a prostitute. I lied to my mom and told her that I was just hosting parties. She did not believe me.

I gave Kalyn her cut from the out of town job and drove to Inglewood to pick up a package from Christian - my play brother who I had been dealing through for years. He was glad that Alonzo was finally out of my life.

His wife Laisyv and I went to Mz. Kizzy's Back Porch in the marina for dinner. Afterwards I dropped off packages to my dealers in Los Angeles.

I stayed over night with Laisyv and the next morning drove home to the Valley. I planned to take a few days off, go fishing with my grandmother, and take my cousins and their friends to the movies.

Next week I would look for an apartment and a square job but today I was going to climb into my king sized bed and sleep. I had not had a decent nights sleep in over a week.

I cried out in my sleep and my grandmother came in and woke me, "What you dreaming about?"

"Oh nothing, just a dream," I could not stop shaking and was relieve to be out of the nightmare.

"You have to tell someone about your nightmare or when you go back to sleep you will dream the same thing again giving the dream too much power, which can make it come true."

"I was dreaming that Alonzo was trying to kill me."

She giggled, "Again?"

I laughed with her, "Well hopefully he is back in Kentucky and won't get another chance."

"You still have to be careful, that boy ain't wrapped too tight. He blames you for all his failures; I wouldn't put it past him to come back. You know your grandfather Melvin and I used to get into fights, some real humdingers but he never tried to actually kill me. He did have a lot of Hoodoo mess in the attic and when I showed it to my mother; she said he had not done it right. She took it to him and told him that she knew how to make his dick fall off if he didn't stop messing around."

"What about Mr. Willie?"

"He tried to fight with me a couple of times when he was drunk. I would wait for him to pass out and beat the hell out of him. When he woke, he had bruises and no clue where they came from. You know both my marriages lasted exactly twenty one years."

"You ever want to get married again?"

"I ain't thinking about men, ain't worth the trouble."

"I know what you mean."

"No, you got a lot of living to do before you throw in the towel. You picked a good apple that turned bad, that don't mean there is anything wrong with you. A strong woman loves hard. You got to remember the good times and move on."

"Things were good with Alonzo; I just knew we would be together forever."

"You want to hear God laugh, tell him your plans for the future. He already got your life planned out for you. Life is meant to be a string of good and bad times. You got a lot more good times in your future. Don't let one bad event make you bitter. I had my life turn around on me more times, than I can count, but I know that God gave me a good heart and somehow we touch everyone who comes into our lives. One day you are going to effect more people than most, I've seen it in my visions, God is going to use you to help a lot of people."

"You know I don't believe in God."

"I don't know why you don't believe, I don't even think you know why. Baby we don't know what in life is going to test our faith, but I know you are strong, you just keep living and mark my words."

My grandmother was something else, I had seen her catch people stealing out of her purse, or shoplifting from her store, and she would turn around and give them more than they were trying to steal. I had also seen those same people come back, tell her that because of her they had gotten their lives together, and pay her back a lot more than she had given.

When she had her café people would come in and order a piece of toast and a cup of coffee, she could tell when people were hitting on hard times. She would plop down a plate of grits, eggs, ham, and French toast in front of them. When they said, "I didn't order this," she knew in translation they meant, I can't pay for this."

"Well you might as well eat it now, I can't serve it to no one else, and health department would close me down. You go on and eat," she said leaving them with their dignity. Sometime she would drop money by their chair or come up with an errand or a job they could do so she could pay them a little something.

Mother always said that what she gave out would come back tenfold. She also said a good plate of food could change a person's life. All you had to do was think pure thoughts and stay joyful while you were preparing it, "Never cook when you are mad, you could kill somebody that way. Your not just feeding the stomach, you are feeding the soul."

Mother had helped hundreds of people, though I had seen her heart broken time and time again by her friends, husbands and children, she never stopped giving with what she called a "pure heart," never expecting anything in return.

"You must be tired, go on back to sleep. Tomorrow is another day that God made. You'll see, things will look better in the morning," she rose to leave.

"Mother?"

"Yeah honey?"

"Can you stay with me tonight?"

She climbed under the covers and pulled my head onto her chest. I felt like a little girl again. I had always felt so safe in my grandmother's arms.

COMING SOON

www.ingramcontent.com/pod-product-compliance
Lightning Source LLC
Chambersburg PA
CBHW051553250626
47157CB00001B/286